The Throwaway Children

DINEY COSTELOE has been writing all her life, including several successful sagas after her children left home.

DINEY COSTELOE

The Throwaway Children

HEAD of ZEUS

First published in the UK in 2015 by Head of Zeus Ltd

9 7 5 3 1 2 4 6 8

A catalogue record for this book is available
from the British Library.

ISBN (HB) 9781784970017
ISBN (TPB) 9781784970024
ISBN (E) 9781784970000

Typeset by e-type, Aintree, Liverpool

Printed in Germany
by GGP Media GmbH, Pössneck

Head of Zeus Ltd
Clerkenwell House
45–47 Clerkenwell Green
London EC1R 0HT

WWW.HEADOFZEUS.COM

For all those who were sent...

Chapter 1

Belcaster 1948

R aised voices again. Rita could hear them through the floor;
her mother's, a querulous wail, the man's an angry roar. For
a moment she lay still in bed, listening. She couldn't hear what
they were saying, but it was clear that they were arguing.

Rosie, her sister, was peacefully asleep at the other end of
their shared single bed, the stray cat, Felix, curled against her.
She never seemed to wake up however loud the shouting downstairs. Rita slid out from under the bedclothes and tip-toeing
across the room, crept out onto the landing. Limpid green light
from a street lamp shone through the small landing window,
lighting the narrow staircase. A shaft of dull yellow light, shining
through the half-open kitchen door, lit the cracked brown lino
and cast shadows in the hall. The voices came from the kitchen,
still loud, still angry. Rita crouched against the banister, her face
pressed to its bars. From here she could actually hear some of
what was being said.

'... my children from me.' Her mother's voice.

'... another man's brats!' His voice.

Rita shivered at the sound of his voice. Uncle Jimmy, Mum's
new friend. Then Mum began to cry, a pitiful wailing that
echoed into the hall.

'For Christ's sake!' His voice again. 'Cut the caterwauling,
woman... or I'll leave right now.'

A chair crashed over, and the shaft of light broadened as the
kitchen door was pushed wider. Rita dived back into her bedroom,

making the door creak loudly. She leaped into bed, kicking a protesting Felix off the covers and pulling the sheet up over her head. She tried to calm her breathing so that it matched Rosie's, the peaceful breathing of undisturbed sleep, but her heart was pounding, the blood hammering in her ears as she heard the heavy tread of feet on the stairs. *He* was coming up.

'Rita! Was you out of bed?' His voice was harsh. He had not put on the landing light, and as he reached the top stair, Felix materialized at his feet, almost tripping him over.

'Bloody cat!' snarled the man, aiming a kick at him, but Felix had already streaked downstairs.

Jimmy Randall paused on the landing, listening. All was quiet in the girls' room. Softly he crossed to the half-open door and peered in, but it was too dark to see anything, and all he could hear was the steady breathing of two little girls asleep.

Must have been the damned cat, he thought. Don't know why Mavis gives it houseroom, dirty stray. If it was my house...

It wasn't. Not yet. But it would be, Jimmy was determined about that. A neat little house in Ship Street, a terrace of other neat little houses; well, not so neat most of them, unrepaired from the bombing, cracked windows, scarred paintwork, rubble in the tiny gardens, but basically sound enough. Jimmy wouldn't mind doing a bit of repair work himself, provided the house was his at the end of it. His and Mavis's, but not full of squalling kids. All he had to do was get his name on the rent book, then he'd be laughing.

Rita heard him close the door but lay quite still in case it was a trick, in case he was standing silently inside the room waiting to catch her out. It was a full two minutes before she allowed herself to open her eyes into the darkness of her room. She could see nothing. Straining her ears she heard his voice again, not so loud this time, and definitely downstairs.

For a while she lay in the dark, thinking about Uncle Jimmy. He had come into their lives about two months ago, visiting occasionally at first, smiling a lot, once bringing chocolate. It was for Mum really, but she'd let Rita and Rosie have one piece every day until it had gone. But Rita was afraid of him all the same. He had a loud voice and got cross easily.

Rita wasn't used to having a man in her life. She hardly remembered her daddy. Mum said he had gone to the war and hadn't come home. He had gone before Rosie was even born, fighting the Germans. Rita knew he had been in the air force, flying in a plane high over Germany, and that one night his plane hadn't come back. There was a picture of her daddy in a silver-coloured frame on the kitchen shelf. He was wearing his uniform and smiling. Wherever you moved in the kitchen, his eyes followed you, so that wherever she sat, Rita knew he was smiling at her. She loved his face, his smile making crinkles round his eyes and his curly fair hair half-covered with his air force cap. Rosie had the same sort of hair, thick and fair, curling round her face. Rita's own hair was like Mum's, dark, thin and straight, and she always wished she had hair like Rosie's... and Daddy's.

Then, a while ago, the photo had disappeared.

'Where's Daddy?' Rita demanded one morning when she sat down and noticed the photo had gone. 'Where's Daddy gone?'

Without looking up Mum said, 'Oh, I took him down for now. I need to clean the frame.'

Daddy had not reappeared on the shelf, and Rita missed him. 'I could clean the frame,' she offered. 'I'm good at cleaning.'

'It's being mended,' explained her mother. 'When I came to clean it I found it was broken, so I've took it to be mended.'

Rita didn't ask again, but she somehow knew that the photo wasn't coming back and that this had something to do with the arrival of Jimmy Randall.

Jimmy Randall had changed everything. He was often there when Rita and Rosie came home from school. Mum used to meet them at the school gate, but since Uncle Jimmy, as they were to call him, had become part of their lives, Mum was too busy, and it became Rita's job to bring Rosie home safely.

'You must hold her hand all the way,' Mum said, 'and come straight home.'

So every school day, except Thursdays, Rita took Rosie's

hand and crossing the street very carefully, walked them home; almost every day when they got home, Uncle Jimmy would already be in the kitchen with Mum.

On Thursdays Gran met them at the school gate and gave them tea. Sometimes she let them play in the park they passed on the way.

'I don't like Uncle Jimmy,' Rita confided to her grandmother one Thursday when they were having tea. 'He shouts. I dropped a cup yesterday, and he sent me upstairs with no tea. It didn't even break, Gran. It's not fair.'

Gran gave her a hug. 'Never mind, love,' she said. 'Perhaps he won't be around for long.' But Lily didn't like him either.

Lily Sharples was Mavis's mother. A widow herself, she still lived in the small brick house in Hampton Road, where she had lived all her married life. It had been spared by the Luftwaffe, when others in the vicinity had been flattened, and despite further raids, Lily remained, stubbornly, in occupation.

'It's been my home for nigh on thirty years,' Lily told Mavis, 'and when I leave it'll be feet first.'

Lily was worried about Mavis and her family. Mavis had been on her own for five years now, and Lily wasn't surprised that she had found herself another man, it was only natural, and anyway, the girls needed a father. It was just that she wished that the man wasn't Jimmy Randall. She could see why Rita was afraid of him. He wasn't used to children and his temper was short. On one occasion, Lily had seen him slap Rita across the face. The child had run to her, burying her burning cheek against her grandmother, and, holding her close, Lily turned on him, saying, 'There was no need for that!'

Jimmy glowered at her and snarled, 'They need a bit of discipline. They've got to learn their place.'

'This is their place,' Lily had snapped. 'It's not yours!' But Lily was increasingly afraid that it was going to be. She decided to speak to Mavis. 'You know the girls are scared stiff of that Jimmy, don't you?' she said. 'It's not right that they should be afraid in their own home.'

'What about me?' complained Mavis. 'I need someone. Now Don's gone, have I got to stay on my own for the rest of my life?'

'No, of course you ain't,' replied her mother, 'but you do have to think about yer kids. If they're scared of Jimmy, is he really the right bloke for you?'

'It's only 'cos he makes them do what they're told,' Mavis said defensively. 'It's only 'cos they ain't used to having a dad around. They'll get used to him. He's just got a short temper, that's all.'

'He don't love 'em,' said Lily mildly.

'Course he don't,' Mavis said. 'They ain't 'is. But he'll look after them, same as he looks after me.'

'Are you going to marry him?'

Mavis shrugged. 'Don't know. Maybe.'

Lily gave her daughter a long look and then said, 'He stays here, don't he? He sleeps here, when the girls is in the house. It ain't decent, Mavis. Your dad wouldn't 'ave stood for it.'

'Things is different now, Mum,' Mavis replied. 'The war's changed everything. Too many men didn't come home. Jimmy did and I'm going to hang on to him.'

'He ain't even got a job,' Lily pointed out. 'How's he going to look after you?'

'He's getting a job,' answered Mavis. 'He's out looking for work now. He's heard they're looking for people on the building sites. His mate, Charlie, says he can get him a job where he works. You'll see.'

The day after Rita had heard the row downstairs, she and Rosie went to school as usual. Uncle Jimmy had not been there at breakfast but poor Mum had a bruise on her face.

'So silly of me,' Mum had said when Rita had reached up and touched the bruise. 'I turned round too quickly and bumped into the door. Silly Mummy!'

'Silly Mummy,' echoed Rosie, beaming at her. '*Silly* Mummy!'

All day the raised voices rang in Rita's ears. Uncle Jimmy shouting, Mum crying, the sound of the overturned chair. Rita thought of little else and was scolded for wool-gathering, but by the end of school she'd made up her mind what to do. She'd go and see Gran. She didn't live far and there were no roads to cross; she would hold Rosie's hand all the way.

When school was dismissed she collected Rosie from the yard and led her out of the gate, turning away from home. Rosie trotted happily along beside her. 'Where are we going?' she asked.

'Round Gran's,' answered Rita, keeping a firm grip on her sister's hand.

'Oh goody,' said Rosie. 'Do you think she'll give us our tea?'

'Expect so,' said Rita, and moments later they were knocking on Gran's door.

When Gran opened the door she was surprised to see them. It wasn't Thursday. 'Hallo,' she said. 'What are you two doing here?'

'We don't want to go home,' began Rita.

'We want some tea!' broke in Rosie, grabbing at her grand-mother's hand. 'Can we have some tea, Gran?'

Lily opened a tin and gave them each a biscuit. Then she turned to Rita. 'Now what's all this about not going home? Course you must go home. Your poor mum will be wondering where you are.'

'I don't want to go home,' repeated Rita. 'Uncle Jimmy might be there.'

'So what if he is?' said Lily. 'He's Mum's friend.'

'They was fighting,' Rita said. 'Uncle Jimmy was shouting and Mum was crying, and I didn't like it.'

Lily put her arms round the little girl. 'No, I'm sure you didn't, pet. But even so you have to go home, you know, or Mum'll be very worried about you. Wait while I get my coat and I'll come with you.'

They walked back to Ship Street, Rosie skipping along holding Gran's hand on one side and Rita walking silently on the other. Lily knew that Rita thought that she, Lily, had let her down. She had come to her for refuge and she was being taken back home.

But what else could she do? Mavis would be out of her mind with worry when the girls didn't come home. She had to get them back as quickly as possible.

When they reached the house and opened the door, Mavis was in the kitchen, sitting at the table with a pot of tea in front of her. She looked up as they came in and her eyes widened with surprise when she saw her mother was with the girls.

'Hallo, Mum,' she said. 'What you doing here?'

'I've brought the girls home,' replied her mother.

'Oh.' Mavis looked vaguely at the kitchen clock. 'Did you meet them in the street?'

'They came to see me,' said Lily carefully. 'Look, Mavis, we need to talk. Why don't you give them their tea and then we can have a chat.'

Mavis shrugged. 'It ain't ready yet. You two go and play out.' She nodded at the door. 'I'll call you when tea's ready.'

Rita grabbed Rosie's hand. 'Come on, Rosie. I saw Maggie outside.'

When the girls had gone, Lily pulled out a chair and sat down. 'What have you done to your face?' she asked as she noticed the darkening bruise on Mavis's cheek for the first time.

Mavis coloured. 'Bumped into the door.'

Lily gave her a long look but then decided to let it go. 'Reet brought them round to me, after school. She didn't want to come home. She said you and Jimmy was fighting.'

'Not fighting, no!' snapped Mavis. 'We was arguing a bit last night, that's all. Nothing in that!'

'Rita heard you,' said Lily. 'It upset her.'

'She don't have to be upset. It was only an argument.'

'Like the one you had with the door.'

'Look, Mum,' Mavis exploded, 'you ain't got no right to come round here, interfering in my life. What I do is my business. Who I see is my business and how I look after my kids is my business.'

'Mavis, they're scared of Jimmy,' Lily persisted.

'Well, they'll just have to get over it,' snapped Mavis. 'He's here to stay, and they'll have to get used to him.' She looked across at her mother and all of a sudden her face crumpled. 'I've been to the doctor today, Mum. Oh, no, not about the bruise. Jimmy's already said he's sorry for doing that. It won't happen again, he's not like that really. No, I went 'cos, well, 'cos I'm in the family way.' She pressed her hands against her stomach. 'About four months.'

'And it's Jimmy's?'

'Course it's Jimmy's! What do you take me for?'

'Is he pleased?' asked Lily, wondering if this had caused last night's row.

'He don't know yet,' admitted Mavis. 'I only went to the doctor today... though I knew really. Haven't had the curse for five months, and I'm beginning to show.'

'So, when are you going to tell him?'

'Don't know. Maybe tonight. Have to pick my moment.'

'And the girls? You'll have to tell them.'

'They don't need to know,' muttered Mavis, 'not for ages yet... and you're not to tell them, Mum. Right? I got to get on with the girls' tea so's they're done before Jimmy comes home.' Mavis went on, and cutting two slices of bread began to spread them with marge. 'You want to go and call them in?'

Lily went to the front door and looked out. She saw the girls further down the street playing hopscotch on the pavement. She watched them for several moments, smiling as she saw Rita flailing her arms as she balanced on one leg, trying to pick up her stone, but her smile faded as she thought about what Mavis had just told her. The lives of her two granddaughters were certainly going to change, but even in her wildest dreams Lily could not have guessed just how much.

Jimmy did not come back to Ship Street that evening until well after the children were in bed, though Mavis had made his tea in the expectation that he would be home by about six as usual. Jimmy actually lived with his widower father, but came round for most of his meals and expected them to be ready on the table when he arrived. Today, however, he had been out drinking with his mate, Charlie, celebrating the fact that he now had a job labouring on a building site. It was not the sort of work Jimmy would have chosen, but at least it brought in some money, cash in hand, and he was short of cash. There was plenty of labouring work about, what with all the bombsites to be cleared and the rebuilding. Then there was stuff you could pick up there, too, if you were careful and didn't let the foreman see you. Clearing the rubble from the bombed-out houses, Charlie told him, you never knew what you might find. On sites reclaimed by weeds and other vegetation, you could often find something worth having, something you could sell on, down the pub. Celebration was in order, so Jimmy and Charlie celebrated.

It was late when he finally staggered into Mavis's kitchen. Mavis was sitting at the table doing her mending, but she did not put down the jersey she was darning; she simply looked up and smiled. That made Jimmy suddenly angry. She ought to jump up to welcome him home and put his tea on the table, especially as he'd got the job, especially as he'd have money in his pocket now, especially as the stupid woman would expect him to contribute to the food bills. Things were definitely going to change around here.

He dropped down onto a chair. 'Where's my tea?' he growled.

'In the oven,' Mavis said, hastily laying aside her darning and getting up. 'I'll get it for you. It may be a little bit dry... I was expecting you a bit earlier than this.' She reached into the oven and brought out a plate of sausage and mash. There had been onion gravy, too, but it had dried into a brown mass on the side of the plate.

Jimmy looked at the food she set in front of him and then turned furious eyes on her. 'What d'yer call this?' he demanded. 'Looks like a plate of shit!' He swept the plate aside and it crashed on the floor. Mavis took a step back as Jimmy got unsteadily to his feet, and glowered at her across the table. 'Get that mess cleared up,' he shouted, 'and get me something to eat!'

As she knelt down to pick up the broken plate and to scrape the food off the floor, she felt him towering over her. Instinctively she cringed away from him, squeaking as she did so, 'Don't hit me, Jimmy! I'm pregnant. I'm expecting your child.'

It made him pause, made him grip the table to steady himself. 'Fucking hell! That's all I need,' he said, and slumped back down onto the chair. Then he put his head onto the table and went to sleep.

Somehow Mavis had managed to rouse him and get him upstairs. Somehow she manoeuvred him onto the bed. She pulled off his shoes and, throwing a blanket over him, left him to sleep it off. She crept out of the bedroom and peeped in at her daughters, asleep in their room. At least, she supposed they were asleep. There was no sign of either of them being awake, but you never knew with Reet. She was a deceitful kid; she must have heard them the previous night and sneaked off to her gran's to tell tales and bring Gran round to interfere. She stood for a long minute outside the door, but nothing stirred.

Mavis went back downstairs, cleared up the mess on the floor and making herself a cup of tea, sat down, exhausted. Would Jimmy remember in the morning? she wondered. It wasn't how she'd meant to tell him about the baby, not blurt it out like that, but the words had burst out all by themselves. Would he remember? Would he react better when he'd thought about it, or would he walk out on her, leaving her to cope with three children?

He'd like the idea of being a dad, wouldn't he? Especially if it was a boy. Surely he'd want a son; all men wanted a son, didn't they?

For a moment she thought of Don. He hadn't minded what they had. 'As long as it's got all its bits, love,' he'd said, patting the bulge of her belly, 'that's all right with me!' And it had been. He'd adored Rita, and would surely have felt the same about Rosie, if he'd been around when she was born.

Surely Jimmy would love his own child, once he got used to the idea he was going to be a father. Then they could get married quickly, so that the baby wasn't a bastard.

Chapter 2

In the morning, leaving Jimmy still snoring, Mavis got the girls ready for school.

'You're to come straight home today,' she instructed Rita. 'Do you hear me, Reet? No going round your gran's and bothering her.'

'Yes, Mum.' Rita was very subdued. She had heard the crashing plate last night, and she'd heard Mum helping Uncle Jimmy up the stairs. She'd stayed still and quiet in the bed and at last drifted off to sleep. But in the morning she remembered it all, and it frightened her. She was pleased when she and Rosie set off for school before he came downstairs.

It was some time later that Jimmy pushed open the kitchen door and peered in.

'What's for breakfast?' he asked by way of greeting.

'Can make you some toast,' Mavis suggested cautiously.

'That's not much for a man to go to work on,' he grumbled, flopping down at the table. There was a pot of tea made and Mavis quickly poured him a cup, before putting a couple of slices of bread under the grill.

'You got the job, then?' she ventured.

'Course I did. Told you that last night when I come home. Start on Monday.' He hadn't, but no point in upsetting him now when he seemed in an affable mood. He drank his tea as he watched her turn the toast and then slide it onto a plate. He reached for the marge and spread some thinly on the toast before taking a huge bite.

The last of my marge, Mavis thought bitterly. We've no more till next week.

'I need your ration book,' she said, as she watched him scrape the last smears onto his second piece of toast. 'I can't cope without it no more.'

Jimmy shrugged. 'It's not as if I'm here all the time.'

'Enough that I need your rations,' she said, surprising herself with her own temerity. 'Jimmy, I can't let the girls go short and now, in my condition...' She let the words hang in the air, waiting.

He looked up. 'Your condition? Oh yes, I remember, you're up the spout.'

'It's your baby, Jimmy!' she said. 'Our baby. I'm having our baby.'

Jimmy said nothing.

'Jimmy,' she ventured again. 'We're having a baby. You're going to be a dad.'

'I heard you,' growled Jimmy. 'What do you want me to do about it? Dance a jig? How do I know it's mine?'

'Oh, Jimmy, of course it's yours. Whose else would it be? You're the only man I've... been with... since Don died.'

'So you say.'

Tears filled Mavis's eyes. 'Jimmy, you know it's true! You know you're the only man in my life.'

'If you say so.'

'I *do* say so. It's our baby, and it'll be born late June, a summer baby.'

'Well, if it's mine, it's mine,' Jimmy said grudgingly.

'It is... but Jimmy, I don't want... I mean it wouldn't be right... I mean we need to think...'

'For Christ's sake, woman, spit out.'

Mavis drew a deep breath. 'I don't want it to be a bastard, Jimmy.'

When he said nothing she took her courage in both hands and went on, 'I want us to get married, Jimmy. Before it's born. That's what I want.'

'Married?' Jimmy sounded incredulous. 'Married?'

'I don't want it born a bastard, Jimmy.'

'Married,' he said again, as if tasting the word.

She waited, knowing if she said the wrong thing, he would say no, walk out and leave.

At last he said, 'I'll think about it. It's a big step, getting married.' He looked across at her. 'If we get married and I move in here, them girls are going to have to go. I told you, I ain't taking on someone else's brats.'

'What do you mean, the girls must go? They're my daughters. Why must they go? Where must they go? Their place is with me! This is their home!'

Jimmy shrugged and got to his feet. 'If it's their home, it ain't going to be mine,' he said. 'It's up to you, Mav. If you want me to stand by you, to marry you, make you respectable like, well, I will, but I won't take on another bloke's kids. Right? Not with my own kid to think of. You got to find them somewhere else.' He reached for his coat and putting it on, went to the door. Looking back at her he went on, 'It's your decision, Mav. I ain't going to change my mind.' And with that he left, closing the door behind him.

Mavis stared after him bemused. What did he mean, the girls had got to go? They were her girls and belonged with her. She thought of Rita and Rosie as she'd seen them that morning, setting off to school, Rosie with her hand trustingly in Rita's as they walked along the street. It was Rita who was the problem. Reet could be difficult, especially recently. She'd been moody, not the sunny little girl she used to be. It was Reet who annoyed Jimmy, who wouldn't do what he told her. It was Rita's fault that Jimmy didn't like her. She was being obstinate and rude and it wouldn't be long before Rosie started to copy her. She always copied Rita. But Rosie was lovely. She looked so like Don.

Mavis hadn't thought of Don much for quite a long time. She got to her feet and went to the drawer in which she had hidden his photograph. Jimmy had 'accidentally' knocked it off the shelf and taking the hint, she had hidden it in the drawer. She got it out now and looked at Don. He smiled back at her as he always had done, as trustingly as Rosie, trusting her with his children. She looked at his face for a long time. He'd never forgive her if she didn't look after his girls. But he wasn't there to forgive her, was he? He was lost, exploded, burned to ashes somewhere over Germany. He hadn't come back and she'd been left to bring up the girls on her own. Now she had a chance to start a new life, with a new man. Surely Don wouldn't begrudge her that. Surely he would say, 'Go for it, girlie. Be happy! Go for it, girlie.' Girlie, his pet name for her. She blinked back the tears that had crept into the corners of her eyes. She had to be strong. Don wasn't here, he never would be again, and she had to get on with her life. She had the new baby to think of. She had to provide for the new baby. She couldn't let it start out life as a bastard.

Mavis didn't have to go to her cleaning job with Mrs Robinson today, and walking through the park on her way to the grocer's she sat down for a rest on a bench, watching a family of tiny ducklings dashing through the water behind their mother. Mavis smiled as one went astray, swimming in the wrong direction. Mrs Duck wasn't at all concerned; she simply swam on, leaving the lost duckling to cheep pitifully behind her.

Not such a very good mother, thought Mavis, then her smile died. I'm not a good mother either. I want this new baby and Jimmy more than I want my girls. And even as she tried to push the dreadful thought from her mind, crush it before it could take root, she knew, in that instant, that it was true. However fiercely she pushed it away, it crowded back. She needed a man, she wanted the baby, and Rita and Rosie were standing in her way.

No, she shook her head hard as if to clear the thought away, no of course they weren't. Of course Jimmy didn't mean it. She could talk him round. As for the girls, they'd get used to the idea that they were going to have a stepdad and a little brother or sister.

She left the peace and quiet of the park and walked along the street to Baillies Grocery. Just as she reached it she met her mother coming out, carrying her shopping bag.

'Hallo, Mum,' she said.

'Mavis.' Lily looked at her daughter carefully. 'You all right, love?' she asked. 'You look a bit peaky.'

'I'm fine, Mum. Just a bit tired, you know how it takes me.'

Lily nodded sympathetically. 'Yes, used to take me in the same way. D'you want a cup of tea? You look as if you could do with one.'

Mavis was about to refuse, and then she thought, why not? 'Yeah,' she said. 'That'd be nice.'

They turned away from the shop and walked the two streets to Hampton Road. Once inside Lily put the kettle on. Mavis dropped onto a chair in the kitchen, watching as her mother put away her shopping. She said nothing. Mavis felt safe in the kitchen of her childhood, in the silence that surrounded them. Lily didn't chatter, or ask awkward questions. She simply put her food away, put cups out on the table and then made a pot of tea. She poured it and waited.

'I told him, last night,' Mavis said, at last breaking the silence. 'About the baby.'

'And?'

Mavis shrugged. 'And he was fine about it.' She sipped her tea. She could feel her mother's eyes on her, and she went on, 'A bit surprised, of course, but he likes the idea of being a dad.' She raised her eyes to meet Lily's. 'We're going to get married... so the baby'll be OK, you know?'

'D'you want to marry him?' asked her mother. 'Really want to marry him? Jimmy, who knocks you about?'

'It's only happened once,' replied Mavis defensively, 'and he was ever so sorry. It was only 'cos he'd had a bit to drink. Won't happen again.'

'Till he's had a bit to drink again,' said Lily wryly. 'What about the girls? What about Rita and Rosie? What do they think?'

'They don't know yet, but they'll be all right.'

'You know they're scared of Jimmy.'

'So you keep saying,' snapped Mavis, 'but they'll get used to him. They'll have to.' Her tone softened a little as she added, 'They'll like having a baby in the house, a little brother or sister.'

'So when are you going to get married then?' Lily knew it was no use tackling the question of the girls at this stage. Mavis had made up her mind. Maybe as the days passed...

That evening Jimmy arrived at the house carrying a suitcase. He dumped it at the bottom of the stairs and pushed open the kitchen door. The children were sitting at the table having their tea, and as he opened the door, they fell silent, watching him with wide eyes. He reached into his pocket and slapped his ration book onto the table.

'There you are,' he said. 'Now perhaps I'll get a decent tea. I'll put my stuff upstairs.' He turned back at the door and added, 'And I want my name on the rent book. Right?' Picking up his case, he marched upstairs to Mavis's bedroom.

'Is Uncle Jimmy coming to stay?' Rosie asked.

'Yes,' Mavis replied. 'He's going to be your new daddy.'

'I don't want a new daddy,' cried Rita, jumping up from her chair. 'I don't want him. I don't like Uncle Jimmy. He's horrid.'

'That's enough of that, young lady,' snapped her mother. 'He's coming to live with us, and that's that.' Mavis reached over and shook Rita hard. 'And I suggest you keep a civil tongue in your head.'

'Why's he coming to our house?' asked Rosie.

'Because we want to be a family,' Mavis answered. 'You'll grow to love him, like I do.'

'I shan't,' stated Rita. 'I shan't love him. He doesn't love me.'

'Well, he certainly won't love you if you talk like that,' said Mavis. 'Now, finish your tea and go out to play.'

Rita crammed the last of her bread into her mouth and without another word went outside.

'Can I play out, too?' demanded Rosie, slipping down off her stool.

'Just for a little while,' agreed Mavis, and Rosie darted out to join her sister in the street.

Mavis was glad to see them go. She wanted them out of the way when Jimmy came back downstairs. She could hear him moving about in the bedroom and wondered what he was doing, but even as she got up to find out, she heard his footsteps on the stairs.

'I'm going out,' he said as he met her in the hallway.

'What about your tea?' she ventured as he opened the front door.

'I'll have it when I come in.'

When he had gone, she went upstairs to her room. The wardrobe door stood open and half her clothes had been pulled out and dumped on the bed. His were still in his case, but Mavis realized that she was expected to hang his up for him in the space he'd made, and she set about doing so, sorting and rehanging her own meagre wardrobe to accommodate his.

While she was busy upstairs, Rita came in from the street. She had seen Jimmy leave as she and Maggie had been trying to teach Rosie to skip.

'Back in a min,' she'd said and leaving Rosie with Maggie, she'd darted back into the house. She could hear Mum upstairs so she crept into the kitchen. Quickly she opened the drawer of the dresser, and there he was. Her daddy, smiling out through the cracked glass of his frame. She'd discovered the photo some days earlier, when looking in the drawer for a pencil. Quickly Rita pulled the frame open and slid Daddy out from under the glass. She looked round for somewhere to hide him. She could still hear Mum moving about upstairs, so she couldn't risk taking him up there. There was nowhere in the hall to hide him, so she opened the door to the front room. They never used the front room, well, only at Christmas when Gran came, so he wouldn't be found in there. She picked up the cushion from what had been her daddy's armchair and slid the photo inside its cover. Then she put the cushion back and slipped out into the street again. Daddy was safe now. She didn't want another dad; her daddy would always be her daddy. If Uncle Jimmy moved into the house, well, let him, but he would never, ever, be her dad.

A few weeks later there was a loud hammering on the front door and Mavis, opening it, was surprised to find her mother on the doorstep.

'How did that child get that cut on her forehead?' demanded Lily. 'How come Reet's got a black eye?'

'She… she fell off her stool last night,' faltered Mavis. 'She hit her face on the gas stove.'

'Hit her face on the gas stove,' echoed Lily scornfully. 'I don't believe you. There's much more to it than that.'

'She fell off her stool…' Mavis began again.

'Knocked off it more like,' asserted Lily. 'By that Jimmy, I bet. You shouldn't have him in the house, Mavis. I've told you before. He's bad news. He knocks you about—'

'No! No, Mum,' Mavis burst out. 'Who said that? Has that Rita—'

'He knocks you about,' repeated Lily, ignoring her interruption, 'an' he knocks the girls about, and whatever you say, he's going to go on doing it. Men like him always go on doing it.'

'Mum, it wasn't like that. Reet fell off her stool. You know what she's like. She was fidgeting… she's always fidgeting, you know she is. An' she fell off and hit her face, poor little kid.' Mavis's eyes challenged her mother to disbelieve her and Lily looked a little less certain.

'That's what she said—' began Lily.

'Because that's what happened, Mum. Did you see her on the way to school?'

'Yes, they were just going in.'

'Look, Mum, I was just leaving. I got to be at Mrs Robinson's in twenty minutes. Walk with me to the bus, eh? I must go or I'll be late.' She edged her mother towards the front door, and Lily allowed herself to be eased out of the house and into the street. Mavis closed the door behind her and, taking her mother firmly by the arm, began walking towards the bus stop.

'Sorry, Mum,' she said, 'but I mustn't be late. The cleaning takes me a bit longer these days and I don't want Mrs Robinson to turn me off. I was going to come and see you when I'd finished. Jimmy's going to the registry office today to get the wedding sorted. You have to put your name on a list for three weeks or something... not sure quite what, but Jimmy knows and he's going to do it in his dinnertime.'

'You really want to marry him, Mavis?' asked Lily, trying to walk more slowly. She wanted to talk to Mavis, to have things out with her, but knew that here in the street wasn't the place.

'Yes, I do,' Mavis asserted. 'He'll make a great dad.'

'Oh, Mavis, you know—'

'Sorry, Mum, here's my bus.' Mavis stuck her hand out to hail the bus and scrambled aboard as soon as it stopped. She turned back, looking at her mother still standing on the pavement. 'I'll come in and see you tomorrow, Mum. Tell you the wedding date and that.'

The bus began to draw away, and Mavis moved inside, waving to her mother through the window.

Lily watched her go with distinct misgivings. She remained unconvinced that Rita had simply fallen off her stool. No, Jimmy Randall had something to do with it. Jimmy Randall was not good news, not good news at all.

Chapter 3

On the bus, Mavis sat back against the seat for the five minutes to took to reach her stop. She realized that all her muscles were tense and she made a conscious effort to relax. She wasn't sure she'd convinced her mother about Rita's black eye, but for now, she'd avoided her questions. She had breathing space to decide what she was really going to do. Tomorrow she'd have to face her questions, but by tomorrow she'd have a wedding date and with luck Lily would be carried along on the tide of preparation.

Last night had been awful. Rita had refused to eat liver for her tea and Jimmy had lost his rag and knocked her off her stool. She'd smashed her face against the corner of the cooker, opening a cut on her forehead, and with a slam of the door, Jimmy had stalked out, leaving Mavis to deal with the blood and two screaming kids. She'd sent them both to bed, furious with Rita for provoking yet another row, and subsided into a chair, burying her face in her hands in despair. She was six months pregnant, always exhausted, and Jimmy still hadn't kept his promise to marry her. He'd moved in, but no wedding date had been set.

When Jimmy finally came back home Mavis was slumped in her chair, half asleep. She started awake as he came in and plonked himself down opposite her. Now he looked across at Mavis. 'Right,' he said, as if they were already in the middle of a conversation, 'tomorrow I'll go to the registry office and you can go to the council and tell them you need a home for your kids.'

Mavis looked at him blankly for a moment and then echoed faintly, 'Registry office?'

'To sort out a date for our wedding. That's what you wanted, isn't it?'

'Yes, oh Jimmy, yes, of course.'

'And you can go to the council and get your girls took in.'

'Took in where?'

'How do I know? They have orphanages, don't they? They have to now, with this new welfare.'

'But they're not orphans.'

'Half orphans, they are. They ain't got no dad.'

'But I want you to be their dad.'

'Well, I don't want to be, do I?' rasped Jimmy. 'And what's more, they don't want me to be, neither!'

'They don't know what they want,' began Mavis, 'they're too young to understand—'

Jimmy cut her off. 'Your Reet understands all right. She don't want me in the house, and I don't want her. Simple as that. She'd be happier living somewhere else. I expect she'll get adopted, and she'll be far better off adopted than living with us.'

'Adopted!' croaked Mavis.

'Well, Mav, there it is. We'll get married just like you want to, and you, me and the baby'll be a family.' He heaved himself to his feet. 'God, I'm tired. Heavy work on the building site. Come on, upstairs.'

In the morning Jimmy's parting words had been, 'I'll go to the registry office in me dinnertime. All right?' He gave her a hard stare and added, 'An' you'll do your bit, right?' Mavis had nodded. She knew she couldn't cope on her own any longer. She needed a man, a man who came home with a wage packet every Friday. A man to take care of the things men do take care of about the home. A man so she wasn't lonely any more. She had Jimmy. And if the price of having him was sending her daughters away for a while... well, it wouldn't be forever, would it? Increasingly it was becoming a price she was prepared to pay... for the sake of the baby. She hadn't quite decided, she told herself, but it couldn't hurt if she went to the council offices to see the welfare after she'd finished at Mrs Robinson's, just to ask. Nothing definite.

At half-past twelve, Mavis left Mrs Robinson's and walked the half mile or so to the Market Square. There, on the far side, were the council offices, housed in a grim, grey stone building, but today, with the sun shining on its windows, it seemed to Mavis to be more approachable. A sign, she thought to herself. A sign she should go in.

She crossed the square and taking a deep breath, mounted the steps and pushed her way through the heavy glass doors into the entrance hall. To one side was a reception desk, manned by a harassed-looking woman, typing. Mavis approached and the woman paused long enough to say, 'Can I help you?'

'I'm looking for...' Mavis gulped and tried again. 'I'm looking for the children's department.'

'Second floor, on the right at the top of the stairs. Room 21.'

The woman returned to her typing, and Mavis turned away. As she looked round to find the staircase, she glanced back through the glass doors at the sunlit square beyond.

I don't have to do this, she thought. I can walk out of them doors, and everything'll be like always.

Like always. No man in the house. A baby coming. No regular money. Reet behaving like a sullen little brat, fighting with Jimmy; Rosie starting to copy her. Shouting and screaming and hitting. If Rita wasn't in the house there'd be peace. If Rita wasn't in the house Jimmy couldn't hit her. Rita would be safer somewhere else. And if Rita wasn't in the house Jimmy wouldn't get so angry and take it out on her, Mavis. It would be better for everyone if Rita wasn't in the house... including Rita. Mavis turned and went up the stairs to find Room 21.

Room 21 turned out to be a sort of waiting room. It was very small, furnished with a couple of old wooden chairs, and on the far side was another door and a glass window with a sort of sliding hatch. Beside the hatch was a bell. Mavis rang it. There was a scuffling behind the glass panel and then the hatch slid open and a pale-faced woman peered out.

'Yes?'

'I want to see someone about having my kids took in,' Mavis said.

'I see,' came the matter-of-fact reply. 'Name?'

'Mavis Stevens.'

The woman made a note. 'Take a seat, please.' The glass hatch slid closed again.

Mavis sat down on one of the chairs. She stared for a moment at the glass hatch. Is that all there is to it? she wondered. Give your name and take a seat?

Mavis waited... and waited. After half an hour she went back to the window again.

'How long have I got to wait?' she asked when the whey-faced woman reappeared.

'It's dinnertime,' the woman replied. 'Miss Hopkins'll be back in a while. She's the one you have to see.' The glass hatch closed.

Mavis knew it was dinnertime, her own stomach was rumbling. She should have guessed the welfare lady might be out for dinner. She wished she'd thought of bringing a sandwich with her. She sighed and began re-reading the notices on the wall.

Miss Hopkins came back into the office a few moments later. She was a heavily built woman, broad in the hips and broad in the shoulders. Her hair was piled up on top of her head in a rather untidy heap and secured with what looked, to Mavis, like two hat pins. She was puffing from climbing the stairs, and she paused on the threshold to get her breath. She looked across at Mavis, but gave no greeting, simply crossed to the door beside the hatch and pushing it open, spoke to the woman inside. 'I'm back, Miss Parker.'

It was another quarter of an hour before Miss Parker appeared at the door and said, 'Miss Hopkins can see you now, Mrs Stevens.' She indicated a glass-panelled door on which were written the words, *Children's Officer.*

Mavis tapped on the glass and opening the door cautiously, went in. Seeing the formidable Miss Hopkins sitting behind a desk covered with papers, Mavis almost turned and fled. But it

23

was too late. She'd had all that waiting time to change her mind, and now, now it was too late. She edged into the room and Miss Hopkins, looking up from a paper she was reading, pointed to the wooden chair that stood in front of her desk.

'Please sit down.'

Mavis sat.

'Name?'

'Mavis Stevens.'

'Address?'

Mavis gave her address and Miss Hopkins made a note on a pad in front of her.

'Husband's name?'

'I haven't got a husband,' stumbled Mavis, unnerved by the woman's brisk efficiency. 'I mean, I'm a widow. He was killed in the war.'

'I see.' Miss Hopkins eyed the well-defined bulge of Mavis's stomach. 'Children?'

'Yes, two girls, Rita's nine and Rosie's five.'

'And another on the way,' stated Miss Hopkins.

'Yes, well, me and Jimmy, we're getting married soon, and...'

'And...?' prompted Miss Hopkins, though she thought she knew what was coming.

'And there ain't room for us all in the house, not with the new baby. We need somewhere for the girls to go, just for a little while, while we get settled, like. Be difficult for us all being crammed in together... with the new baby an' all.'

'I see.' Miss Hopkins sat back in her chair and steepled her fingers. 'I see, so you want to move the girls out to make way for the baby.'

'Just for a little while,' Mavis reiterated, 'just while, you know...' Her words tailed off. Silence.

'And where do you want them to go?' enquired Miss Hopkins at last. 'Why have you come to me?'

'Well,' Mavis looked a little confused, 'well, you're the welfare, ain't you? I mean, you're the children's department. You have to look after children that don't have no homes.'

'But your children do have a home,' pointed out Miss Hopkins.

'Well, they do and they don't,' said Mavis, and when Miss Hopkins made no comment to this rather cryptic statement, she went on, 'They do just now, but they won't when Jimmy and I get married.'

'You mean he won't give them a home,' stated Miss Hopkins bluntly.

'He will, but it ain't easy. They ain't his family, are they? Not like the baby'll be.' Mavis leaned forward earnestly in her chair. 'They ain't his kids. He don't feel about them the way I do.'

And you'd rather have him than them, thought Miss Hopkins. Aloud she said, 'I see.'

She did see too, a woman at her wits' end. Needing to get married to have support for the new baby, and for herself, but knowing that this was not going to happen unless her daughters were removed from the household. Well, it wouldn't be the end of the world. Miss Hopkins knew of a place that would happily accept such children. Perhaps...?

'Do the girls get on all right with... your fiancé?' she asked.

'Yeah, yeah... mostly... well, not all the time. Rita gives him a bit of cheek sometimes and he don't like it.'

'Does he strike her?'

'No! Course not!' Mavis filled her voice with indignation, but when Miss Hopkins' eyes bored into her, Mavis dropped her gaze and said, 'Well, not often. But I mean, she cheeks him... says he's not her dad and that.'

'Well, he isn't, is he?' pointed out Miss Hopkins. Silence again. Mavis stared at the floor. 'So he doesn't love them... the girls?'

'Well, they're not his, are they?' Mavis demanded. 'I mean, it's natural that he don't love them like he'll love the baby. He ain't never going to love them like he'll love the baby, is he? 'Cos the baby's his, ain't it?'

'You'll have to fill in a form,' Miss Hopkins said, 'requesting assistance with housing your daughters, that's if you're serious about asking for them to be fostered for a while.'

'Just till we're sorted,' Mavis said. 'Shall I fill it in now? The form?'

'It's quite complicated,' replied Miss Hopkins. 'I think you should take it away and look at it very carefully. Go through it with your... fiancé. It's not a thing to be rushed, you know. Once you've made your application it will be considered, but I must warn you this doesn't mean that it will be granted. The decision will take time, but if accepted, places will be found for your daughters.' Miss Hopkins rose to her feet. 'It's too important to be hurried.'

Mavis stood as well, clutching her handbag in front of her, a barrier between her and the formidable woman behind the desk.

'No,' she said. 'All right, I'll take it with me and bring it back tomorrow.'

'Very well.' Miss Hopkins rang a bell and Miss Parker appeared at the door.

'Ah, Miss Parker. Please give Mrs Stevens application forms for temporary foster care and adoption.'

'Adoption!' exclaimed Mavis.

'I think that's what you're actually asking for, Mrs Stevens, isn't it? Someone to take Rita and Rosie off your hands so that you can start a new life with your new husband?'

Mavis didn't reply, and Miss Hopkins continued, 'In that case, please fill in both sets of forms and bring them back with the children's birth certificates. We can take it from there. Good afternoon, Mrs Stevens.'

As the door closed behind her visitor, Miss Hopkins put down the paper and looked thoughtful. It was clear to her that the two little girls weren't wanted at home. But she knew someone who wanted them, and if the mother returned with the right documentation, she was sure that she could hurry the application through. As the newly appointed acting Children's Officer, with several years' experience in welfare work, she was the dominant person on the new Children's Committee and decisions she made were normally rubber-stamped by those who deferred to her experience. She reached for the telephone and asked the operator for the number she needed.

Chapter 4

Emily Vanstone stared out of the window. It was raining and the garden beyond looked damp and depressing. On the desk in front of her was a brochure showing a wide and open landscape, basking in warm sunshine. At the top were the words, *EVER-Care taking children to a better world and a better life.*

It was ten years since she, Emily Vanstone, spinster daughter of the late George Vanstone, sister-in-law of Sir Edward Sherrington and pillar of the Crosshills Methodist Church, had set up a charity to rescue children whom she described as 'Guttersnipes' from their poor and feckless families.

When her father, George Vanstone, mill-owner and philan-thropist, died, he left his money in four equal parts. One quarter went to each of his three daughters, Amelia, Emily and Maud. The last quarter of his substantial estate was in a trust to be administered jointly by Emily and by Maud's husband, solicitor, Martin Fielding, *'for the benefit of those in need'.* And who could be in more need than children who lived in the gutter?

Emily had visited Amelia and her brother-in-law, Sir Edward Sherrington, to tell them of her grand scheme. Not to ask them to contribute financially, that would have been a pointless exer-cise, but to use them in an entirely different way. What was the use of having an aristocratic brother-in-law if you didn't take advantage of the fact on occasion? She had told Amelia she wanted to discuss something with them and Amelia had, rather reluctantly, asked her to dinner.

'My orphanage will give these girls a home,' Emily explained.

'Girls only?' interjected Amelia.

'Certainly girls only,' replied Emily. 'It's girls who need rescuing before they are dragged into prostitution... or worse.'

'Is there anything worse?' wondered Amelia vaguely.

Emily ignored her and went on, 'They will be fed and clothed, but more importantly, they'll be taught good Christian values. They will learn to work and they will learn to pray. They will learn to behave as a good citizen should. They will learn their place in life. They will not slide into a life of crime like their parents. The home will be run on strict principles, there'll be no laxity, only strict discipline will turn these street Arabs into upright and worthwhile citizens. Early rescue is the key. Haul them out of the gutter before it's too late.'

Sir Edward looked at the middle-aged woman in front of him, her greying hair swept back into a tight bun at the nape of her neck, her eyes holding a fanatical gleam, and thought, Emily's a real chip off the old block.

Despite his superiority in education and social standing, Edward Sherrington had been in awe of his father-in-law, and though he would never admit it, even to himself, he was a little afraid of his formidable sister-in-law as well.

George Vanstone had had no sons, but Emily was as shrewd a business woman as ever her father had been. The mills still turned and produced increasing profits, and Emily had refused to hand over the reins to either of her brothers-in-law. This suited them all. Neither man wanted to be linked to 'trade' and provided their wives received their share of the profits, they had little inclination to interfere, leaving Emily able to do much as she pleased. She had invested in numerous projects, and now, Sherrington thought, she's investing in children.

'I've talked to Martin about it,' Emily continued, 'and he agrees that I can set up an orphanage with the money Father left in the trust. I've already heard of a suitable house. It's in Russell Green, just over Russell Bridge. Martin and I are going to see it tomorrow.'

Edward Sherrington shrugged. 'Well, you're the trustees,' he said. 'Just as long as you don't expect *me* to put money into it.'

'No, Edward,' Emily said smoothly, 'not your money.' Not that it is your money, she thought, it's Amelia's, but she won't put any in either. 'Not your money, Edward, your name.'

'My name?' Edward looked startled.

'I want you to be the patron. You know, with your name as patron on the headed notepaper.'

'Well, I don't know...'

'A baronet would look very well on a letterhead, don't you think?' remarked Emily, turning to her sister. No harm in reminding Edward that he had traded his title for their money.

'Indeed,' Amelia agreed. She was far too clever to remind Ned what he owed her; she was quite happy with the bargain. Moving in the upper echelons of society as Lady Sherrington, she wanted reminders of her lowly origins as little as Ned did. However, she also enjoyed playing Lady Bountiful, and the thought of the Sherrington name on the letterhead of a charitable foundation was a tempting one.

'You know, Ned,' she went on, 'Emily's right. It would look very well.'

Edward actually agreed. 'Well,' he said, 'if you invite me to be your patron, I can hardly decline, can I? But,' he looked at Emily over the rim of his wine glass, 'it's all I will do. I'll have no other part in this venture. Is this understood between us, Emily?'

'Oh, absolutely, Edward,' replied Emily, suppressing a smile. The last thing she wanted was Ned meddling in her affairs. 'I'll ask you for nothing else, I promise.'

The next morning Martin Fielding collected Emily and they drove out to Russell Green to look at the house she had found. Laurel House. As soon as she saw it, Emily was sure it would suit her perfectly. It was a substantial, rather ugly Victorian house standing in a large garden, the front of which was surrounded by the high laurel hedge that gave the house its name. Built in grey stone, its bleak exterior was made even more austere by a squat tower at one end. In the 1920s someone had added a brick-built wing, making the house an 'L', and providing some much needed kitchen space. At the back was a much larger garden, with a shaggy lawn and overgrown kitchen garden, beyond which was an orchard, surrounded by a high stone wall. Clearly it hadn't been lived in for some time.

The heavy door creaked open reluctantly and they stepped inside. Immediately Emily began assessing Laurel House's possibilities. Taking a notebook and pencil from her handbag, she began to make notes, already seeing the house as it would be, once it was furnished ready for the children.

The entrance hall was wide and high with a staircase that rose to the floor above in a broad sweep. Downstairs there were several reception rooms, including a morning room and a study. The old kitchen had been turned into a laundry, and from it a door led down into a large cellar that ran the length of the house. Emily did not venture into the cellar, merely opening the door and peering down into the gloom, but she was pleased to know it was there, offering plenty of storage space. The kitchen in the new wing was adequate and as she wandered through the empty rooms, Emily became certain that this was the house for her orphanage.

'We'll buy it,' she announced to Martin. 'It's perfect. We can easily accommodate at least thirty children in here. Maybe more.'

'My dear Emily, we can't rush into this, you know,' Martin said, concerned. He thought it a dreadful house, grey and forbidding. Much time, effort and money would have to be spent on it to make it habitable. 'We need to consider long and hard before we decide. There may be other houses that would be even better. It would be stupid to buy the first one we saw.'

Emily turned on him at once. 'Martin,' she said briskly, 'we've agreed to use the trust money for an orphanage. This house provides all we need, there is no point in waiting.'

'It will take a while... all the legalities of setting up a charity,' Martin pointed out.

'That's your job,' she said cheerfully. 'You sort out the legalities, and all the other paperwork. That's why Father made you a trustee. You arrange the purchase of the house, I'll get the work started.'

It had all taken longer than Emily had envisaged, but she spared no one in her determination to get the orphanage up and running. She did not squander money on furnishing the place. She had the walls painted, but kept to dark colours that wouldn't show the dirt. She bought metal beds with thin mattresses, which were now crammed, six to a room, in the five bedrooms upstairs. Long wooden tables and hard wooden chairs furnished the dining room, the erstwhile drawing room, and two second-hand sofas and some ancient easy chairs were in the newly designated 'playroom'. In the kitchen were a heavy duty kitchen table, a deep Belfast sink and a solid fuel range. There were several cupboards set against the walls and some shelves which housed an assortment of pots and pans.

Emily proudly showed Martin a new gas cooker standing in the corner. 'Two stoves, you see? Plenty of room to cook for thirty children.'

'Who's going to do the cooking?' Martin asked.

'Oh, the children will prepare their own meals,' Emily said. 'Under supervision of course. But the whole point is that it will be part of their training, you see. We're going to teach these creatures to become useful citizens.'

The orphanage had opened a few weeks later, with fourteen children and a live-in staff of four. Three, the matron, the cook and a housemaid, lived in bed-sitting rooms built into the loft above the kitchen, and the superintendent in a small flat at the top of the tower. The children were sent from an overflowing home several miles away.

Over the years the home had been run with strict discipline and at minimal cost. The children cooked, cleaned, mended and tended the garden. They were fed and clothed and went to the local schools until they were fourteen, when they were found a job and expected to hand in their pay packet at the end of each week. At sixteen, if they had a job, they were allowed to leave the house, and most of them did. Many of them went into service, where they lived in, all found, and were only paid minimal wages. A few chose to stay at Laurel House and go out daily to jobs in shops, or as live-out domestics, but they were expected to hand over half their pay packet to the orphanage for their keep.

The numbers grew, the home always full, and Emily Vanstone considered buying another house. She was actively looking for something suitable, when she received a letter that turned her attention to Australia. Her cousin, Daphne, had married an Australian service man, Joe Manton, after the war, and gone to live in Carrabunna, a small town north-west of Sydney. It was she, writing to Emily, who mentioned a nearby farm school that took children from the slums in England and taught them to be farmers.

I thought you might send some of your orphans here, Daphne wrote. *It's a beautiful country and it would be a new start for them, away from evils of the city.*

'Australia?' snapped Edward when she told him.

'Yes. Fairbridge and Dr Barnardo's have been doing it for years.'

'Yes,' scoffed her brother-in-law, 'but they are large and well-known societies, not a small orphanage like yours.'

'We may be small, Edward, but we are well respected,' retorted Emily, adding in a more conciliatory tone, 'due, doubt-less, to your patronage.'

'But, Emily,' Amelia said, staring at her sister in amazement, 'will the parents let you send their children to Australia?'

'Most of my children don't have parents,' replied Emily, 'and the parents of those who do signed legal guardianship over to me when they put their children in my care. Martin drew up all the papers, and we made sure they were watertight. I am their legal guardian. I can send whoever I want wherever I want. It's all arranged. The house is bought and I'm going over to get it all set up.'

'*You're* going to Australia?' Edward was incredulous.

'Certainly,' agreed Emily, 'I leave next week.'

Emily Vanstone had sailed for Australia, and when she returned six months later, the EVER-Care migrant home was ready to receive its first children. Though she'd had to change her 'farm school' idea, something she had realized that Daphne and Joe were in no way equipped to run, she had set out the principles on which the Australian home was to be organized. She had no doubt that the children who were sent there would benefit from the same firm regime as at Laurel House. Law-abiding, hard-working citizens would emerge... and be a credit to her and the EVER-Care name.

Laurel Farm, Carrabunna, was established. Though not a farm as such, it sought to feed itself as far as was possible, and the labour was supplied by its inmates. For three years Emily had, without any consultation, sent children from her orphanage twelve thousand miles across the world to a new country and a new life. She had never again visited the Australian EVER-Care home, leaving the running of it to Daphne and Joe Manton, in whom she had complete confidence. However, she liked to have her finger on the pulse of all her enterprises and she kept in close contact by letter. Then Hitler intervened and the child migration scheme was put on hold.

The war changed everything. There were even more children needing a home, children orphaned by the war, and EVER-Care accepted them all. The flow of children continued, not least because Emily Vanstone had a new admirer: a new member of the congregation at the Crosshills Methodist Church. Miss May Hopkins. Miss Hopkins was the social worker for the local council in charge of children's affairs. She admired the zealous and philanthropic Miss Vanstone greatly, and whenever she had children to place in care, it was to the EVER-Care home at Laurel House that she turned first.

The end of the war had also brought a change of government and with it plans for a new welfare system. Things began to change. There was a shift in public thinking and the new

Children's Departments were expected to explore other ways of providing care for needy children. Different arrangements were to be made and the newly appointed Children's Officers were placing such children with foster families rather than residential homes like Laurel House. Miss Hopkins was expected to do the same. Public opinion on the child migration scheme had changed too. People began to think that perhaps children as young as three should not be plucked from all that was familiar and shipped off to the other side of the world. English children should be brought up in England. Sir Edward Sherrington's thoughts that the riff-raff should be sent somewhere else, preferably as far away as possible, were no longer publicly expressed.

Miss Hopkins did not agree with the changes, and whenever possible she still sent girls in need of care to Laurel House. From what she'd just said on the phone, it sounded to Emily as if she might soon have two new inmates for Laurel House.

Chapter 5

Rita lay in bed, listening. She could hear the sound of Mum's voice downstairs, high and excited. There was the rumble of Uncle Jimmy's voice as he replied, but Rita couldn't hear what they were saying.

When Uncle Jimmy had come home, Mum had put a plate of sausage and mash on the table and said, 'Here's your tea, love. We must talk later. Got things to tell you... you know.' She nodded her head. 'You know,' she repeated.

'What things?' asked Rita. Why was Mum nodding and smiling like that?

'Nothing to do with you, Miss Nosey Parker,' said her mother. 'Now, you girls go out to play till bedtime.'

Listening to the voices downstairs now, Rita knew they were talking about the things that had nothing to do with her, and she wondered what they were. She crept out of bed and edged halfway down the stairs. She dared not go any further or she'd have no hope of escaping if Uncle Jimmy came out unexpectedly. She strained to hear what was said, but she could only hear snatches... something about the baby.

Mum was asking about going to an office. Had he been as he promised? Rita couldn't hear Uncle Jimmy's answer, but her mother sounded pleased. Then he said something else, and Rita heard Mum say, 'Yes, I went, I said I would.'

Uncle Jimmy's voice again and then Mum said, 'The welfare woman said just fill in the forms, and I...' then the clatter of china drowned her next words. Rita strained to hear but the scrape of a chair on the kitchen floor made her scurry upstairs. She was just in time as the kitchen door opened and Uncle Jimmy came out.

'Jimmy, where are you going?' Mum's voice was quite clear now.

'Out for a pint.'

'But what about the forms? I need your help with them. We've got to decide.'

'We have decided,' answered Uncle Jimmy. 'You fill them in. I'm going for a pint.'

Rita heard the front door slam and her mother's plaintive 'Jimmy!' to the empty kitchen.

Rita lay in bed thinking about what she'd heard. The baby. Well, she knew Mum was having a baby. It was growing in her tummy and making her very fat. She wasn't at all sure how the baby was going to get out. When she'd asked, Mum had said that when the time came the nurse would come and the baby would be born. Rita knew there must be more to it than this and she talked to Maggie down the street, who had a new baby brother.

'The nurse came,' Maggie told her, 'and she pulled him out through Mum's belly button.'

'Did you see him come out?' asked Rita in wonderment.

'No,' Maggie admitted. 'I was sent round my nan's.'

Rita had given Maggie's answer a lot of thought since. She couldn't quite believe that a baby could get out through a belly button, but what other explanation was there? Now, she wondered, was it something to do with the welfare woman Mum had mentioned? Did you have to go to the welfare office and fill in forms for the baby to be able to come out? Mum had decided it was time to fill in the forms so that the baby could be born.

As Rita finally drifted off to sleep, she thought, I'll ask Gran. She'll know.

The opportunity to ask came the next afternoon. It was Thursday, and Gran was waiting for them at the school gate in Capel Street as usual. On the way home Gran let them stop at the playground where they went on the swings, laughing as she pushed them higher and higher. Rita loved the tall slide and was soon scrambling up the ladder to the top.

'Look at me, Gran,' she called. 'I'm very high!'

'So you are, love,' Gran cried, 'and too high for you,' she said to Rosie as she ran to climb up behind her sister. 'Come on, love. I'll push you on the roundabout.' Moments later Rita was there too, clinging to the bars of the little roundabout and scooting it with her foot to make it go faster.

Lily stood back and watched the two little girls shrieking with excitement, carefree on a warm afternoon and love for them welled up inside her, threatening to spring as tears from her eyes. Her beautiful granddaughters, growing up like so many after this dreadful war, with no father in their lives.

Does that matter? wondered Lily. Of course it matters! she admonished herself. Every child needs a dad, but must it be Jimmy Randall?

As they walked on to Gran's house Rosie skipped trustingly beside her, swinging their joined hands.

'What's for tea?' she asked.

'Have to see what we can find, won't we,' answered Gran. 'How does bread and dripping sound?'

'Yippee!' cried Rosie twisting away and dancing backwards along the path. She beamed at her grandmother and said, 'I love coming to your house, Gran. I wish it was always Thursday.'

When they were sitting at Gran's kitchen table eating the promised bread and dripping, Rita said, 'Gran, when it's time for Mum's baby to be born, how does it get out of her tummy?'

'Well,' said Gran, 'when it's time, the nurse will come and the baby will be born.'

'But how does it get out?' persisted Rita. 'Does Mum have to fill in forms for the welfare woman?'

'Welfare woman?' Gran sounded puzzled. 'What welfare woman?'

'Mum said the welfare woman had said she just had to fill in the forms.'

'Start again, Reet,' said her grandmother, frowning.

'I heard Mum and Uncle Jimmy talking about the baby. Mum said she'd been to see the welfare woman, and all she had to do was fill in the forms. She asked Uncle Jimmy to help, but he said they'd already decided and that she could do it.'

'When was this?' asked Gran, a frightening suspicion invading her mind. She immediately pushed it away. No, it was impossible. Mavis would never... would she? No, certainly not. Rita must have got hold of the wrong end of the stick. 'When did you hear all this?' she asked.

'I was in bed, and I heard them talking down in the kitchen,' Rita said, 'only I couldn't hear properly so I went out onto the stairs, and that's what I heard them say.'

'You shouldn't have been out of bed,' said Gran sternly. 'Eavesdroppers never hear any good of themselves.'

Rosie looked up from her dripping sandwich. 'What's an eavesdropper, Gran?'

'Someone who listens to other people's conversations when they should be in bed,' answered Gran. 'Like your naughty sister.' She turned her attention back to Rita. 'I expect your mum was talking about the forms she has to fill in to get a ration book for the baby when it comes. Now, eat your tea and then we'll have a game of snap.'

'But how does the baby—' persisted Rita.

'I'll tell you all about it another time,' Gran cut in hastily. 'There's no time now if we're going to play snap before you have to go.'

That evening, Lily sat in her kitchen and considered what Rita had said. The child was no fool. If she said she'd heard them talking about filling in forms for the welfare, then that's what they'd been saying. But why on earth would Mavis be talking to the welfare? She didn't need anything from them. And what had Mavis and Jimmy already decided? Perhaps they'd finally fixed a date to get married. Rita had said that Jimmy was going to the registry office yesterday to find out. They'd certainly need to fill in forms for that. Perhaps that was it. That *must* be it. Rita had got confused about two different parts of the conversation and misunderstood; after all, she'd said that she hadn't heard it all.

Still, Lily thought, I'll talk to Mavis tomorrow and find out what's going on. I suppose it's for the best if they get married with a little'un on the way, but I don't like that Jimmy. I don't like him and I don't trust him.

Next morning she went round to Ship Street early to catch Mavis before she went to work. Mavis looked flustered when she opened the door and found her mother, yet again, on the step.

'Mum,' she groaned. 'What are you doing here?' She didn't say 'again' but it was in her voice.

Lily gave her a broad smile and said as she eased herself into the hallway, 'I just came to see how Jimmy got on with the registry office. You said he was going on Wednesday, and I wondered if he'd got a date. Have you got the kettle on, love? Let's have a cup of tea and you can tell me all about it.'

Mavis sighed, led her mother into the kitchen and topped up the teapot. When she'd poured tea for each of them, she sat down across the table from Lily and forced a smile. 'Jimmy went, like he said he would,' Mavis said. 'We have to fill in the forms and then I have to show them Don's death certificate.'

'So lots of forms, then?' suggested Lily, relief in her voice. That's what Rita overheard, she thought.

'Well, we tell them we want to get married and they put the form up on the noticeboard outside the registry office. Then after three weeks we can get wed. We want to get married next month, before...' Mavis laid a protective hand on her bump. 'Jimmy's taking the forms back and he'll book us in for a date then.'

'The girls'll be excited,' Lily said. 'Have you told them yet?'

'No, not yet,' answered Mavis, looking away. 'Not till everything's sorted, for definite, you know.'

'You've got to get Jimmy to go easy on them, Mavis,' said her mother. 'It'll be hard for them at first, having to share you with him... and the baby. Reet, particularly, is going to find it difficult.'

'Mum...' Mavis began and then stopped.

'What?' Lily looked at her, and saw the anguish in Mavis's eyes. She reached a hand across the table and said, more gently, 'What's the matter, Mavis? What's wrong?'

'It's the girls,' Mavis whispered. 'Jimmy won't have them here.'

'Won't have them here?' echoed Lily. 'What d'you mean, won't have them here? It's their home. Where else should they be?'

'He wants them took into care,' murmured Mavis, not looking up. 'He don't want them here, he just wants us to be a family, him, me and the baby.'

'But the girls, Reet, Rosie, they're your family.' Lily stared at her daughter's bowed head uncomprehendingly. 'Mavis, they've only got you!'

'He won't have them.'

'Then tell him to sod off,' flashed Lily.

'I can't, Mum. He's the baby's father. I need him here. I've got to choose!'

'And you choose him?' Lily was outraged. 'You choose that violent brute... 'cos he is violent and you know it... you choose him over your own kids? Your own flesh and blood?'

'I have to,' wailed Mavis. 'The baby's my own flesh and blood too, and I can't cope on my own, Mum, not any more.'

'You're not putting my granddaughters into no home,' Lily exploded. 'How can you even think of such a thing?'

'If you really want to know, I think they'd be happier there,' Mavis shouted back. 'Reet would, I know she would. She don't like Jimmy. She makes no effort to get on with him, and now she's encouraging Rosie to cheek him as well. Every day it's getting worse and I can't stand it no more!' Mavis burst into a flood of tears. 'What am I going to do, Mum? I can't keep them. They've got to go and live somewhere else. It's for their own good.'

Lily watched her as she struggled with her tears, and then said, 'But a home, Mavis? An orphanage, you mean? They ain't orphans.'

'Lots of kids in orphanages ain't orphans,' sniffed Mavis. 'After this bloody war lots of men ain't come home. Lots of mothers are like me, been left alone with kids and can't cope with them. It won't be forever...'

'Rubbish!' snapped Lily. 'If Jimmy won't have 'em now, when they're just little kiddies, he won't take 'em back when he's got more of his own.' Lily looked despairingly at her daughter. 'Oh, Mavis,' she cried, 'you ain't really going to do this, are you? Give your daughters away? What would Don think of you? Him going off to fight, trusting his precious girls to you. Don't you owe him nothing?'

'Don's dead,' answered Mavis bleakly. 'He's gone. He was another part of my life and it's over. He ain't coming back, is he? So I've got to get on with the rest of my life. I'm another person now.'

'You certainly are,' replied Lily tightly, 'and not one I want to know. I'm ashamed to think you're my daughter.' She got to her feet and stared down at Mavis.

'You won't tell them yet, will you?' begged Mavis.

'I won't tell them at all,' retorted Lily, 'in the hope that you come to your senses and realize exactly what you're intending to do.' She went to the door, but as she put her hand on the handle she turned back. 'Oh Mavis, love, don't do it! Don't let him bully you into it. We'll manage without him, even with the new baby. We'll manage. You and me and Rita and Rosie will be the baby's family. We can manage, I promise you.'

'It'll be a bastard,' Mavis said flatly.

'Well,' Lily replied, 'there's plenty of those around... you're even planning to marry one!'

'Get out, Mum!' Mavis started up from the table, glaring at her mother. 'Get out. It ain't nothing to do with you. If you don't like what I'm doing, get out and don't bother coming back!'

Lily gave her daughter a long look and then without another word turned and walked out of the house. The brilliance of the day outside made her blink, the heat blasted back from the pavement, but the chill that gripped Lily made her feel as cold as ice.

For the rest of the day and all that night, Lily thought of nothing else. She lay in bed unable to sleep, her mind churning. She could still hardly believe that Mavis was going to put her daughters into an orphanage. Surely she'll think better of it and change her mind, thought Lily. Mavis loves her kids, how could she bear to be parted from them? How could she even begin to consider sending them away... on the orders of that man?

'I won't let her,' Lily announced suddenly to her bedroom. 'I won't let her. If that brute won't let her keep them in their own home, then they can come here to me. I won't let them grow up in some dreadful place, thinking no one wants them.'

It was the obvious solution. She'd go and tell Mavis first thing. This decision made Lily fall into an uneasy doze, waking only an hour or so later, unrefreshed but determined.

It was Saturday, the girls would be at home, and so might Jimmy, but that couldn't be helped. She must speak to Mavis again, tell her the girls should come and live with her, before it was too late.

When Mavis opened the door to find her mother on the step, she immediately tried to push it shut again, but expecting such a reaction, Lily was ready and thrust against it.

'Go away!' hissed Mavis. 'You're not welcome here.'

'Mavis!' Lily's voice brooked no argument. 'I have to speak to you.'

'You spoke to me yesterday,' snarled Mavis. 'We ain't got nothing left to say.'

'I'll have them,' Lily said urgently, still leaning on the door to prevent it from shutting. 'I'll have the girls to live with me.'

The pressure on the door eased a little, but still Mavis wouldn't open it. 'What d'you mean?' She spoke softly as if afraid of being overheard.

'I'll have the girls to live with me,' repeated Lily. 'Mavis, love, listen. Let me in so we can talk about it.'

'Jimmy's here.'

'That's OK,' replied Lily. 'He can be part of the discussion. We all need to agree on what's to happen... what's for the best.'

'You're not to make him angry,' warned Mavis. 'He was mad when he heard what you'd said about him yesterday.'

More fool you for telling him, thought Lily, but aloud she said, 'No, I won't make him angry, promise. I'll simply explain my idea. I'm sure we can work something out that will please everyone.'

Reluctantly, Mavis opened the door and let Lily step inside. She led the way into the kitchen where Rita and Rosie were sitting at the table.

'Gran!' cried Rosie in delight, jumping down from her stool for a hug.

Rita stayed where she was, but smiled and said, 'Can we come to your house today?' She turned to her mother. 'Can we?' she said. 'Can we go round Gran's?'

'Perhaps later,' said Lily.

'You girls go and play upstairs,' said Mavis, 'and don't you go waking your Uncle Jimmy.'

'But I want...' began Rita, but her mother reached over and took her arm, pulling her roughly from her stool. 'You'll do as you're told, my girl, or you'll feel the weight of my hand.'

Rita scowled, but she did not reply. She simply took Rosie's hand and said, 'Come on, Rosie, let's go upstairs.'

Mavis flopped into a chair and turned to face Lily. 'All right,' she said belligerently, 'what's your plan? You can see how difficult Reet's being.'

'I thought it might be best if Rita and Rosie came to live with me,' replied Lily. When Mavis made no response she went on, encouraged, 'That way you wouldn't lose them, would you? They'd be just round the corner and you could see them whenever you wanted to. They could go to the same school. They'd still be with their friends. They wouldn't feel pushed out, they're happy enough when they're with me.' She paused, and as Mavis still said nothing she added, 'No one would think you'd rejected them, they'd see that you'd simply given yourself a little breathing space... with a new husband and a new baby.'

'I don't know,' Mavis said gruffly. 'After all you said yesterday.'

'Yesterday... well, yesterday I was surprised, and upset. You did rather spring it on me, your idea of a home.' Lily pulled out a chair and sat down opposite Mavis. 'But it needn't come to that. If they come to live with me for a bit, they'll be out of Jimmy's hair and you'll be able to concentrate on him and the baby. If they come to me they'll be going somewhere they know, not to some strange place with strangers to look after them.' Lily reached out a hand. 'Mavis, love, I know you love your kids, that you want what's best for them, and you're probably right, it is better for them to be out of this house for a little while, but please don't put them in a home. Let them come and stay with me where you know they'll be safe.'

Mavis still didn't answer, but Lily could see that she was giving consideration to the idea, so she allowed the silence to lengthen. It was eventually broken by a cry from upstairs and then a thud, followed by the sound of heavy footsteps on the stairs. Mavis came to her feet as the door opened and Jimmy Randall came in.

Unshaven and dressed only in pyjama trousers and a string vest, he stopped dead when he saw Lily at the table. 'And what the 'ell are you doing 'ere?' he demanded.

'I've come to talk to Mavis about Rita and Rosie,' replied Lily, trying not to shrink back as he towered over her.

'Come to meddle, more like,' he said. 'Well, we don't want your meddling, right? So you can push off. Go on, out.' He pushed back the door and pointed to the street.

'She's only come—' began Mavis.

'To bloody interfere. We don't need her, right?'

'She says the girls can live with her,' Mavis said. 'She says she'll take them and—'

'Then get up them stairs and pack their bags,' snapped Jimmy. 'She can 'ave 'em, but they go today.'

'Today...' stammered Mavis, paling visibly.

'Why not?' shrugged Jimmy. 'She wants 'em, we don't. They can go today.'

'Jimmy...' wailed Mavis, but he had turned on his heel and was stumping back up the stairs.

Lily had been going to suggest that today they tell the girls about coming to live with her, let them get used to the idea, and then move their things the following weekend. She'd have had time to prepare their room, and given herself time to get used to the idea too, but Jimmy's reaction decided her. She wanted those girls out of this house and out of his way at once. She had felt intimidated by him, and she was a grown woman, well used to looking after herself. What must those children feel when he came into the room? She turned to Mavis, who had buried her face in her hands.

'Come on, Mavis,' she said briskly. 'Call the girls down and let's tell them they're coming to me. But tell them, mind, that it's just till you've had the baby and got settled again. All right?'

Mavis didn't answer, simply moaned into her hands. Lily reached over and shook her roughly by the shoulder. 'Pull your-self together, my girl,' she said. 'This house ain't no place for them.'

Lily went to the bottom of the stairs and called the girls. They came down into the kitchen and looked expectantly at their mother and grandmother. When Mavis still said nothing, Lily said, 'I've got something to tell you both. Poor Mummy is very tired, what with the baby coming soon, and she needs more rest, so I thought it would be a good idea if you two came and stayed with me for a bit.'

Rita stared at her incredulously for a moment, while Rosie clapped her hands and cried, 'Are we going to stay in your house, Gran? And sleep the night? Can we have bread and dripping for tea?'

'Come and live with you, you mean?' asked Rita. 'All the time?'

'For now,' replied Lily. 'Just to give Mum a rest, until she has the baby.'

Rita nodded as if she were considering the idea. 'What about school?'

'You can go to school from my house,' answered Lily. 'Mum'll come and see you, and bring the baby when it's born.'

'Will Uncle Jimmy come and see us, too?' asked Rosie.

'No!' It was Rita who spat out the answer.

'No,' her grandmother agreed more softly, 'he'll be too busy to come. Now, let's go upstairs and pack up some of your things, then we can take them to my house.'

Packing took little time. Their few clothes fitted easily into the small cardboard suitcase that Mavis produced, and favourite toys were crammed into a shopping bag. Rosie clutched Knitty, a strange-looking creature that Lily had knitted from an unravelled jumper. He had buttons for eyes, an embroidered nose and smiley mouth, and Rosie loved him dearly, always sleeping with him tucked under her arm. Both girls had their school satchels with their plimsolls for drill, and Rita slipped the photograph of Daddy into the pages of her sum book. She was careful not to let Mum see him, in case she took him away.

Once they were packed and ready, they set out for Lily's house. Walking along the street, carrying the suitcase, the shopping bag and their satchels, they looked for all the world, Lily thought, like the refugees you saw on the cinema newsreels.

Chapter 6

As the next weeks slipped by, the girls settled into their new home, and their new routine. Rosie had shed a few tears at bedtime the first few nights. She wanted Mum to come and kiss her goodnight, and when Gran tucked them in and kissed them she whispered on a sob, 'I want my mummy!'

'Course you do, lovey,' soothed Gran. 'But don't cry, she's coming to see you tomorrow when you get home from school. Now you snuggle down with Knitty, like a good girl, and it'll be tomorrow in no time.'

Rita missed her mother, too, but she was determined not to say so. Mum had sent them to Gran's so that she could be with Uncle Jimmy. Well, thought Rita, I don't care. I don't want to live with Uncle Jimmy, I'd rather stay with Gran.

But she did care. She missed the familiar kitchen with its own peculiar smell, its cluttered shelves and scarred wooden table. Gran's kitchen, though familiar, wasn't the same. Rita missed her bedroom, too, with its faded roses on the wall and cracked window pane. She had a bed to herself now, but she missed sharing with Rosie and very often she crept in beside her, curling round her as she always had, so that they were as warm and cosy as two kittens in a basket.

School was just the same and if it wasn't raining, Gran let them play in the park on the way home most days now, but Rita missed running on home to tell Mum about her day afterwards; she missed Mum as she used to be, Mum-before-Uncle-Jimmy.

Mavis and Lily had gone to school together to see Miss

Hassinger, the head teacher. Miss Hassinger had been at the school for over thirty years and had taught Mavis herself when she was eight years old. Walking into her office now, Mavis felt as if twenty years had dropped away and she was still only eight years old, about to be scolded for some misdemeanour. Miss Hassinger offered them a chair each, and when they'd sat down she looked expectantly from one to the other.

Miss Hassinger was a small, bird-like woman, with completely white hair wound into a pleat at the back of her head. She had bright, darting eyes that missed nothing and these were turned on her erstwhile pupil now. Uncomfortable under her scrutiny, Mavis looked away and gazing out of the window, left the explanations to her mother.

Lily also turned to Mavis, waiting, but when it was clear that she wasn't going to speak, she said, 'It's about Rita and Rosie.'

Miss Hassinger nodded encouragingly. 'Yes?'

'We've come to tell you that Rita and Rosie are moving in with me,' Lily explained. 'Just for a while. Mavis is getting married in a few weeks...'

Miss Hassinger's glance flicked to Mavis's protruding belly and the expression in her eyes said 'and about time too'.

'... and when the baby's born... you know... it'll be easier for her if the girls are with me for a bit,' Lily finished.

'I see.' Miss Hassinger was one of the old school. Strict she certainly was, demanding instant and unquestioning obedience from the children she taught, but no one ever doubted that she was concerned for the welfare of those children and wanted the best for them. 'I must say I did wonder if something was happening at home. Rita, particularly, has been very unsettled of late. She's normally such a happy little soul, bright and outgoing, you know, but recently she's been... well, difficult. Not disobedient exactly, but not polite and not easy to handle.' Miss Hassinger looked across at Mavis. 'I was thinking of asking you to come in for a chat, Mrs Stevens.'

Mavis shifted uneasily in her chair. Miss Hassinger was always punctilious in how she addressed her old pupils, treating them with the courtesy and respect due to their attained adult-hood, but Mavis had never felt comfortable with it. She wished that her old teacher would forget about 'Mrs Stevens' and call her Mavis as she always had. Even now she did not respond, still leaving the explanations to her mother.

'Mavis's fiancé is in and out of the house, as you'd expect,' Lily went on, 'and the girls have found it unsettling. They don't remember their dad, see, and ain't used to having a man about the place.'

'I do see,' Miss Hassinger said, her eyes bright with under-standing. 'I'm sure this arrangement's for the best, then, just for a while.' She got to her feet and Lily and Mavis stood up too. 'I wish you every happiness in your new marriage, Mrs Stevens,' she said, holding out her hand. 'Perhaps,' she added to Lily as Mavis turned away in embarrassment, 'you'd be good enough to give Miss Granger your address on your way out, Mrs Sharples, just so we can keep our records straight. We need to know who to contact in an emergency.'

'She should contact *me* in an emergency,' snapped Mavis as soon as they were outside. 'I'm still their mother!'

'Of course you are,' agreed Lily, 'but to be honest, Mavis, I'm not sure you always remember that.'

Mavis glowered at her mother. 'You don't know nothing,' she spat. 'I miss them all the time.' And she did. Mavis did miss the girls, more than she could have believed. The house seemed empty first thing in the morning when there was no rushing round to be ready for school, and at half-past three when they would have come home, the place was too quiet; but life was certainly easier without them. There was only Jimmy to think about; she could devote all her attention to him. They were even able to go out together on a Saturday night because she didn't have to stay at home with the girls. Without them in the house, Jimmy was less demanding. He came and went as he pleased, but finding Mavis waiting for him, her attention undivided when he did come in, made their relationship much less stressful.

Mavis could relax and be herself; she no longer had to act as a buffer between her lover and her daughters. There were times when she felt guilty that she was happier without them, but as the days passed she managed to convince herself that she had made the right decision, not for herself, but for them.

After all, she kept telling herself, they're happy at Mum's... and I do have the baby to consider too.

She had passed over the girls' ration books and gave Lily eight shillings a week for their keep, but though she went to see them every Wednesday after school, it seemed as if a gap had opened up between them. They were pleased enough to see her, Rosie in particular ran into her arms, but with Rita it was different. She would say hallo and accept a kiss, but it was to Lily she turned and told about her day; of Lily she asked questions; into Lily's lap she snuggled. Almost, Mavis thought resentfully, as if I was some distant auntie, not her mother at all.

The day of the wedding dawned bright and clear. It was a Friday; the girls had a day off school and that in itself made the day special. They woke early, and when they'd had their breakfast they waited, barely containing their excitement until the time came to have their hair brushed, tied with a white ribbon and then to get dressed. They each had a new dress for the occasion, cotton frocks fashioned from a pair of curtains that Lily had kept in an old trunk in the attic. They were patterned with red roses, and though they still looked like curtains to Lily, the girls were delighted with them, twirling and spinning so that the skirts flew out like parasols.

'Won't everyone think we look lovely!' cried Rosie, as she made a wobbly curtsey to herself in the mirror. 'I wish I could wear my party dress every day.'

'Then it wouldn't be a party dress, silly,' pointed out Rita as she took her turn in front of the looking glass. 'Anyway,' she went on, pouting, 'we ain't going to the party.'

'Never mind, love,' comforted Lily. 'We'll have a party of our own back here.'

Lily was to take the girls to the register office for the actual wedding, and then they were to make themselves scarce and leave the grown-up guests free to enjoy themselves at the Red Lion.

'It won't be the same,' whined Rita. 'Why can't we go to the real party? It's not fair!'

'You're not allowed into a pub,' Gran explained. 'It isn't Mum saying you can't go in, it's the government.'

'Well,' scowled Rita, 'it's still not fair.'

Lily rather agreed. She had offered to have the reception at her house, but Jimmy had poured scorn on the idea. 'Who'd want to come there?'

'Better in the Lion, Mum,' Mavis had said, trying to be conciliatory. 'Far less work for you... and less expense for us all.'

Lily hadn't thought of that, but she ought to have realized that Jimmy would have. If they all went to the Red Lion, Mavis and Jimmy would provide the sandwiches, and the cake, but everyone would buy their own drinks.

'But they won't see our new dresses,' wailed Rosie.

'Course they will,' Gran assured her, as she brushed Rosie's fair hair, tying it carefully with two white bows on the top of her head. 'Everyone at the registry office'll see you. Now for goodness sake, stand still, child, or I'll never get your hair done.' She finished Rosie's hair and started on Rita's. Straight and dark and fine, it had to be plaited or it wouldn't hold a ribbon. Rita looked at her sister's silky, blonde hair, now caught up with the two white ribbons.

'Why can't I have hair like Rosie's?' she grumbled.

'You've got lovely hair,' said her grandmother soothingly, 'dark like Mum's.'

'Rosie's isn't like Mum's.'

'No,' agreed Lily, still plaiting the fine hair. 'Hers is like your daddy's was.'

'I wish I had hair like Daddy's,' Rita said. 'How did Rosie get it? She didn't even know Daddy.'

Lily smiled. 'Well, some children look like their mothers and some like their fathers, you don't know till they're born.'

'Will Mummy's new baby look like Uncle Jimmy?' asked Rosie with interest.

'No!' Rita snapped. 'We don't want a brother or sister who looks like him. He's fat and ugly.'

'Now, Rita, that's enough!' said her grandmother firmly. 'This is Mum's special day, and you ain't going to spoil it for her by being rude to Uncle Jimmy.' She took Rita by the chin and looked into her eyes. 'You understand, my girl? You behave yourself, or I'll bring you straight home and there'll be no party tea for you here either. Understand?'

Rita pulled free and muttered, 'Yes, Gran,' but her eyes were mutinous as she turned away.

They gathered outside the register office and waited for the arrival of the bride. The girls jumped up and down the steps, their skirts flying round their legs. Gran had made them each a matching pair of knickers, so that there was the occasional flash of rose-patterned underwear.

Jimmy arrived wearing his demob suit and accompanied by his father, his best man Charlie and a couple of his work-mates with their wives. When he saw the little girls playing on the steps, he glowered at them. Lily, seeing his expression, called them over to her and held each firmly by the hand.

Mavis arrived in a car. Her best friend, Carrie, from down the street, was her matron of honour, and she'd asked her brother to drive them both to the register office.

Mavis stepped out onto the pavement, her face alight with happiness. Lily, looking at her, thought she had never seen her looking so lovely, and she had to blink back unexpected tears. Mavis has had a difficult life since her Don was shot down, Lily thought as she watched her, she deserves some happiness now. I just hope she can find it with Jimmy Randall.

Carrie fussed round Mavis for a moment, straightening her dress where it had been crushed in the car. The dress was cream, patterned with tiny yellow rosebuds. Loose and flowing, it floated from Mavis's shoulders but did little to disguise her burgeoning state. She had found the material in the market and bought it off the ration. Carrie had made the dress for her and she'd used a strip of the material to trim the jaunty straw hat that now perched on Mavis's head. To complete her outfit, Mavis carried a tiny bunch of yellow roses, tied with yellow ribbons.

'Mummy!' cried Rosie, and pulling free of Lily's hand she darted over to her mother. 'Mummy! You've got a new dress too!'

Mavis held out a hand to her, smiling, and bent to kiss her daughter. Rosie put her arms round Mavis's neck and hugged her hard. Lily let go of Rita's hand, and Rita was about to run to her mother as well, when Jimmy strode over to his bride and grabbed her by the hand.

'Come on,' he said, pulling her towards the steps. 'Let's get married.'

Mavis smiled up at him and gripping his hand tightly, murmured, 'Oh yes, Jimmy. Let's.'

It seemed to take no time at all. They all went into the register office and stood round the bridal pair as they made their vows, and then they were pronounced man and wife, and Mr and Mrs Jimmy Randall emerged into the sunlight.

Rita was disappointed. She wasn't sure what she'd expected, but it wasn't just a man asking Mum and Uncle Jimmy questions. The sun streamed in through the windows, and little dust motes danced in the sunlight. Rita watched them disconsolately, wishing she'd hugged Mum before they went in, like Rosie had. When Uncle Jimmy put a ring on Mum's finger, Rita suddenly wondered what had happened to the one she used to wear, the one Daddy had given her. She looked carefully, but Mum certainly wasn't wearing both.

Carrie's husband, John, had a camera, and he took some pictures of Mum and Uncle Jimmy standing on the steps. He took one of Rita and Rosie in their new dresses, and then he asked Gran to take one of him with Carrie.

'I don't know how to use one of these,' Gran protested, but John said, 'It's easy, Mrs Sharples. Just make sure you hold it still and press the button.'

Then it was over. Mum and Uncle Jimmy got into the car and were driven round the corner to the Red Lion, the rest of the guests following on foot.

Lily took Rosie's hand and, calling to Rita, set off in the other direction, back to her own home in Hampton Road. Rosie skipped cheerfully along beside her. She hadn't been disappointed in the wedding. Several of the ladies she didn't know had told her how pretty she looked. No one had said it to Rita.

When they reached the house, they found the party tea waiting. Before the girls had got up that morning, Lily had put a white cloth on the table in the front room, and had laid out plates and glasses. On each plate was a piece of chocolate, and in the middle of the table was a jug of orange squash.

'Now, Rita,' Lily said, 'you come and help me.' They went into the kitchen and Rita was given a plate of sandwiches to carry through. There was a cake as well, and when they had eaten all that, Lily gave Rita a shilling and sent her to the corner shop for ice cream.

Later, when the children were safely in bed, Lily sat in her armchair and thought about the day. The weather had been perfect, the sun shining, and Mavis looking happier than Lily had seen her for years. The tiredness that had left her pale throughout her pregnancy seemed to have left her, and she'd looked blooming with health as she'd taken Jimmy's hand and walked into the register office. Lily poured the last of the orange squash into a glass and raised it in a toast.

'Here's to you, my darling girl,' she whispered. 'I wish you every happiness.' But even as she said it, Lily knew that the life Mavis had chosen was not going to be an easy one. 'And I'll keep your girls safe until they can come back to you, however long that is.'

On Monday it was back to school, but the girls had lots to tell the other children. Lily had explained to Rita and Rosie that when two people got married they went away together for a few days to have a little holiday on their own.

'It's called a honeymoon, and that's why Mummy and Uncle Jimmy have gone to the seaside by themselves. They'll be back on Saturday and I'm sure Mummy'll be straight round to tell you all about it.' She was going to say that perhaps Mum would bring them a stick of rock as a present, but she didn't, in case Mavis didn't.

After Lily had dropped the children off at school on Monday morning she went round to Baillies, the grocer's.

'How did the wedding go?' Fred's wife, Anne, emerged from the back of the shop. 'You had a lovely day for it. I bet the little girls enjoyed it.'

'They certainly did,' Lily agreed, 'it *was* lovely.'

'Where've they gone for their honeymoon?' Anne asked.

'Southend,' answered Lily. 'Be nice there if this weather holds.'

'Anything else I can get you?' asked Fred when he'd wrapped her ration of cheese and carefully placed three eggs into her shopping basket.

'No thanks, Fred, that's all for today.'

Lily never saw the car that hit her. Her mind still on the wedding, she walked out into the street, straight into its path. There was the squeal of brakes, as Lily and her shopping were thrown up over the bonnet and thudded onto the windscreen. She made no sound, but pedestrians in the street shrieked as they ran to help, or simply stood, transfixed with horror at what they had just seen.

Fred Baillie, hearing the commotion, ran out of his shop and found the driver of the car out on the pavement, his face pale with fright, his hands shaking, saying over and over, 'Not my fault! She just stepped out. Right in front of me. Just stepped out.'

Lily had slid off the car and was now lying face down in the gutter, blood running from a cut on her head, and one of her legs bent back at an alarming angle. Her eyes were closed and, though people were gathered round her, no one moved to touch her.

'It's Lily Sharples,' cried Fred Baillie. 'Is she dead?'

'Wouldn't know, mate,' said a small man in overalls who had been peering down at her and now drew hastily back. 'Looks like it.'

Fred Baillie bent down and lifted Lily's wrist. He'd been an air-raid warden during the war, and he was used to dealing with the injured and the dead. He found a slight pulse and looked up at the circle of faces. 'She's alive. I'll go and ring for an ambulance from my shop. Don't move her.'

'Shouldn't we try and make her more comfortable?' suggested a woman. 'I mean, she's face down in the gutter. If we just try to turn—'

'No,' Mr Baillie insisted. 'Don't touch her. I'll call an ambulance and find a blanket to put over her, but then we leave it to the ambulance men. They'll know what to do.' When he was sure the ambulance was on its way and knew where to come, he went back outside and gently laid a blanket over Lily's still form. He couldn't hear her breathing, there seemed to be no movement of her chest, but he had definitely felt a pulse and could only hope that she would hold on until the ambulance arrived.

A young police constable had appeared and was speaking to the pale-faced driver. 'If you could just tell me your name, sir,' he said, 'and then tell me exactly what happened here.'

'Sidney Short. It wasn't my fault, officer, she simply stepped right out in front of me. I hadn't a chance of stopping... right out in front of me. Just stepped out.'

The constable took out his notebook and licking his pencil, said, 'Does anyone know who she is? Did anyone else see what happened here?'

'Her name's Lily Sharples,' supplied Fred Baillie. 'The ambulance'll be here directly.'

The constable turned his attention to him. 'Did you see the accident, sir?'

'No,' admitted Fred, 'but she'd just left my shop when it happened.' As he spoke he reached down and picked up Lily's basket from where it had fallen, leaving a smear of broken eggs on the pavement. He glanced into the empty basket and then round on the road. The cheese had disappeared.

At that moment they heard the clang of the ambulance bell. Yet again people paused and turned to see what was happening. This was more excitement than the street had seen since the last raid in 1944. The little crowd gathered again as the ambulance men jumped out and hurried across to the still form in the gutter.

One bent down and felt for a pulse and when he succeeded in finding the faint throb under her chin, he said softly, 'She's still alive, Ernie. Get the stretcher.'

'Right-ho, Jack.' Ernie hauled a stretcher out of the back of the ambulance and laid it on the pavement. Gently the ambulance man lifted Lily's hair and looked at the head wound. It was still bleeding and her hair was matted with blood. Very carefully he placed his fingers onto her neck, feeling the line of vertebrae at the top of her spine. She moaned a little but didn't open her eyes, drifting off into unconsciousness again.

'As much as we can do here, Ernie,' Jack said straightening up. 'Let's get her aboard and back to casualty. You, constable, give us a hand. You support her head... don't let it loll as we lift her onto the stretcher.'

The young constable hesitated and Fred Baillie said, 'I'll do it. I know how from the war.'

With extreme care the two ambulance men lifted the inert form of Lily Sharples onto the stretcher, with Fred Baillie holding her head as straight and level as he could.

'Well done, mate,' Jack said as they finally slid her into the back of the ambulance and strapped her in. 'Know her name, do you?'

'It's Lily Sharples,' replied Fred.

When the ambulance had driven off, Fred looked at the shaken Sidney Short and said, 'Think you'd better come and sit down in my shop, mate. My missus'll make you some tea. That's what you need for shock. You come on inside.' Sidney Short looked at him with gratitude and followed him into the shop.

'What's happened, Fred?' cried Anne as they all trooped inside. Fred explained and Anne said, 'But we must let Mavis know.'

'We don't know where she is,' Fred said.

'Southend.'

'Yes, well, Southend's a big place. They could be anywhere. How're we going to find her?'

'Carrie Maunder might know,' suggested Anne.

'I'd better go round and see her,' said Fred. 'Ship Street, isn't she? Number 5?'

'Yes, I think so,' said Anne.

Fred nodded and set off for Ship Street.

Carrie was surprised to see him when she answered her bell. 'Mr Baillie,' she said, 'what can I do for you?'

'Carrie, d'you know where Mavis Stevens what-was has gone on her honeymoon?'

'Mavis? She's gone to Southend. Why?'

''Cos her ma's been knocked down in the street and took to the hospital. We need to get hold of her, straight away.'

'All I know was Southend. I don't know where they was staying,' said Carrie in dismay. 'I think they was just going to find a boarding house when they got there.'

'There must be some way of getting hold of her,' Fred said. 'If she don't come home quick, she might be too late.'

Carrie shook her head. 'Poor Mrs Sharples,' she said. 'Who'd have thought it.'

'And then there's the kiddies,' Fred said suddenly, as the thought struck him. 'They was living with her, wasn't they? Where're they going to go now, with their gran in hospital and their ma away?'

'Well, I suppose they could come here for a bit,' Carrie said. 'It'll only be till Saturday, won't it?'

'Could they? That's good of you. You sure?'

'Yes, it'll be a bit of a squeeze, but we'll manage. I'll go round the school and let them know what's happened. I'll tell Miss Hassinger I'll have them until Mavis gets home. John won't mind for a few days and Maggie'll think it great fun having them to stay.'

Carrie was as good as her word and went straight round to the school to explain the situation to Miss Hassinger.

'There's nowhere else for them to go,' she said when she'd told the headmistress about the accident. 'I'll have them at mine until Mavis gets home again.'

'That's really very good of you, Mrs Maunder,' Miss Hassinger said. 'Do you know how Mrs Sharples is?'

'No, but it doesn't sound very good. I think Mrs Baillie from the grocer's is going to the hospital to find out. I'll let you know when I know anything.'

'I'll just get the girls here to tell them what's happened,' said Miss Hassinger, 'and then we'll explain that they're going to stay with you till their mother gets home.' She reached for the bell on her desk and sent for Rita and Rosie.

A few moments later there was a knock on the door and the girls came in, Rita holding Rosie by the hand, looking nervously at the headmistress.

'Ah, come in girls,' she said smiling at them. 'It's all right, you haven't done anything wrong. You know Mrs Maunder, don't you?'

Rita nodded, and Rosie said, 'She's Maggie's mum.'

'Well, she's going to collect you from school today. You're going home with Maggie.'

'Where's Gran?' demanded Rita. 'Why ain't we going there?'

'I'm afraid there's been an accident,' Carrie said gently. 'Your gran is in the hospital, so I thought you could come and stay with us for a few days, just till Mum gets back.'

Rita stared at Carrie for a moment and then said, 'Is she dead?'

'No, but she was hurt, so they took her in an ambulance to the hospital. The doctors are looking after her, but she'll have to stay there for a while, till she's better.'

Rita nodded, but Rosie's bottom lip began to tremble. 'I want Mummy,' she whimpered. 'Where's Mummy?'

'She's on her honeymoon,' replied Carrie. 'She'll be home on Saturday.'

'So will Uncle Jimmy,' whispered Rita.

Miss Hassinger looked at her sharply, but decided not to hear the remark. However, when the girls had been taken back to their classrooms by Miss Granger, and their teachers told what had happened, Miss Hassinger sat deep in thought. Just when the two children had a little stability at last, she thought. It couldn't have happened at a worse time.

Chapter 7

'I know where Gran keeps a key,' Rita said to Carrie when she met them at the school gate that afternoon. 'We'll need our things.'

'So you will,' Carrie agreed with relief. She'd been wondering how she was going to clothe the Stevens girls till Mavis got home. 'Let's go to your gran's then and fetch them.'

Once again Rita and Rosie's meagre belongings were put into the old suitcase, Knitty was retrieved from the bed, and they all walked back to Ship Street.

'I've made you a bed on the floor in Maggie's room,' Carrie told them. 'You'll have to snuggle up together on that eiderdown, all right?'

Maggie was thrilled that they were coming to stay. 'Can we play out?' she asked once the girls had put their things into her room.

'Just till I get tea ready,' Carrie said, and shooed them out into the street.

'I couldn't do anything else,' she said to her husband later that evening, when the three girls were finally asleep. 'They'd nowhere else to go. It's only till Mavis gets home on Saturday.'

'You did right, girl,' John assured her. 'She'd do the same for you.'

'Course she would,' agreed Carrie, but in truth she wasn't so sure. She'd known Mavis from schooldays, but Mavis had changed since Jimmy had come on the scene.

Mavis and Jimmy arrived back in Ship Street late Saturday

afternoon, to find a postcard pushed through the letter box. On it Carrie had simply written, *Your Mum in hospital. Come round our house when you get back. Carrie.*

She stared at the card for a moment and then, putting her hat back on, said to Jimmy, 'I've got to go round Carrie's.'

'What you got to go round there for?' demanded Jimmy. 'What about my tea?'

'Carrie says Mum's in hospital. I got to find out what's wrong with her, and what's happened to the girls.'

'Well,' said Jimmy, 'if you ain't getting me tea, I'll go down the Lion. I'll get a pie down there.'

Although Mavis knew this meant he wouldn't be home until late and probably with a skinful inside him, she didn't want to argue. There had been very few arguments while they'd been in Southend, and she didn't want them to start again as soon as they got home.

'All right, love,' she said. 'Good idea. I'll go and find out what's been happening. I might have to visit Mum in the hospital, but I can probably leave that until the morning.' Before he could object any further, she let herself out of the house and waddled down the street to number 5. She had become so large that it was almost impossible to hurry anywhere now. She couldn't wait for the baby to be born and for her body to be her own again.

It was Maggie who opened the door to her and seeing Mavis on the step, called back over her shoulder, 'Reet, your mum's here.'

Rita flew to the door and flung herself into her mother's arms. 'Oh, Mum,' she cried, 'Gran was hit by a car and she's in hospital and she's very bad.'

Mavis hugged Rita to her, and then Rosie, hearing Mavis arrive, erupted from the kitchen and she, too, flung herself at her mother, simply saying, 'Mummy, Mummy, Mummy,' over and over again. Mavis moved into the house, pushing the front door closed behind her.

'Now then,' she said as she finally disentangled herself from her daughters, 'where's Auntie Carrie?'

'She's gone to see Gran,' Rita said. 'Uncle John is here.'

At that moment John appeared from the kitchen. 'Hallo, Mavis,' he said. 'You back?'

'John, tell me quick. What on earth's happened to Mum?'

'Quite a lot's happened since you went away,' John replied. 'Come in and take the weight off. I'll put the kettle on and tell you all about it.'

Mavis followed him into the kitchen, the two girls still swinging on her arms. She sat impatiently at the table while John made tea, and when he'd finally poured them each a cup she could contain herself no longer.

'John, for God's sake, tell me what's happened. What happened to Mum?'

'Your mother was knocked down by a car,' he said. 'The ambulance came and took her to the General, and she's been there ever since.'

'But how bad, John?'

'Pretty bad,' he admitted. 'She was thrown up over the bonnet, I heard from Fred Baillie, and then knocked into the gutter. He called the ambulance. She bashed her head and her leg was broke in two places. Outside Fred's shop. He come round to tell Carrie, and she agreed to have the kids till you come home again.'

'But how is Mum now, John? Do you know?'

'Well, Carrie went in that same day, but they wouldn't let her visit. She weren't allowed 'cos Lily was unconscious for a bit. She's come round now, though, and can have a visitor. Carrie's there now.'

'I must go and see her,' Mavis said, heaving herself off the chair.

'Well, you can try,' John said, 'but they're only letting one person in at a time. The nurse Carrie talked to said she was still in a bad way.' He looked at his watch and added, 'Doubt if there's any point in going now, anyway, visiting's over. They're very strict. The nurse said that the matron's a right tartar. Carrie'll be home in a minute. I should sit down and wait for her.'

'But I must see her!' cried Mavis. 'Oh, why didn't you try and find me? You should have sent for me.'

'How could we?' asked John reasonably. 'All we knew was that you was in Southend. It's a big place. Now, best thing is for you to sit down and wait here till Carrie gets back and she can tell you all the latest.' He drained the last of his tea and got to his feet. 'Well, now you're here, Mavis, I'll just pop out for a pint. Maggie, be a good girl till your mum gets home, OK?'

Mavis sat down again to wait for Carrie and Rosie clambered up onto her knee. She wriggled, trying to get more comfortable. 'I can't sit on your knee,' she grumbled, 'your baby's sitting on your knee.'

Mavis set her down on the floor again as she said, 'Never mind, pet, it won't be long before it's born, then there'll be room.'

'When is it coming? Can we come home then?' asked Rosie hopefully. Rita, still standing close to her mother, stiffened a little as she waited for the answer.

'Why don't you girls go outside in the sunshine?' Mavis suggested. 'Your mum'll be home soon, Maggie.' When the girls had gone, Mavis squeezed another cup of tea from the pot and considered the situation. Rosie had asked if they were coming home again. It was a fair question, but Mavis didn't know the answer. It wasn't that she didn't want them there, not really, Jimmy certainly didn't, but where else could they go? The baby was due in the next couple of weeks, and would come when it chose. Who would look after the girls then? How long was Mum going to be in hospital?

'Oh Mum,' Mavis cried, 'why did this have to happen now? Why didn't you look where you was going?'

At that moment the door opened and Carrie came in. 'Mavis,' she said with a smile, 'you're back.'

'Yes, we got back an hour ago. How's Mum? Is she all right?'

'Well,' said Carrie. 'I saw her for the first time, today. She's as all right as you can be with your leg in plaster, and a cracked head.'

'At least they let you see her? John said you hadn't been allowed before.'

'Only for a little while. I just sat by the bed. She's not up to much, her leg's up in a sort of sling thing. She don't look well, very white. All she could ask was, was the girls all right? I said I'd got them for now, and you'd be home today. Then she fell asleep, so I come away.'

'But what do the doctors say?' asked Mavis.

'They didn't talk to me, I'm not family, but one of the nurses said that Mrs Sharples was lucky to be alive. She said it'll take time and they don't know how well she'll walk again. She'll probably need a stick to get about.'

'Will she be able to manage on her own?' wondered Mavis.

'Don't know,' Carrie said, 'but it'll be some time yet, anyway.'

'It was very good of you and John to take them in like this.'

'Well, it was only for a few days, wasn't it? You'd have done the same for me.' Carrie got up and put the kettle on the gas. 'Why don't we have another cuppa, and then you can pack up the girls' things and get them settled at home.' She spoke firmly. She had done her bit and now it was time for Mavis to take responsibility for her own kids.

Seeing the bleak look on Mavis's face, Carrie softened a little. 'Don't suppose you've got any food in the house, have you? Look, leave them with me another half hour and go down Baillies and get some stuff in. Here.' She opened a drawer and pulled out two ration books. 'I picked these up when we went round to your mum's to get their things. I used a few coupons, had to, but you'll get enough to see you over the weekend.'

When Jimmy finally came home he was several sheets to the wind, and though Mavis immediately put some supper on the table, he simply put his head down beside the plate and went to sleep. When he snorted awake half an hour later, Mavis helped him up the stairs as she had so often before, and he fell into his bed still unaware that his stepdaughters had come home.

The girls were safely asleep in their old bedroom, sharing their old bed, and though Rita hated being back at Ship Street, it was comforting to snuggle down with Rosie in the familiar bedroom. When they woke next morning, the girls crept downstairs, afraid of waking Uncle Jimmy, and shut the kitchen door tightly before looking for some breakfast. There was no milk, but Rita found a packet of cornflakes in the cupboard and they each ate a bowl of these, softened with water.

When Mavis woke she slid out of the bed, leaving Jimmy snoring heavily on his side, and peeped into the girls' bedroom. The bed was empty, so she went down to the kitchen where she found Rita had made the tea and was now making toast under the grill.

They were eating their toast when they heard the bang of a door upstairs and then the thud of feet coming down. Both girls turned frightened eyes on their mother. The look on her face did nothing to reassure them, and they sat, as if frozen, until Jimmy opened the door and stumbled in.

He stopped in the doorway, glaring. 'What are they doing here?' he demanded.

When Mavis did not immediately answer he roared the question again. 'What are they doing in this house?'

Rosie shrunk against her mother, but Rita simply sat stock still, staring at him. He slouched into the room and, leaning over her, his breath foul in her face, growled, 'What you staring at, eh?'

'Nothing, Uncle Jimmy,' she whispered, and white-faced she looked away.

Jimmy turned his attention to his wife. 'So, I asked you a question, didn't I?'

'I brought them home last night,' Mavis began, and then broke off, speaking abruptly to her daughters. 'Go and play out,' she said. 'Go round Maggie's and play there.'

Rita and Rosie were only too glad to escape, and edged past him, through the door, and ran out into the street as fast as they could.

Jimmy slumped down on a chair and Mavis hastily poured him a cup of tea, before spreading margarine on her own piece of toast and sliding it onto his plate.

Jimmy slurped a mouthful of tea and then said, 'Well?'

'I had to bring them home, Jimmy. I had to. Mum's in the hospital and won't be out for weeks. Carrie's been minding them while we've been away. They have to come home now Mum can't have them.'

'No!' Jimmy bellowed. 'No, we agreed before, they don't live here. If they can't stay with your mother, then they'll have to go into a home... like we said before.'

'But Jimmy,' she wailed, 'it's not forever, it's only till Mum's out of hospital. Then they can live with her, like before.'

'Oh yeah? And when's that likely to be? This year, next year, sometime, never! That's when.'

'It won't be long.' Mavis was determined that Jimmy should not discover the full extent of her mother's injuries. 'The nurse told Carrie that she was doing well. It'll only be for a little while.'

Jimmy got up from his seat and very deliberately pulled Mavis out of hers. Gripping her tightly by the shoulders so that his fingers dug into her flesh, he shook her hard and long, shouting as he did so, 'Don't you understand the word "no", you silly cow? I... will... not... have... those... girls... in... my... house!' And with each of these last words he slammed her back against the gas stove. For good measure he gave her a final punch to her stomach, then, letting her go, flopped down onto his chair again.

Mavis sagged against the table, her knees weak, tears streaming down her face, and even as she clutched the back of her chair to steady herself, she felt water draining down her legs.

'Oh my God,' she whispered, staggering again before collapsing onto the chair. 'Oh my God, me waters have broke!'

'What?' demanded Jimmy testily. 'What's the matter now, you miserable cow?'

'Me waters have broke. The baby's coming!'

'Coming? Coming now?' Jimmy was disbelieving. 'Course it ain't! It ain't due for another two weeks.'

'It's coming now,' repeated Mavis, panic in her voice. 'We

have to get the midwife. Fetch Carrie. Jimmy, for God's sake, fetch Carrie. She'll know what to do.'

Jimmy gave her one final hard look and then, realizing that she wasn't making it up to frighten him, ran down the street to find Carrie. Rita and Rosie were playing hopscotch with Maggie outside the house; all three drew back fearfully as he came rushing up.

'Maggie, where's your mum?' he demanded, and when she pointed to the front door which stood ajar, he burst in without knocking, shouting, 'Carrie! Carrie! You've got to come! Mavis is having the baby.'

Rita and Rosie stared wide-eyed as he ran back out of the house, swiftly followed by Carrie. She paused by the staring children.

'Don't worry, kids,' she said, 'it's time for your brother or sister to be born, that's all. You stay with Maggie, I'll be back in a while.'

She found Mavis doubled up in the kitchen, pale and sweating, her breath coming out in ragged spurts. Immediately Carrie was at her side, her arm round her, murmuring words of comfort, but Mavis didn't seem to hear her. Carrie looked back at Jimmy who was standing helplessly by the door.

'How long's she been like this?' she asked.

Jimmy shrugged. 'Not long, just before I come round to you. She said her waters had broke and then told me to get you. Said we need the midwife.'

'We certainly do,' agreed Carrie. She reached up for the card that was tucked in beside the clock on the mantelpiece and handed it to him. 'Here's the number. You go down the phone box and ring her. Tell her we need her now.'

Jimmy took the card and then hesitated, looking down at Mavis. 'For goodness sake, Jimmy,' Carrie urged him, 'go and ring!'

When he'd gone, Carrie turned her attention back to Mavis. 'Come on now, Mavis love. Let's get you upstairs onto the bed. Easy does it.'

Very carefully she eased Mavis up onto her feet and supporting her as best she could, managed to get her to the foot of the stairs. 'Lean on me,' she said, 'and up we go. Come on, Mavis, you'll be better once you're lying down. Jimmy's gone for Sister Hooper, she'll be here in no time.'

Slowly they made their way upstairs. The bed, unmade as Jimmy had left it, did not look inviting, but Mavis didn't care, and she collapsed onto it with a moan.

'Are you having contractions?' asked Carrie, trying to straighten the bedclothes under her. 'How often are they coming? We need to get you into your nightie, then once you're comfy, I'll make you a nice cup of hot tea. That'll make you feel better.' She chatted on as she manoeuvred Mavis into her nightdress, but got no response. As she slipped the nightie over Mavis's head, Carrie saw some faint bruising on her shoulders. How had Mavis come to bruise herself there? she wondered, but as Mavis was suddenly seized by a contraction, she gave it no more thought, simply held her friend's hand as the waves of pain flowed over her and then, mercifully, subsided again.

Jimmy was soon back, saying that Sister Hooper was on her way, but it seemed to Carrie an age before she heard the midwife's bicycle bell and her cheery voice on the stairs.

After that things moved very quickly. Sister Hooper examined Mavis and said the baby was a breach. 'Hospital for you, my girl,' she said briskly and sent Jimmy back to the phone box to summon an ambulance. As they got Mavis ready, Sister Hooper also noticed the bruises on Mavis's shoulders, and Carrie saw they were more distinct than they'd looked earlier. The two women exchanged glances, and then went on with what they were doing.

When the ambulance arrived, a small crowd gathered outside in the street to see Mavis carried down the stairs and driven off. Jimmy had climbed into the ambulance as well, and Carrie was left with Rita and Rosie, standing forlornly on the pavement.

She looked at them and said, 'You'd better come back and have your dinner with us. Uncle Jimmy'll come and find you when he comes back with news about the baby. Won't it be exciting to have a new baby brother or sister!'

By the time Jimmy returned from the hospital to say that he had a son, Carrie had given up waiting for him and had again put the girls to bed on the eiderdown in Maggie's room.

The next morning she sent them off to school as usual, and assumed Jimmy would make arrangements for them at home-time. Jimmy did not, and the girls, not knowing what to do, walked home to Ship Street and let themselves in. And that was where Jimmy found them, eating cereal and toast when he came home from work.

'I can't look after them,' he said to Mavis at visiting time that evening, sounding more reasonable than she'd ever heard him. 'I got to go to work. I can't be there to make their tea when they come in from school, can I? I got to earn our living. Can't afford to lose me job now that we've got another mouth to feed, can I?'

Mavis, still tearful after a difficult birth, agreed that he couldn't.

'So,' he went on in the same reasonable voice, 'I've brought them forms you had from the social. The ones you was going to sign before they went to Lily's place. I think you'd better sign them now, and we can get things settled.' He gave her a reassuring smile. 'Got to get things settled before you come home with our Richard.'

'But I don't want them to go into a home,' pleaded Mavis.

'Course you don't, but it ain't going to be forever,' Jimmy said encouragingly, 'just till your mum gets out of the hospital and can have them back. I saw the doctor,' he lied. 'Once her leg's out of the plaster she'll be right as ninepence. Only a month or so.'

He put the documents that he'd retrieved from the kitchen drawer onto the bedside locker. 'Look, I've filled them in for you, so you don't have to bother with any of that. All you have to do is sign them at the bottom, right?'

With a delicacy entirely foreign to him, he reached over and kissed her forehead lightly. 'I'd better get back to them,' he said. 'You get some sleep, love. Just think about what I've said, and you'll see it's for the best.' And with these gentle words, he left the ward and headed for the Red Lion, delighted with his strategy. Softly, softly!

Mavis did think about what he'd said. She was exhausted, she couldn't remember ever being as tired as this, not after Rita, not after Rosie, and she'd had Mum to help her then. There'd be no Mum this time, she'd have to cope on her own. She thought about coming home, with baby Richard. Life after the girls had moved in with Lily had been so much easier, so much more peaceful. She'd missed them, she knew she loved them, they were her kids after all, but she also knew, if she were honest, that life was easier when her daughters lived somewhere else. Jimmy said Mum would be home soon and if she signed these forms, they could be properly looked after in the meantime.

Mavis reached for the forms and without reading through the several pages they contained, signed her name at the end of them both. Then with the quietness of mind that comes from having, finally, made a difficult decision, she turned over and went to sleep.

Chapter 8

'I beg your pardon?' For a moment Miss Hassinger seemed to have lost her habitual restraint. She stared incredulously at the woman who sat across the desk. 'You have authority to do what?'

'I am May Hopkins, the local Children's Officer, and I have written authority,' she emphasized the word 'written', 'to remove two of the children currently at your school and take them with me to their new place of accommodation.'

'But why are you taking them? Where are you taking them?' Miss Hassinger looked perplexed. 'Where is their mother? Where is Mrs Stevens... I mean, Mrs Randall?'

'I understand she is in hospital, having just given birth,' came the reply. 'The children's stepfather is unable to look after them at home and Mrs Randall has requested places for her daughters in the EVER-Care children's home. I have documents signed by Mrs Randall, asking for her children to be accommodated at EVER-Care, and assigning legal guardianship to the EVER-Care Charitable Trust. It is EVER-Care who are now the legal guardians and Mrs Randall has given up her rights as their parent.'

'She's what?' Miss Hassinger was incredulous. 'Show me,' she demanded, holding out her hand for the papers. She studied them for several minutes, reading each clause carefully, and finally realizing that Miss Hopkins had, indeed, all the rights she was claiming. She could remove Rita and Rosie Stevens from the school forthwith and take them to live at Laurel House

EVER-Care orphanage, and there was nothing she, Miss Hassinger, or anyone else could do about it. She stared blankly at the typed pages for several more moments. What had that stupid girl, Mavis Sharples, or Stevens, or Randall as she was now, what had she done? Signing away her rights to her own children.

Miss Hassinger had always considered Mavis a good mother. The children had always come to school clean and tidy, with brushed hair and proper shoes. They were well fed, and though pretty little Rosie with her blonde hair and wide blue eyes was the one who attracted notice, Rita had always been the determined one, obstinate her mother had called it, with a strong streak of common sense. Mavis had coped very well since her husband had been killed. It was, Miss Hassinger knew, difficult for a woman on her own, but why had Mavis suddenly given up now? Now, when she had a new husband to help in the task of bringing up her children.

'Isn't there any way we can delay this?' she asked Miss Hopkins. 'It's all very sudden. I mean, have Rita and Rosie been prepared for this change? Has it been explained to them?'

'I think you may safely leave that to us,' said Miss Hopkins. 'From now on they are no longer your responsibility, they have become ours.' She looked steadily at the headmistress. 'If you will be so kind, Miss Hassinger, to have the children fetched now...'

Miss Hopkins sat back in her chair and waited. Her thoughts drifted back to the day, earlier in the week, when Jimmy Randall had first come to her in her office, and placed the signed papers on her desk.

'We want these kids took into care,' he'd said and turned to walk out of the room.

'Just one moment, Mr... er...' Miss Hopkins glanced down at the documents in front of her.

'Randall.'

'Mr Randall. I'm sorry, but what is all this about?'

'We want these kids took into care,' he repeated. 'There isn't room for them in our house, and with the new baby, we can't look after them. My wife did come to see you previous. You gave her the papers.' He pointed to the sheaf of papers he'd put on the desk. 'That's them. The papers. They're all signed.'

'Excuse me, Mr Randall. It isn't just a question of bringing in signed papers, you know. Each case has to receive careful consideration, and then I have to see if I can find a place for these girls... It's very short notice—'

'Because it's an emergency,' said Jimmy Randall. 'My wife is in hospital with our new baby and when she comes home with him, well, there won't be room for them. Anyhow, there's no one at home to look after the girls now. I'm at work all day, and there's no one to mind them, to get their tea and that. I don't get home till late. It's not right.'

'Is there no family member who can step in and help?' asked Miss Hopkins. 'Surely there must be someone.'

'No,' replied Jimmy firmly. 'No one.' He looked at the woman who sat opposite him, behind the desk. She was fat and she was ugly, her hair like a bird's nest with two sticks stuck through it. She was the sort of woman that Jimmy instinctively disliked. He wanted to say, 'Look, you fat cow, find these kids somewhere to stay, and sharpish. That's your job, ain't it?' But he needed to keep on the right side of her, so that things could be settled as quickly as possible, certainly before Mavis came home again and could change her mind.

He drew a deep breath and after a struggle with his natural belligerence, said in his most reasonable voice, 'It's best for the girls to move as soon as possible. It's not right that they are left on their own. Their mother's signed the forms you gave her. We need to get this sorted as quick as we can, for their sakes.'

'Well, yes, I rather agree with you,' said Miss Hopkins. 'It certainly isn't desirable for them to be left at home on their own. I will make some enquiries. Are you on the telephone? No? Well, perhaps you could call in again tomorrow and I'll be able to tell you then what we can do for the poor little creatures.'

This time when the large and rather frightening man in front of her made to leave the room, she simply bade him goodbye, relieved that the interview was over. Despite his reasonable words, there had been an underlying violence in the way he had said them which Miss Hopkins found quite intimidating.

Carefully she checked the papers he'd left. Yes, all correct. He had brought the girls' birth certificates as the forms requested, and the mother's signature was in the right places.

She picked up the phone, dialled the number for the EVER-Care home at Laurel House and asked for Miss Vanstone.

'I think I have two more children who need a home with you after all, Miss Vanstone,' she said when the preliminary courtesies were over. 'You may remember that I had a woman in a few weeks ago wanting to have her children put into an orphanage, and I suggested to you then that they might come to you?'

'Yes, I remember,' said Miss Vanstone. 'What about them?'

'Well, their stepfather has just brought in the forms, completed and signed by the mother. There's no reason why they shouldn't come to you straight away if you have room for them.'

'I see,' Miss Vanstone spoke thoughtfully, while in fact her mind was racing. If all the documentation was completed and signed, that made her the children's legal guardian... and that would mean...

'Both sets of forms, Miss Hopkins?' she asked. 'For guardianship and adoption?'

'Oh yes,' replied Miss Hopkins happily. 'Once the EVER-Care name and address are inserted, they'll be yours.'

'What about the Children's Committee?'

'Oh, my dear Miss Vanstone,' cooed Miss Hopkins, 'you can leave the Committee to me. There'll be no problem with them, I do assure you.'

Jimmy Randall had returned to the Children's Office the next day and was shown straight in to see Miss Hopkins.

'I have good news for you, Mr Randall,' she told him as soon as he was sitting down. 'I have managed to place your daughters—'

'Stepdaughters,' corrected Jimmy.

'Your stepdaughters, in an excellent home. EVER-Care. You've heard of it?'

'No.'

'Well,' Miss Hopkins went on, a little disconcerted by his abrupt answer, 'it is a charitable trust set up by a lady named Miss Emily Vanstone. The children are very well cared for, and taught to look after themselves, to be good—'

'When can they go?' interrupted Jimmy. Mavis had been told that she could probably come home after the weekend, and he wanted Rita and Rosie gone before she did.

'Once I am certain that it is in the best interests of the children and that their mother isn't—'

'Their mother's already signed the forms, hasn't she?' snapped Jimmy, trying to keep hold of his temper. What more did this bloody woman want?

'Indeed she has,' agreed Miss Hopkins, 'but—'

'So, when can they go? Today? Tomorrow?'

'I have arranged with the home that they will be brought there tomorrow, if that's convenient to you.'

'Tomorrow,' repeated Jimmy, his eyes glinting.

'They'll need their belongings packed into one case,' went on Miss Hopkins. 'Then if you'll bring them here after school tomorrow—'

'I can't bring them,' said Jimmy firmly. 'I'll be at work tomorrow afternoon. I can't just walk out in the middle of the day. You'll have to fetch 'em. Get 'em from school and take 'em to this EVER-Care place. I'll drop off the case here in the morning.' When Miss Hopkins did not answer immediately he added harshly, 'You got them papers, all signed. My wife's already passed them kids over to you.'

So here she was, sitting in the headmistress's office waiting to collect her new charges and take them to Laurel House. She could see that the head was upset, but so what? The Stevens girls would be leaving with her, and she would have done her duty. She would put them safely into Laurel House and they'd be safe, away from that horrible man who was now their stepfather and their ineffectual mother. Miss Hopkins felt the warm glow of righteousness as she waited for them to appear.

There came a knock on the door and the school secretary came in.

'Rita and Rosie Stevens, Miss Hassinger,' she said, as if Miss Hassinger had never seen the children before, and pushed them forward with a gentle hand.

The two children stood, silent, in the middle of the room. Rosie looked at Miss Hassinger with anxious eyes, while Rita stared balefully at Miss Hopkins. She had no idea who she was or why she was there, but there was something about her which made Rita mistrust her.

She's got piggy eyes, Rita thought as she looked at her. Her face is all fat, and her eyes are piggy eyes.

'Come here, Rita, Rose,' said Miss Hassinger softly, and surprisingly held out her hand to them. Both girls edged forward, Rita taking Rosie's hand as they did so.

'This lady is called Miss Hopkins,' began the headmistress. Rita flashed another look at the woman sitting in the chair. 'She's—'

'I'm the Children's Officer,' interrupted Miss Hopkins, 'and I've come to take you to your new home.'

'I don't want a new home,' Rita said fiercely, looking from one to the other. 'We've got a home, Rosie and me.'

You're a courageous little thing, thought Miss Hassinger as she watched the child face up to the Children's Officer. And ready to look out for your sister as well.

'I'm afraid you can't live there any more,' said Miss Hopkins. 'Your mother is in hospital and can't look after you.'

'We've got a new baby brother,' Rosie said conversationally. 'He's called Richard.'

'We won't go with you,' Rita said. 'We ain't got to. Mum's coming home.'

'Come along, now,' said Miss Hopkins, ignoring Rita's outburst and getting to her feet. 'We've got to collect your luggage and then we're being fetched in a car.'

'Never been in a car,' remarked Rosie.

'Well, you won't go in one now if we don't get a move on,' replied Miss Hopkins briskly. 'Now come along, both of you.'

She held out a hand to each girl. Rosie took one, trustingly enough, but Rita thrust her own hands behind her back and turning her gaze on Miss Hassinger, said, 'I want to go home. I don't want to go with her.'

'I'm afraid you must, Rita,' said Miss Hassinger gently. 'She has come to take you somewhere to be looked after...' She hesitated and then added softly, 'until your Mum can have you home again.' Then she took Rita by the hand led her to the door. 'Come along, Rita, there's a good girl. You've got to look after Rosie, you know. That's what Mum would want you to do.'

'Now then, Rita, Rose,' she said when they reached the street, 'be good girls and do what Miss Hopkins tells you.' She turned to the Children's Officer and said, 'Good afternoon, Miss Hopkins. I hope you are satisfied with this day's work.' Then she turned and walked, ramrod straight, back into her school.

Chapter 9

Rita stared at Laurel House. It was grey and grim and she hated it before she'd even passed through its heavy front door. Why were they here? It must be a mistake. They lived in Ship Street with Mum. But she knew there was no mistake. Uncle Jimmy didn't want them and somehow he had got this piggy-eyed woman to take them away.

Still, Rita thought, it won't be for long. When Mum brings baby Richard home from the hospital, she'll come and find us. While we're here, decided Rita, I'll look after Rosie.

Miss Hopkins had led them away from the familiarity of Capel Street with its elementary school and its park, to the centre of town, bustling with people. The sun was beating down from a clear blue sky and the air was hot and sticky. Rita dragged her feet as she was towed through the streets, and though Rosie skipped along cheerfully enough at first, eager for the promised ride in a car, her legs were soon tired and she, too, dragged her feet, making Miss Hopkins snap, 'Pick up your feet, child, and come along.'

When they finally reached a big building in the middle of the town, the piggy-eyed woman had picked up a small suitcase that Rita recognized at once.

There was no car. Miss Hopkins walked them to a bus stop where they stood in a queue and waited for a bus.

A number 37 bus came at last and the two girls scrambled aboard, followed by a lumbering Miss Hopkins with the little suitcase in one hand and her capacious handbag in the other. She pushed the two girls into a seat near the back and sat behind them.

'One and two halves to Russell Green,' she told the conductor as she paid the fares. The bus was a novelty, and Rosie knelt up on the seat, her nose against the window, watching the town pass by.

Rita looked out of the window too, trying to remember where the bus went, but it was impossible, it drove down unfamiliar streets, over a river and past shops that Rita had never seen before. How far they were going? How far from home and from Mum and Gran?

When they finally got off the bus Rita watched it trundle away. Number 37. Mum would come to fetch them on a number 37.

Five minutes' walk through suburban streets finally brought them to Laurel House. Rita reached for Rosie's hand as they waited for the front door to open. When it did they were greeted by a pale-faced girl, wearing a black dress and a white cap.

'Miss Hopkins to see Miss Vanstone,' announced Miss Hopkins, pushing her way into the hall. 'Please tell her we are here, Betty.'

'Yes, mam.' The girl bobbed a curtsey, and disappeared. As they waited, Rita looked round the hall. It was painted a dull green and sparsely furnished, with a bench along one wall and a chair opposite. A wide staircase led to a landing above and, standing in the curve below it, a tall grandfather clock ticked solemnly in a corner, ticking-tocking the time away.

After a few minutes another lady came into the hall. 'Ah, Miss Hopkins,' she said, 'here you are at last.' She glanced down at the two girls who edged closer together. 'And you must be Rita and Rose Stevens.' The girls didn't reply and she said sharply, 'Answer when you're spoken to.'

'Yes, miss,' whispered Rita. This woman was not like the fat, piggy-eyed Miss Hopkins. She was tall and straight, her hair pulled back into a severe bun. Her eyes were grey and penetrating, drilling into them. Instinctively Rita was afraid.

'Yes, *Miss Vanstone*,' said the lady. She looked at Rita expectantly and Rita murmured, 'Yes, Miss Vanstone.'

'That's better. Now then, follow me.' Glancing behind her, she called, 'Betty, ask Mrs Hawkins to come to my office.'

Miss Vanstone led them into her office. It was furnished with a large desk and a filing cabinet on either side of a window which looked out onto the front garden. It was sunny outside, but the room was gloomy and rather forbidding. Miss Vanstone sat down behind her desk, waved Miss Hopkins to a chair in front of her and said to the girls, 'Sit on the floor and cross your legs.'

Paying them no further attention she addressed Miss Hopkins. 'You've brought the relevant paperwork with you?'

'Oh, yes, Miss Vanstone,' Miss Hopkins replied. 'It's all here.' She delved into her handbag and brought out the papers. 'All signed. All correct.'

Miss Vanstone took the papers and began to peruse them. As she was reading there was a knock on the door. Without glancing up she called, 'Come.'

The door opened and a small, dark woman came in. 'You wanted me, Miss Vanstone?'

Miss Vanstone set the papers aside. 'Ah, Mrs Hawkins. Yes. Here are Rita and Rose Stevens. They've arrived today. I'll pass them over to you now.' She looked down at the girls. 'Now you two, up you get and go with Mrs Hawkins. Do as you're told, and you'll do very well here. Disobey, and you will be punished. Do you understand?'

Rita had scrambled to her feet, pulling Rosie up as well.

'Do you understand?' Miss Vanstone repeated.

'Yes, miss,' muttered Rita.

'Yes, Miss Vanstone.'

'Yes, Miss Vanstone,' echoed Rita.

'Rose?'

Rosie looked across at her. 'I'm called Rosie,' she said.

It was as if she hadn't spoken. 'Do you understand, Rose?'

Rita crushed Rosie's hand in hers and muttered, 'Say "yes, Miss Vanstone".'

Rosie looked at her and then obediently said, 'Yes, Miss Vanstone.'

'That's better. Off you go with Mrs Hawkins, now.'

Mrs Hawkins picked up the small suitcase and they followed her along the passage to a narrow stairway. 'These are the stairs you use,' she told them. 'Not the main staircase.' When neither girl replied, she looked at them sharply and snapped, 'You're to answer when you're spoken to. Do you understand?'

'Yes, miss,' murmured Rita.

'Yes, Mrs Hawkins,' corrected the woman.

'Yes, Mrs Hawkins.'

'Everyone here has a name,' Mrs Hawkins said. 'Miss won't do. Now then, let's see where you'll sleep.'

At the top of the stairs was a long landing with doors opening on either side. Halfway along were the main stairs, and at the far end another staircase led up to the tower. Pointing to it, Mrs Hawkins said, 'That's the way to my rooms. You are never to go up those stairs unless I have sent for you. Do you understand?'

Rita had now learned to answer so she said, 'Yes, Mrs Hawkins.'

Mrs Hawkins opened a green door and led them into a bedroom. 'This is Green Dormitory,' she said, 'where you'll be sleeping, Rose.'

It was a small room with six narrow beds crammed into it, and just enough room to walk between them. Each bed had a stool at the end, a wooden locker beside it, with a metal basin on the top. A wide window looked out onto the garden below, but the view was marred by the black iron bars that crossed it. No child could fall... or escape... through that window. The only thing green about the room was the door.

Mrs Hawkins pointed to one of the beds and said, 'This is your bed, Rose, and that is your locker. That is where you'll keep your things.' She opened the suitcase and took out the small washbag that contained their toothbrushes and flannels. She opened the locker and put one of each inside.

'Please, miss... Mrs Hawkins,' Rita corrected herself hastily, 'that's my toothbrush. Rosie's is the pink one.'

Mrs Hawkins said nothing, simply gave her a long look and closed the locker door.

'Sit on the stool, Rose, and wait here until I come back,' she instructed. 'Rita, come with me.'

She turned and walked out of the room and Rita whispered to Rosie, 'Sit on the stool and wait, Rosie. I'll be back in a minute.' Rosie's lip began to tremble, but Rita gave her a push and she sat down.

Rita followed Mrs Hawkins to another room on the opposite side of the landing. Apart from its purple door, it was identical to Green Dormitory.

'You'll sleep in here, Rita,' Mrs Hawkins said, and pointed to a bed under the window. 'That's your bed.'

'Please, Mrs Hawkins,' began Rita, and then paused as her courage failed her.

'Well, what is it?'

'Please, Mrs Hawkins, can't I sleep in the same room as Rosie? She'll be scared without me.'

'No, you can't,' replied Mrs Hawkins calmly. 'Green Dormitory is the baby dormitory, Purple is the under elevens. That's you.'

'What about our other things?' asked Rita. She had seen their new dresses in the case, and some pants and vests and socks. They were wearing their school uniforms, but there should be another skirt each and a blouse and a jersey.

'They'll be put away in the general wardrobe,' replied Mrs Hawkins. 'You'll be given what you need to wear.'

'But we've got new dresses—' began Rita.

'Everything is shared here,' replied Mrs Hawkins briskly. 'Some of the girls here have never had a new dress. You'll wear it when it's your turn and not before. Now put your satchel into your locker and come along.'

Rita had been at Laurel House for less than an hour, but she had already learned there was nothing to be gained from arguing, and guessed that there was plenty to be lost. She quickly put her satchel into the locker, her picture of Daddy still safely inside it.

They collected Rosie who was still sitting on her stool, pink and tearful, and Rita hurriedly put her sister's satchel into her locker. Knitty was inside it and she was determined that Mrs Hawkins wasn't going to make Rosie share Knitty with everyone else.

Mrs Hawkins showed them the bathroom and then led them back downstairs to a large room at the back of the house over-looking the garden. Several girls were sitting in a circle, sewing; others sat round a large table, doing school work. They were all dressed in faded, blue-checked cotton frocks, all wore black plimsolls, all had their hair in plaits or held back with a hair band. They all stood up when Mrs Hawkins came in.

'This is the playroom,' Mrs Hawkins said. 'This is where you do your homework after school when you've finished your chores. Sheila Nevin!'

A large girl wearing wire-rimmed spectacles who had been darning a sock put down her work and stood up. 'Yes, Mrs Hawkins?'

'We have two new girls come to join us. Rita and Rose Stevens. I have shown them their dormitories, you're to make sure they are in the right place for the rest of today. Their names are already on the rota board.' She waved a hand towards a cork noticeboard on the wall, 'so you can explain what they have to do. Rita, Rose, listen to what Sheila tells you.'

The minute the door closed behind her there was a buzz of conversation. Rita and Rosie stood by the door, Rosie still clutching Rita's hand. They looked round at the sea of faces staring at them. The girl, Sheila, glared across at them. She was older than either of them, about thirteen, with a big round face and dark hair. She peered short-sightedly at her charges, and scowled.

'Why do I always have to do the nannying?' she moaned. 'Come here, you two, and let's have a look at you.'

When neither child moved Sheila got to her feet and gripped Rosie by the wrist, jerking her forward and making her cry out. 'I said, come here.'

'Let her go,' cried Rita, 'you're hurting her.'

'And I'll hurt her some more if she don't do what I tell her,' snapped Sheila. Rosie was wailing now and the older girl turned on her. 'Shut up!' she hissed. 'Shut up, you snivelling kid.'

'Let her go!' Rita shouted, but Sheila simply laughed, tightening her grip.

'Make me!' she jeered and then gave a screech of pain. Without warning, Rita had bent down and sank her teeth into the bigger girl's arm. She bit hard and Sheila released Rosie, jerking her arm free. Rita grabbed Rosie and pulled her away. There was a burst of laughter from the girls who were sitting in the mending circle, and Sheila rounded on them, her face flaming with humiliation.

'And you lot can shut up an' all!'

'Leave the poor kids alone,' said a voice from the door. 'Don't you remember what your first day was like?'

Rita spun round to see another girl had come into the room. She was older than anyone else in the room, almost grown up. She stood surveying the scene, Rita and Rosie cowering together, Sheila on her feet nursing her arm where the marks of Rita's teeth stood out, a dark red on her pale skin.

'Yes, I remember,' growled Sheila. 'It was tough. Life is tough here and the sooner these kids learn that the better.'

The newcomer walked over to Rita and said, 'Hallo, I'm Frances. If you want to know anything you can ask me.' She bent down to Rosie and taking a handkerchief out of her pocket, wiped the little girl's eyes and helped her blow her nose. 'Stop crying,' she said gently, 'it's all right. Now, tell me your names.'

'I'm Rita, and this is my sister Rosie, and she's only five. I have to look after her.'

'Of course you do,' agreed Frances, 'but you don't have to bite people. I think you should say sorry to Sheila.'

'No,' Rita said fiercely. 'She should say sorry to Rosie.'

For a moment Frances looked from one to the other and then shrugged. 'I've come for the mending,' she said. 'Have you finished? I've got to take it up to Matron.'

'Nearly,' came a murmur from the sewing group and the girls returned to their mending.

'Now then, you two,' Frances said, turning back to Rita and Rosie, 'let's have a look at the rota board to see what you should be doing.' She led them across to the board and looked at the chart.

'Here's your name, Rita,' she said. 'Tomorrow you are on cleaning Purple Dorm in the morning, and helping in the garden when you get home from school. After breakfast you're on kitchen duty, so go to the kitchen and you'll be told what to do. Now, let's find you, Rosie. You have to help clean your dorm, too, and then after breakfast you'll be helping to feed the chickens and collect the eggs.' She smiled down at the little girl. 'You'll like that, won't you?'

Rosie looked back at her, round-eyed. 'I don't know where the chickens are,' she said.

'Don't worry,' said Frances, 'someone will show you.'

'Not her.' Rosie looked back fearfully at Sheila who was now sitting, head bent over her darning. 'I don't like her.'

A bell sounded and at once everyone stood and lined up in pairs at the door.

'Stand in the line with the others,' Frances said to Rita as she collected up the finished mending. 'When you get to the dining room you'll be told where to sit.' She walked to the door pausing beside the still crimson-faced Sheila. 'Go easy on them, Sheila, they're only kids.'

Frances hurried off to give Matron the mended clothes. She knew it would be tough for the Stevens girls from now on, Rita in particular, for she had made an enemy of Sheila, but they would have to get used to Laurel House, as everyone else had.

Another bell rang, and the line of girls led down the passage into the dining room. Each of three long wooden tables was laid with ten places. Across the top of the room was a smaller table with six chairs, and in a corner on either side of this were two separate chairs with no table in front of them. As the line of girls filed in, each went to her allotted place. Rita and Rosie hesitated by the door, not knowing where to sit. Sheila went over to them.

As she approached, Rosie shrank away from her, but Rita, her heart thudding, held her ground.

'You,' Sheila pointed at Rosie. 'You sit at the babies' table.' She jerked her thumb towards the table by the door where some much younger girls were standing behind their chairs. Rosie looked across at them and gripped Rita's hand more tightly, not moving. 'And you,' Sheila glared at Rita, 'you sit over there, at the junior table.' Having given her instructions she turned away, unconcerned whether the two new girls followed them.

Rita took Rosie over to the babies' table and whispered, 'You got to sit here, Rosie. I'll come and find you after.'

Rosie's eyes immediately filled with tears. 'But I want to sit with you!' she wailed. At the sound of her cries everyone turned to look at her.

'Shh, Rosie!' hissed Rita, turning scarlet as she felt the eyes staring at them. 'You can't. I got to sit over there. Stay here.'

She pulled her hand free and went across to the next table where some girls she'd not seen before were waiting in silence behind their chairs. She took her place behind an empty one from where she could still see Rosie.

'Not there,' hissed the girl opposite. 'That's Beryl's chair. Come round here next to me.'

Rita moved to her new place, listening to Rosie's continuing wails.

'What is that disgraceful noise?'

Rita looked over her shoulder and saw that Mrs Hawkins had come into the room. The superintendent strode over to Rosie and with one swift movement, slapped her cheek. The wailing stopped abruptly as Rosie was startled into silence.

'That's better,' said Mrs Hawkins. 'Now, no more of your nonsense.' And ignoring the subsequent whimpering, she walked to her place at the top table.

The dining room was full now. Rita saw that there was a senior girl standing at each of the tables. It was with relief that she saw Frances take her place at Rosie's table. Frances had been kind to them before, surely she would be kind to Rosie now.

The other senior girls sat at the small, top table from where Mrs Hawkins presided. There was one space at Rita's table, and another at the table where Sheila and her friends were sitting. Rita was wondering who was missing when two girls were brought in and were led to the chairs standing in the corner. Rita, looking over at them, realized they must be punishment chairs.

Mrs Hawkins intoned grace, then, with a scraping of chairs, everyone sat down. A creaking sound heralded the arrival of a fat woman in white overalls pushing a trolley. On it were four large dishes, steam pouring from under their lids. Beryl pointed to the girl sitting next to Rita. 'Daisy,' she said.

Daisy got up and went to the trolley and collected one of the dishes. She set it down in front of Beryl and then returned to her place. Beryl picked up a spoon and began dishing food onto the plates piled in front of her and when every girl had her plate, at a signal from Beryl, they all began to eat. All except Rita. She looked at the pale yellow mess on her plate and wondered what it was. The other girls scraped away with their forks, scooping the food into their mouths quickly, as if it might disappear. No one spoke; the only sound in the room was the chink of cutlery on china as everyone ate their cauliflower cheese.

'Eat your tea, Rita,' Beryl said, her voice sounding very loud in the surrounding silence.

Rita looked again at the food in front of her. Pieces of cauliflower floated in a pale yellow juice, with occasional lumps of... something. She picked up her knife and fork and cautiously speared a piece of cauli. She put the piece into her mouth and almost gagged. It was warm and soggy, and the sauce tasted of soap. She spat it out again, and heard the intake of breath as the other girls at the table watched to see what would happen.

'Eat your food properly,' said Beryl.

'You've got to eat it,' murmured Daisy, 'or you'll get it again at breakfast.'

'No talking, Daisy,' snapped Beryl, and Daisy lowered her eyes to the table, but she dug a finger into Rita's leg to emphasize her point. Rita looked at her plate. If she refused to eat it now, would it really be back for breakfast? She took another forkful forcing herself to swallow it. There was a glass of water beside each place. Rita reached for hers, and by taking a mouthful of water with each mouthful of food, she managed to get it down without being sick. At last it was done. Daisy had collected a plate of bread and marge from the trolley and had put it on the table. Everyone had helped herself, and by the time Rita had finished her cauliflower cheese, there was none left.

'If you had eaten up properly in the first place,' Beryl told her, 'you'd have had your bread and marge, but as you didn't, someone else has had it. You'll know another time.'

When the meal was over, Mrs Hawkins got to her feet and so did everyone else.

'Purples on washing up,' she announced, and then stalked out of the room, leaving the girls to file out after her.

'That's us,' Daisy said. 'We're Purples. Come on. I'll show you.' She led Rita out of the room, and with four others went along a passage to the kitchen. The kitchen maid followed, pushing the loaded trolley, and they were all met by the fat woman in the white overalls.

'Right, you lot,' she said as they came in, 'get started. You.' The cook pointed at Rita. 'You're new! Who're you?'

'Rita Stevens.'

'Well, Rita Stevens, I'm Mrs Smith. You do as you're told and we'll get on all right. Isn't that right, Daisy?'

'Yes, Mrs Smith,' replied Daisy obediently.

'Right. Well, get on with you.'

Daisy went over to the deep sink and turned on the taps. 'You bring them plates over,' she said to Rita. 'You and I can wash, Dora and Mary can dry and Joan can put away. I'll do the plates, you do the knives and forks.'

It took them half an hour to finish the washing up, then they had to wipe down the surfaces in the kitchen and hang the tea towels on the airer over the range before Mrs Smith, having inspected the now tidy kitchen, said, 'Right, off you go!'

'Come on,' said Daisy, and scurried off down the passage. 'We got quarter of an hour before prayers.'

'Prayers?'

'Bedtime prayers, in the playroom. We all got to be there.'

Rita hurried after her, anxious not to lose her new friend. 'But I got to find Rosie,' she panted. 'I promised.'

'She'll be going to bed,' Daisy said.

'I better go and find her,' Rita replied. 'Will she be in her dorm?'

''Spect so, but you can't go in there.'

'Why not?'

'Not allowed. No dorm visiting. They'll be having dorm prayers in a minute. Babies have bedtime prayers in their dorm.' She caught hold of Rita's hand. 'Come on, we can go in the playroom now.' But Rita pulled free. She wanted to see Rosie, and check she was all right. She darted back and went upstairs. The door to Green Dorm stood open and she peeped in. Most of the girls were in their nighties. Rosie was sitting, fully dressed, on the stool at the bottom of her bed, tears streaming down her face. Her locker door was open and her satchel was lying on the floor. Knitty was nowhere to be seen.

Rita marched into the room and said, 'Who's got my sister's teddy?'

The girls all stared at her, but no one answered.

'Who's got Knitty?' she demanded again. Still no answer, so she turned to Rosie. 'Who's got him, Rosie?'

Rosie pointed to a girl with red hair who was sitting on the edge of her bed. 'Her,' she whispered.

Rita crossed the room and grabbed the girl by the wrist. 'Have you got Rosie's teddy?'

The girl stuck her tongue out.

'Susan, that's the girl what bit Sheila!' muttered the girl on the next bed.

'An' I'll bite you an' all if you don't give him back right now!' hissed Rita, pulling Susan's arm towards her mouth. Susan gave a squeal and tried to jerk her arm free, but Rita was holding on too tightly. Lowering her mouth to the girl's arm, Rita repeated, 'Where's Knitty?'

'Under her pillow,' called Rosie.

With a firm grip on Susan's arm, Rita reached under the pillow and retrieved Rosie's beloved toy. She tossed him over to her. 'You can all remember that I'm the one who bit Sheila, and if any of you touch my sister again, I'll come back and bite you all over. OK?'

Her words were greeted by silence. 'OK?' she repeated, lowering her mouth towards Susan's arm again.

'Yes!' squeaked Susan. 'OK!'

Rita let her go and turned back to Rosie who was clutching Knitty to her, tears still streaming down her cheeks. 'Stop crying, Rosie,' she said. 'Come on, you'd better get undressed. Put Knitty under your pillow for now.' She took the teddy from Rosie and hid him quickly under the pillow. She was just in time, for at that moment the matron came into the room. She paused in the doorway, looking at Rita in surprise.

'And just what do you think you're doing in here, young lady?' she demanded.

'I just wanted to say goodnight to Rosie. She's my sister and—'

'Dormitory visiting is not allowed,' said the matron, as if Rita hadn't spoken. 'Out you go, and no coming back.' She fixed Rita with a steely eye. 'You should be in the playroom by now for evening prayers, you'll be in trouble if you're late.'

Outside Rita stood in the passage for a moment, long enough to hear Matron saying, 'Come along now, Rose, you haven't even undressed. Susan, I thought I told you to look after Rose and tell her what she has to do.'

'Please, Matron, I did, but she...' began Susan.

Rita didn't wait to hear any more; she daren't risk Matron catching her again.

Chapter 10

Rita was only just in time for evening prayers. When she walked into the crowded playroom Daisy waved at her, and Rita edged her way round to join her.

'We all have to stand in dorms for prayers,' Daisy said. 'Did you find your sister?'

'Yes, but Matron came in and turned me out.'

'The Dragon,' nodded Daisy. 'Don't want to get in her way!'

The door opened and Mrs Hawkins stalked in. There was a shuffling of feet as all the girls stood up and waited for the evening roll call.

When the superintendent had finished she said, 'Step forward, Rita Stevens.'

Rita could feel the colour flood her cheeks, but at a shove in the back from Daisy, she took one pace forward.

'This is Rita Stevens,' Mrs Hawkins said to the assembled girls. 'She and her sister, Rose, have come to live here. It's up to all of you to teach her how we behave here at Laurel House. Step back, Rita.'

Rita stepped back, her face still flaming. One or two of the other girls smiled. Everyone knew who Rita Stevens was, the new girl who had bitten Sheila Nevin. She'd already made one enemy.

'Two girls were late getting into croc after school today,' Mrs Hawkins went on, 'Joan Cameron and Pamela Wynn. We do not tolerate tardiness here. If anyone is late tomorrow it'll be dormitory stools on Saturday for everyone.' She paused and then added, 'Is that understood?'

There was an answering chorus of 'Yes, Mrs Hawkins.'

'What's dormitory stools?' whispered Rita to Daisy, but Daisy stood hard on her foot and she fell silent.

'Ready for prayers, please,' said Mrs Hawkins, and all the girls put their hands together and closed their eyes. Rita did the same.

'Oh Lord,' intoned Mrs Hawkins, 'teach these poor, weak girls a due sense of gratitude for all Your mercies to them; for their good fortune in being in this place where all their wants are supplied. Teach them to be duly grateful for the generosity they are shown in this house. Let them learn to be obedient to those set in authority over them, each to know her place. Teach them to work hard and keep them from the evils of idleness, laziness and the devil's work that comes with these sins. Punish those who transgress, oh Lord, that they may learn humility and obedience. Amen.'

'Amen,' came the murmured response.

Rita opened her eyes, but on finding Mrs Hawkins glaring at her hastily closed them again.

'Oh Lord, bless our benefactress, Miss Emily Vanstone. Bless her for her kindness to these unfortunate girls, her generosity in taking them from the gutter and providing them with a home and all the comforts of life. Amen.'

'Amen.'

'Our Father...'

They all joined in. Rita kept her eyes shut until she felt Daisy move beside her and heard a low buzz of conversation. When she dared open them again she found that Mrs Hawkins had left the room, and most of the girls had flopped down on the chairs and sagging sofas.

'We have to go to bed now,' Daisy said. 'Juniors go up straight after evening prayers.'

'What's dormitory stools?' asked Rita again.

'If someone's late for croc again, we'll have to sit on our dormitory stools for three hours on Saturday afternoon.'

'What's croc?' asked Rita anxiously.

Daisy stared at her in amazement. 'Don't you know nothing? Croc's how we walk to school. In twos. We line up in croc and then we all walk to school. Same when we come home. You'll see tomorrow morning.'

'Go to bed,' said a harsh voice and Rita looked up to find Sheila standing over her. 'Or I'll report you to Matron.'

'We're just going, Sheila,' Daisy said hastily. 'Come on, Rita.'

The other Purples had already left the room, and Daisy pulled Rita along the passage after them. At the bottom of the stairs they met Frances. Daisy pushed Rita back against the wall to let the senior girl pass, but Frances stopped.

'Daisy,' she said, 'you'd better look after Rita. Make sure she's in the right place at the right time, especially not late for croc.'

'Yes, Frances.'

'And you, Rita, listen to what Daisy tells you, she knows what's what.'

'Yes, Frances,' answered Rita meekly.

Frances nodded. 'Bed, then,' she said and walked off down the corridor.

'She's nice,' Rita said as she watched Frances disappearing.

'She's all right,' conceded Daisy. 'Better than most of them, anyway. Come on.'

In the dormitory Daisy showed Rita where to fill her bowl. 'Hands, face and teeth at night,' she explained. 'Strip wash in the morning. Bath night once a week. You have to look at the list to see which is your night.'

There was supposed to be silence in the dormitory, but the other five girls exchanged whispers as they got ready for bed. Rita watched, doing what they did, but all the time she was fighting a lump in her throat. Tears filled her eyes as she put on the nightie lying on her bed. She blinked fiercely, trying to hold them back. She wanted her own bed in Ship Street, she wanted Mum and Gran, but they didn't even know where she was. A sob escaped her, and then another.

Matron came in at that moment with a blue-checked cotton

frock like the other girls all wore. 'Here's your dress for tomorrow, Rita,' she said, as she placed it on her stool and gathered up the school dress Rita had been wearing. 'You get clean knickers and socks on Saturday.' She saw the tears on Rita's cheeks and added, 'And you can stop that snivelling. We don't want cry-babies here.'

The lights went out five minutes later, and the six girls in Purple Dorm settled down to sleep. There was an occasional whisper, but before long there was only the sound of regular breathing as one by one they drifted off to sleep. All except Rita. She lay in bed, her face buried in her pillow, trying to stifle her sobs, but homesickness washed over her, filling her with a misery so deep, she even wished she were back with Uncle Jimmy. Everything at Laurel House was so strange, Rita ached for the familiarity of her own home, her own bedroom, of Rosie curled up beside her.

The thought of Rosie made her tears flow again. Poor little Rosie, alone in her new bed, too. Was she all right? Was she asleep, or was she lying awake as well?

As the summer light fled the sky, the dormitory was lit with an eerie green light from the street lamp in the road outside. Cautiously Rita stood up on her bed and peered out through the bars. Below the window was the front garden, patterned with dark shadows. A shaft of light from a downstairs window lay across the path, but even as she watched, it disappeared as the light was switched off. For a long time Rita stared out of the window. Her tears were dry now, but she felt a deep and aching loneliness; an emptiness that was beyond tears.

Laurel House was silent. Very quietly, Rita got off her bed and with her eyes accustomed to the pallid light, crossed to the door. She eased it open and crept along the passage to Green Dorm, its door standing ajar. For a moment she stood outside, listening to the quiet breathing of its inmates; the quiet breathing and the muffled sobs. Rita pushed the door open a little wider and slipped inside. It was darker in here, but she could see enough to creep over to Rosie's bed. The little girl was curled up into a ball, crying in her sleep. Rita twitched back the blanket and lay down beside her, putting her arm round her and snuggling into shape behind her. Rosie stirred and opened her eyes, muttering.

'It's all right, Rosie,' whispered Rita. 'It's me, Reet!' She felt her sister relax against her, and it was only moments before they both fell into a deep and exhausted sleep.

The clanging of a loud bell shook them awake, and for a moment neither of them knew where they were. Then the events of the previous day crowded back to them, and Rita was filled with rising despair. She was just crawling out of Rosie's bed when the door was flung open and Frances came in. She was wearing a dressing gown, and her hair stood in a halo round her head.

'Come on, kids,' she began and then broke off, staring at Rita. 'What d'you think you're doing in here?' she demanded. 'Get back to your own dorm, and be grateful it was me found you, not Matron. Go on, scoot!'

Rita scooted.

'Where were you?' hissed Daisy, when she saw her.

'Went to the toilet,' lied Rita.

'Well, hurry up and strip your bed,' said Daisy, who'd folded her bedclothes into a neat pile on her stool. 'Come on,' she said, placing her clothes on the bare mattress. 'You've got to fill your bowl and get washed.' She grabbed her own bowl and scurried out of the room, returning moments later with her bowl full of water. She stared at Rita.

'Come on, Rita,' she implored. 'Strip your bed. Look.' She put her bowl down and showed Rita what to do. 'Hurry up,' she scolded as Rita struggled to fold the sheets and blanket. 'Matron'll be here in ten minutes, and we have to be dressed, with our beds made and ready for inspection.'

She turned back to her own preparations, leaving Rita to fill her own bowl. By the time she was dressed, all the other girls in the room had remade their beds, and were waiting for Matron to carry out her inspection. They could hear her voice, loud with disapproval in another dorm, and Daisy grabbed Rita's bedclothes and swiftly remade the bed.

'Hospital corners,' she muttered as Rita tried to tuck them in. 'Like this!'

'You're very slow this morning, Purples!' Matron said as she walked in and found Rita struggling with her blanket. She looked at her and sniffed. 'Well, as it's your first morning, I won't be putting you on report,' she said. 'But you'll have to learn to be quicker.'

She looked round the room where the other girls were all standing by their beds, waiting for her approval. Glancing at a notice on the back of the door she said, 'You're on dormitory work this morning, Joan. You and Rita. Show her what to do. The rest of you, get off to your chores.'

They got to the playroom just in time for morning prayers and listened, hands together, eyes closed, as Mrs Hawkins droned out exactly the same prayers as the night before, only adding, 'Teach these girls to make the most of this day You have given them, to waste not a minute of Your precious time in idleness, but fill each moment with work and praise.'

Breakfast was porridge and bread and marge. Rita smiled across reassuringly at Rosie, sitting at the babies' table, but Rosie simply stared down at the plate of cold porridge she'd pushed away. It was still Frances taking her table, and Rita saw her encouraging Rosie to eat. The next time she looked, the plate of porridge was in front of red-headed Susan, and Rosie was left with one piece of dry bread.

When the meal was over Rita found that it was still the Purples' turn to wash up, and she followed the rest of her dorm to the kitchen to do so. There were other girls in the kitchen at the same time.

'It's Orange on veggies today,' Daisy said as they washed the porridge bowls. 'It'll be us tomorrow.'

There was no time to spare once the clearing up was done.

'Croc in the garden, in five minutes,' came the call, and Rita followed Daisy to collect her satchel from her locker, ready for school. In a moment when there was no one near her, Rita unbuckled the flap and slipped her hand inside. There, tucked into the pages of her sum book, was her picture of Daddy. Quickly she slipped him inside her pillowcase before she hurried out to join the croc forming up in the garden.

The crocodile moved off, through the gate into the street beyond. Rita's partner, Angela, looked at her and said, 'Did you really bite Sheila?'

'Yeah,' answered Rita shortly, 'she was hurting my sister.'

Angela nodded. 'Yeah, she's a bully. She often hits the little kids.'

'Frances stopped her,' Rita said.

'Yeah, well, Frances won't always be there,' Angela said. 'She's got a job now. You better watch out for Sheila. She's got it in for you.'

The walk to school took ten minutes. On the way they were overtaken by a number 37 bus. Rita watched to see where it stopped. The number 37 was the way home, back to Mum and back to Gran, but the bus didn't stop; it swept round the corner and was lost to sight. Rita looked at the name of the road they were in. Meredith Lane. Me-red-ith. She sounded the name out to herself. Well, at least she knew where to look for the bus, even if she didn't know where the stop was.

When they reached the elementary school, the juniors and babies branched off into the playground, while the rest of the crocodile continued to the secondary school. Rita found Rosie in the playground and took her hand.

'We go to school here now, Rosie,' she said.

Rosie clung to her. 'I'm hungry,' she wailed.

'You didn't eat no breakfast,' pointed out Rita. 'You let that Susan have it. You got to eat your breakfast, Rosie.'

'I don't like porridge,' whined Rosie. 'It was nasty.'

'I didn't like it, neither,' Rita said, 'but we got to eat it, or we'll be hungry.'

At that moment Angela came up to them. 'Miss Harrison wants to see you both,' she said and pointed towards the school door. Rita looked over to where Miss Harrison was waiting. 'Come on Rosie,' she said, and led her across.

'Rita and Rose?' asked the teacher with a smile. 'Welcome to St George's School. I'm Miss Harrison and I'm your new headmistress. Miss Hassinger phoned me and told me all about you. Come on inside and I'll show you where your classrooms are.' She reached for Rosie's hand, but Rosie drew back and hid behind Rita.

'Rosie's shy, miss,' Rita explained.

'So she is,' agreed Miss Harrison cheerfully. 'Never mind, you just bring her in with you. Come along.'

The morning passed very quickly. Everything was new and different at St George's; for a start it was girls only and Capel Street Elementary had been mixed, but when Rita went to find Rosie at playtime, she was happily playing with a girl from her class, and so Rita left her to it.

At the end of morning school the Laurel House girls were marched back to the home for lunch. It was fish and mashed potato, and though Rita didn't like fish very much, she was so hungry that she, like everyone else at the table, ate it all. A rather soggy suet pudding followed, and then it was washing up again. Rita couldn't believe it was still their turn.

'We'll be late for croc,' she wailed when Daisy dragged her into the kitchen.

'Better not be!' warned Daisy. 'Don't want no dormitory stools!'

All the Purples agreed with that, and hurriedly set to work on the dishes.

'No more washing up for a week,' crowed Daisy as they left the kitchen and rushed out to join the crocodile. 'Yahoo!'

'Warning, Daisy Smart, for making unseemly noises in the corridor!' Mrs Hawkins was emerging from the dining room. 'Another sound like that and you'll be on punishment.' She swept on down the passage, leaving Daisy mutinous, if pale-faced, behind her.

'Watch out for the Hawk,' she muttered to Rita. 'She comes from nowhere!' Then she stuck her tongue out at the retreating figure. 'Don't mess with the Hawk, Reet.'

By the end of afternoon school, Rita was beginning to feel at home in her new classroom and she was sorry that it was Friday and there would be no more school until Monday. Miss Davis, her teacher, had given them all some spellings to learn, and said there would be a nine times table test on Monday. Rita had the words carefully written in her new spelling book. She wasn't worried about the table test; Miss Hassinger had been very strict on learning tables and Rita already knew her nine times. But the thought of no school till Monday made Rita's heart sink. Just Laurel House. A weekend of being shut up in Laurel House, with no escape... Unless, of course, Mum came to take them home. But as the crocodile wound its way in through the gate, Laurel House closed round her, so that for a moment Rita felt she couldn't breathe. She looked round for Rosie, but she was much further back in the croc, with the other babies, and she couldn't see her. The moment they were indoors, Daisy was pulling her into the kitchen.

'Come on,' she urged, 'or we'll get blackcurrants!'

'What?' Rita had no idea what she was talking about, but she hurried anyway. She had quickly discovered that Daisy knew her way around, and if she stuck with her she'd be all right. They were first into the kitchen and Mrs Smith gave them a large basket each and sent them out to pick gooseberries.

'And don't let me catch you eating any,' warned Mrs Smith. 'I want them baskets full, sharp as you like.'

It took Rita and Daisy over half an hour to fill their baskets, and while they were picking Rita plucked up courage and asked her new friend some questions.

'How long you been here, Dais?' she asked.

Daisy paused in her picking for a moment. 'Here at Laurel House? Forever.'

'My mum'll come and get me an' Rosie when she gets home,' Rita said.

'Sez you!' retorted Daisy, adding as an afterthought, 'Home from where?'

'From fetching baby Richard from the hospital.'

'Is that where she is?' asked Daisy.

'Yes, and when she gets home, she'll come and get us.'

'No!' Daisy spoke emphatically. 'She won't. They never do.'

'What?' Rita turned sharply. 'What you mean, "they never do"?'

'They never come. Mums, or dads.'

'Mine will,' stated Rita.

Daisy shrugged and went on picking the gooseberries. 'Betty ain't got no mum or dad, but she thought her auntie would come, and she's still here. Her auntie never come for her, and she helps in the home now. You seen her. Wetty Betty what answers the door and runs round after them all.'

'The maid?'

'Yeah,' Daisy said. 'She's been here forever, an' now she has to stay an' work 'ere.'

'Why? Why's she got to stay?'

''Cos she ain't got nowhere else to go. She left school last year, but couldn't get no proper job, so she has to work here, helping the Dragon an' that.'

'You got names for all of them,' remarked Rita, looking across her basket and thinking how brave Daisy was. She'd stuck her tongue out at Mrs Hawkins at lunchtime. You'd have to be brave to do that, Rita thought.

'Yeah, the Hawk, the Dragon, Ole Smithy and Wetty Betty.'

'There was another lady when we come in,' Rita said, 'in her office. Who was that?'

'That? Oh,' Daisy said a little less nonchalantly, 'that was Miss Vanstone. You belong to her now! Even if your mum does come, she can't have you.'

'Why?' asked Rita fearfully. Daisy seemed to know everything. Suppose she was right. 'Why can't she?'

''Cos Miss V's got the papers.'

'Papers? What papers?' But Rita remembered Miss Vanstone looking at some papers Miss Hopkins had brought.

'The papers what say that you've got to stay here. She's got papers about all of us.'

When the baskets were full at last, they took them into the

kitchen where Mrs Smith set them to the topping and tailing. By the time the bell went for high tea, their fingers were stained and sore, but they had finished.

Daisy grabbed Rita's hand. 'Come *on*!' she hissed as they hurried to line up for tea. 'We've only got laundry drop to do tonight, and then we're off.'

'What's laundry drop?' asked Rita hurrying after her.

'We have to collect the clean clothes from the Dragon and put them out on dormitory stools. Saturday tomorrow, ain't it! Clean clothes day, sweets and no school. Best day of the week.'

The laundry drop was quite easy. Rita took a pile of clothes to Green Dorm. As she put a set of clothes onto her sister's stool, she muttered, 'Hide Knitty properly.'

Rosie pulled the pillow more firmly over Knitty's head. 'Will you come and see me later?' she asked.

'If I can,' Rita said, and went on with her clothes drop.

In the dorm that evening, Rita got ready for bed with the others, but she had already decided that she would creep into bed with Rosie again when everyone else was asleep. She had seen her briefly after tea and Rosie had told her about feeding the chickens.

'Can we have chickens when we go home?' Rosie had asked. 'I like feeding chickens.'

'Don't think Mum likes chickens,' Rita said.

'Why not?' asked Rosie, surprised. 'We could have eggs. One of the big girls was collecting the eggs.'

'We ain't got a hen house, Rosie.' Then to soften her words she gave her a hug. 'What's your teacher like?'

'She's called Miss Coucher,' Rosie informed her, 'and she shouts a lot. We did number-work and painting, and she told us a story about a circus. And Milly's my friend.'

The day had been so busy, Rita had had little time to think, no time to feel homesick for Mum and Gran, but now, as she collected washing water in her bowl and cleaned her teeth with Rosie's toothbrush, she felt a sudden rush of homesickness. She hated Laurel House, the chores, the food. She hated the dreary dormitory. She wanted to go home. She wanted to see Gran. But most of all she wanted Mum. She fought back the tears. No one cried at bedtime, and she was determined no one should see her crying. She locked herself in the lavatory and there she stayed until she heard the Dragon. She flushed the toilet, and scurried back to the dorm.

'Hurry up, Rita,' scolded the Dragon, 'it's lights out.'

'Sorry, Matron, I was being excused.'

'You should have thought of that before, young lady,' said Matron turning off the dormitory light, leaving Rita to find her way to bed in the gathering twilight.

Rita waited until she was sure everyone else was in bed, and then crept to Green Dorm. She slipped in beside Rosie and curled up together, they both fell asleep.

Saturday was not a bad day. They put on the clean clothes they had been given. No school uniform today, just the skirt and blouse left on the stool. There were always chores to do. The older girls worked in the laundry, some of them washing clothes in the big sink, others standing over ironing tables.

Rita and Daisy were given a tin of Gumption and a cloth each and sent to clean the bathrooms. Daisy explained what had to be done and then they chatted companionably as they worked.

'What happens for the rest of the weekend?' Rita asked as she scrubbed at a line of scum on one of the tubs.

'We got to do the veggies for dinner next,' Daisy told her. 'Then, when chores is finished, we have to do our homework. After dinner there's sweets before we go out to play.'

'Play out?'

'Yeah, if we ain't on punishment, or nothing. We go outside until teatime. Evening chores is the same. It's Sundays that's boring with church an' that.'

When the midday meal was over, they each chose two sweets from a huge tin that was passed round the table, and then went out into the garden. There was a hopscotch grid painted on the paved yard. Beyond was the kitchen garden where they'd picked the gooseberries, and the hen run where Rosie'd fed the chickens.

A grassy area which Daisy called 'the Patch' had a couple of swings and a seesaw, and a dirty-looking sandpit in one corner.

Most of the girls sat or played on the Patch. Rita saw Rosie happily digging in the sand, making a castle with her bare hands.

'Come on,' Daisy said as Rita paused to look round. She grabbed Rita's hand and dragged her across the Patch, through a gate into the orchard beyond. 'I'll show you.'

At the end of the orchard was a clump of bushes by the old stone wall. Daisy pushed her way through these and Rita followed. She found herself in a little clearing, surrounded by bushes on three sides and the wall on the fourth. An old piece of tarpaulin was draped over some of the branches, making a rough shelter beneath.

'This is my camp,' Daisy said. 'I come here to get away from that lot.' She jerked her head towards the house. 'I keep my stuff here, safe like.'

'What stuff?' Rita looked round the hidey-hole curiously.

'Private stuff... you know.' Daisy crept under the tarpaulin roof and pulled out an old biscuit tin. 'It's in here,' she said, opening the tin to show Rita what was inside. There was a pencil and some paper, a green stone with a hole in it, and a piece of string, a stale-looking biscuit and four threepenny bits. She picked up the stone and held it out.

'That's my lucky stone,' she said. 'I found it on the way to school, just lying it was, in the gutter.'

Rita took the stone in her hand, admiring it, but her eyes were on the threepenny bits. She handed back the stone and said, 'Where d'you get that money from then, Dais?'

'That's mine,' Daisy said fiercely.

'Didn't say it wasn't,' said Rita. 'Just wondered where you got it, that's all.'

That evening, hidden in the bathroom where none of the others could see, Rita showed Daisy the picture of Daddy.

'He looks nice,' Daisy remarked. 'You're lucky. I ain't got no pictures of me mum.'

'Or your dad?' ventured Rita.

'Don't know who he is, do I?' snapped Daisy. 'Come on. Get that hid again. The Dragon'll be here for lights out in a minute.'

'Sunday's always the worst day,' Daisy informed Rita as they lined up after breakfast, ready to go to church. They were paired together in the crocodile that marched all the children from Laurel House to the Crosshills Methodist Church.

'Why?' Rita wasn't really listening. She was wondering if Mum was home yet, and if she was, when she would come to find them.

'Cos we have to go to church, which is boring, and we ain't allowed to do nothing but our chores.'

The day proved quite as dreary as Daisy had described. When they reached the church, the Laurel House girls were all seated in pews at the back. The Hawk, the Dragon and Ole Smithy each sat at the end of a pew containing the younger girls. The working girls, including Betty Grover, sat behind. The rest of the church was filled with the ordinary parishioners.

Rita stared round the church. She'd only been into a church a few times. Mum didn't believe in church; she said that if God was really there He wouldn't have let Daddy die in the war, and Rita had given God no further thought. At school they had scripture, she knew the Lord's Prayer, and could recite the everyday prayers in school assembly, but they meant nothing to her. Now, as she waited for the service to begin, Rita looked round with interest. The church was not large, its walls red brick, pierced by arched windows, through the plain glass of which the sun was streaming. There was no other decoration.

There was a buzz of conversation from the rest of the congregation as they waited for the minister to appear. Sitting near the front Rita saw the pig-faced woman. She was nodding and smiling to the people around her. She ignored the rows of girls at the back, and she wasn't the only one. None of the people, dressed in their Sunday bests, who filled the other pews, paid any attention to the girls from Laurel House.

Just before the service started one last woman arrived. Expensively dressed, wearing a stylish hat, she walked up the aisle and took her place in the front pew. Rita recognized her as the other lady from Laurel House, Miss Vanstone, the one Daisy said owned the place. She saw the pig-face raise her hand in a sort of wave, trying to catch Miss Vanstone's eye, but Miss Vanstone looked neither right nor left as she moved into the front row. The moment she had taken her place, as if it were a signal that the proceedings could begin, the minister glided out from behind a curtain, and the service began.

It was as boring as Daisy had promised and Rita's thoughts were soon far away, drifting back to Mum and Gran and baby Richard, and she felt a lump in her throat as she pictured them at home in Ship Street. She was startled back to her surroundings by a sharp nudge in the ribs from Daisy when they all had to stand to sing another hymn while the collection was taken. On arrival at the church, each girl had been given a threepenny bit to put in the collection bag when it came round.

'I reckon they take the threepences out at the end of the service and give them to us again next time,' Daisy muttered as they were handed theirs.

Rita remembered the threepenny bits Daisy had in her tin. Had she kept them instead of putting them into the bag? Had Daisy really dared do that? She glanced sideways at her new friend, but Daisy was staring straight ahead of her. As the bag came along the row, everyone, including Daisy, dropped her coin into it before passing it on to the next girl.

Daisy had been right. Sunday was a dead bore and as she slipped into bed in Purple Dorm that evening, Rita found herself looking forward to school the next day. She'd done her home-work, practised her nine times and learned her spellings. She had no fears about school, and school would be away from Laurel House.

Chapter 11

In the days that followed, Rita gradually settled into the strict routine at Laurel House. She was not happy, she still missed Mum and Gran desperately, but somehow she was not unhappy either. The rigid routine gave a framework to her days, which was oddly comforting. She quickly learned to keep her head down and conform to what was expected. Punishments were given for the most minor infringement of the rules, and there was nearly always someone sitting on one of the punishment chairs. Daisy and she had become firm friends, and this brought them to the attention of the staff, who frowned upon 'particular friendships', and when the chores rota was posted in the playroom, they found they were no longer paired to peel potatoes, or to scrub the bathrooms.

Daisy was picking blackcurrants, which caused her to scowl, especially as Rita was still picking gooseberries. 'All right for some,' she moaned. 'Hate doing blackcurrants!'

'I'll probably get them next week,' Rita said, hoping as she spoke that she wouldn't be here next week.

'Yeah, well,' was all Daisy muttered as, hearing Mrs Smith coming out of the kitchen door, she scurried off to the blackcurrant bushes.

At school it was different. They played together in the playground, and when asked to get into pairs for any activity they always chose each other. Rita had never had such a close friend before. She'd known Maggie, down Ship Street, forever, their mothers were good friends too, but they had not been inseparable.

Daisy, on the other hand, was Rita's rock in the still-uncertain world of Laurel House, and her grip on their friendship was firm. And Daisy? Daisy had found a kindred spirit; from the moment that Rita had faced up to Sheila Nevin, Daisy had realized that Rita was different. The way she had stuck up for her sister had drawn Daisy to her, and from being a bit of a loner, Daisy finally found she had a friend.

Despite the growing friendship, however, Rita did not confide completely in Daisy; she did not tell Daisy where she slept each night. For every night she continued to slip out of her bed and creep along the landing to Green Dorm and Rosie. She and Rosie seldom had a chance to see each other during the day, but as soon as the house was quiet, Rita went to find her, each comforted by the familiar warmth of her sister, in the bed, beside her. Since Frances had caught her that first morning, Rita had been careful. She'd always managed to wake up before the rising bell, sliding quietly out of Rosie's bed and tip-toeing back to her own, with no one the wiser.

'You mustn't tell no one that I come in,' she warned Rosie. 'The Dragon'll be very cross if she finds out. OK?'

Rosie nodded solemnly. 'I won't tell,' she said, adding, 'I don't like the Dragon, Reet. She's scary!'

'Yeah, I know. So don't tell no one, or she'll find out.'

It wasn't the Dragon who found out, it was the Hawk.

One Friday night Rita had slipped out of Purple Dorm, and not closed the door properly behind her. Later that night Mrs Hawkins, coming along the landing on her way to her flat in the tower, noticed the door open and looked in. All was quiet, she heard nothing but the soft breathing of six little girls, asleep in bed. She paused by the door, and then flicked on her torch, flashing it round the peaceful dormitory until the beam fell on the bed by the window. It was empty. Whose bed was that? She turned her torch onto the dormitory list on the back of the door. Bed number 4. Rita Stevens. Rita Stevens was not in bed... so where was she?

Mrs Hawkins was about to wake the whole dorm to ask where Rita was, when she had a better idea. First she would go and see if Rosie Stevens was there. She turned back to Green Dorm and softly easing the door open she flashed her torch round the room. Rosie Stevens was asleep in her bed, but so was Rita.

Mrs Hawkins switched on the light and strode across to Rosie's bed. With a grunt of anger, she threw back the covers, leaving the two little girls exposed, curled up in each other's arms. Rita's nightdress had ridden up, so that her bare seat was on view. The slap that resounded on her bottom and her cry of pain woke the rest of the dormitory.

'Get out of that bed,' Mrs Hawkins snarled, dealing out another slap. Rita leaped from the bed, the marks of the super-intendent's hand red on her pale skin, and Rosie began to cry.

The other children stared, round-eyed, as the Hawk aimed another blow at Rita before turning to the hysterical Rosie. 'Be quiet, Rose, or you'll get a hiding too.' She turned back to Rita. 'Get back to your own bed,' she hissed. 'I'll deal with you in the morning.'

Rita fled and jumping into her bed, buried herself under the covers. Her bum hurt like fury, and she was humiliated that the 'babies' had seen her slapped like that. She could still hear Rosie's wails until they stopped abruptly. The Hawk must have slapped her too, or terrified her into silence in some other way.

Purple Dorm was still and quiet. No one had heard the com-motion from down the landing. Rita lay among the peacefully sleeping girls, the thin blanket over her head, shivering, waiting for the Hawk to call her out again, but she heard nothing and eventually she drifted off into an uneasy sleep.

When she woke, it was still dark. The light from the street lamp filtered into the room and Rita lay looking at the ghostly shapes, her mind swirling with what had happened in Green Dorm. How had the Hawk found them? What had she done to Rosie, and what was going to happen to *her*?

I'll deal with you in the morning! The Hawk's words echoed in her brain. What was she going to do? What could she do? The more these thoughts churned in her mind, the more frightened Rita became.

When the rising bell rang, Rita felt almost sick with fear. She got out of bed and stripped it, but somehow she couldn't move quickly enough. When it was time to go down for morning prayers and breakfast, though she was dressed, Rita's bedclothes were still piled onto her stool.

'Come on, Reet,' hissed Daisy. 'You'll get us all into trouble.' She pushed Rita aside and swiftly shook out the sheets and blanket, so that when the Dragon came into the room, Rita was just straightening her pillow, feeling the picture of Daddy safely in the pillowcase.

Matron made a quick inspection to see that each bed had the required hospital corners and then said, 'You're all behind in here. Hurry up and go down for prayers.'

The six girls scurried along the passage to the stairs, but as they passed Green Dorm, Rita glanced in. The room was empty, except for Rosie. Rosie was standing on her stool with her sheet draped over her head and round her shoulders. Rita stopped dead in her tracks.

'Rosie?' she said. 'Rosie, what…?'

'Come *on*.' Daisy caught her hand and dragged her along the passage.

'But Rosie—' began Rita, trying to go back.

'She's wet her bed,' said Daisy. 'That's all. Matron will make her stand there until after breakfast, and then she'll have to wash the sheet. Come on, Reet,' she insisted, 'or we're in trouble too.'

When Rita still held back Daisy said, 'You can go back and help her after breakfast.' But by the time breakfast was over, Rita was in no position to help her sister.

The Purples were the last into the playroom, reaching their usual place by the window only moments before Mrs Hawkins came in. She glanced round the room and for a moment her eyes rested on Rita, before she raised them to heaven and said, 'Let us pray.'

When prayers came to an end, she looked round the room again allowing her gaze to fall on several girls before it finally fixed, once more, on Rita.

The inmates of Laurel House knew their superintendent well. They had recognized the signs. Someone was in deep trouble, and for an awful, long moment as the Hawk's eyes roved the room, each wondered if she had strayed or failed in some way that she had forgotten.

'Stand forward, Rita Stevens,' said the Hawk at last. Even as Rita took a small step forward, she could feel the rest of the room relaxing round her. It was Rita, the new girl, who had transgressed.

'This girl has broken one of our most important rules,' the Hawk announced. 'Last night, not only was she out of bed and out of her dormitory after lights out, she was in another dormitory and in another girl's bed!'

There was an audible gasp from the assembled girls.

'Please, Mrs Hawkins,' began Rita, 'it was my sister, Rosie's, bed—'

'Keep silence, girl,' thundered the Hawk. 'When I want you to speak I shall ask you to. It is forbidden to leave the dormitory at night for any reason. You are on punishment for the rest of today, Rita, and if I hear another back answer from you, it will be for the whole week. Do you understand?' Rita, almost mesmerized by the superintendent's glare, nodded.

'Do you understand?' The question was put even more loudly, and at a dig in the back from Daisy, Rita mumbled, 'Yes, Mrs Hawkins.'

'You will remain in this room while everyone goes to breakfast. I will send for you when I want you.' With this the Hawk stalked from the room.

The rest of the girls filed out, and Rita was left standing by the window. She had no idea what being 'on punishment' meant, but clearly she was in for big trouble.

Some minutes later Sheila entered the room. 'Mrs Hawkins says to come into the dining room.' She smirked at Rita. 'Not so brave now, are you, Rita Stevens? Not biting anyone today? Going to bite Mrs Hawkins?' She took Rita by the arm and marched her into the dining room, saying, 'Punishment chair in the far corner. There ain't no breakfast for you today.'

Mrs Hawkins said grace and then everyone sat down to their breakfast. As it was Saturday it was eggs, collected from the hens that Rosie had been feeding yesterday. Rita had her back to the room, so she couldn't see if Rosie was in her place at the babies' table. She knew that Rosie still wet her bed occasionally when she was frightened or worried; she'd done it several times when Uncle Jimmy had first moved in. Mum had been cross and scolded her, but she'd never made her stand wrapped up in the damp and smelly sheet.

Breakfast seemed to go on forever. Rita was hungry, but she was given no food. At the end of the meal, when grace had been said and everyone had filed out to get on with their chores, Sheila came and fetched her.

'You got to go up to Mrs Hawkins' room,' she told her.

'Where's that?' asked Rita.

Sheila laughed unkindly. 'Up the stairs,' she pointed to the main staircase, 'and then up again. That's the Hawk's nest.' She gave Rita a push towards the stairs. 'Go on, she's waiting and she don't like to be kept waiting.'

Rita hurried up the stairs and turned along the landing, almost bumping into the maid, Betty Grover, as she did so.

'You ain't supposed to use them stairs,' Betty whispered.

'But Sheila said...'

'That Sheila's a bully,' said Betty. 'She meant to get you into more trouble 'cos you bit her. Good thing you only bumped into me an' not the Dragon.'

'I got to go up to Mrs Hawkins.'

'Yeah, I know,' Betty nodded, 'but when you come down again, look under your pillow. I put a bit of bread and marge there. Don't get caught eating it, mind, or we'll both be in trouble.'

Rita stared at the maid in surprise. Why would she give her some food when she knew that she was in disgrace? Was it a trap?

Betty seemed to read her mind, because she said, 'I'm glad you bit that Sheila, an' I'm not the only one!' She gave Rita a little push towards the stairs. 'Go on up,' she urged, 'or it'll get worse.'

Betty scuttled away and Rita turned her steps towards the tower and Mrs Hawkins. When she reached the door she plucked up her courage and tapped.

'Come in.'

Rita opened the door and found herself in a large room, with sunlight pouring in through wide windows that overlooked the garden. The Hawk was sitting in an armchair, her feet up on a sturdy footstool, reading the paper. Beside her was a coffee table, and on it rested a leather strap, a broad belt with a large buckle on the end. She glanced up as Rita came in. 'Oh,' she said. 'It's you,' as if she'd been expecting someone else. 'Stand over there.'

Rita moved to the spot she had indicated, and waited... and waited.

The Hawk continued to read the paper for a while and then looked up again. 'Take your knickers down,' she instructed.

Rita stared at her in amazement, not sure she'd heard correctly.

'I said, take your knickers down... and then come over here.'

'Please, Mrs Hawkins,' whispered Rita, 'I don't want to.'

'You'll learn to do as you're told, my girl,' snapped the super-intendent, 'and the sooner you do, the better.' She paused and fixed Rita with a gimlet glare. 'Now, take your knickers down and come here.'

Shaking with fear and mortification, Rita approached.

'You heard what I said,' purred Mrs Hawkins, her eyes gleaming. 'If you don't take your knickers down now, I'll do this in the dining room in front of everyone else. Take them down and bend over the stool.'

She was standing up now, and at last Rita did as she was told, tears of humiliation streaming down her face. With her bare bottom exposed, she knelt face down across the footstool. She heard the Hawk pick up the belt, heard the rasp of the leather as she ran it through her hands. Then nothing. For nearly five minutes she knelt there; to Rita it could have been five hours as she waited, tensed and terrified, for the first lash of the belt across her backside, but nothing happened. Just as she was beginning to think that the Hawk had changed her mind, she heard it... and felt it. The swish of the belt through the air, the sharp sting as the leather licked across her buttocks. Rita let out a cry of pain and anguish. Her tears slid, unchecked, down her cheeks, and she tasted their salt on her lips.

Then nothing. Another wait. Was that it? When was the next lash coming? In one minute? Or two? It was nearly three. The anticipation was far worse than the actual strike, and the Hawk knew it. She had seen the rebellion in Rita's eyes from the first, had heard how she had bitten Sheila Nevin, a girl nearly five years older, and she knew that she had to break Rita's spirit once and for all, or she would continue to cause trouble and unrest among the other girls.

It was more than twenty minutes later when Rita found herself back downstairs. Six lashes with the belt, but they had taken twenty minutes.

'You'll go to your dormitory and sit on your stool,' commanded the Hawk when she finally let Rita stand up. 'You will stay there until I send for you. Do you understand?'

Though still choking with tears of pain, mortification and anger, Rita managed to say, 'Yes, Mrs Hawkins.'

'This punishment is a private thing between you and me,' the Hawk said. 'If you mention it, or discuss it with anyone else, I shall call you in again, and next time I'll use the other end of the belt. Do you understand, Rita?'

'Yes, Mrs Hawkins.'

'Good. I hope you do. Go to your dormitory and speak to no one for the rest of the day.'

Rita went to the dormitory, and sat on her stool. That hurt, but she dare not disobey, and she found that if she sat still, it was bearable. Her tears dried on her face as she sat in the silence of the room, listening to the other girls going about their Saturday chores. Girls who had been here for years. Girls like Daisy, who had learned to work the system, girls like Sheila who got her own back by bullying where she herself was bullied, girls like Wetty Betty, the maid, who had been here forever and still hadn't managed to escape. Thinking of Betty, Rita remembered the promised bread, and though she did not feel hungry, she crept off her stool to look, and to check with sudden panic that the picture of Daddy was still there. It was. She still didn't risk taking it out to look at him, in case the Dragon came in, but she could feel the shape of the photo, and under the edge of her pillow was a bread and marge sandwich.

Rita strained her ears to hear if anyone was outside in the passage, and when she heard nothing, she bit into the sandwich. Suddenly she was ravenous, and crammed the whole thing into her mouth. She looked on the floor and retrieved the few crumbs that she had dropped, eating those as well. No crumbs for the Dragon or the Hawk to find.

At lunchtime Sheila Nevin came to fetch her. Once again it was the punishment chair and no food. As she walked to the chair, she looked across at the babies' table and saw Rosie standing behind her chair with all the others. She had red blotches on her cheeks, the traces of earlier tears, but she gave no sign of having seen Rita, keeping her eyes firmly on the table.

Rita longed to go and give her a hug, but she knew that it would be the worse for both of them if she did. At least Rosie was having her meals. Rita was very hungry, and very thirsty, but no one came near her as everyone else ate Saturday lunch. At the end of the meal she was brought a large glass of water by Sheila, who stood over her until she had drained it, then she was sent back to her dormitory stool, to spend the afternoon alone. Her bottom still hurt, but the first pain had subsided, and Rita had other things on her mind. Escape and revenge. Revenge would be impossible, but escape might not be.

We're not staying in this place a day longer than we have to, she thought, I have to get us out and home again.

Saturday afternoon was the only time in the week when the inmates of Laurel House had any time to themselves. She could hear them now, their voices and laughter drifting up on the summer air as they played hopscotch in the yard, or took turns with the skipping rope. She imagined Daisy hurrying across the Patch through the orchard and into her secret den.

Could they escape from the garden next Saturday if Mum hadn't come for them by then? wondered Rita. Perhaps they could climb over the wall behind Daisy's den. No, that was hopeless. She might manage it, but Rosie couldn't. And it wasn't just getting out of Laurel House that was the problem; even if they managed that, how would they get home? She didn't know where home was from here. She knew that the number 37 bus went in the right direction, but she had no money for fares and she knew Rosie could never walk that far. Her mind churned with ideas as she sat alone on her stool, but she came no nearer a solution.

The door to the landing stood open, and once the Dragon had looked in, saying nothing, simply nodding, and once, more alarmingly, the Hawk had stood silently at the door for a full minute before going up to her room. Rita had simply stared at the floor until she heard the Hawk's footsteps on the stairs and then the closing of a door. For the moment she was safe from the Hawk. She wasn't the only one who realized that. A few minutes later Betty crept into the room. In her hand she had an apple.

'Here.' She held it out.

Rita looked first at the apple and then at Betty. Then with a swift movement she snatched it, sank her teeth into it and began to munch.

'You'll have to eat the core too,' Betty told her. 'There's nowhere to hide it, and if they find it, we're both for the high jump.' Rita nodded and continued to munch.

'Don't keep nothing special in your locker, neither,' Betty advised. 'They always search your lockers when you're at school. And you'd be better not to keep that picture in your pillowcase,' she added. 'If they find that, it's gone.'

So Betty had found the picture of Daddy after all. 'It's my daddy,' Rita said, 'but I've nowhere else to put him.'

'Carry him with you,' Betty advised. 'Keep him in your clothes, or in your desk at school. They don't search that if you keep it tidy.' She was silent for a moment and then said, 'If you've got a dad, why're you in here?'

'He's dead,' Rita said flatly. 'He was killed in the war.'

'Mine too,' said Betty. 'Went to the war and never come back. Me mum died in an air raid. When me dad didn't come home, me auntie stuck me in here.' She looked across at Rita and then said, 'You got a mum?'

Rita thought about Mum... Mum and Uncle Jimmy. She nodded. 'Yes, I got a mum, but she's having a baby. We'll be going home, me an' Rosie, when she come out of the hospital.'

'Lucky you... if you do,' Betty said, turning away. 'I got to go.' She had only taken a couple of steps along the landing when she heard footsteps and the Dragon emerged from the staircase.

'Betty, what are you doing up here?' Rita heard her demand. With her mouth still crammed full, Rita pushed the remains of her apple up under her skirt, as Betty replied, 'Just brought up the laundry for Mrs Hawkins, Matron. Going back down now.'

'Well, hurry up, I'm sure Mrs Smith has something for you to do in the kitchen.' Without waiting for a reply she pushed open the door to Purple Dorm and looked in on Rita, who sat, rigid, on her stool, her mouth full of apple, but her jaws unmoving. The Dragon stood there for a long moment and then went out again without a word. Rita, sagging with relief, swallowed her mouthful, and taking the rest of the apple out from under her skirt, ate it quickly, core and all.

It was five o'clock before the Hawk came into the room and said, 'Are you sorry for your behaviour now, Rita?'

Rita kept her eyes lowered; she was afraid. Afraid of this terrifying woman who stood over her now, her eyes cold and dark and malevolent, so she murmured, 'Yes, Mrs Hawkins.'

'I'm glad to hear it. Now go down to the dining room and join your table for tea. And let me have no more trouble from you, do you hear?'

Rita took her place beside Daisy in the dining room. Saturday tea was the only meal at which they were allowed to talk, and when grace had been said there was an immediate buzz of conversation.

'You have to go up to see the Hawk?' asked Daisy as she reached for the bread and marge and made herself a thick sandwich to dip into her soup.

'Yeah,' Rita answered briefly as she did the same. She was very hungry. Apart from the bread and the apple Betty had brought her, she had had nothing to eat since the corned beef hash the night before.

'What she do?'

'Ticked me off and put me on punishment,' replied Rita, not meeting her eye. Nothing would induce her to tell anyone, not even Daisy, exactly what had happened in the half hour she had been in the Hawk's room.

Daisy eyed her for a moment and then nodded, accepting what she said, but clearly not believing it.

'Got an egg for you in the playroom,' she said.

'An egg?' Rita looked startled.

'Yeah, from breakfast. They're always hard-boiled, so I put yours up me knickers and brought it out.' She laughed at Rita's disgusted expression. 'It's still in its shell, silly,' she said. 'I'll eat it if you don't want it!'

'No,' Rita said hastily, 'I'll have it. Thanks, Dais.'

Daisy grinned at her. ''S all right.'

Rita didn't tell Daisy she was planning to escape. She liked Daisy, and was grateful for her kindnesses, but Rita had learned a hard lesson in the past few weeks. Trust no one. Everyone she'd ever trusted had let her down in one way or another, and today, during the long afternoon spent sitting on her dormitory stool, she had realized that the only person she could trust was herself. Only Rita was going to look after Rita.

She lay in bed that night trying to think of a way out. She'd talked to Rosie in the playroom soon after tea. 'You all right, Rosie?' she asked.

'Where you been, Reet?' Rosie asked tearfully. 'I couldn't find you.'

'Busy,' Rita said. 'Look, Rosie, you got to try not to wet your bed, OK? Dragon'll get cross if you do it again. If you need to do a wee in the night, you have to go to the bathroom.'

'I had to wash my sheet,' Rosie told her. 'I had to put it in the bath. A nice lady called Betty helped me.'

'Well, don't do it again, Rosie, just go to the bathroom, all right?'

'It's dark,' whined Rosie. 'I don't like the dark.' She looked up at Rita. 'Are you coming in with me tonight, Reet?'

'No,' Rita told her firmly. 'I ain't. You got to learn to sleep on your own, Rosie.' She softened as she saw the tears begin to well up again in her sister's eyes. 'I can't come, Rosie,' she said. 'They won't let me.'

'I don't like them,' said Rosie miserably.

'No, nor do I,' agreed Rita.

''Cept Betty,' said Rosie. 'She's nice.'

Why was Betty helping them? Rita wondered as she lay awake in bed watching the light from the street lamp play on the dormitory ceiling. She had brought Rita some bread and an apple, and she'd helped Rosie with her wet sheet. Why? Was it really simply because Rita had bitten Sheila? Was it revenge for the way she had been treated over the years? Rita wasn't sure; all she knew was that she didn't trust Wetty Betty any more than anyone else.

Sunday followed its usual routine, and as the croc wound its way through the streets to the church, Rita wondered if there was any way they could slip away coming back. She could see Rosie further forward in the croc, holding hands with another of the Green Dorm babies, but there was no way she could get to her.

If it was just me, Rita thought as they crossed a side road and passed the open gate of a park, I could nip in there and hide.

She looked at the bushes behind the fence that created the boundary with the road. She might be able to hide there until the rest of them had gone past and then find her way home, but she couldn't leave Rosie.

Outside the church two of the seniors came round handing each girl her threepenny bit for the collection, and it was as Rita put the coin in her pocket that the idea came to her. At first she dismissed it as impossible, but as the service progressed on its dull and boring way, she kept coming back to it. As usual, Miss Vanstone had come striding into church. Rita looked at her stern face as she took her place in the front pew and wondered if she knew that the Hawk beat the girls with a belt. If she did, Rita thought, she probably didn't care. Nobody cared.

It was this thought that finally made her decide to take the risk. The risk of stealing from the church. She glanced along the row to where Ole Smithy stood, singing away, head held high, eyes raised to heaven. The Hawk was at the end of the row in front, so it was really only the Dragon who might see. Rita stole a quick look at the matron who was standing at the end of the pew behind. She, too, was singing, but her eyes were directed at the girls in the pew across the aisle. There were only a couple of minutes to decide, as the collection bag drew nearer; and Rita decided. She would not put her threepence in, she would keep it towards the bus fare home and...

Rita kept her coin in one clenched fist, and when the bag reached her, she put the other hand in, as if dropping in her own offering. Pinching her fingers round an earlier coin, she managed to extract it in her closed fist as she passed the bag on. She now had sixpence towards their fares and she kept the two coins clenched in her hand as they walked home.

'What you going to do with that money?' asked Daisy casually. 'I saw you take it out the bag.'

Rita rounded on her. 'I never! I didn't take nothing.'

'You did too,' retorted Daisy. 'You'll be in dead trouble if you're caught, but what d'you want it for?'

'I never took nothing,' Rita maintained, stoutly.

Daisy shrugged. 'OK,' she said. 'Suit yourself. I won't tell no one, anyway. Only where you going to hide it?'

It was indeed a problem. She decided her satchel would be as safe as anywhere. If anyone found the money there, she could say it had always been there, that her mother had made her carry sixpence as emergency money.

After all, she thought, I've only got to hide it till tomorrow. As the minister had intoned the final prayers, Rita made another decision. Now she had some money for the bus, she would take Rosie home tomorrow.

When they reached Laurel House Rita went to the lavatory beside the downstairs cloakroom. She hurried to where her satchel was hanging on her peg, and, after a quick glance round to see that she was unobserved, slipped the two coins under the flap. Moments later she was in the playroom, lining up for lunch with the others.

Chapter 12

When the bell went for afternoon play the next day, Rita hurried out into the playground to find Rosie. Passing the cloakroom, she unhitched her satchel from its peg and took it with her. Rosie was already outside, playing with her friend Milly.

'We got to go now, Rosie,' Rita said, taking her hand.

'Where are we going, Reet?' Rosie asked.

'You'll see. Come on.'

'Can Milly come, too?'

'No, she can't,' snapped Rita. 'Come on!' Rita was anxious to slip away as quickly as possible, so that they would be well clear of school before their absence was noticed. She had decided on afternoon playtime for their escape. Afternoon register had already been taken, and after break it was hymn practice for the whole school, so they might not be missed immediately.

Reluctantly Rosie allowed herself to be detached from Milly and led away behind the toilet block.

'We're going to go home now, Rosie,' Rita said. 'But we got to go quickly and you got to do what I say, OK?'

'Aren't we going home with everyone else?' asked Rosie, bewildered.

'Not home to Laurel House, silly,' Rita replied. 'We're going home to Ship Street. We're going home to see Mum and baby Richard. Now, come on.'

She took Rosie's hand again and they edged their way towards the gateway and the street beyond. As they reached the open gate, the whistle went for the end of break. 'Come *on*, Rosie.' Rita dragged her little sister out of the gate, and turning right, hurried along the pavement, round the corner out of sight. The only person who saw them go was Daisy. She stared after them, feeling suddenly lonely. Rita had disappeared, taking her sister with her. All of a sudden, Daisy wished that she had a sister. Someone of her very own.

She stood irresolute in the playground as the rest of the school filed back inside. Should she tell? Now was the time to do it if she was going to. It won't do me no good, she thought. And when Rita came back, as Daisy was certain she would, she'd have lost her only real friend.

'Hurry up, Daisy,' called Miss Harrison. 'Time for hymn practice.'

'Coming, miss.' Daisy turned and went inside. Reet'll be back soon enough, she thought. No one gets away from Laurel House, and when she's back, I'll still be there.

Once they were safely out of sight, Rita slowed her pace a little. Rosie was already dragging on her hand.

'Where're we going, Reet?' whined Rosie. 'Don't go so fast.'

'Told you, we're going home. We're going to find Mum.'

'Will Uncle Jimmy be there?' asked Rosie, coming to a complete stop.

Rita shrugged. 'Don't know,' she admitted. 'Maybe. Baby Richard will be.'

'Is he our brother?' asked Rosie.

'Yes, you know he is. Look,' Rita cried, setting off again and pulling Rosie along behind her, 'there's a 37. That's our bus, come on.' She hurried them along to the bus stop, and they both climbed aboard just before the bus moved on. When the conductor came down from the top deck, Rita had her money out, ready.

'Two threepenny halves, please,' she said and handed over the coins.

The conductor punched the tickets and moved on down the bus. Rita looked out of the window, hoping to see something she recognized, but the streets all looked the same. Some were tree-lined. There weren't many trees in the streets near Ship Street, so she knew they weren't near home yet. Each time the bus stopped she peered out of the window, hoping to recognize a street name. She felt a rising panic welling up inside her. How was she going to know where they should get off? She thought back to where they had got on the bus with the pig-faced woman; in the centre of the town, near the town hall. She wasn't sure she could find her way home from there, but at least she would be quite near and she could ask someone.

Rosie was sitting beside her, legs swinging, and singing to herself as she often did. Suddenly she grabbed Rita's arm. 'I haven't got Knitty!' she wailed. 'I want to go back.'

'No, we can't,' Rita said firmly. 'We'll ask Mum to get him... when we get home.'

'But I won't have him for tonight,' Rosie cried, tears beginning to slip down her cheeks. 'I want him.'

'You'll have me with you tonight,' Rita reminded her. 'You won't be on your own.' But Rosie wasn't to be comforted, and other passengers began to look at them. Rita was still trying to quieten her when the conductor reappeared.

'Here,' he said, 'you girls should've got off by now. Threepence don't take you to the end of the line, you know. Come on, off you get!'

'But we ain't got to our stop yet,' protested Rita.

'Oh yes you have,' said the conductor, and then added, 'Which stop was it then?'

Thinking fast, Rita said, 'The town hall.'

The man gave a bark of laughter. 'The town hall,' he repeated, 'then you certainly need to get off. We're going the other way.'

'The other way?' faltered Rita. 'What d'you mean?'

'I mean the other way. We're going away from the town hall. Looks like you caught the bus from the wrong side of the street.'

'But this is a number 37...' began Rita.

'So it is, dearie,' the conductor agreed, 'but it went to the town hall before you got on. So, off you get, both of you.' He rang the bell and moments later the bus drew up at its next stop, and Rita and Rosie had to get off. There was a bench in the bus shelter, and Rita sat down, with Rosie beside her. Despair rose up inside her, making her feel sick. They had been on the bus for ages, been going the wrong way for ages.

'I'm hungry,' Rosie announced. 'Are we nearly home now?'

'No,' answered Rita. 'Quiet, Rosie, I'm thinking.' They'd have to walk, she decided. They couldn't stay where they were, and she'd no more money. They'd have to go back along the road and see if they could find someone to ask the way. There were quite a few people about, but Rita knew she wasn't supposed to speak to strangers, Mum and Gran had both drummed that into her. She'd have to find someone who looked safe. Someone in uniform, Mum used to say. The bus conductor had been in uniform, but he'd just dumped them off the bus.

'I'm hungry,' moaned Rosie again. 'Can we have tea soon?'

Rita was hungry too. It seemed a long time since they had trailed back to Laurel House for cottage pie and cabbage lunch.

'Come on then,' Rita said, getting off the bench and taking Rosie's hand. 'Let's go home for tea.'

They walked through the streets, as far as possible in a straight line. When they came to a side road, Rita crossed them over carefully and kept on going straight. Every now and again she found a bench at a bus stop, or outside a pub, and she let Rosie have a rest. Her own legs were tired, and Rosie was walking more and more slowly, dragging her feet.

They reached a bridge which crossed over the river, and Rita remembered the 37 had gone over a bridge on their way to Laurel House, but was it the same bridge? She gave them another rest, sitting on a bench beside the river, and watched the water slipping away under the arches that spanned it. She was exhausted, and she knew Rosie couldn't go much further. Tears welled up in her eyes and, despite her determination not to cry, they spilled down her cheeks. Her throat hurt with trying not to sob, but Rosie saw her tears and immediately began to cry too.

'Well, now, what have we here?' asked a voice. 'You both look pretty miserable.'

Rita looked up to see a tall policeman standing beside them. He was looking down at them and as she raised her eyes he gave her an encouraging smile. 'Are you lost?' he asked. 'You shouldn't be out on the streets by yourselves, you know.'

'I'm looking after Rosie.' Rita's voice came out croakily through her tears.

The policeman crouched down beside them. 'I'm sure you are,' he said, 'but even so, you don't look very happy. You should be at home. Where do you live?'

Rita, still struggling with her tears, said, 'Ship Street.'

'Ship Street?' The policeman sounded surprised. 'Well, you are quite a long way from home, aren't you? Perhaps I'd better take you there. Would that make you happier, if I walked with you?'

'Do you know the way?' asked Rita.

The policeman nodded. 'Yes, I know the way. It's quite a step from here, though.' He stood up again and added, 'My name's Constable Chapman. What's your name then, love?'

'Rita. And this is Rosie. She's tired. She's only five.'

'Perhaps I can carry her a bit,' suggested Constable Chapman. 'But I think we should get going again. Your mother will be wondering where you are, won't she?'

Rita didn't reply to this but simply slipped off the bench, saying as she did so, 'Come on, Rosie, it's all right. He's got a uniform.'

The policeman picked up the little girl and hoisted her onto his back, then he took Rita by the hand and they set off. Rita felt safe with her hand held firmly in Constable Chapman's large, warm one. At first he didn't speak as they walked in the early evening sunshine, but after a while he couldn't contain his curiosity any longer.

'What were you doing so far from home, Rita?' he asked.

For a long minute Rita didn't answer, and then she said, 'We was going home, and we got on a bus going the wrong way by mistake. The conductor put us off. I ain't got no more bus money, so we had to walk.'

'Going home?'

'From school, only we got the wrong bus by mistake.'

'I see,' said the policeman, but he didn't. He couldn't imagine why the two little girls were so far from home. He asked no more questions. They could wait until he had reunited the girls with their parents, who must be frantic with worry. School probably came out at about half-past three, and the church clock was striking six now.

At last Rita began to recognize the streets, and she knew they were nearly home. 'I know the way from here,' she said, coming to a standstill and pulling her hand away.

'I'm sure you do,' Constable Chapman replied easily, 'but I think I'll deliver you to the door. Rosie's still tired.'

'Well, she's had a ride,' Rita said. 'She can walk the last bit, can't you, Rosie?'

'I want Mummy,' was all Rosie said, and clung more tightly to the policeman's neck.

'That's all right, love,' he said. 'Nearly there. Bet she'll be pleased to see you!' It was Rita dragging her feet now, but Constable Chapman ignored her dawdling, thinking she was afraid of getting into trouble for being so late.

'Which is your house?' he asked as they turned into Ship Street. Rita hesitated, but Rosie cried out with delight, 'There it is!' She pointed to one of the small terraced houses. 'We live there.'

'Right, come on then, let's tell Mum you're home safe and sound.' He walked up to the front door and rang the bell. At first there was no reply, and he wondered if the parents were out looking for the two girls, but as he was about to press the bell again, the door opened.

'Yes? What d'you want?' A man peered out at them, the tall policeman with Rosie on his back, peeping over his shoulder, Rita shrinking behind him. His eyes widened as he took in what he was seeing. 'What they doing here?' he demanded.

'I understand they live here,' replied the policeman, surprise in his voice. 'Isn't this their home?'

'No, it ain't!' replied the man fiercely. 'Not any more it ain't.'

Constable Chapman could feel Rita's body rigid against him, and Rosie burst into tears, burying her face in his neck. 'Is their mother here?' he asked the man.

'No, she ain't...' began the man, but the kitchen door behind him opened and a young woman carrying a small baby came out.

'Who is it, Jimmy?' she asked, but as she saw who was standing on her doorstep, she gave a little cry, her hand flying to her mouth as if to stifle it.

'Good evening, madam,' said Constable Chapman. 'Are these your daughters?'

He didn't have to wait for her reply as Rosie let out a shriek. 'Mummy!' She let go of the policeman's neck and slithered to the ground. The man stood unmoving, blocking the doorway. He glanced over his shoulder. 'I told him, Mav, they don't live here no more.'

'And you are...?' Constable Chapman disliked the look of this man, standing so belligerently in the doorway.

'Jimmy Randall. And this is my house.'

'I see.' Constable Chapman took a step forward. 'Perhaps we could all come in and discuss this.'

'There ain't nothing to discuss,' Jimmy Randall replied.

'But you, madam, are their mother?' The policeman looked past Jimmy and made eye-contact with the woman who cowered behind him. She said nothing but gave a brief nod.

'Then I think we do have something to discuss,' he said. 'These children are exhausted, they need food and a bed. I'm sure you don't want any trouble, Mr Randall, so perhaps we can all come indoors...'

Jimmy Randall glowered at him, but he stood aside to let them in. Rosie was now clinging to the constable's leg, and Rita still stood, frozen behind him. Constable Chapman gave a hand to each and, with a reassuring smile, took them indoors, following their mother into the kitchen. A baby's bottle was lying on the table, and it was clear that Mavis had been feeding the baby when they had arrived. She sat down and reaching for the bottle, began to feed him again. The two girls still kept close to the policeman as if for protection as Jimmy Randall followed them into the kitchen.

'Now then,' Jimmy said, 'what you brought these girls here for?'

'I found them wandering the streets,' replied Constable Chapman, 'and they said they lived here.'

'Well, they don't,' asserted Jimmy, looking challengingly at the copper who'd pushed his way into the house. 'We ain't got room for them. They live in an 'ome now, where they can be looked after proper. Their mother, my wife, signed all the papers, so it was done proper. Best all round, eh?'

'Is that right, Mrs Randall?' asked Constable Chapman.

Mavis looked up from the baby and nodded.

'They must have run away,' said Jimmy. He pointed at Rita. 'She'll be behind it. She's always trouble, that one.'

As he was speaking, Rosie let go of the policeman's hand and edged her way to where her mother sat. She put a hand on the baby. 'Is that my brother?' she asked.

Her mother nodded, unable to speak, the tears streaming down her cheeks. She reached out an arm and gathered her daughter to her, burying her face in the blonde curls. Rita stood beside Constable Chapman, watching. She longed to run to her mother too, but something held her back.

The policeman turned to her. 'Have you run away?' he asked gently.

Rita nodded, and PC Chapman crouched down beside her and took her hand in his. 'Why? Why did you run away?'

Rita gulped and then whispered, 'I wanted to come home. I want my mum.'

The simplicity of this statement brought unexpected tears to the big man's eyes. He blinked them away, saying, 'I'm sure you do. Why don't you give her a hug now?' He gave her a little push, and she moved round the table.

'Mum,' she said and reached out her arms. Mavis looked at her stricken; with baby Richard in one arm and the other round Rosie, she had no hand to extend to Rita. Rita saw this and stopped. For a moment they were still, a family group that wasn't a family, then Constable Chapman stepped forward and gently took the baby from Mavis's arms, so that Rita could take his place.

'Here,' growled Jimmy, 'that's my baby.'

Chapman turned to him, and without a word passed him the child. Turning back he saw the mother had gathered both her daughters against her, and all three were weeping.

A ring on the doorbell, loud and long, demanded entry. Mavis didn't look up and as the sound was repeated, louder and longer, Jimmy answered the door. A woman's voice sounded in the narrow hallway, harsh and strident. It was the pig-faced woman.

'There you are,' she cried. 'You wicked, wicked children. How dare you run off like that!'

Chapman stepped forward, barring her way forward. 'Good evening, madam,' he said. 'May I ask who you are?'

The woman faltered for a moment in the face of his uniform but then said, 'Good evening, Constable, I am May Hopkins, Children's Officer for this district. I have come to retrieve these naughty girls and return them to their home.'

'Which is...?'

'Laurel House EVER-Care home. They disappeared from school today. Everyone has been so worried.' She turned again to the two girls, still clinging to their mother. 'You're very bad girls,' she told them. 'You've caused a great deal of trouble. Now then, you're coming with me.'

Rosie immediately began to scream, a high-pitched scream, and Rita simply allowed the tears to flood down her cheeks.

'We just wanted to come home,' she gulped. 'We wanted to see Mum.'

'Well, now you've seen her,' growled Jimmy, 'you can go back where you belong.'

'Don't they belong here?' asked the policeman quietly.

'No they bloody don't,' said Jimmy. 'We signed the papers, right and tight. She ain't their mum no more.'

'Jimmy, couldn't we just—' began Mavis, her eyes pleading, her arms still tight about her girls.

'No, Mavis. I told you,' he snapped, holding the baby up in the air, 'you and me and Rick's a family now.'

'Just for tonight, Jimmy, let them stay just for tonight? I promise—'

'I'm sorry, Mrs Randall,' interrupted Miss Hopkins, 'but that won't be possible. I have to take them with me now. Miss Vanstone's sent a car.'

'Miss Vanstone? Who's she?' asked the constable.

'She is the founder and benefactress of the EVER-Care children's home,' announced Miss Hopkins. 'When she heard that these children had gone missing, she very generously sent a car so I could bring them back.'

'I don't want to go back,' cried Rita, finding her voice at last. 'It's horrible there. When Rosie wet her bed, they wrapped her in the wet sheet, and...' She took a deep breath. 'And they beat me with a belt.'

''Spect you deserved it,' retorted Jimmy.

'Rubbish,' snapped Miss Hopkins, with a quick glance at the policeman. 'There's no such chastisement at Laurel House.' She turned on Rita. 'You're a wicked child to tell such lies. Everything is provided for you at Laurel House, you lack nothing.'

Except love, thought Constable Chapman, but he kept his thought to himself. He could see that, however much he hated the idea, these two little girls were going to be returned to the orphanage. The stepfather refused to have them, the weak mother was unable to withstand him, and the Children's Officer was determined that her authority to take them was assured.

'You may kiss your mother goodbye,' Miss Hopkins said, as if she were granting the girls a great favour, 'and then we must go.'

Mavis gave one last despairing look at her husband, but Jimmy turned away, jogging his son up and down in his arms, and ignoring everyone else in the room. She held both girls close for a moment, kissing their wet cheeks, and then she too turned away.

Miss Hopkins pushed past the policeman and took each of them by the hand. 'Come along,' she said briskly, and led them, still weeping, out of the room. Rosie's screams of 'Mummy! Mummy! I want Mummy!' echoed through the house as Miss Hopkins dragged her out to the street and into the waiting car.

'An' you can get out, an all,' said Jimmy, swinging round and addressing Chapman. 'You've interfered enough!'

Constable Chapman ignored him and looked over at Mavis who had collapsed, sobbing, back onto her chair. 'Will you be all right, Mrs Randall?' he asked gently.

'Course she will,' snapped Jimmy. 'I'll look after her. Now, get out of my house.'

Unable to do more, Constable Chapman left the house without saying another word. He was more affected by the events of the last hour than he could have imagined. The sound of Rosie's cries resounded in his head, and he knew it would be a long time before he forgot the despair in her childish voice. How could a mother let her children be taken from her like that? He walked to the end of the street, and then, on hearing a door banging, he turned and looked back the way he had come. Jimmy Randall had come out of the house, slamming the door behind him, clearly heading for the pub at the end of the road.

Emily Vanstone was at Laurel House when it was discovered that the Stevens girls had gone missing.

'I'm afraid that Rita Stevens has been a problem ever since she arrived here,' Mrs Hawkins said. 'Within an hour of her being here she had bitten one of the older girls who'd been asked to keep an eye on her. She's a sullen little thing and unfortunately has palled up with Daisy Smart, another of our more difficult children.'

'I see,' said Miss Vanstone, 'and how have you dealt with her?'

'Fairly leniently at first,' replied Mrs Hawkins, 'after all Laurel House was new to her, but when she continued to flout the house rules, I was more severe and she was put on punishment for a whole day.' She gave Miss Vanstone a thin smile. 'It is usually enough to bring a child to heel, spending a day on her own, and having only bread and water.'

'I see.' Miss Vanstone looked thoughtful. She did not know the extent of the punishments that her superintendent used, nor did she want to. As long as the home ran smoothly she never enquired into the day to day running. Occasionally there were problems, but she could not remember the last time a child had absconded. Most of the children had nowhere to go anyway, but the Stevens girls? Perhaps the punishment day had been too severe.

'How has the little one, Rosie, settled in?' she asked.

Mrs Hawkins shifted a little and said casually, 'Not as difficult as her sister. She's a bed-wetter. Of course, she's been reprimanded for that.'

Emily Vanstone nodded. 'And you're quite sure that they're missing?'

'Quite sure,' insisted Mrs Hawkins. 'They were not in the crocodile when it reached Laurel House, and no one can say for sure whether they were there at the end of school.'

'Is there no roll call?' asked Miss Vanstone.

'Not before they leave school,' admitted Mrs Hawkins, 'but of course,' she added with a thin smile, 'if they walked out during school hours, that would be the school's responsibility, wouldn't it?'

'Have you spoken to the headmistress?'

'Oh, yes, as soon as I heard they weren't home here, I rang the school. Luckily Miss Harrison was still there. She checked the registers. They'd both been there at afternoon registration. When I suggested that the class teachers should have noticed their absence, she said that the whole school was together for hymn practice, with the music teacher. Class teachers don't sit in on that, and the children are dismissed from the hall. No one would have noticed if two of the children were missing.'

'The other children would have,' remarked Miss Vanstone. 'You say Rita and Daisy Smart are friends?'

'Yes,' answered Mrs Hawkins, 'unfortunately.'

'Have you spoken to Daisy?'

'Certainly, straight away. I asked her if she knew where Rita was, but she said she didn't.'

'Let's have her in and ask again,' said Miss Vanstone. 'We can be almost certain that they've gone home, but we need to be sure.'

While the superintendent was fetching Daisy, Emily Vanstone reached for the phone and rang the Children's Office at the town hall but was told that Miss Hopkins had already left for the day. Thoughtfully, she replaced the receiver. She had a home number for Miss Hopkins, but first she would speak to Daisy. Rita hadn't simply run away because she'd been punished, she had taken her little sister with her. She had planned her escape carefully. Surely Daisy would have known about it.

'Thank you, Mrs Hawkins,' she said when the superintendent arrived back with Daisy in tow. 'I'll give you a call if I need you.'

Mrs Hawkins flushed. She didn't like being dismissed like that in front of one of the children, but she turned for the door, saying as she did so, 'I'll be in the dining room.'

'Please make sure that some tea is saved for Daisy,' instructed Miss Vanstone. 'I'll try not to keep her too long.'

When the door shut behind Mrs Hawkins, Miss Vanstone looked at the little girl standing in front of her. 'Come and sit down, Daisy,' she said, pointing to a chair by the desk. Daisy edged forward and perched on the chair. She guessed why she was here, so she wasn't surprised when Miss Vanstone said, 'You know Rita and Rosie Stevens are missing?'

'Yes, Miss Vanstone.'

'Rita's your particular friend, isn't she?'

'She's in my dorm,' Daisy replied carefully. Rita was already in trouble, but Daisy wanted to stay out of it.

'And in your class at school.' It was a statement, not a question.

'Yes.'

'We think Rita and Rosie have run away. Do you know where they might have gone?'

Daisy shrugged.

'I expect they've gone home, don't you?'

'Don't know, miss.'

'The thing is, Daisy, that if they are wandering about in the town they could be in danger. Little Rosie's only five, isn't she? How were they going to get home, do you think?'

'Don't know, miss.'

'I mean,' continued Miss Vanstone, almost as if talking to herself, 'they won't have had any money, will they? Not even enough for a bus fare.'

'Don't know, miss.'

'Yes, Daisy, I think you do. Rita must have planned how they were going to go...' She let the end of the sentence hang in the air, but Daisy said nothing.

'Did you know that Rita's mother had just had another baby?' Emily Vanstone tried a different tack. Daisy didn't answer.

'Come on, Daisy, I'm sure she told you that. You were her friend.'

Daisy nodded.

'And because you're her friend you don't want to tell on her now, do you?'

Daisy shook her head and Miss Vanstone smiled. 'So, you do know what she planned.'

'She didn't tell me,' Daisy maintained, 'but I 'spect she went home to her mum.'

'Thank you, Daisy,' said Miss Vanstone. 'You can go and have your tea now.'

When the girl had left the room Emily Vanstone leaned back in her chair and considered her options. She didn't want to report the children missing to the police, not yet. She would ring May Hopkins and send her round to see if the girls had gone home.

Indeed, thought Miss Vanstone, I'll send her in my car and

she can bring them straight back without any fuss. She reached for the telephone.

Within an hour Miss Hopkins returned to Laurel House with the two runaways, and brought them straight into Miss Vanstone's office. Both children were clearly upset. Rita, white-faced and tear-streaked, stood mute, as Miss Hopkins described how she had found them. Rosie was still whimpering, crying for her mother.

'Thank you, Miss Hopkins,' said Miss Vanstone, when the Children's Officer had finished. 'My driver will take you home.' She looked across at the two miserable children. 'I'll look after them now.'

Miss Hopkins turned towards the door, but was unable to leave the children without saying, 'You're very naughty girls. I'm sure you'll be severely punished.'

Miss Vanstone waited for the door to close behind her before saying, 'She's right, you know. It was naughty to run away like that. Everyone's been so worried about you.' She looked across at Rita. 'You shouldn't have taken your sister out of school, Rita. It wasn't safe to wander about in the streets like that. Thank goodness the policeman found you.'

Rita said nothing. Rosie murmured, 'I want Mummy.'

'Have you nothing to say for yourself, Rita?'

Rita was certain that nothing she said would make any difference, but she answered. 'Rosie wet her bed, and they made her stand on her stool with the wet sheet over her head.'

'I see,' said Miss Vanstone. 'And what about you? What were you punished for?'

'Rosie was frightened. I just went into her dorm to sleep. We've always slept together. We was asleep in bed, that's all.' She did not tell this frightening lady about the Hawk and the beating. She wouldn't believe her any more than the pig-faced woman had.

'I see,' said Miss Vanstone again. 'Well, things are different at Laurel House, Rita. We don't allow that sort of thing.' She turned her attention back to Rosie. 'You can stop that moaning, young lady,' she said. 'Your mother isn't here and isn't going to be. She has sent you here to be looked after, and this is where you'll stay. We'll have no more of this nonsense. No more wet beds, no more sleeping with Rita. You're a big girl now. Laurel House is where you live, and you'd both better get used to it.' She paused and looked at the two children standing in front of her. 'Now, go to your dormitories and go to bed. I want to hear no more of you. Tomorrow you'll start afresh.'

'I'm hungry,' whimpered Rosie.

'You'll be even hungrier by breakfast,' retorted Miss Vanstone. 'Now off you go, and I don't want to see either of you in here again.'

When the door had closed behind them, Miss Vanstone sat back in her chair and considered what had happened. Mrs Hawkins was right, Rita Stevens could make trouble. The problem is, she thought, that they're really living too close to their mother, and suppose the mother changed her mind too? She rang the bell and sent for Mrs Hawkins.

'You were right about Rita being difficult,' she agreed, 'so we'll have to do something about them both, and quickly, before she causes any more trouble. I think we'll send them in the group going to Carrabunna.' She looked up at Mrs Hawkins. 'It'll get them out of your hair. I'll get the documentation sorted out. You can organize their passports. In the meantime, please watch them extremely carefully. We don't want a repeat performance of this, it gives the home a bad name. I gather the police were involved.'

'Just one policeman,' Mrs Hawkins assured her. 'He found them wandering about and took them home.'

'Well,' said Miss Vanstone, 'if anyone from the police does come round, please ensure you refer him to me.'

'Yes, indeed, Miss Vanstone.' The superintendent was relieved. She had no wish to be interviewed by the police about any punishment that she had meted out to Rita. 'I'll get on to their passports straight away.'

Chapter 13

Lily Sharples sat on a chair in the hospital dayroom, waiting to go home. The plaster was off her leg, her hair was beginning to cover the puckered scar on her head, and the recurring headaches came less often.

'I can't wait to get home,' she told Nurse Marsh. 'Nothing like being in your own home, is there?'

'No,' the nurse agreed, 'but is there anyone there to help you?'

'Not living in, no,' said Lily, 'but my daughter'll come over every day to see I'm all right.' She gave the nurse a conspiratorial smile. 'I told the almoner she'd be there, so you don't have to worry.'

'So, really, you're going to be on your own,' Nurse Marsh said sternly.

'Well, some of the time,' admitted Lily.

'Will you be able to cope? Your plaster is off, but you're still on crutches.'

'I'll be fine,' asserted Lily. 'My neighbour's been in and put my bed down in the front room, so I don't have to do stairs yet, and when my granddaughters move back in they can be my legs, can't they?'

'Your granddaughters?'

'Yes, Rita and Rosie. They live with me, you see.'

'Do they now?' Nurse Marsh was pretty sure Lily hadn't mentioned granddaughters to the almoner either.

'And my daughter's had a baby since I come in here,' Lily

said. 'I haven't seen him yet. She didn't want to bring him into the hospital in case of infection.'

That's what Anne Baillie had told her when she'd visited and told her she had a grandson. It was Anne who had been her most regular visitor. Carrie had come in once and told her that she had been looking after the girls until Mavis got back from her honeymoon, but she didn't come again. Anne came often, and it was Fred and their son, Martin, who'd moved her bed downstairs. It was Fred, she knew, who had come to her aid after the accident, and today he was coming in his van to collect her and take her back home.

'You've both been very good to me,' Lily had said, touched at their thoughtfulness.

'Don't be silly,' Anne had chided gently. 'What else are neighbours for?'

'Well,' said Nurse Marsh, looking at the determined woman sitting in the chair waiting, 'don't you overdo it, Mrs Sharples, or you'll find yourself back in here.'

'I won't,' promised Lily. 'I'll take it steady, and get back to normal gradually.'

Fred arrived then, peering in through the door of the dayroom.

'Ah, there you are, Lily,' he said. 'Your carriage awaits.'

Lily beamed at him. 'Thank you, Fred. I'm ready.' She got to her feet a little unsteadily and, grasping firmly hold of her crutches, walked slowly across the room. At the door she turned back and smiled at the nurse. 'Thank you for everything, nurse. You've all been so kind. Please thank all the others, too.'

'You make sure she doesn't do too much too soon,' the nurse warned Fred as he picked up Lily's bag. 'She's a lady with a mind of her own.'

'Don't you worry, nurse,' he replied, 'my wife'll keep an eye on her. She's only round the corner.'

Ten minutes later they drew up outside the house in Hampton Road where Anne was waiting.

'Welcome home, Lily,' cried Anne. 'I've got the kettle on.'

'Thank you, Anne, just what I need.' Lily struggled into the house and headed straight for the kitchen, its warm familiarity calming her.

Anne made the tea and all three of them sat round the table drinking it.

'I got some food in for you,' she said, 'just to keep you going until Mavis can do a proper shop.'

'Thank you, Anne, you've thought of everything.' Lily took a sip of her tea. 'Mavis knows I'm coming home today, don't she?'

'Yes,' Anne said cautiously, 'I did tell her.'

'Then they'll be round later,' Lily said. 'I can't wait to see the girls, and of course the new baby. Richard, you told me. Lovely. Named for his granddad.'

Once they'd seen Lily safely settled into the house, had shown her the front room bedroom, and made sure she had everything she needed to hand, the Baillies left her alone.

'Soon as you can manage them stairs again, Lily,' Fred said as they stood at the front door, 'Martin and me'll move your bed back upstairs for you.'

They've all been so kind, Lily thought as she closed the door behind them. She moved slowly back to the kitchen, remembering to sit in an upright chair as they'd told her in the hospital. The house was very quiet and she sat still, relishing the peace after the busyness of the ward. She'd missed Rita and Rosie dreadfully while she'd been in hospital. She'd imagined them getting to know their new little brother, helping Mavis to look after him, with Rita learning to change him and give him a bath. Surely they'll be round later and, in the meantime, perhaps she'd have a little rest on the bed. Take it steady, the nurse said.

She was awoken an hour later by the shrill of the front doorbell. Slowly she got to her feet and, grabbing her crutches, went to open the door. It was Mavis.

'Mum,' she cried, lifting the baby from the pram and holding him out in front of her, almost as if he were a shield, 'meet your new grandson, meet Richard.'

Lily looked at the bundle in Mavis's arms. 'Oh Mavis, he's

beautiful. Come on in and let me see him properly.' She turned, awkwardly making her way back to the kitchen, and Mavis followed her.

Once she was sitting down, Lily took the baby, holding him close, pressing her cheek to the softness of his dark hair. She looked up again at her daughter. 'He's beautiful, love,' she said again, 'and the image of you when you was a baby.'

Mavis gave a half laugh. 'Think so? Jimmy thinks he looks like him.'

'Well, a bit of both of you,' Lily said diplomatically. 'Where's the girls? I can't wait to see them. I thought they'd come with you.'

'I'll make some tea, shall I?' suggested Mavis, reaching for the kettle.

Lily, however, was not to be diverted. 'Where's Rita and Rosie?' she asked again. 'It's Saturday and they ain't at school.'

'No,' agreed Mavis. 'Look, Mum, let me make the tea and I'll tell you all about them. Richard needs a feed, d'you want to give him his bottle?'

Lily smiled. 'It's a long time since I did that, not since Rosie was a baby.' She watched as Mavis made tea and warmed Richard's bottle, all the while cuddling the warm bundle that was Richard close against her. When the tea had at last been poured, and Richard was sucking hungrily at his milk, Lily said, 'Well, come on Mavis, tell me about the girls.'

'When you was run over, Mum, and I was on my honeymoon, Carrie took them in and minded them. They didn't have no address for us, see?'

'Yes, I know all that, she told me.'

'Then when we got home again they come back to Ship Street. You can guess Jimmy weren't too pleased.'

Lily said nothing, simply nodded.

'Anyway, then my waters broke and when the midwife come she said the baby was breach and I had to go to the hospital. So Jimmy got an ambulance.' Mavis sighed and for a moment lapsed into silence.

'And the girls?'

'The girls went back to Carrie's for the night.'

'They ain't still there?' asked Lily, surprised.

'No, course not. But I was in the hospital and Jimmy couldn't look after them, could he? I mean... well, he had to go to work. We need his pay packet, don't we?'

'You didn't let them come home to an empty house after school, did you?'

'No, course not,' said Mavis, and latching on to this as a reason for what she had done she added, 'I wanted them looked after proper, didn't I? Couldn't ask Carrie to have them every day, could I? And when Jimmy got home from work he was coming to see me in the hospital.'

'So?' Lily's voice was dangerously low. 'So what did you do, Mavis?'

But she knew. Before Mavis, still blustering, admitted that she'd put the children into the council's care, Lily knew and she grew cold. 'You put them in an 'ome, didn't you?'

'Mum, don't look like that,' begged Mavis. 'What else could I do? I couldn't expect Carrie to have them that long, Jimmy was working and you was in the hospital...'

'But it'd have only been till you was out of hospital,' said Lily. 'How long was you in there? Ten days?'

'Two weeks, Mum, because Richard—'

'Two weeks,' Lily interrupted her. 'Two weeks and then you were home to look after them yourself. Couldn't Carrie have had them just for that two weeks?'

'I couldn't ask, Mum. She'd already had them for nearly a week. They was sleeping on Maggie's bedroom floor.'

'They could have gone to her till Jimmy got home and then slept in their own beds.' Lily sounded desperate. Surely something could have been arranged.

'Mum—'

'So you put them in an 'ome,' said Lily flatly. 'Your own kids. You let that Jimmy persuade you.' She looked up at her daughter with bleak eyes. 'And when you did come out the hospital? What then? Why didn't you fetch them home?'

'I couldn't, Mum, not right away. Richard's a colicky baby. I weren't getting any sleep and the house was getting on top of me. Jimmy was out all day and of course he was tired when he come home at night. It's heavy work labouring on a site. I couldn't have the girls there too, it was too much.'

'It'd have only been till I got home again,' Lily cried. 'Just a few weeks.'

'We didn't know that, Mum,' whined Mavis. 'We didn't know if you'd be well enough to have them back.'

'Why wouldn't I be?' demanded Lily. 'I ain't old, you know.'

'You'd had a bang on the head, you might have been left a bit funny.'

'Gaga, you mean? Spit it out, Mavis. Let's not mince matters. Well, I might have been, but I ain't and you didn't bother to wait and find out. You simply shunted them off into an 'ome. And now they've gone, Jimmy ain't going to have them back, is he?' Still cuddling the baby, who had now finished his bottle and fallen asleep in her arms, she stared into space. Her beloved Rita and Rosie were in a home somewhere thinking that nobody wanted them. 'Who took them there?' she asked. 'Did Jimmy take them? Did he pretend they could come home again soon?'

Mavis couldn't meet her mother's eyes. She shook her head. 'The woman from the council took them,' she whispered. 'She went round the school and took 'em from there.'

'And that Miss Hassinger let her?' Lily was outraged. 'Surely she could've stopped her.'

'The woman, Miss Hopkins, had all the papers,' Mavis said. 'Miss Hassinger couldn't have done nothing.'

'And you'd signed these papers? You'd signed away your own kids? Your own flesh and blood? Oh, Mavis, how could you?'

'I had to,' sobbed Mavis, the tears which had been filling her eyes now flooding down her cheeks. 'I had to, Mum, what else could I do? At least they're looked after properly there, and that Miss Hopkins said it wasn't true when Rita said she'd been beaten—'

'Rita said she'd been beaten?' broke in Lily. 'You've been to see her then?'

'No,' admitted Mavis, realizing she'd let slip too much. 'No, she brought Rosie home... to see Richard.'

'Brought Rosie home?' echoed Lily incredulously. 'They let her bring Rosie home, by herself?'

'No. They'd run away. Rita took Rosie out from school and a copper brought them home.'

'A copper did?' Lily stared at her for a long minute. 'Come on, Mavis, spit it out. Tell me what happened. Rita said she'd been beaten?'

'That's Reet just making up her stories again,' sniffed Mavis, dabbing her tears. 'That Miss Hopkins said they don't beat the girls there.'

Don't they? wondered Lily to herself. I think I know who I'd rather believe. But she simply said, 'So, they come home...'

'And that Miss Hopkins come round in a car and picked them up again. That's all.'

'And you let her? You let her take them?'

'I couldn't stop her, Mum,' whined Mavis, the tears continuing to flow. 'How could I stop her? She had the papers, she had the right—'

'Only 'cos you'd signed the bleedin' papers,' snapped her mother. 'I don't know what you're crying for, Mavis, it's your fault, and no one else's.' Lily held the baby out to his mother and continued, 'Well, all I can say is I hope you look after this one better than you've done with the girls. Now, where are they?'

Mavis took the proffered baby and hugged him close. 'I don't know,' she muttered.

'Don't know!' Lily's voice was almost a shriek. 'What d'you mean you don't know?'

'Miss Hopkins didn't say.'

'But it must have been on the papers or something.'

Mavis did know, but before coming today, Jimmy had given her a sound talking to.

'Now don't you go telling that interfering mother of yours

where them girls have gone or she'll be round the 'ome sticking her oar in where it ain't wanted and causing us more grief.' He grabbed Mavis by the shoulders and shook her hard. 'You understand, Mav? If you tell that old cow where them girls are, I won't be answerable for the consequences, right?'

'I won't tell,' promised Mavis, and now, even with her mother's eyes boring into her, she didn't.

'She didn't say,' she said, 'and I was in a right state, wasn't I? I didn't ask.'

'And what sort of state was the children in, I wonder,' said Lily bitterly, but she didn't expect an answer, and she didn't get one. She looked up at Mavis who was now cradling Richard just as she had once cradled Rita and then Rosie.

'I think you'd better go home,' she said. 'I can't bear the sight of you just now.'

'But Mum, I—'

'Go home, Mavis. Go back to Jimmy. You deserve him.'

'Mum, that's not fair—' began Mavis, but Lily cut her off.

'Fair? What d'you mean fair?'

'Jimmy's Richard's dad...'

'Indeed he is,' said Lily wearily. 'I just pray there isn't an ounce of that man in him, precious babe.' She raised her eyes to her daughter once more. 'Go home, Mavis, and look after Richard, he's going to need you.' She turned away and stared steadfastly out of the window until Mavis had finally left. It was then, and only then, that Lily gave way to her emotions and allowed her pent-up tears to course down her cheeks, the sobs racking her body until she could cry no more.

She was completely drained, and as she sat in her kitchen, utterly exhausted, she allowed herself to wonder if she could indeed cope alone. There'd be no Mavis to help now.

'Pull yourself together, woman,' she said through gritted teeth. 'You've no alternative. Get yourself going. You're going to find those girls, wherever they are, and bring them home, where they belong.'

Chapter 14

It was a struggle. For the next few days Lily shuffled her way from her bed in the front room to her chair in the kitchen. Balancing on her crutches she made tea and toast, and opened tins from her meagre store. She leaned against the sink and washed the dishes and she listened to the wireless for company. She was delighted to be in her own home again. However, by the time the next weekend was approaching, she knew she was going to have to get out of the house and get some groceries in.

On Saturday morning she got dressed, a performance in itself, and, opening the front door, she stepped out into the street. She was far better at manoeuvring herself on her crutches by now and she made slow but steady progress along the pavement to the Baillies' shop.

Fred heard the bell ring announcing a customer and, looking up, saw Lily at the door. He hurried round from behind the counter and immediately set a chair for her.

'Lily,' he cried. 'Surely you shouldn't be struggling out and about on your crutches like this? Where's Mavis? She hasn't left you to do your own shopping, has she?'

Grateful for the seat and catching her breath after the effort of walking the few hundred yards from her house, Lily smiled at him. 'Thanks, Fred, I need to rest my pins.'

'Should you be out on them crutches so soon?' asked Anne, appearing from the back.

'I wanted to thank you again for all you've done for me,' replied Lily. 'And I just popped in for a couple of things to keep me going over the weekend, just till Mavis can come round and do me a proper list.'

'I expect she's busy with the baby,' Anne said and Lily agreed that she was.

'Well, you just tell me what you need,' Fred said, 'and I'll get Martin to deliver it.' Lily sat on the chair and Fred packed all the things she asked for into a cardboard box, ready for his son to deliver later. Since it was all going to be brought home for her, Lily stocked up her cupboard, handing over her coupons to Fred.

'You let me know when you want anything else,' he told her as she hobbled out of the shop. 'Anne'll pop in after the weekend and see what you need.'

By the time Lily closed her front door behind her and shuffled to her chair, she was exhausted, but triumphant. She'd done it! She'd gone out of the house by herself and got to the corner shop. Next time she'd go a little further, and by the end of next week, when she was off her crutches, she would be ready to walk to the bus, and she could begin the search for her granddaughters.

She didn't see Mavis in the days that followed and she wasn't really surprised. She'd been hard on her, she knew, but the thought of what Rita and Rosie must be going through still made her angry. How could Mavis have done it? In her heart of hearts, she knew the answer. Jimmy had made her, and Mavis was afraid of Jimmy. If Lily were honest she was afraid of Jimmy too, but she was determined to find her granddaughters, and if that meant braving a confrontation with Jimmy, then so be it. Lily began to make her plans. When she only needed a stick, she would go round to Ship Street, on the pretext of visiting the baby.

Not just a pretext really, she thought, I'd love to have another cuddle with Richard.

The following Saturday, when Lily could limp along with only a walking stick, she made her way slowly to Ship Street, arriving late morning and hoping Jimmy would be in the Lion for his lunchtime pint. When Mavis saw who was on her step, her face hardened, and she barred the way, greeting her mother with a gruff, 'What do you want?'

Lily forced a smile to her lips and said calmly, 'I've come to see how Richard's doing. Haven't seen him for two weeks, have I? And they change so quickly at this age.'

'He's all right,' began Mavis, but was interrupted by a shout from inside the house.

'Who is it, Mav?'

Jimmy had not yet left for the pub. He appeared behind Mavis and, seeing Lily outside on the step, growled, 'Oh, it's you, is it? What the hell do you want?'

'I came to see how Richard was doing,' Lily replied. 'Can I come in?'

'Suit yourself,' he answered, pushing past both the women. 'I'm going out, but if you start interfering in our business again,' he warned Lily, 'it'll be the last time you come into my house.'

They watched him stride away and then Mavis stood reluctantly aside. 'You better come in,' she said.

Richard was in his pram in the front room. 'I'd rather have him in the kitchen with me,' Mavis said as they both looked down at the sleeping baby, 'but Jimmy says there ain't room, and I s'pose he's right.'

'Well, he's gone out,' pointed out Lily, 'so, we could wheel him in there now.'

But Mavis shook her head. 'Better not,' she said. 'Never know when he's coming back, do we? We'll leave the door open, that's what I do when I'm on my own. Jimmy don't like him crying, see, so most of the time I keep the door shut.' She smiled down at the baby, the first time Lily had seen the light of love in her daughter's eyes, and said, 'Poor little mite. He gets colic something dreadful. Little knees pulled up against his chest.'

'Are you getting any sleep?' asked her mother.

'Not much,' admitted Mavis. 'He's often fretful in the night, so I get up to him a lot. Don't want him to wake his dad, do I?'

'Isn't his cot in with you, then?'

'No, he's in the girls' room.'

Mention of the girls brought a sudden, uneasy silence between them. Lily decided to grasp the nettle. 'You ain't going to have them back, are you?' she said quietly. 'Not ever.'

'I can't,' Mavis's voice broke on a sob. 'Jimmy won't have them here.' She looked across at her mother with agonized eyes. 'I've lost them, Mum. They've gone.'

Lily reached over and gripped her daughter's hands. 'No, Mavis,' she said, 'you haven't. We'll find them, get them back. They can come and live with me, like before. Jimmy didn't mind that, did he?'

'He didn't like it, and now he don't want them anywhere near.'

'But where are they, Mavis? You must know.'

Mavis didn't answer, simply picked up Richard and began to feed him.

'Where are they, Mavis?' Lily asked again.

'I don't know,' muttered Mavis.

'You must do,' said Lily, gently. 'You must know where they are.'

'Well, I don't.'

'But you signed the papers, they must have named the place, didn't you read them?'

'Jimmy filled them in, I just signed, all right!' Mavis finally looked over at her mother. 'Leave me alone. If Jimmy hears you're looking for them I don't know what he'll do!'

'He can't stop me looking,' Lily said, 'and nor can you. I must have some rights as their grandmother—'

'No you fucking don't!' came a growl from the door. Both women spun round to find Jimmy standing in the doorway. 'It ain't nothing to do with you, and I told you not to interfere. That's why I come back. I knew you'd be fucking interfering again.' He advanced across the room and, towering over Lily, said menacingly, 'and if I find you here again in my house, it'll be the worst for you. Understand, do yer? Get it?'

It took all Lily's courage not to flinch away from him as he stood glowering down at her.

'What I understand, Jimmy Randall, is that you're a bully, and them girls is a damn sight safer away from a vicious brute like you.' She struggled to her feet, leaning heavily on her stick, but coming upright so they were face to face.

Jimmy shoved his face, now mottled with rage, into hers. 'Get out,' he almost spat at her. 'Get out of this house and don't never come back.'

Mavis watched this exchange with horror, believing that Jimmy was about to attack her mother. The bottle fell from Richard's mouth and he began to wail, his cries quickly increasing in intensity and volume.

Jimmy spun round on Mavis, shouting, 'Shut that baby up! I can't stand that caterwauling.'

Without a word Mavis gathered up baby and bottle and rushed out of the room. Lily heard her footsteps on the stairs and then the closing of a door. The wails diminished and then suddenly stopped. Mavis must have given him the bottle again.

Lily grasped her stick, almost as if it were a defensive weapon, and turned to Jimmy. 'Where's my granddaughters, Jimmy? Where's Rita and Rosie?'

'Gone,' he said and smiled. 'Gone for good, and good riddance.'

Lily tried once more. 'But they could live with me, Jimmy. They wouldn't have to come and live here.' She tried to sound conciliatory. 'I can see that wouldn't work, but if they lived with me, Mavis could still see them. She loves her kids and they love her. They need her... and she needs them.'

'She don't need them no more,' retorted Jimmy. 'She's got us now, me and young Rick. That's all she needs. She don't need them girls and she certainly don't need you, coming in here and meddling. So get out, now, before I throw you out and you end up back in the hospital.'

When Lily reached home again she sank exhausted onto her bed. Her body felt heavy, her legs ached from the unaccustomed exercise, and her mind was numb.

How on earth was she going to rescue Mavis and Richard from the monster they lived with, let alone find Rita and Rosie and bring them home? She lay, bone-weary, on the bed for several hours. She did not sleep, simply replayed the scenes in the Ship Street kitchen over and over in her head. Mavis was terrified of Jimmy, not only for her own sake, but for Richard's too. Jimmy, always on a short fuse, couldn't bear the sound of a crying baby. If Mavis couldn't keep Richard away from his father when he cried, how long would it be before Jimmy tried to stop Richard crying himself?

Eventually Lily bestirred herself and went into the kitchen. She opened a tin of soup and made a cheese sandwich. The food revived her spirits a little, and as she sat drinking a cup of tea after her meal, she began to plan her next move. For despite Jimmy Randall's threats, Lily was still determined to find the girls and bring them home to live with her in Hampton Road.

On Monday morning she set off to the council offices to see the Children's Officer. She had been involved in the placing of the girls, had been the one who took them from school, so she would know where they were. Leaning heavily on her stick she climbed the council office steps and pushed open the door. From the reception desk in the entrance hall, she was directed up the stairs to room 21 on the second floor. There were several women sitting in the tiny waiting room, and all of them looked up as Lily came in. She looked about her and then went to the hatch and tapped on the glass.

The window slid open and a pale, pinch-faced woman peered out at her. 'Yes?'

'I would like to see the Children's Officer, please,' said Lily.

'Have you got an appointment?'

'No, but...'

'I'll make you an appointment.' The woman reached for a desk diary.

'I don't need an appointment,' Lily said. 'I only want to ask her one question, in fact you may be able to help me.'

'I'm only secretarial,' replied the woman. 'I can't tell you anything.' She glanced down at the open diary. 'Miss Hopkins has got meetings for the rest of today and tomorrow, but she could see you on Wednesday. 11.30, all right?'

'But you may have the information I need,' Lily tried again.

'I doubt it,' replied the woman, 'but I couldn't give it you anyway. Name?'

'Name?'

The woman sighed. 'Your name, so's I can write you in the diary. 11.30, Wednesday. Half hour appointment.'

'Half an hour? I don't think I'll need that long.'

'Name.'

Lily gave her name, and the woman put it in the diary, then snapped the window shut.

Lily arrived early for the appointment on Wednesday. Though she was walking better every day, she was still slow on her feet, and she was determined not to be late and miss her allotted time. The waiting room was empty, but even so it was well after half-past eleven before Lily was summoned into Miss Hopkins's office.

The Children's Officer waved her to a chair. 'Good morning,' she said. 'Sorry to keep you. What can I do for you...' She glanced down at a piece of paper in front of her. '... Mrs Sharples?'

'I've come to find out where my granddaughters are,' Lily said.

'I beg your pardon?'

'I've come to find out where you've took my granddaughters to.'

'I'm sorry, Mrs Sharples, I'm afraid I don't know what you're talking about. You'll have to explain. Who are your granddaughters?'

'Rita and Rosie Stevens,' replied Lily. 'Their mum had them took into care while she had her baby, and I was in the hospital after an accident and couldn't have them, but I'm fine now, so they can come back to me as they was before.'

Miss Hopkins' face twitched at the names, but she simply said, 'I'm sorry, but that was a bit difficult to follow. Your grand-daughters are Rita and Rosie Stevens?'

'Yes, I said.'

'And their mother has put them into care?'

'Yes, and now I'm out of the hospital I want them back. They was living with me, before, you see.'

'Before...?'

'Before I got knocked down. And then their mum had to go into the maternity to have the baby, 'cos he was breach, see, so they got put into care. But now I want them back.'

'I'm afraid that's impossible, Mrs Sharples,' said Miss Hopkins smoothly. 'You see they have been signed into our care by their mother. She gave up her rights as their mother when she did that. They have been placed in suitable accommodation by the Children's Committee, and that is where they are now, awaiting probable adoption.'

'Adoption!' Lily sagged back against the chair. 'But they don't need to be adopted, they've got me. I can look after them better'an anyone. I'm their gran. They love me and I love them!'

'I'm sure you do,' agreed Miss Hopkins, 'and as you do, you'll want what's best for them. I believe they were at some risk from their stepfather. Their mother was anxious to get them right away.'

'Jimmy Randall,' exploded Lily. 'My Mavis is scared of him.'

'Then they are almost certainly better off where they are, well looked after, with everything they need.'

'But can't I see them?' asked Lily.

'No, I'm afraid not. They're settled now, and seeing you would only unsettle them again.'

'How d'you know they're settled?' demanded Lily. 'They ran away and come home not long ago. Someone took them back. Was that you?'

'I'm sorry, Mrs Sharples, I'm not prepared to discuss this case any further with you. All such cases are confidential.'

'So you ain't going to tell me where they are, then?'

'No, I am not.'

'Not even so's I can write to them, to let them know they ain't forgotten?'

'No. It would not be appropriate. Now if there's nothing

more...' She got to her feet to indicate that the interview was over. For a long moment Lily sat where she was, defeated.

'Mrs Sharples, I do have other people to see,' said Miss Hopkins, and so Lily stood up and walked to the door.

'I expect you haven't got children,' she said, turning back to the woman behind the desk.

'I am unmarried,' replied Miss Hopkins thinly.

'Yes, well, that don't surprise me,' remarked Lily. 'Good thing too, if you ask me. I wouldn't wish you as a mother on any child.'

That evening Lily sat in her kitchen, going over and over the meeting with Miss Hopkins. It seemed as if there was nothing further she could do to discover the whereabouts of the children. Jimmy wasn't going to tell her and nor was Mavis. Perhaps she really didn't know. They'd been taken from school, picked up without any warning, probably by that dreadful woman she'd met today. Armed with the papers Mavis had signed, poor Miss Hassinger wouldn't have been able to prevent it. Then it struck her. Miss Hassinger; Miss Hassinger might know. In the morning she'd go to Capel Street Elementary and see if Miss Hassinger could help her.

The girls were happy here, she thought as she waited to see the headmistress.

'Mrs Sharples?' Miss Hassinger's voice broke into her reveries and Lily got to her feet. 'I'm so glad to see you out and about again,' said the headmistress as she ushered Lily into her office. 'We heard all about your accident, it sounded dreadful. Do please sit down.' She pulled a chair out for Lily and then seated herself opposite. 'Well now,' she said, 'what can I do for you?'

'It's good of you to see me,' began Lily. 'The thing is, Miss Hassinger, well, the thing is, I wanted to ask you something.'

'I see,' said Miss Hassinger, smiling reassuringly, 'and what was that?'

'You know our Rita and Rosie was taken into care while Mavis was in the hospital having the baby.'

Miss Hassinger's smile faded. 'Yes,' she agreed, 'I know all about that.'

'Do you? Do you really?' Lily's heart leaped. 'Do you know where they was took to?' She looked across the desk and said, anguish in her voice, 'I can't find them, miss. I don't know where they are.'

'Surely Mavis knows.'

'Well, if she does she ain't saying. Her new husband don't want them in the house, and that's all there is to it. Mavis is scared of him, and she does what he says.' Lily looked earnestly at Miss Hassinger. 'All I want is to bring them back home to live with me, like before.' Her voice trailed off as she whispered, 'I just want to find them, that's all.'

'It must be very difficult for you,' sympathized Miss Hassinger, 'but I'm not sure how I can help.'

'Mavis told me they was took from school,' explained Lily. 'She said that the welfare come here and took them away. She'd signed some papers or other, silly girl, which let them be fetched. Did you see them papers, Miss Hassinger?'

'Yes, the Children's Officer showed them to me.'

'And was that a Miss Hopkins?'

'I believe that was her name, yes.'

'And did she let you read them, all through, like?'

Miss Hassinger nodded. 'Yes, I read them.'

'Didn't it say where they was going? It must have put an address or the name of the place or something.'

Miss Hassinger thought hard, considering what to do. She knew they had been sent to Laurel House, the EVER-Care children's home. Now she had to decide whether to tell Mrs Sharples where they were, or whether to maintain the strict confidentiality as she ought, and refuse to do so. She knew Lily Sharples of old, both as Mavis's mother and as Rita and Rosie's grandmother. Surely, and she was positive about this, the two little girls would be far better off living with their gran, whom it was clear they loved dearly, than in an institution.

'I can tell you where they were taken,' she said when she'd

decided to take the risk, 'but whether they're still there or not, of course, I don't know. Children in care don't always stay in the same place, you know. The move these days is to find them a foster home, where they can become part of a family, rather than keep them in residential care. I'll give you the name of this place, it's called Laurel House EVER-Care home and it's in Russell Green.'

Lily looked at the headmistress, tears of gratitude in her eyes. 'Thank you,' she whispered, 'thank you *so* much.'

Miss Hassinger smiled ruefully. 'Well,' she said, 'I shouldn't have told you, it's breaking confidentiality, but I'm sure you'll forget where you heard it.' She stood up and held her hand out to Lily. 'Good luck, Mrs Sharples. I hope you find them and can bring them home. I look forward to having them back in my school.'

Miss Hassinger watched from her window as Lily Sharples made her way out of the school gate, still hobbling with her stick, but armed with the information she'd been able to give her.

I hope you find them, she thought, but even if you do, I doubt if you'll get them back.

On her way home, Lily stopped at the bus station and looked at the timetables. The number 37 bus was the one she needed to get to Russell Green.

'Russell Green! Russell Green!' called the bus conductor, and gave Lily his hand to help her step off the bus. Once on the pavement she looked round her. It was an area of the city that she didn't know. The bus had dropped her outside a parade of shops. Lily decided to ask in the newsagent's. If they delivered papers in the area, they would be sure to know where Laurel House was. She pushed open the door and went in.

'Laurel House?' said the woman behind the counter. 'You mean the abandoned children's home?'

Abandoned children? The words cut through to Lily's heart. If that's how the place was known locally, Rita and Rosie must truly feel they'd been abandoned. 'Yes,' she replied, 'the children's home.'

'That's in Shepherd Street,' said the newsagent.

With the directions in her hand, Lily found her way to Shepherd Street, and walked slowly along, looking at the big old Victorian houses that lined it. Halfway along she found Laurel House. The name was on the gate, as if it were a private house, like the others around it, but inside the front wall was another sign announcing it to be the EVER-Care Home for Girls.

Lily pushed open the gate walked up to the heavy front door and rang the bell. As she waited for someone to answer, she looked up at the house. Were her girls really inside this bleak, unwelcoming place? For a while it seemed that no one was going to answer the bell. She was about to ring again when she heard footsteps inside, and stepped back.

A maid opened the door. 'Yes?'

'Good morning,' Lily said, surprised, all her carefully rehearsed words deserting her.

'Did you want something?' asked the maid.

'Yes,' answered Lily gathering her wits. 'Yes, I want to see whoever's in charge here.'

'You mean Mrs Hawkins?'

'If she's the one who runs the place.'

'You'd better come in.' The maid stood aside and Lily entered, finding herself in a large hallway. 'If you wait there,' the maid said, indicating a chair, 'I'll go and see if Mrs Hawkins can see you. What name shall I say?' she added as an afterthought.

'Mrs Sharples.'

It was some ten minutes before she returned to say, 'Mrs Hawkins will be with you in a minute,' and another five minutes before a small, dark-haired woman emerged from the corridor. She looked at Lily and said, 'Mrs Sharples?'

'Yes, Lily Sharples.'

'I'm Mrs Hawkins, the superintendent of Laurel House. Perhaps you'd like to come through to my office.'

'Now, Mrs Sharples,' she said as she closed the door behind them, 'how may I help you?'

'I've come to find my granddaughters,' Lily said. 'I've come to find Rita and Rosie.'

'Rita and Rosie?' The superintendent's voice remained calmly enquiring, but Lily caught a flash in her eyes; the woman knew them.

'Rita and Rosie Stevens. I know they're here, 'cos that Miss Hopkins brought them here.'

'I'm sorry, Mrs Sharples,' said Mrs Hawkins, 'I'm not sure I can help you. We never reveal the names of the children we care for to outside parties.'

'I'm not an outside party!' cried Lily indignantly. 'I'm their grandmother.'

'I don't doubt it,' said Mrs Hawkins reasonably, 'but the children here are in our care—'

'Well, Rita and Rosie shouldn't be,' interrupted Lily. 'That's what I'm trying to tell you. They was living with me but I had an accident, and while I was in the hospital they was brought here. I'm out now, so they can come home again.'

'I'm sorry, Mrs Sharples,' replied Mrs Hawkins, 'but I'm afraid it's not as easy as that. We've become their legal guardians, it is we who decide what is in their best interest. We don't simply hand them over when someone walks in and asks for them.'

'I understand that,' Lily said, trying to sound as reasonable as the superintendent. 'But I'd like to discuss it, explain, like.'

'Of course,' Mrs Hawkins' lips twitched, 'but that would mean speaking to our benefactress, Miss Vanstone. She makes the decisions with regard to the children here, I simply have the day to day care of the girls.'

'So Rita and Rosie *are* here,' said Lily.

'I can say nothing about our children,' Mrs Hawkins said firmly, thinking that this Mrs Sharples spelled trouble. The determined look in her eye said she wouldn't be fobbed off. Mrs Hawkins dare not let the Stevens girls be returned to their grandmother. She had tried to break Rita Stevens' spirit, to bring her to heel, as she'd done with other rebellious girls, but if Rita went to live with this grandmother, who seemed so like her, had the same determination in her eyes, who knew what the child would say, what stories she would tell? Mrs Hawkins wanted no report of her treatment of those in her charge escaping into the fresh air beyond the laurel hedges. She already had the passports Miss Vanstone had asked for, and soon the two girls would be safely out of reach.

'So,' she continued, 'if you wish to make further enquiries, I suggest you make an appointment to see Miss Vanstone.'

'And how do I do that?' asked Lily.

'I will give you a telephone number,' replied Mrs Hawkins.

'Isn't she here? Can't I speak to her now?'

'No, I'm afraid not. But please do phone, I'm sure she'll be happy to help if she can.' She rang a bell on her desk, and the maid appeared.

'Ah, Betty, kindly show this lady out, will you?'

The superintendent handed Lily a piece of paper. 'Here is the number to ring if you wish to pursue this matter further, Mrs Sharples.'

Lily took the paper and put it in her bag. She stood up. 'Thank you,' she said, 'I certainly shall. I intend to find Rita and Rosie.'

Mrs Hawkins looked at Betty Grover standing by the door and was annoyed she'd given her the chance to overhear Mrs Sharples' business. Mrs Hawkins considered Betty a sly little thing, so she wouldn't give the grandmother a chance to speak to her alone.

'That's all right, Betty, I don't need you after all,' she said. 'I'll see this lady out. You can go back to the kitchen.'

The superintendent escorted Lily to the door, but once outside, Lily turned back. 'I'm going to find my girls, you know,' she said, 'and you nor nobody else ain't going to stop me.'

Mrs Hawkins smiled and said, 'Good afternoon, Mrs Sharples.'

When she had shut the front door, Mrs Hawkins went back to her office and sat down to think. Clearly the Sharples woman wasn't going to be put off; she'd soon be on the phone to Miss Vanstone asking about the Stevens girls. Mrs Hawkins picked up the phone.

'Will you be coming into Laurel House today?' she asked when Emily Vanstone answered.

'No, why?'

'I've had a visitor, and we need to discuss things.'

'I see,' sighed Miss Vanstone. 'Perhaps on my way into town. I have a meeting at the council offices.'

'In that case,' said Mrs Hawkins, 'we definitely need to talk before you go there.'

'Why, what's happened? Who came to see you?'

'A Mrs Sharples, says she's the Stevens girls' grandmother. I think she's going to be trouble. She wants to see you. She's going to ring you for an appointment.'

'I'm far too busy to see her,' declared Miss Vanstone. 'I'll instruct Miss Drake to say so. You did give her the office number, didn't you?'

'Yes, but I doubt if she'll accept a refusal,' answered the superintendent. 'If you don't see her, I think she'll try and take it further.'

'There's no further to take it,' said Miss Vanstone. 'What did she want, anyway?'

'She wanted them back,' replied Mrs Hawkins.

'Wanted them back?'

'To live with her. Apparently they used to live with her before they came to us. Now she wants them back.'

'Well, that's not going to happen,' asserted Miss Vanstone.

'I know that,' said Mrs Hawkins, 'but she won't accept that from me. She needs to hear it from you, then she may give up trying. But she looks like a trouble-maker to me.'

'I'll give her an appointment in a week or so,' conceded Miss Vanstone, 'and then it will be too late. They'll have left for Carrabunna,' adding, 'I'll deal with this from now,' before she disconnected.

Mrs Hawkins sat back in her chair. Not my problem, she thought with relief.

Mrs Hawkins was pleased enough to be employed by the EVER-Care Trust; her salary and living quarters were reasonable and it gave her scope to exercise authority over those beneath her, but she had no feeling for the children in her care. Rita's continued intransigence vexed her, she was not used to defiance, and though Rita now seemed subdued, there was defiance in her eyes. Well, thought Mrs Hawkins, she's on her way to Australia now, and she can take her defiance with her.

Emily Vanstone leaned on her desk and considered what she'd just heard. Everything was arranged for the Stevens girls to travel at the weekend, and she'd allow nothing to interfere with those plans. She rang for her secretary, Miss Drake.

'If a Mrs Sharples rings for an appointment, please be very polite, but no appointment until Friday week, understood?'

'Certainly, Miss Vanstone.'

We'll have to see about this grandmother, Emily thought as she dialled the Children's Office. When May Hopkins answered, Emily said, 'I need some information, background information, on the Stevens girls.'

'Oh dear,' cried Miss Hopkins. 'They're not in trouble again, are they?'

'Their grandmother has been to Laurel House looking for them,' replied Miss Vanstone, 'and she'll be back. I need to know their family circumstances, exactly where they came from and why, before I see her. I need a proper report from you.'

'Oh, I see, well, yes...' Miss Hopkins sounded flustered. 'Well, I must think—'

'We have a meeting scheduled for this afternoon,' interrupted Miss Vanstone. 'I shall expect all the information to be available for me to take away then.' She rang off before the Children's Officer could reply.

When they met that afternoon Miss Hopkins handed Emily Vanstone a folder. 'It's all in here as far as I can remember it,' she said. 'The mother remarried and there was a baby on the way. They'd been living with their maternal grandmother, but she was taken into hospital. The stepfather is a violent man, we had to remove them from his care while his wife was having the baby.'

'They'd have been at risk if they'd stayed with him?'

'Oh yes, almost certainly,' replied Miss Hopkins, and seeing that her answer pleased Miss Vanstone, she added, 'Nasty piece of work he is.'

'I see. And when you went to fetch them, after they'd run away, was the grandmother there then?'

'Oh no, I only met her for the first time the other day.'

'You met her?' Miss Vanstone raised an eyebrow. 'You didn't mention it.'

Miss Hopkins flushed. 'I'm sorry, Miss Vanstone, I didn't know it was important. She came in here demanding to know where her granddaughters were.'

'And you told her.'

'No, of course not. I refused to tell her anything and she left.'

'I wonder how she found out,' Miss Vanstone mused. 'Well, it's clear she's not going to drop the matter. Now that I understand the background, I can deal with her. Now, where's everyone else? I thought this was a meeting of the Children's Committee.'

'It will be, I just wanted to brief you first.' Miss Hopkins sounded more confident. 'There's a directive come down from the government encouraging fostering children in families. This means there will be fewer children coming through the system to you. I'll do what I can, of course, Miss Vanstone. I have great faith in institutions like Laurel House. But,' she gave a small shrug, 'we are now obliged to consider family foster care first.'

'I see.' Emily Vanstone's expression did not change.

'And the thing is, well, if we do continue to send children to you, the home will have to have regular inspections.'

'And you think we'd fail these inspections?'

'It'll be a question of staff qualifications, and well, none of your staff are properly qualified, are they?' She took her courage in her hands and went on, 'Mrs Hawkins, for example. She has great experience, I know, but I think she can be hard on the girls. That Rita Stevens accused her of beating her... with a belt. All lies, of course, but she did make the accusation in front of a policeman...' She let her words hang in the air. When Miss Vanstone made no comment, she said, 'If he follows it up... if it came out that I and the Children's Committee knew of such accusations and did nothing about them... well, it could prove extremely difficult for me. I'm sure you understand.'

Still faced with Miss Vanstone's silence, May Hopkins lapsed into a silence of her own. For a long moment they sat there, and then Miss Vanstone got to her feet.

'I don't think you need to worry about Rita Stevens and her accusations,' she said. 'She won't be with us beyond the end of the week. Please give my apologies to the Committee, I shan't be attending the meeting today. Good afternoon, Miss Hopkins.'

That evening Emily Vanstone called a staff meeting at Laurel House.

'Ten girls will be leaving for Carrabunna on Sunday,' she said. 'Sheila Nevin, Angela Gardner, Dora French, Mary Shannon, Joan Cameron, Daisy Smart, Rita and Rose Stevens, Sylvia Brown and Susan Hart.'

'Sheila's a bit old, isn't she?' asked Mrs Smith.

Miss Vanstone looked surprised at her intervention. 'I have my reasons for sending Sheila,' she said, but gave no further explanation. None of the other staff commented on the children who had been chosen. Few ever queried Miss Vanstone's decisions. If anyone thought that Rosie, Sylvia and Susan, all aged five, were a little young to be sent to the other side of the world, she didn't say so.

'I also wanted to warn you that a woman called Mrs Sharples has been nosing her way round here. She's the Stevens girls' grandmother. If she should approach any of you, please refer her to me. Do not mention Australia or get into discussion with her about Rita and Rose. They are not her concern.

'Now then, the usual preparations will have to be made, but I will tell the girls myself on Friday evening. Until then there is no need to mention their departure to any of them. Any questions? Everybody understand?'

There were murmurs of assent, they all understood. The

children concerned would only be told what was happening after they had finished school on Friday and by Monday they would have gone. Their schools would have no more warning than the children. The meeting broke up. As they were leaving the office, Miss Vanstone called Mrs Hawkins back.

'There have been accusations about your treatment of some of the girls,' she said. 'I'm not going to enquire into those, discipline is something for you.' She gave her superintendent a hard stare. 'But in future I advise you to be a little more circumspect in how you discipline these girls. From now on Laurel House will be inspected on a regular basis, and I will not have the whole project put at risk by... shall we say, overzealous disciplinary measures. Should that happen, I should have to seek a new superintendent. Do I make myself clear?'

'Yes, Miss Vanstone,' murmured Mrs Hawkins.

'Good. Now, make sure all those going have the usual sets of clothes ready, and a decent pair of shoes each, and I'll authorize the expenditure. Good evening to you.'

Chapter 15

The children had almost no notice of their departure for Australia. Rita and the other Purples were laying the tables on Friday evening, when they were summoned to Miss Vanstone's office.

'Just leave that,' said Ole Smithy brusquely, 'and get along to the office, sharp as you like.'

'What on earth have we done now?' wondered Rita as she and Daisy headed along the corridor.

Daisy shrugged. 'Don't know, but you can bet it ain't nothing good.'

At that moment Sheila Nevin appeared, dragging an unwilling Rosie along behind her.

'Here, what are you doing with my sister?' Rita demanded.

'Nothing,' glowered Sheila, 'just sent to fetch her, that's all. Got to take her and these,' she jerked her thumb at Sylvia and Susan trailing behind, 'to Miss Vanstone's office.'

'Let go of her,' Rita said fiercely, adding more gently, 'Come here, Rosie, you can come along with me, we got to go too.'

'I didn't want to come with her, Reet,' whispered Rosie, 'she hurt me.'

'Never mind that now, Rosie,' Rita said taking her hand, 'we got to go to the office.'

'Why, Reet?' asked Rosie, following willingly now.

'Don't know, do I? Going to find out.'

When they reached the office door, Sheila stepped forward and knocked.

'Come in.'

Sheila turned the handle and they crowded into the small office. Miss Vanstone was sitting behind her desk where they'd always seen her. She looked up and smiled.

'Ah, there you are,' she said. 'Close the door, Sheila. Sit down on the floor, please.'

Rosie sat close to Rita, still holding tightly to her hand and looking at Miss Vanstone with anxious eyes.

'Now then,' began Miss Vanstone, 'I've some very exciting news for you all. You've all been chosen to have the adventure of a lifetime.' She beamed round at them. 'Look, I've got something to show you.' She picked up a picture from her desk, holding it up for them to see. 'Just look at this!'

It was a wonderful sight, a wide green landscape, rolling hills with occasional patches of woodland and far away in the distance the sparkle of water.

'You've been specially chosen to go on holiday,' Miss Vanstone said. 'You'd like that, wouldn't you?'

For a long moment they all stared at the picture in silence, not really understanding what she was talking about. A holiday? Where? To the place in the picture? Where was the place in the picture? And most of all... why them?

'But what about school?' It was Sheila who was brave enough to ask.

'It's the end of term next week,' Miss Vanstone reminded her. 'You'll only miss a couple of days, and I'll tell the school you're going.'

'Where are we going, then?' asked Rita, suspicion in her voice.

'You're going to this wonderful place called Carrabunna,' replied Miss Vanstone, thinking as she did so, Mrs Hawkins is right, that Rita is a nuisance. 'It's a lovely place, warm and sunny, just like in this photo, and out in the countryside.' She put down the picture. 'Now then, Matron has been getting your clothes ready for you, and tomorrow she'll take you all to buy new shoes. That'll be fun, won't it?'

There was an immediate buzz of interest; none of the girls could remember when they last had new shoes of their own, not simply another pair from the communal box.

'Can I take my party dress?' piped up Rosie, suddenly brave as she saw Miss Vanstone's smile.

'What party dress?'

'Mine,' said Rosie.

'We had new dresses for our mum's wedding,' Rita said in explanation when Miss Vanstone looked at her enquiringly. 'Matron took them away.'

Seeing this as a way to bring Rita back into the fold, Miss Vanstone said, 'I'll ask her to pack them in your case, shall I? Would you like to take them?'

'Yes!' cried Rosie in delight.

'Very well, then.' Miss Vanstone looked back at Rita, but the little girl had looked away. 'Now then all of you, go and have your tea.'

'Please, miss,' ventured Joan Cameron. 'When do we go?'

'You're leaving on Sunday,' came the reply. 'Mrs Hawkins and I shall be taking you to London on the train.'

'But where is Carra... Carra...' asked Angela Gardner. 'Is it in London?'

'No, much further away than that... across the sea!'

'Are we going on a boat?' asked Daisy, wide-eyed.

'Yes, indeed you are,' answered Miss Vanstone. 'Won't that be an adventure? Now, run along all of you and have your tea.'

'Why is it us?' wondered Daisy as soon as they were outside the office.

Rita shrugged. 'Who knows? Probably wants to get rid of us.'

'But for how long?' demanded Joan, who had joined them in the passage. 'I mean, how long is the holiday? When are we coming back?'

'Don't reckon we are,' said Sheila, coming up behind them. 'Reckon she's sending us to another home, for good.'

'Another home?' Joan sounded scared. She knew no other home.

Sheila shook her head. 'Don't know, do I?'

'But she said we was going in a boat,' pointed out Rita.

'Can't be that, going to another home, by boat!' scoffed Angela.

'New shoes!' Daisy said in wonder. 'Think of that! I never had a pair of new shoes!'

Later that night, lying in bed, Rita thought about their forthcoming 'great adventure'. She had no real idea of where they were going, but at least she and Rosie were going together. She wondered if Sheila was right and they weren't coming back.

Suppose it don't matter where they send us, she thought as she watched the summer twilight fade into darkness, we ain't going home again. It was the first time she had actually admitted this fact to herself. When the pig-faced woman had returned them to Laurel House, Rita had expected severe punishment. She had imagined that the Hawk would send for her again, and the thought made her feel sick, but no summons came from the tower and the next day it was as if nothing had happened.

'Knew they'd catch you,' Daisy said as the croc formed up for the walk to school. 'Where did you go? They tried to get it out of me, but I didn't tell them nothing.'

'You didn't know nothing,' pointed out Rita.

'Well, saw you sneaking off, didn't I? Didn't tell them that. Did you go home and see the baby?'

'Yes,' replied Rita shortly. She was fighting back the tears that seemed to come so easily since she'd been home and then dragged back again. Daisy saw and in a rare gesture of comfort, put her arm round her friend and hugged her.

'I think you was very brave, Reet,' she said. 'And you took Rosie with you. I never dared run away, and I'm on my own. Wish I had a sister,' she added wistfully.

Rita returned the hug. 'I ain't going to let them see me cry. Not ever again. I don't care what they do. Even if the Hawk beats me with the belt.'

'Is that what she did?' breathed Daisy. 'Did you tell?'

'Tell who?' scoffed Rita, but then added, 'I did say, when I was at home, but they didn't believe me.'

'I believe you,' Daisy said stoutly.

'Yeah, well, you're my best friend, ain't you? Like another sister. You're s'posed to believe me.'

'You could tell them at school,' suggested Daisy. 'Miss Harrison might believe you.'

'Waste of time.' Rita dismissed the idea. 'Even if she did, it'd mean more trouble. The Hawk would say I was telling lies and I'd still be stuck here.'

Now it seemed there was a chance of escape. Not as they had escaped by running back home to Mum, but by moving to live somewhere else. Somewhere far away from the Hawk and the Dragon. Surely she and Rosie would be better off anywhere that wasn't Laurel House.

The news of their 'holiday' was soon common knowledge in the house. The three younger girls from Green Dorm simply accepted it at face value, a holiday in the country, and were the envy of their dorm-mates. The Purples were all going, and somehow that made it easier. They were going together to a new place, but at least there'd be familiar faces.

It was their night for washing up, and Daisy, cornering Ole Smithy in the kitchen, asked bluntly, 'Will we be coming back here, Mrs Smith?'

Ole Smithy looked uncomfortable and said, 'I don't know, Daisy, do I? Miss Vanstone says you're all off somewhere exciting.' She smiled awkwardly and added, 'Be nice to have a change from here, won't it?'

'Where's this place we're going to?' Daisy asked.

'Place called Carrabunna,' answered the cook. 'It's a lovely place, by all accounts. You'll love it. Now then, Daisy Smart, stop wasting my time and get on with them dishes.'

Daisy wasn't satisfied. She had nothing to lose now by pestering the cook, and she knew Ole Smithy was the person most likely to give them the answers, so she turned again from the dishes and announced, 'But you know where we're going, don't you, Mrs Smith? Come on, tell us.'

'Yeah, where is this Carrabunna place?' asked Angela.

'Yeah, where're we going?' demanded Joan.

'And how long for?' Mary asked.

'When will we be back?'

'Is it a long way? Miss Vanstone said a boat.'

Once Daisy had had the courage to broach the subject, they'd all fired questions at the unfortunate cook.

Ole Smithy looked taken aback for a moment and then she made her decision. Why on earth shouldn't these kids know where they were going? They'd had no preparation for this enormous change in their lives. No one had explained where they were going to, or why. Ole Smithy didn't approve of them being sent away at all, but at least she could try and tell them a little about where they were going.

'You're going to Australia,' she said. 'It's a country a long way away, and you'll have to go on a big ship to get there. But when you get there it'll be lovely! Nice and warm, with lots of open space and lots of things to do.'

Australia! They stared at her in amazement. Australia meant, if it meant anything, kangaroos and koala bears.

'I don't want to go to Australia!' Rita burst out, thinking of Mum and Gran. Of all the children selected to go, Rita and Rosie were the only ones who had a family. Tears sprang unbidden to her eyes, but she forced them back, determined to maintain her resolution never to let anyone see her cry... ever again.

'Might be better than here,' pointed out Daisy a little uncertainly.

'Couldn't be worse,' muttered Angela, and Dora nodded.

'So we ain't coming back,' Joan said tremulously. 'Not ever?'

Ole Smithy had seen the mixture of fear and expectation in their eyes and hating what she saw, wished she could do something to alleviate it.

'Why don't you go and look at the atlas?' she suggested. She wanted them out of the kitchen, so she could forget their dismay. She had thought it right to tell them, but now she had, she wanted to turn away from their confusion and leave it for someone else to sort out.

They found Sheila in the playroom and they told her where Carrabunna was. She opened the old atlas and found Australia on the far side of the world.

'Well,' she said, snapping the atlas closed, 'roll on Sunday. We ain't coming back from there.'

When they arrived at Tilbury dock, the Laurel House girls stood on the quay, labels pinned to their coats, their small suitcases at their feet, an anxious group, staring in bewilderment at the people eddying round them. Other children were standing in similar groups. One, a large group of both boys and girls, was standing round a tall man wearing some sort of uniform, listening intently as he spoke to them; another, made up of boys only, was being led up the gangplank, while yet another, a small group of girls, was lining up, ready to board. Each child wore a brown identity label, each child carried one small suitcase, and all stood around not knowing where to go or what to do.

'Stay here,' Miss Vanstone ordered and leaving the girls standing with Mrs Hawkins, she bustled away to speak to the man at the foot of the gangplank.

As they waited the girls stared up in awe at the ship towering above them. White-painted with an orange line sweeping its length and pockmarked with portholes, she was taller than any of the office buildings they had seen on their way through London. A tall funnel, standing proud above the upper decks, puffed smoke out into the summer sky, and the whole ship seemed too huge, too heavy, to stay afloat.

'Are we really going on that?' Daisy whispered to Rita.

Rita, standing beside her with Rosie clutching her hand, peered up at the towering vessel. 'S'pose so,' she said. 'It's very big.'

'Australia must be a long way away,' said Joan, nervously.

'It's the other side of the world, stupid!' snapped Sheila, though she too was a little shaken at the size of the ship that was to take them there.

Miss Vanstone reappeared. 'Come along, you girls,' she commanded. 'Follow me.'

The ten girls picked up the cases that contained their worldly possessions and straggled up the gangway, the Hawk bringing up the rear. On deck there were children everywhere, some large groups, some small; some scuffling and noisy, others standing silent and forlorn shrinking away as adults struggled past them, carrying suitcases and bags.

Miss Vanstone spoke to a crew member who directed them to a glass-fronted office, but it was nearly twenty minutes before it was their turn to be met by a harassed-looking woman in a white uniform who held a clipboard.

'These are the girls from the EVER-Care Trust,' said Miss Vanstone, passing over a list of names and a handful of passports. The woman consulted her clipboard and began ticking off names, checking the name against that on the label each girl wore on her coat. While she dealt with the paperwork, the little group of girls gazed round them.

'It's a very big ship,' whispered Daisy. 'Look at all those other people. Are they all coming too?'

'Don't know,' replied Rita. 'S'pose so.' Her grip tightened on Rosie's hand. 'Stay close to me, Rosie,' she ordered. 'You might get lost.'

As long as she was beside Rita, Rosie was not afraid. She looked about her at all the hustle and bustle, and asked, 'Are we nearly at Australia now?' Australia to Rosie could be anywhere, the next street, the next town or a million miles away.

'No, course not, silly,' snapped Sheila Nevin, overhearing the question. 'We're going to be on this ship for weeks and weeks.' Sheila, as the eldest girl in the group, had assumed its leadership and for the time being the others had accepted this, all hostilities laid aside as they turned to each other in their strange new situation.

Now they were on the ship, it made Rita realize the enormity of their journey. They would have to stick together, and fend for themselves and her job would be to look after Rosie.

'Right,' the woman in the white uniform said, 'I'm the purser in overall charge of you children. But you have two chaperones who'll keep an eye on you during the voyage. Miss Dauntsey and Miss Ellen Dauntsey. They're two teachers, going to Sydney. If you have any problems they're the first people you go to. If necessary they'll come to me.' She looked the little group over and said, 'All right?'

'And where are the Miss Dauntseys?' asked Miss Vanstone, looking round.

'Dealing with another group at present,' replied the purser. 'If you take your group into the lounge on "F" deck, they'll come and find you there.'

Miss Vanstone and the Hawk shepherded them to the deck above. Miss Vanstone carried the suitcases belonging to Sylvia and Susan, and instructed the Hawk to take Rosie's.

They found the lounge, a wide saloon furnished with tables, chairs and several deep sofas. The evening sun flooded in through the windows, disguising the rather tired state of the furniture.

'Come and sit down here,' ordered Miss Vanstone, leading them to a table. She opened her capacious handbag and pulled out a packet of sandwiches, giving one to each child. Overawed by their surroundings, they ate in silence, and were just finishing when two young ladies crossed the room towards them.

'Good afternoon,' said one, extending her hand to Miss Vanstone. 'These are the EVER-Care children, am I right?'

'You are indeed,' said Miss Vanstone. 'Stand up, girls, and say good afternoon to Miss Dauntsey.'

Obediently, they all rose to their feet and chanted, 'Good afternoon, Miss Dauntsey.'

'And this is my sister, Miss Ellen Dauntsey,' said the first lady. 'You may call her Miss Ellen, so that you don't get us muddled up.' She smiled at the forlorn-faced children, and added, 'Cheer up, we're off on a wonderful adventure.'

'Well,' said Miss Vanstone, picking up her bag, 'we'll leave you to it, Miss Dauntsey. Be good, children. Do as Miss Dauntsey tells you on the voyage. Remember, you carry the good name of Laurel House with you.' And with that she walked out of the lounge and followed closely by the Hawk who had said no good-byes, disappeared down the stairs. Ten pairs of eyes tracked them to the door, and then turned miserably back to the two Miss Dauntseys.

'Now then,' said Miss Ellen, speaking for the first time, 'you know our names, so we need to know yours.' She pointed at Rita, still holding tight to Rosie's hand. 'Who are you, then?'

'Rita Stevens,' replied Rita softly, 'and this is my sister, Rosie.'

One by one they said their names and Miss Ellen checked the labels pinned on their fronts. When they'd finished, Miss Dauntsey said, 'You must wear your name tags for a few days, but we'll do our best to remember which of you is which. If we get it wrong after that, you'll have to tell us. Now, come along everyone, let's find your cabins.'

The cabins each had two bunks. Rita and Rosie were together, sharing with Daisy and Sylvia.

'Get yourselves settled in,' said Miss Ellen, 'and I'll come and find you later.' Rita closed the door behind her, and the four girls looked round the cabin that was to be their home as they crossed the world.

'We'd better have the top bunks,' she said to Daisy. 'Don't want the babies to fall out.'

'I ain't a baby,' protested Rosie, glaring at her.

'Nor am I,' said Sylvia.

'OK,' agreed Rita, 'you ain't babies, but you ain't having the top bunks, neither.' She opened Rosie's small case and took out the clothes that Matron had packed for her. Included was the dress she'd worn to the wedding.

'My party dress,' cried Rosie in delight, grabbing at it.

'And here's Knitty,' Rita said, pulling the beloved creature out of the case.

'Knitty!' screamed Rosie, clutching him to her as she waltzed round the cabin.

'Careful,' Daisy admonished her, 'you nearly had me over.'

Rosie didn't care, she had her beloved Knitty. Rita had asked Wetty Betty to see if she could slip him into the case once the

Dragon had finished with it, and Betty, wishing she'd been included in this strange adventure, had managed it.

'You've been very kind to us,' Rita said before they left.

''Cos you got some spunk,' Betty said. 'Wish I had your spunk. You never give in to the Hawk, even after she beat you.'

'How d'you know she beat me?' demanded Rita.

''Cos she did the same to me,' answered Betty, 'but I give in, and now she knows she can make me do anything with the threat of doing it again.'

'But you're grown up,' said Rita in surprise.

'Not really,' replied Betty, 'but I will be one day, and I'll get my own back. One day she'll be sorry.' She looked across at Rita. 'You still got your picture? The one of your dad?'

Rita nodded.

'Want me to put that into your case for you?'

'No thanks, Betty,' Rita said firmly. 'I'll look after it.'

They unpacked their few belongings into the four drawers of the chest that was the only storage space.

'We got a basin, though,' marvelled Daisy. 'D'you think them taps really work?' She turned one on and water gushed out. 'They do!' she cried in delight. 'We don't have to fetch our water no more!'

Above the basin were a shelf and a small cupboard for their washing things and beside it was a rail on which hung four towels. Daisy climbed up to one of the top bunks, and flopped down.

'This is a bit of all right,' she announced. 'Never had such a soft bed.'

Rosie and Sylvia immediately bounced on theirs with cries of glee, and Rosie tucked Knitty carefully under the covers.

'I should keep him hidden for a while,' advised Rita. 'Don't know what these teachers are like yet, do we? Don't want them to take him away.'

Rosie pushed Knitty down further under the covers, hiding his head under the pillow.

Rita climbed up on the other top bunk and carefully slipped the picture of Daddy into the pillowcase.

'This ain't half bad,' she agreed, sitting up and dangling her legs over the edge. She leaned forward. 'I can see the dock through our window.'

'Porthole,' corrected Daisy, leaning forward as well. 'There's still loads of people on the dock. How'll they all fit on this ship?'

'Don't know,' laughed Rita, 'but they ain't having my bed.'

'They ain't having my bed,' echoed Rosie, standing on her bunk to look out.

Miss Ellen came to fetch them, and took them back up to the lounge where they'd first met her. The others were there, and a crowd of children they didn't know, some chattering and laughing, others sitting silently, staring round with anxious eyes.

Miss Dauntsey was already there, and when Rita's group came in she clapped her hands for silence.

'Now then,' she said, 'listen, all of you.' The noise faded away as everyone paid attention. 'We're going to be on this ship for a long time, so we just need a few rules.'

Here we go, thought Rita. Do this, do that.

'Meal times are posted on the board in this room,' began Miss Dauntsey. 'You are not to be late for meals, understood? They will be taken in the dining room, on the next deck up. I'll take you all up there and show you in a minute. You may go almost anywhere on the upper decks of the ship, provided you don't get in the way of the crew. If they tell you to scoot, you scoot, OK? And remember there are other people travelling on this ship, and they don't want to be plagued by a lot of noisy children. This room is reserved for you. Grown-ups won't come in here, they have a lounge reserved for them upstairs. You don't go in there. Understood?'

There was a murmur of assent and she went on, 'We want you to enjoy the voyage, but if anyone is a nuisance, they'll be made to stay in their cabin… which would be very boring, don't you think?'

More murmurs of assent. 'Good, well, I think that's it. Off you go and explore if you want to, but supper is in half an hour in the dining room. Don't be late.'

And so it was that they were all in the dining room, tucking into fish, chips and green beans, as the *Pride of Empire* was towed away from the quayside and nosing her way slowly out of Tilbury on the evening tide, slipped away into the river, taking with her the hopes and fears of the migrants who made up her passenger list, all headed for a new life in Australia. Adults, tired of the bleakness of post-war, war-torn Europe, following earlier pioneers to what they hoped was a new and better life; children who had no say in whether they wanted to go or not.

Chapter 16

The morning after her visit to Laurel House, Lily Sharples went to the phone box at the end of the road, and rang the number Mrs Hawkins had given her. She was determined to get an appointment to see Miss Vanstone. The number was answered almost immediately with a sing-song 'Vanstone Enterprises! May I help you?'

For a moment Lily was thrown. She had thought the number she'd been given would connect her straight with Miss Vanstone.

'Oh, er...' she began, 'I, er, I need to speak to Miss Vanstone.'

'Putting you through,' carolled the operator. There was a click and a whirr and then a woman said, 'Miss Vanstone's office.'

'Miss Vanstone?' asked Lily, hesitantly.

'No, I'm afraid Miss Vanstone isn't available just now. This is her secretary, Miss Drake, may I help you?'

'Maybe,' Lily was unfamiliar with the workings of an office. 'I need to see Miss Vanstone.'

'I see,' the voice on the other end said calmly, 'and may I ask in what connection?'

'Pardon?'

'What did you want to see her about?' asked Miss Drake, patiently.

'That's between me and her,' replied Lily stiffly, adding, 'It's about EVER-Care and it's urgent.'

'I see,' said the secretary again. 'May I ask who's calling?'

'Mrs Lily Sharples.'

'Thank you, Mrs Sharples,' said Miss Drake, remembering her instructions. 'Would you hold the line one moment, while I fetch her appointment book?'

Lily waited. She could hear noises on the other end of the phone as if someone were searching for something, then Miss Drake's voice again. 'Sorry to have kept you, Mrs Sharples, the diary was in the other office. Now then, let's have a look.' Another pause. 'Ah yes, well, I'm afraid the first appointment I can offer you is Friday of next week, in the afternoon.'

'But it's urgent,' cried Lily. 'Can't she see me sooner than that?'

Miss Drake was all apology. 'I'm so sorry, Mrs Sharples, but I'm afraid not. Miss Vanstone's away on business and won't be back until next Thursday night, and she's instructed me to keep her diary clear on the Friday morning. I shouldn't really be putting you in, in the afternoon, but, well, you did say it was urgent. Shall we say at Laurel House, Friday 6 August at four o'clock?'

It was clear Lily couldn't see this Miss Vanstone any sooner, so she agreed to the time and date and rang off. Disappointed she went back home. Ten days until she could find out any more about the girls. It seemed to stretch an eternity before her.

That afternoon the doorbell rang and she was surprised to see Carrie Maunder's husband, John, outside on the step.

'John!' Immediately she feared the worst. 'What's the matter? Is Mavis all right... and Carrie?'

'Far as I know, Mrs Sharples,' John said cheerfully, 'nothing's happened to no one. Just thought I'd pop in and see you was all right... see if you'd got the kettle on.'

John Maunder had never been to her house, she hardly knew the man, but she opened the door wide and smiled. 'Of course, John. Come on in.'

He followed her into the kitchen. 'I've got a pot on the go,' she told him, 'but it might be a bit stewed. I'll make a new pot.'

'No, don't worry about that, Mrs Sharples,' said John. 'I like my tea strong.' He took a sip. 'Lovely,' he said, 'just the ticket.'

He put the cup down and reached into the pocket of his jacket. 'We thought you might like these,' he said, and handed Lily a large envelope.

She took it, saying, 'What's this, then, John?'

'Little present. Thought they might cheer you up.'

Lily opened the envelope and pulled out three photographs. She stared at them for a moment, and then looked up at him with tears in her eyes. 'Oh, John, what a dear man you are!' she breathed. In one hand she held a photo of Mavis in her wedding dress, and in the other a picture of Rita and Rosie standing together in their rose-patterned-curtain dresses, beaming at the camera. The third was of Mavis and Jimmy newly married on the steps of the register office. She looked back down at the girls, and the tears slid silently down her cheeks.

'Now then, Mrs Sharples,' said John in alarm. 'No water-works! I thought you'd like them.'

Lily smiled up at him through her tears and reassured him, 'John, I just love them. It's the only snap I got of them girls. I'll put it in a frame on the mantelpiece. And the one of Mavis is lovely too,' she added, almost as an afterthought. 'She did look happy that day, didn't she?' She pulled her hankie from her sleeve and mopped her eyes. 'Thank you,' she said. 'It was very thoughtful of you.'

'Carrie said you'd like them,' said John, clearly relieved that the tears had stopped. 'Glad you do.' He downed the rest of his tea and got to his feet. 'Well, better be off. Only popped in for a mo, just to give you the snaps.'

Lily began to get to her feet, but he put a restraining hand on her arm. 'Don't get up, Mrs Sharples, I can find my way out. Ta ta for now.'

As she heard the front door close behind him, Lily looked again at the pictures, and this time she allowed the tears to flow. How long, she wondered as she gazed at the little girls' beaming faces through the mist of her tears, how long would it be before she saw them again? How long before she could bring them home, here to Hampton Road, where they belonged?

Next morning Lily decided to walk round to Ship Street, once Jimmy had gone to work, and see how Mavis and baby Richard were getting on. Lily loved babies, and longed to have her new grandson in her arms again. When she reached the house she knocked on the door, and as she waited for Mavis to open it, she realized that she could hear Richard crying. She knocked again, and then, trying the door, found it on the latch. 'Mavis?' she called as she went into the hall. 'Mavis? Is everything all right?' There was no reply, but the crying was coming from upstairs, so Lily grasped the banister and hauled herself up to the landing. The wails came from Richard's bedroom and when Lily opened the door she found the baby lying in his cot, scarlet-faced from screaming. She scooped him up into her arms and realized at once that he needed a nappy change. His clothes were wet through, and the cot sheet was soaked as well. She held him close and soothed him, rocking him comfortingly against her until his bellows died away to nothing more than a whimper, then she sat on a chair and with swift and practised movements stripped off his wet clothes and sodden nappy. Wrapping him in a cot blanket she carried him out of the room and into Mavis's bedroom.

Mavis was in bed. She lay absolutely still with her head under the covers. For one dreadful moment Lily thought that she was dead, but, approaching the bed fearfully, she saw the faint rise and fall of the bedclothes and realized Mavis was deeply asleep.

She must be exhausted, Lily thought, if she slept through the racket young Richard's been making. Seeing she was all right, Lily gave her attention to the baby.

'Now then, young man,' she murmured, 'let's get you comfy, eh?' She pulled open a drawer and found a pile of terry nappies. Moments later he lay on her lap, clean and dry, as she pulled on a clean vest and romper. 'There,' she said, 'that's better, ain't it? Let's go down and find you some milk. We'll leave your mummy to sleep. Looks as if she needs to. Did you have her up all night? Bet you did, you monkey.'

She carried Richard to the top of the stairs and then stopped. It was difficult enough for her to negotiate the stairs on her own, let alone carrying a small baby. Reluctantly she took him back to his cot. 'Now, you stay there, darling,' she said, 'and Gran'll go and find your bottle.' Even as she left the room, Richard began to whimper again, and by the time she was in the kitchen he was going strong. When she struggled up the stairs again with the bottle, there was still no sound from Mavis's room.

Sleeping the sleep of the dead, thought Lily as she gathered Richard up into her arms once again and offered him the teat. As if she had turned off an electric switch, his wails stopped and he latched onto the bottle, clearly very hungry indeed. Lily rocked him gently as he sucked, wondering as she did so when he'd last been fed. She looked at her watch. It was past eleven, no wonder he was hungry, he'd probably had his last feed at about six.

Richard finished his bottle and Lily swung him up onto her shoulder to burp him. Moments later, exhausted from his extended crying and with his stomach once more comfortably full, he was asleep in her arms, his little body relaxed against her, his head nestled under her chin. Lily sat holding him close for a while, before gently returning him to his cot. Mavis was still asleep in the next room and as far as Lily could tell, hadn't moved an inch since. She stared down at her daughter for a long moment before leaving the room, quietly pulling the door to. Poor kid, she thought, she ain't having an easy time of it, she needs her sleep.

Lily went back down to the kitchen and looked round. It was a disgrace. Not like Mavis to have it so bad. Lily sighed and rolling up her sleeves, set to work. It was nearly two hours later when she finally sat down with a cup of tea, but glancing round she decided all the hard work had been worth it. The kitchen was clean again. Lily was just looking into the meat-safe outside the back door when she heard footsteps, and turning round found Mavis coming blearily into the room.

'Mum! What you doing here?' Mavis looked dreadful. There

were dark circles under her eyes, and a fading bruise on her fore-head. Her hair, unwashed, hung in lank rats' tails round her pale cheeks.

Lily, shaken by just how worn out Mavis looked, tried to school her expression. 'Just clearing up a bit,' she replied care-fully. 'You was fast asleep and Richard was crying. Didn't want to wake you, so I changed and fed him. He's asleep as well now.'

'Yeah, I know,' said Mavis, smothering a yawn. 'I looked in on him.' She glanced round the kitchen, suddenly aware that it was not as she'd last seen it. 'You done the kitchen,' she said.

'Well, it needed a bit of a going over,' her mother said, smiling. 'Thought you might not have time to do it when you woke up.'

'Thanks, Mum.' Mavis flopped down on a chair and rested her head on the table. 'Still not quite with it yet,' she admitted.

'Never mind, love.'

Lily poured them each a cup of tea, then said, 'I was just looking to see what you've got for Jimmy's tea. See you've got a couple of hearts in the safe. S'pose I stuff them for you, and you can pop them into the oven in time for when Jimmy come home. 'Spect he's hungry when he come off the site, ain't he?'

Mavis nodded. The tea had revived her a little and she smiled wanly at her mother. 'Thanks, Mum, that would be lovely of you.' She gave a shuddering sigh. 'I don't seem to be able to cope with Richard like I did with the girls. He cries a lot, which Jimmy hates, and I'm so tired. Jimmy don't understand, he says how can you be tired when you've only been looking after a baby at home? He don't see that as work.'

'No, well, he wouldn't, would he?' replied Lily. 'He's a man!'

Lily prepared the hearts for Jimmy's tea, but she made sure she was well away before he came home. She dare not come to the house when he was there, but she was determined to visit when he wasn't. She knew Mavis needed her, and more to the point so did Richard. Lily had been horrified at the state in which she'd found him. She said nothing to Mavis about her search for Rita and Rosie. Mavis would never be able to keep it from Jimmy. She had no intention of saying anything about the girls until she had them safely back in her own home.

For the next few days she popped in regularly to see how Mavis was getting on. On more than one occasion she found her deeply asleep in bed, while Richard was left wet and unfed in his cot. Each time Lily sorted him out, and each time she encouraged Mavis to make the effort to look after him herself. Mavis was tearful, but she did seem grateful for Lily's support.

On the day before Lily had her appointment with Miss Vanstone, she went round to Ship Street during the morning, ostensibly to see if Mavis wanted anything from the shops. When she got there she found Mavis doing the washing at the kitchen sink. Richard was lying, gurgling, in his pram in the yard outside the back door.

'He sounds happy enough,' Lily remarked.

'Yeah, he's OK.' Mavis didn't turn round, but simply continued doing the washing.

'You look busy, love,' said Lily cautiously. 'Shall I put the kettle on?'

'Can if you like,' replied Mavis, still not turning, still pummelling clothes in the soapy water.

Lily picked up the kettle and moved across to the sink to refill it. Mavis edged aside, keeping her face averted. Lily filled the kettle and set it to boil on the stove, then she turned back to her daughter and, with a hand on her shoulder, turned her round.

For a moment she stared in shocked silence at the state of Mavis's face, then she hissed, 'The bastard! When did he do this?'

'Last night,' whispered Mavis. 'He come home and Richard was crying, and I was upstairs with him, and the tea wasn't ready.'

'But what the hell did he do? Your face is a mess!'

'You don't have to tell me that, Mum! I got a mirror, haven't I? He pushed me down the stairs. Hit my face on the banisters.'

'Bastard! Bastard!' Lily almost spat the words.

'He was sorry after,' Mavis said. 'He didn't mean to push me down the stairs, course he didn't, just gave me a bit of a shove to hurry me up and I toppled over. My fault really.'

That was too much for Lily. 'Don't be ridiculous, Mavis. Course it weren't your fault.'

'He said sorry after. Said he won't ever do it again.'

'You could've been killed, falling down them stairs,' said Lily, unable to let the matter go.

'Leave it, Mum, it was only a tumble.' Mavis seemed determined to make light of what had happened, but Lily wasn't going to let Jimmy off so easily.

'You could've been holding the baby!'

'He wouldn't have pushed me if I'd been holding Richard,' said Mavis. 'He loves that baby.'

Lily bit back the retort that Jimmy loved no one but Jimmy, and said, 'You must be bruised all over. Have you been to the doctor?'

Mavis gave a bark of laughter. 'The doctor? Where do I find money for the doctor?' Then seeing the concern on her mother's face she said more gently, 'I'm fine, Mum, really I am. A bit bruised, that's all. Nothing broken.'

Lily didn't stay long, she needed to get out of that house. Mavis was up and about, Richard was happy in his pram, and you never knew when Jimmy might walk in, and today, if she met Jimmy, she would be unable to control her anger at what he'd done.

Next afternoon Lily set off to Laurel House. This time she was expected and when the pale-faced maid opened the door, she was shown into a small parlour and told Miss Vanstone was expecting her. Five minutes later Miss Vanstone sailed into the room full of apologies at having kept her waiting. She led Lily to her office and settled her into a chair, before taking up her own place, behind her desk.

'Now, Mrs Sharples, what can I do for you?'

Lily came straight to the point. 'I come to find my granddaughters, Rita and Rosie. I know they're here, 'cos that woman from the Children's Office brought them.'

'I'm very sorry, Mrs Sharples, but I'm afraid you've had a wasted journey,' said Miss Vanstone smoothly. 'We never discuss the children in our care.'

'But surely I'm entitled to know where they are!' cried Lily. 'They're my grandchildren after all, my flesh and blood.'

'That I quite understand,' said Miss Vanstone, 'but when they were signed into our care, we became their guardians, and they no longer "belonged to you" as it were. However,' she raised a hand to cut off Lily's riposte, 'in your case I will make an exception. You are clearly a loving grandmother and want to be sure that your granddaughters are well and cared for. So, this much I will tell you. We did indeed have Rita and Rose with us for a while. Miss Hopkins was extremely concerned that they should be removed from the vicinity of their new stepfather, who I understand is a violent man. She was rightly concerned for their safety. I am sure you've seen evidence of his violence?' She cocked her head to ask the question and Lily found herself nodding.

'So, you see,' she went on, 'they were brought here for their own protection. These days, however, that is a short-term measure. It is better to place such children in a safe, family environment. With this in mind, Rita and Rose have moved on... to be adopted.'

It was the first time, in her edited version of the truth, that Emily Vanstone told Lily an outright lie, justified in her own mind by the need to ensure this woman caused no more trouble. 'We've found a charming couple, up north, who are prepared to take both of them, so they won't be separated. They'll grow up together in a happy home as sisters should. It is the best possible chance for them, as I'm sure, when you've thought it through, you'll agree.'

Lily didn't agree. She stared, dumbfounded, at the woman who had, without reference to anyone, put them up for adoption.

'Adopted?' she croaked at last.

'Yes,' nodded Miss Vanstone, 'much the best option.'

'And the Children's Officer, that Miss Hopkins, has she agreed to all this?'

'She's been kept informed, naturally, as the children came to us through her, but she's quite happy with the arrangement, yes.'

'And they've already gone?' whispered Lily. 'To this new home?'

'Yes. After they ran away from here, it was decided that we should move quickly to establish them somewhere safe in a permanent home.'

'Can I see them?' asked Lily, still struggling to take it all in. 'Can I go and see them in this new place?'

'No, I'm afraid not,' replied Miss Vanstone regretfully. 'That would not be appropriate.'

'What d'you mean, not appropriate?' demanded Lily, beginning to fight back. 'Why can't I see them? You just going to let them think that their mum and their gran simply forgot about them? It may be best, as you said, for them being with this new family. Maybe they can give them things what I can't, but they need to know I'm still their gran and that I still love them.'

'I can understand your feelings,' sympathized Miss Vanstone, 'but what you have to realize is that this would certainly unsettle them again, just when they've begun to find their feet with their new parents.'

'New parents,' echoed Lily with a catch in her voice. For a moment there was silence, as she wondered what to say next, and Miss Vanstone waited her out.

'Can I write to them?' Lily asked at last. 'At least give me an address where I can write to them… tell them I love them.'

Miss Vanstone's expression softened. 'Well,' she said, 'I can't actually give you the address, of course, but I tell you what I will do. If you want to write them a letter, and you give it to me, I will see that it's posted on to them. How's that? Even that's bending the rules.'

'You mean if I write them a letter, you'll see that they get it?'

'Of course,' agreed Miss Vanstone smoothly, 'but just the one.'

'So if I write to them and bring you the letter, you'll send it on?'

'Yes, Mrs Sharples, I've just said I will,' came the patient reply.

'And you won't open it or read it or nothing?'

'Certainly not!' Miss Vanstone sounded most affronted. 'I don't make a practice of reading private correspondence.'

'No, no, course you don't.' Lily backtracked hastily; she didn't want Miss Vanstone to change her mind. She'd simply have to trust her.

'Why don't you write to them now?' suggested Miss Vanstone. 'I'll give you notepaper. Then you needn't come all the way back again.'

'Well,' Lily hesitated, 'I'm not sure.' She'd much rather sit down at her own kitchen table, and take her time; but suppose Miss Vanstone wasn't here when she came back? Suppose it was only the Hawkins woman? Lily certainly didn't trust her. Safer, really, to take advantage of the offer, and give the letter to Miss Vanstone now.

Miss Vanstone opened a drawer and took out a sheet of notepaper and an envelope. Picking up a fountain pen from the desktop she said, 'Here you are.' She got to her feet as she spoke. 'Now, I'll take you back to the parlour and leave you to write your letter in peace, and when you have, just bring it back to me here. I'll be here for at least half an hour.'

Swept along by the other woman's briskness, Lily took the proffered writing materials and followed her back to the parlour.

'You won't be disturbed in here. All right?'

'Yes, thank you,' replied Lily, and with a smile Emily Vanstone closed the door.

Lily sat down at the table and looked at the notepaper. It was not a large piece; she would have to write concisely. It was so difficult to know what to say. She didn't want to upset Rita and Rosie by sounding upset herself. She wanted to assure them they would never be forgotten, but she knew that, if she loved them, and at this moment she ached with love for them, she needed them to settle into their new home and be happy. At last she drew the sheet of notepaper towards her and began to write.

Dearest Rita and Rosie,

I hear from Laurel House that you have moved away and are living with a new family. How exciting! I'm sure they will be kind to you and you'll be very happy in your new home. I just wanted to tell you that I'm out of hospital now, back at home in Hampton Road and going on all right. I don't know exactly where you are, but Miss Vanstone says she'll send this letter on to you. Remember, wherever you are you are my best girls. Look after Rosie, Rita. I know you will, and be very good for your new Mum and Dad.

Lots of love to you both,

Gran. xx

Lily read the letter through, it seemed very cold and unemotional, but she decided that was better than pouring out her grief at their being taken away. That would help no one. She also had to recognize that the adoptive parents would almost certainly read the letter, so she hoped that her comments about them would help make life easier for her girls. She added two more kisses on the bottom and then, with quiet resolution, folded the paper, and sealed it in the envelope.

Turning it over she wrote, *Miss Rita and Rosie Stevens*, leaving plenty of room for the address to be added below. She held the sealed letter in her hand for a moment and went back to the office.

Lily held out the letter. 'Here you are,' she said, and Miss Vanstone took it and laid it on her desk.

'Aren't you going to address it?' asked Lily.

'I'll get my secretary to look out the address,' replied Miss Vanstone with a smile. 'I'm afraid I don't carry all that sort of information in my head. Rest assured, Mrs Sharples, I'll deal with your letter as soon as I can.'

The two women shook hands and Miss Vanstone walked Lily to the front door. When she had closed the door behind her visitor, she returned to her office. She picked up the letter that lay on her desk, spinning it round in her fingers, but she didn't open it. She had promised not to; she simply tossed it into the wastepaper bin.

Chapter 17

The days on board ship did indeed seem like the holiday Emily Vanstone had promised to the children from Laurel House. Before the war the *Pride of Empire* had been a three-class ocean liner, regularly plying her trade from London to Sydney. Her war work as a troop ship over, she'd had a refit, and was back in service on her old route. Now, she transported migrants in search of a new life across the world, rather than the pre-war, rich passengers, but to the migrant children, she was the grandest place they'd ever been in. None of them slept well that first night. It was far too exciting to be going to bed in a cabin, and feeling the movement of the ship as she ploughed through the English Channel.

'Now, you're all to go to sleep and no chatting,' warned Miss Ellen. 'I'm going to turn out the light and you're to settle down. It won't be completely dark, there's a night-light up there.' She pointed to a tiny green light, high up in a corner. 'I'll come and tell you when it's time to get up, but until then you stay in the cabin, understood?'

'Yes, miss.'

'Right, well, goodnight.' She turned off the light, and shut the cabin door.

After morning prayers, a bell sounded, the signal to go into the dining room. The children had never seen so much food.

'You seen what there is?' whispered Daisy, pointing at a plate of food being served at the next table. 'Them's fried eggs, two, and bacon. D'you reckon we can have some of them?'

'Don't know,' Rita sounded doubtful. 'P'raps it's just for that lot, you know. Maybe they're special or summat.'

'What can I get you, miss?' said a voice, and Rita turned round to see a dark-faced waiter wearing a smart white jacket, smiling enquiringly.

'What?'

'What would you like to eat?' he asked. 'Would you like some egg and bacon, or a sausage? I bring toast after.'

'Yes,' said Daisy, quickly. 'I'll have all of that.'

'Me too,' said Rita, and looking at Rosie, she added, 'and the same for my sister.'

'Certainly, miss,' said the waiter. 'Just a few minutes.'

He was back in less than five minutes bearing three plates, piled with the food the children had asked for. They couldn't believe their eyes, and when he offered orange juice they all nodded yes please, their mouths already too full to make an audible answer.

Though several of them, Daisy included, were feeling distinctly queasy as the ship continued down the English Channel, they all devoured everything they were offered. Afraid such food might not be there again, they all stuffed themselves, despite their seasickness. Rita didn't feel too bad, as she adjusted quickly to the motion of the ship; Rosie did not.

'Reet,' whimpered the little girl, 'I feel sick.'

'You can't be sick here,' cried Rita looking round the posh dining room in agitation. 'Come on, Rosie, we got to get to the cabin.' Leaving the last of her own breakfast on the table, she grabbed her sister's hand and dragged her out of the room, back down to their cabin two decks below. Rosie was beginning to retch as Rita pulled her inside and they only just made it in time for Rosie to return her breakfast into the basin. Rita held her head, muttering soothingly, until at last Rosie, pale and scared, lifted her head.

'I don't like it,' she wailed. 'I don't feel very nice.'

'Get on your bunk and lay down,' advised Rita. 'I'll stay here with you. OK?' She helped Rosie onto her bunk, but within moments she was up again, leaning over the basin. When there was nothing left to come up Rita helped the little girl back to bed, where moments later she fell asleep.

Daisy and Sylvia felt seasick too, and it wasn't long before they were lying on their bunks, eyes closed, fighting to keep their breakfasts down.

'You silly girls,' cried Miss Ellen when she came to see how they were faring, 'you shouldn't have eaten so much. You'd better not eat anything else until you've got your sea-legs.'

'What's sea-legs?' quavered Rosie. 'Where do we get them?'

Miss Ellen laughed. 'Sea-legs just means getting used to the ship moving. Then you can eat to your heart's content.'

'Will we get breakfast like that every day?' asked Rita in wonder.

'Of course,' replied Miss Ellen. 'And lunch and tea and dinner, so you don't have to eat yourselves sick!'

At first there was still confusion about the meals that would be served. As far as most of the children were concerned, lunch was a mid-morning snack, dinner meant the midday meal, and tea was the evening meal. No one expected four meals a day.

'Tea's awful early,' said Rita to Daisy when the bell summoned them to the dining room at half-past four, the first afternoon.

'Not much of it neither,' said Daisy, looking in disgust at the bread and jam set out on the table. 'We won't half be hungry by breakfast.'

'Cake!' cried Rosie, pointing to slices of cake arranged on a dish. 'There's cake!' They helped themselves to several slices of bread and jam, piling pieces of cake onto their plates in case it disappeared.

'For goodness sake, children,' admonished Miss Ellen, seeing the food stacked up on their plates, 'if you eat that lot, you won't have any room for dinner.'

'But we had dinner, miss,' pointed out Sheila, taking the lead. 'Fish pie and ice cream.'

Miss Ellen laughed. 'Silly girl! That was your lunch. Tea is in the afternoon, just to keep you going, and then dinner is at seven in the evening.'

They all stared at her in amazement. 'You mean we got another meal to come, miss?' asked Daisy.

'Certainly you have, so leave some room for it.'

'Is that the same,' ventured Rita, 'every day?'

'Every day,' Miss Ellen assured her, and seeing the incredulity on their faces, she suddenly realized how little these children normally had to eat. For the first time, she took in their skinny bodies, their pallid faces and their lacklustre hair.

'Enjoy your tea,' she said, 'but leave room for your dinner.'

Life slipped into an easy pattern and the children began to enjoy their unaccustomed freedom. The Laurel House girls roamed the ship freely, exploring the different decks, finding a library and a games room, and were soon making friends among the other children who were also being sent to a new life in Australia. They hardly saw Sheila; she had palled up with two older girls who were travelling out with their parents to live in Perth. If any of the Laurel House girls bumped into her during the day, she scarcely gave them a glance as she and her new friends sauntered past.

'I'm in charge of our group,' Rita and Daisy heard her say on one occasion, 'as I'm the oldest. They have to do what I say.'

Rita stared after her and remarked scornfully, 'She ain't in charge of nofink, and I ain't going to do nofink she tells me, neither.'

'P'raps I'll tell her stuck-up friends that you bit her,' said Daisy with a grin. 'That'd learn her.' And both girls burst out laughing.

The days began to merge into each other. Each morning started with prayers, and each evening, between tea and dinner, Miss Dauntsey read to any children who were in the children's lounge. To begin with few children were interested in going to story-time, but as the word got round that she was reading a really exciting book, *Five Children and It*, more and more of the children came in to listen. Miss Dauntsey made no comment as the numbers increased, but each evening she read the next instalment, always leaving them waiting for more.

'Where'd you get that book, miss?' Rita plucked up the courage to ask her.

Miss Dauntsey smiled at her. 'I found it in the library, Rita. Have you been in there?'

Rita shook her head. 'Not really, miss, not looking at the books, like.'

'You should,' said Miss Dauntsey. 'The shelf by the window has the children's books on it. You can choose one to read yourself.' She looked at Rita speculatively. 'You can read, can't you, Rita?'

'Course I can.' The scorn in her voice made Miss Dauntsey smile. 'I was the best reader in my class at school.'

'Well, that's excellent,' answered Miss Dauntsey. 'There's nothing like reading a good book. Why don't you go and have a look tomorrow? I'll be in there in the morning, so I can help you if you like.'

'What on earth d'you want to go to the silly old library for?' scoffed Daisy when Rita told her. 'Dull as ditch-water in there.'

But Rita loved *Five Children and It*, and wanted to see if there were other exciting stories that she could read for herself.

Miss Dauntsey was already there. She had several books out on the table in front of her. She looked up as Rita came across to her. 'Ah, there you are, Rita, that's good. Sit you down and have a look at these.' She smiled across at her. 'Choose one you like the look of and read me a bit.'

'You like reading, don't you, Rita?' Miss Dauntsey said when Rita had read her several pages.

'I liked reading at school, and I used to read to my gran, when I lived with her. Gran read to us sometimes, me and Rosie when we was in bed.' There was a quaver in her voice that didn't escape Miss Dauntsey, and she wondered what on earth Rita and Rosie were doing going to Australia if they had a grandmother who loved them back in England. Not wanting to upset the child further, she said, 'It doesn't matter what you read, as long as you read. Books are meant to be fun, so if you're enjoying one, keep reading it.'

'I like the one you're reading us,' Rita said. 'It's good, isn't it?'

'I think so,' agreed Miss Dauntsey, smiling. 'There are other books written by the same lady, you know. Shall we see if we can find another one?'

When she left the library five minutes later, Rita was clutching a battered copy of *The Phoenix and the Carpet* and Miss Dauntsey sat staring into space and thinking how sad it was that a child as bright as Rita was being sent thousands of miles away from the grandmother she so obviously loved.

Once the *Pride of Empire* had progressed through the Straits of Gibraltar into the Mediterranean, the children began to blossom. Properly fed, and spending most of the day out in the warm, fresh air, there was little to see of the pasty-faced urchins who had boarded the ship at Tilbury. As the weather grew hotter the cover was removed from the small swimming pool, and here once a day the Miss Dauntseys allowed their charges a supervised swim. Few of the children had swimming costumes, but the boys were allowed to swim in their shorts, and the girls, swimming at a different time, wore their vest and knickers.

'Hey, Reet,' cried Daisy on the first swimming day, 'you been in a pool before?'

'Nope,' replied Rita, 'and I'm not sure I want to go in one now.'

'Cowardy Custard,' taunted Daisy, and to show she wasn't afraid, she jumped in, disappearing under the water. It seemed an age to the anxious Rita before Daisy came spluttering back to the surface, only to disappear once again.

'Miss, miss!' called Rita, running over to Miss Dauntsey, who, having finished her own swim, was lying on a sunbed. 'Quick, miss, Daisy's fell in. She's drowning, miss!'

Miss Dauntsey took one look at Daisy, coming to the surface spluttering for the third time, and diving across the pool grabbed her as she began to sink again. 'You stupid child!' she admonished, as she hauled the still-spluttering Daisy onto the side. 'If you want to go into the pool and you can't swim, you must come down to the shallow end and walk in.'

'Don't want to go in, miss,' muttered Daisy.

'Well, you're going to,' insisted Miss Dauntsey. 'Everyone should learn to swim. Come on, Daisy, back into the water. You too, Rita.'

After that, she gave swimming lessons every day, and over the next few weeks most of them learned to swim, enjoying the cool water as the skies above them remained blue and hot, and the sun toasted their pale skins brown. The routine swim had become the high spot of the day.

The Miss Dauntseys were not strict; they were chaperoning several groups, but the children only saw their guardians at the obligatory meeting before breakfast each day, at the afternoon swim and story-time after tea. It wasn't long before the Laurel House girls were making friends with both boys and girls from other homes. All the children revelled in their freedom. When they passed through the Suez Canal, they leaned over the side of the ship watching little Egyptian boys diving for pennies thrown overboard by some of the passengers.

'Wish I could swim like that,' moaned Daisy as she watched a dark head burst upward through the water. She had got over the fright of her first dip in the pool, and could now dog-paddle from end to end with confidence. Rita wasn't anything like as keen as Daisy.

She joined in the swimming lessons, but she was happy to get out as soon as she was told. There were books to read and quiet corners in which to read them, either out on the deck, enjoying the increasingly hot sunshine, or in the cool of one of the smaller saloons.

It was there, one afternoon, she met Paul Dawson. He was sitting at a table writing in an exercise book. He didn't look up as she walked over to him, his concentration complete as his pencil flew across the paper. Rita wondered what he was doing. Surely he wasn't doing school work. Nobody was doing school

work. Suddenly Paul stopped writing and gazed up at her, unsee-
ing and chewing the end of his pencil.

'What are you writing?' ventured Rita.

Paul noticed her for the first time. 'This is my journal,' he
replied. 'I'm writing about what's happening on this ship.'

'Can I read it?'

'No,' said Paul, firmly. 'You can't. Write your own.'

'Write my own?' said Rita. 'I couldn't.'

'Don't you do composition at school?

'Yes, course I do. That's just composition.'

'Composition is writing,' said Paul. 'Writing a journal is just
long composition. If you can do composition, you can do that.'

Rita thought for a moment. 'I'd rather read,' she said, and
taking her book, curled up in an armchair in the corner, and
within moments she was no longer on board the ship, but running
to the railway embankment to wave to the old gentleman on the
train. Later she thought about what Paul had said. She had
always enjoyed composition at school; perhaps if she began to
write about their journey to Australia, like Paul, that might get
her started.

That evening, she asked Miss Ellen if she could have a book
to write in.

'I'll see if I can find an exercise book for you, Rita,' she said,
'but if I can't, I can probably find you some paper.'

Daisy was very scornful when Rita returned to the cabin carrying a new pencil and a thin exercise book.

'What's got into you, Reet?' she demanded. 'Why've you gone
all goody-goody and started doing school stuff? Reading and
writing and that! You're dippy, you are. No school for two
months and you're writing compositions.'

But Rita, having decided she would write a journal, was not
to be put off. 'I'm writing about our voyage,' she explained.
'What we've seen and that.'

The days slipped by, merging one into another, so that Rita
found she had no real idea as to how long they'd been travelling.
She found the ship's daily routine, marked off by the sound of

bells, comforting. There was nothing around the ship to remind her of the past, nothing to trigger memories that might ambush her; and as for the future, well, she had no idea what that might hold. She thought of her mother and grandmother, but somehow they had faded, like an old photograph, and seemed only shadows of themselves.

Rosie, to Rita's relief, had at last stopped asking for Mum. She seemed content to settle into the new and strange life on board, playing happily with her friends, romping like a water baby in the swimming pool. At bedtime, provided she had Knitty, she settled down to sleep without fuss. Just occasionally she climbed up the little metal ladder and crept into bed beside Rita, but not every night.

The day came when they had their first sight of Australia, and the *Pride of Empire* steamed into Perth. Some of the migrant workers and one large group of children disembarked there before the ship resumed her journey, docking again in Adelaide for two days, before sailing on to Sydney. One evening the captain announced that, the day after tomorrow, they would reach their destination. There was a ragged cheer from some of the migrant workers still on board, but the Laurel House girls were less happy, anxious about what awaited them when they arrived.

'Perhaps this Carrabunna place won't be the same as Laurel House,' suggested Rita.

'Course it will,' scoffed Daisy. 'Any place that Vanny has her fingers in will be the same, you'll see!'

Chapter 18

Wetty Betty Grover shut the door of her tiny bedroom and wedged the back of its single chair under the handle. There was no privacy for Betty, no respect shown to her beyond the allocation of a tiny attic room to herself above the kitchen wing. Its furniture consisted of an iron-framed bed, a sturdy wooden upright chair and a bedside locker. A cramped, cold and uncomfortable room, it was the only place Betty Grover had to call home.

She had lived at Laurel House for much of her life, first as an orphan and now as a maid, working as a skivvy, with no love or affection, simply cheap labour, available because she had nowhere else to go. For a twelve-hour day, and sometimes longer, she received her keep and half-a-crown a week, her only free time being late evenings and two hours on Saturday and Sunday afternoons. She was treated with contempt by the staff, and she resented it, but there was little she could do about it. Yet.

Betty had left school soon after her fourteenth birthday, with no qualifications, no particular natural aptitude, and when no job was found for her, she'd been obliged to stay at Laurel House and earn her keep.

However, Betty was made of sterner stuff than many imagined. She had plans; she had no intention of staying a day longer than she must, and from the day she'd first put on the hated maid's uniform, she'd begun to make plans for her escape. She was certain that someone, probably the Dragon, regularly went through her few possessions. Betty couldn't prevent the search, but she managed to keep her secrets safely hidden.

Now she was safe from interruption, Betty pulled the locker away from the bedside, and with an old kitchen knife levered up the piece of loosened floorboard beneath it. From the hollow revealed, she lifted out a home-made bag and tipped its contents onto the bed and looked at them. There was a small pile of money, some newspaper clippings, some trinkets and a stub of pencil. From her pocket she took an envelope and once again stared at the names on it before adding it to the collection on the bed.

Earlier that afternoon Betty had been coming out of the laundry, when she'd almost bumped into Miss Vanstone.

'Ah, there you are, Betty,' said Miss Vanstone. 'I don't know when you last cleaned my office, but it's in a terrible state, thick with dust and the windows are a disgrace. Please make sure it has been thoroughly cleaned by the time I come back tomorrow.'

'Yes, Miss Vanstone,' murmured Betty, eyes downcast, standing aside to let her pass.

'You'll have to pull your socks up, Betty,' remarked Miss Vanstone. 'I've noticed several times recently that you've been skimping on your work. Don't make me have to sack you. You owe Laurel House a great deal, you know. It would be a pity if we had to turn you out to fend for yourself.' She raised her eyebrows, clearly expecting an answer.

'Yes, Miss Vanstone.' Betty kept her eyes lowered until her benefactress had walked on. Then, with an expression of hatred on her face that would have astonished Miss Vanstone had she seen it, she went to the scullery to collect the cleaning things.

Once in the office, she looked about. She knew that important documents were stored in the two filing cabinets which stood either side of the window, but they were of no use to her and she ignored them. She went straight to Miss Vanstone's large oak desk. It had a central drawer, which was normally locked, and three drawers down each side, which were not. Quickly and methodically, Betty went through each of the unlocked drawers.

They held little of interest, some sheets of writing paper, blotting paper, paper clips, pencils and a new bottle of ink. Nothing of value. On one occasion the middle drawer had been left unlocked, and inside she'd found stamps, a few silver coins in a small tin, a cheque book, a small black address book and some letters. Betty had taken nothing from the drawer, simply noting what was in there for future reference. Seldom was there anything on the top of Miss Vanstone's desk except her blotter, a pen, a bottle of ink and a small steel paperknife. If there was anything else, Betty had always replaced it, in case it had been a test; something of value left by Miss Vanstone to see if she were stealing.

Betty was stealing, whenever she got the chance. She was saving up to walk out of Laurel House, and kick its dust from her heels. Whenever she found anything that might have the minutest value, she squirrelled it away under the floorboard in her room; but she knew better than to take anything of Miss Vanstone's. On the day she finally left, she would break into that drawer and take everything of value, one last, defiant act before she broke free of Laurel House forever.

Today the desk was clear. Betty took the duster she'd brought with her and set to work, lifting the blotter, pen, ink and paperknife, and setting them on the chair to polish the smooth oak surface. There was rubbish in the wastepaper basket, so she put it beside the door to empty. It was then she noticed that a letter had fallen into it. She picked it out and glancing at it, saw the names *Miss Rita and Rosie Stevens* written neatly on the envelope.

Betty stared at it: a letter, addressed to Rita and Rosie, in the bin? Why hadn't it been addressed and put into the hall box, for posting? They had left for Australia more than a week ago, so why was Miss Vanstone writing to them? One of Betty's chores was to take the letters to the post office, and now she saw that the writing on the envelope was not Miss Vanstone's, but a small, neat script, written by someone else. But who? Then she remembered the woman who'd come to see Miss Vanstone only this afternoon.

It was the second time she'd come to Laurel House, and Betty suddenly remembered that the first time she'd asked for Rita and Rosie. Betty stood for a long moment, holding the letter in her hand, wondering. Their grandmother? Too old to have been their mother. Whoever she was, she must have written the letter, and Miss Vanstone, cruel bitch that she was, had simply thrown it away when the lady had gone.

At that moment, Betty, always alert to the sounds of the house, heard footsteps in the corridor outside and stuffed the letter into her pocket; when the Hawk opened the office door, Betty was vigorously polishing the sides of Miss Vanstone's desk.

'Ah, there you are Betty,' cried the Hawk. 'I've been looking for you everywhere.'

'Miss Vanstone told me to clean her office straight away,' Betty said, adding, with no hint of apology in her voice, 'sorry if you was looking for me, Mrs Hawkins.'

'I see. Well, when you've finished in here, come and find me. I've several jobs for you.' The Hawk stalked out of the room, leaving the door ajar behind her.

'Bitch,' muttered Betty as she returned to her polishing. She still had the windows to do, and if the Hawk had jobs as well, she knew that meant that she'd be working till late. She was sure that the Hawk had left the door open on purpose, and as she couldn't risk being caught off guard, Betty simply finished her cleaning and emptied the wastepaper basket, before closing the door on the office. As she'd expected, the Hawk kept her busy all evening and it wasn't until she crept up to bed at last that she had time to consider the letter again, and decide what to do with it.

It lay, still sealed, on her bed. She was sorely tempted to open it, to discover who had written it. She hesitated; she could open it easily enough, but she had no way of resealing it, and she would have to do so if she sent it on to the Stevens girls.

Betty thought of the two girls: Rosie, a tearful and bewildered little girl, clinging to her sister in the alien world of Laurel

House, and Rita, who had stood out so bravely against the bully Sheila Nevin; who had dared to run away, and take her little sister home. Rita had never jeered at Betty like the other girls. They had talked and Rita had told her how her mother had had another baby, but that she would soon be fetching them home.

Rita had been wrong there of course, but, thought Betty, picking up the letter once again, it looked as if there was someone who was trying to find them.

Rita and Rosie had been shipped off to Australia thinking no one cared what happened to them. Betty, on the verge of making the break from Laurel House herself, wanted them to know that someone had come to ask.

Next time I've to post a letter to Carrabunna, thought Betty, I'll copy the address and I'll send Rita her letter and maybe she'll get found again. That, she thought with satisfaction, will be one in the eye for old Vanstone.

As she put the letter into her cloth bag, she counted the money she had hidden there. Two pounds, fifteen and threepence, the sum of her wealth. Among the coins so carefully hoarded, folded into a tiny square, was a green pound note. She had been collecting the coins for months, but the pound note had been a gift from God. It had swirled past her, a flash of green among the yellow and brown autumn leaves. It was a moment before Betty registered what it was, then darting out into the road she snatched it up, stuffing it into her pocket before anyone else could lay claim to it. A whole pound! It was the pound note that had sealed her determination to escape from Laurel House once and for all. If she could save another pound or two maybe, she'd head for London. Two pounds, fifteen and threepence until she stole the petty cash from Miss Vanstone's desk... but only on the day she left.

That day came sooner than she'd dare hope. Three days after she'd found the letter, the Hawk called her into her office and said, 'There's post to go today, Betty.' She handed Betty a package, wrapped in brown paper. 'I want you to post this parcel, and Miss Vanstone has letters to go as well. Collect them from her office.' She pulled out her purse, and peered into it, then she extracted a ten shilling note and handed it to Betty. 'I've no change,' she said crossly, as if it was Betty's fault. 'You'll have to take this. Now, mind you bring me a receipt for the parcel, and make sure I have the right change.'

'Yes, Mrs Hawkins,' replied Betty dutifully. 'Matron needs me to sort the laundry upstairs. Will it be all right if I go to the post when I've done that?'

'Just as long as you catch today's post with that.' The Hawk nodded at the parcel. 'It's for my niece's birthday.'

'Of course I will,' promised Betty. 'I'll just leave it on the hall table for now and pick it up as I go.' The ten shilling note she folded and slipped into her pocket, where it seemed to generate a warmth of its own.

This is my chance, Betty thought. I've an extra ten bob in my pocket. Today's the day.

She felt suddenly hollow inside. Could she really do this? She clenched her hands into determined fists. Today was the day. It had to be. If she didn't leave today, then she'd never leave. She'd be stuck in this God-awful Laurel House for the rest of her life. This last thought brought her out in a cold sweat, and the decision was made.

Betty went to the office. 'Excuse me, Miss Vanstone, but Mrs Hawkins said you had some letters for me to post.'

'Ah, Betty, yes.' Miss Vanstone looked up from what she was writing. 'I should have them finished in about half an hour. I'll leave them in the hall box when I go. Please make sure they catch today's post.' She opened her desk drawer and reached inside, handing Betty a florin. 'That should cover the postage,' she said, adding, 'you may keep the change, Betty, it'll only be a few pence.'

It was the chance Betty had been waiting for and she scurried up to her room to get ready. Having wedged the chair against the door once more, she retrieved her hoard from under the floor and laid it out on the bed. She took her Sunday frock from the hook on the back of the door and her change of underwear, comb and toothbrush from the locker by her bed. All she had in the world. With a quick glance round the room, she stuffed everything into the cloth bag and then tied it round her waist under her black stuff skirt. It made a peculiar bulge, so she retied it so that the bag hung down behind her knees. It made her walk with a strange waddle, but it was concealed, and she only had to get through the kitchen and hide it in the yard ready to pick up later.

With a final look at her bleak little attic, she closed the door. Never again would she go into that room.

When she reached the kitchen, Ole Smithy was standing, red-faced, at the stove.

'There you are, Betty!' she cried. 'Where've you been? I need you to take over here,' and without further explanation she handed Betty the huge wooden spoon she'd been using to stir a vat of custard, and disappeared. Betty gave the custard a hefty swirl and darted out of the door into the yard. She stashed her bag behind the dustbins and was back at her post, dutifully stirring the custard when Ole Smithy returned.

'Now, my girl,' she said, 'you keep on with that, and mind you don't let it burn. What were you doing upstairs, anyway?'

'Just went up to be excused,' replied Betty, trotting out the answer which had to be accepted.

'Well, don't disappear again, do you hear?'

Betty ducked her head submissively. 'No, Mrs Smith.'

As soon as lunch was over and the girls were set to their chores once more, Betty went into the hall and collected the letters from the box. She was about to go back through the kitchen, when a thought struck her. Perhaps Miss Vanstone had already gone. Betty hurried along the passage and knocked on the office door. There was no answer. Betty knocked again just to be sure, and then eased the door open.

The room was empty. Betty went inside, closing the door quickly behind her. Then, she crossed to the oak desk. She pulled open the unlocked drawers, but as usual, there was nothing of value, so she turned her attention to the central drawer. It was locked. Betty pulled hard at the handle, but although it moved a little, it didn't give. Frustrated, Betty rattled it hard, pulling and jerking in an effort to break the recalcitrant lock. She was about to give up, when she caught sight of the little metal paperknife lying on the desktop. She snatched it up and with all her strength, jammed its point in beside the lock, twisting it hard against the wood. Something seemed to give a little and she did the same again. At the third attack, the lock gave way and the drawer was open.

It was the work of a moment for Betty to empty the petty cash tin and grab the stamps, but just as she was about to shut the drawer again, she saw a small black address book and remembered the letter. She snatched it up and stuffed it into her pocket with the money. Then, pushing the drawer closed, she pocketed the paperknife and went to the door.

Now was the dangerous part. She opened the door an inch and listened. Silence in the corridor outside, and so, clutching the letters in her hand, she slipped out into the passage and hurried towards the kitchen.

'Betty!' The Hawk's harsh tone brought her up sharp. 'What are you doing there?'

'Just going to the post, Mrs Hawkins,' murmured Betty, the colour flooding her cheeks. She held up the letters.

'In that corridor?' The Hawk's voice was laden with disbelief.

'I just went to see if Miss Vanstone had any more letters before I went,' answered Betty, falling back on her prepared excuse, 'but she's not there.'

'No, she's gone home.' The Hawk raised an eyebrow at her. 'You haven't forgotten my parcel, I trust.'

'No, Mrs Hawkins,' she lied. 'I was just going to collect it.'

'I've several jobs for you,' the Hawk told her. 'Make sure you come up to the flat as soon as you get back.'

For the last time, Betty Grover ducked her head and replied, 'Yes, Mrs Hawkins.' She fetched the parcel from the hall-stand and went through to the kitchen, gathering up her coat and slinging it carelessly over her arm. In the yard, she collected her bag and concealing it beneath her coat, walked out through the back gate. In the road outside she turned in the direction of the post office, aware that the Hawk might be watching from a window. She walked quickly, heading for the nearest bus stop. A bus pulled up beside her and she got on. She had no idea where it was going, and she didn't care. She simply needed to be far away from Laurel House before they realized that she'd broken into Miss Vanstone's desk and wasn't coming back. And by then, thought Betty, I'll have disappeared, swallowed up by the world. Swallowed up by the world. She liked that idea and for the first time in days, Betty Grover smiled.

Betty looked out of the bus window. No one knew she was escaping, and no one cared. She wondered what the Hawk would do when she realized that Betty wasn't coming back. Would she care? Or would she simply shrug and say, good riddance to bad rubbish?

The Hawk'll be furious, thought Betty, 'cos I've had the courage to walk out, and I've taken her ten bob with me!

The bus stopped at the railway station and Betty jumped off and went to the ladies' public convenience. Ten minutes later, she emerged with combed hair, wearing her Sunday frock. She'd been about to throw away the hated black uniform, but remembering she had little else, she reluctantly stuffed it into the bottom of her bag. With her coat over her shoulders and her bag on her arm, Betty walked to the ticket office and bought a third class ticket to London. One way. She was never coming back to Belcaster.

She'd counted her money and with the ten shillings the Hawk had given her, the florin from Miss Vanstone, and the money from the office desk as well as her savings, she now had almost four pounds.

If I'm careful, she thought, I can make that last until I find some work.

Sitting in a compartment by herself, Betty opened the Hawk's parcel. Inside was a small brown teddy bear. He lay in tissue paper, and looked up at Betty with bright boot-button eyes. Betty lifted him out and pressed his soft furry face against her own. She had planned to sell whatever was in the package, but now she changed her mind.

'You'd better come with me, Tedda,' she told the bear, 'you're my lucky mascot,' and she tucked him carefully into the top of her bag.

She opened each of the letters in case there was money enclosed, but there wasn't, and she tore them up and watched as the fragments were whipped away in the turbulence of the train's slipstream. Then she sat back and considered her future.

'Whatever it is, Tedda,' she said to the bear who regarded her solemnly from the top of her bag, 'it has to be better than Laurel House.'

It was a week later, in London, that she wrote the Carrabunna address, found in Miss Vanstone's address book, on the letter to Rita and Rosie Stevens and using all the stamps she'd taken from the desk, dropped the letter into a pillar box.

Chapter 19

The *Pride of Empire* steamed into Sydney Harbour, on a chilly September dawn, giving a blast on her foghorn as she approached the great bridge.

'Cor! Look at that!' breathed Rita, staring up in amazement at the incredible steel structure arching across the harbour mouth.

'This ship's too big,' cried Daisy as they drew nearer. 'Our funnel ain't gonna fit under there!'

'Course it is,' scoffed Sheila who was standing with them, 'ships like this come in here all the time, stupid!'

'It's very high,' whispered Rosie, clutching her sister's hand. 'Will it fall down?'

'Don't be silly, Rosie,' muttered Rita. 'Course it won't.' But, as they steamed slowly beneath it, they could hear the thunder of a train passing over their heads, the steady rumble of its wheels seeming so close that they were all glad when the ship was through and making her way up the inner harbour towards Pyrmont, where they would finally disembark.

They, along with all the other migrants left on the ship, were standing on the main deck, crowding the rails to gaze in wonder at the huge bridge and the city around it; the town stretching away to their left, with strange buildings clinging, higgledy-piggledy, to a rocky headland. Wharves, jutting out into the water with boats tied up alongside, were topped with warehouses, some of which seemed derelict. There were boats everywhere, ferries hurrying fussily across the water to pick up and deposit passengers all around the harbour, other small, private craft that chugged about on business of their owners, and boats under sail, skimming across the bay, seemingly unaware of the vast liner passing under the bridge.

The *Pride of Empire* continued her stately progress up the harbour. All round the deck there was a buzz of excited conversation, a babble of languages from the melting pot of migrants aboard, as with a mixture of fear, hope, excitement, expectation and resignation, they gazed at the city, spreading amorphously away on either side of them. Their long voyage was finally coming to an end and they were about to be expelled from the safe haven of the ship into this strange, unknown city at the end of the world. The six-week journey, a curious interlude between their past lives in war-scarred Europe and their uncertain, future lives in Australia, was at an end.

The ship finally docked at Pyrmont. With much noise and shouting she came alongside the wharf and was made fast. When they at last disembarked, streaming down the gangplanks onto the quay and into the customs sheds, the crowd of immigrants fell into untidy lines, their meagre luggage at their feet, the buzz of their conversation muted by anxiety.

The Miss Dauntseys had gathered their charges together the evening before, speaking to each group in turn, giving them instructions on what to do when they disembarked.

'All your luggage must be packed and ready this evening,' Miss Dauntsey told the EVER-Care children. 'We arrive early in the morning, and have to get off the ship straight away. Make sure you leave nothing behind or you'll lose it.'

'You're to wear your best clothes,' Miss Ellen added. 'We don't want Mrs Manton to think we've brought her a lot of scruffs.'

'Sheila, you're in charge of your group,' went on Miss Dauntsey. 'Make sure everyone stays together. I'll be handing you over to Mrs Manton once all the formalities have been dealt with.'

'What's "formalities"?' murmured Daisy.

'Showing passports and telling them what you've got in your suitcases,' Miss Ellen explained. 'Don't worry, it won't take long.'

She was wrong. It took ages. Once ashore the children were separated into their original groups. The Laurel House group was the smallest, and as they stood together waiting for someone to come and collect them, they saw the other, larger groups of children shepherded away. Miss Ellen and Miss Dauntsey waited with them, looking anxiously about. Until they had handed over their charges they couldn't leave the port themselves. Various groups of children were called, and either Miss Dauntsey or Miss Ellen came forward with the necessary papers, escorting each group out to where they were to be collected, passing on their guardianship.

The Laurel House girls shuffled their feet, sat on their cases, moaned and grumbled. Rita looked round the enormous shed at the stream of people who had disembarked from the *Pride*, pushing and shouting and gesticulating. All these people, she thought. All these people coming to live here... because they want to. I don't want to.

'How much longer?' whined Susan Hart.

'I'm hungry,' wailed Rosie.

'So am I!' said Daisy.

They were all hungry. The excitement of their passage into the shelter of Sydney Harbour had kept the children on deck. None of them had gone below for their breakfast. Six weeks earlier, none of them would have missed the chance of a meal for any reason; but with six weeks of regular and satisfying meals, the fear of hunger had faded.

'You should have gone to breakfast when you had the chance,' remarked Miss Ellen, overhearing as she returned from handing over another group. 'Never mind, Rosie, I expect Mrs Manton has made arrangements to feed you very soon.'

Paul had been part of the previous group, and as they'd stood waiting to be called forward, Rita had asked him where he was going.

'Place called Molong,' he replied. 'Looks all right. It's a farm.'

They'd said goodbye, and as he turned to rejoin the rest of the Molong group, he said, 'Keep writing your stories, Reet. They're quite good.'

'And you,' replied Rita, giving him a half wave as he followed the others out of the shed. He didn't look back.

Rita watched him disappear, sad to see him go. Over the final few weeks, they'd become friends. While the other children continued to race round the ship, playing hide and seek, and deck tennis, running races and inventing new games to amuse themselves, Paul and Rita had spent many hours curled up in the library, reading, writing and sharing their thoughts. Watching him walk away into the new world which was Australia, Rita felt bereft, and fighting the tears that threatened her, she turned back to find Rosie. Rosie was still her responsibility, and it was with a rush of affection that she saw her sister sitting on her suitcase, kicking her heels against its cardboard sides.

'You all right, Rosie?'

'Yeah,' replied Rosie, surprised. 'Aren't you?'

'Me? Course I am.'

Eventually they were allowed to straggle out of the customs shed to a concrete yard beyond where a formidable-looking woman sat on a bench: Mrs Manton, Superintendent of Laurel Farm, Carrabunna, waiting to collect her new charges.

The woman stood up as they approached. She was tall and thin, her greying hair scraped back into an untidy bun under a small black hat. Her face wrinkled, her mouth downturned with permanent discontent, she peered at the children from small, mistrustful eyes. Dressed in a long black overcoat which almost reached her spindly, black-stockinged ankles, she wore black gloves and carried a capacious, black handbag.

'She looks like a witch,' muttered Daisy. 'Or a spider. She's going to be worse than the Hawk.'

'May be OK,' Rita murmured in reply.

'Huh!' Daisy looked her new guardian up and down. 'Don't you believe it, Reet.'

The little group came to a halt in front of her, all of them realizing as they saw the expression on her sallow face that their 'holiday' had indeed come to an end.

'Here you are at last,' said the woman by way of greeting. 'I was beginning to think you were never coming through.'

'Mrs Manton? I'm so sorry, but they dealt with the larger groups first,' explained Miss Ellen. 'I'm afraid your girls were last.' She turned to the silent group at her heels and said brightly, 'Well, girls, here's Mrs Manton. She's going to look after you from now.'

No one moved. Rita stared at Miss Ellen, suddenly realizing how important she'd become during the journey. She had shown her charges a kindness which was new to most of them. She and her sister had read to them, played with them, talked to them; something few adults had done before. Of all the children in their small group, only Rita and Rosie remembered being with loving adults, and those memories were fast fading. Looking at Miss Ellen now, Rita wanted to clutch hold of her and beg her not to leave them, but she knew with bleak certainty that there was nothing Miss Ellen could do.

'Well, I must say goodbye,' Miss Ellen said awkwardly. She hated the idea of leaving these girls to the mercy of the dry stick of a woman who was about to take them away. They'd been her particular charges during the voyage and she'd become fond of them, especially the little ones. She glanced at Mrs Manton, but that lady's expression had not relaxed into one of welcome for the children who had come so far.

Rosie, suddenly aware that Miss Ellen was going away, let out a wail of misery. Miss Ellen reached out to her and gathered her into a hug. Moments later she'd hugged each of them, even Sheila, who at nearly fourteen might have rebuffed her, and then with tears burning in her eyes, she turned on her heel, hurrying away to collect her own luggage and join her sister in the immigration queue.

Mrs Manton turned to her charges. 'Stop that yowling,' she ordered, glaring at the three youngest, who, at the sight of her expression and at the tone of her voice, gulped down their sobs and dashed the tears from their cheeks.

Satisfied, Mrs Manton gave an abrupt nod, then looking over to the gate, she waved an imperious hand at a young, tow-headed lad wearing dirty overalls. 'Colin!' she called. 'Get over here.'

The boy peeled himself away from the wall and, picking up the handles of a handcart, ambled over to them.

'Load up the luggage, Colin, and be quick about it, we've got a train to catch.'

The lad stepped forward and grasping two of the suitcases, hefted them easily onto his cart. In a matter of moments he had all the cases stacked, and set off with the cart.

'Form up in twos,' directed Mrs Manton, turning back to the waiting children, 'follow me and keep up.'

'Please, miss,' ventured Sheila, 'where're we going?'

'To catch a train,' replied Mrs Manton briskly. 'Now, you older girls make sure the little ones don't get lost.' She waited for a moment as the older girls took hold of the younger ones, and then she turned on her heel and strode off, leaving her charges to follow. Rita held Rosie firmly by the hand, and from habit the rest of the group came together in pairs, forming a loose crocodile as they straggled out into the windswept street. Sydney was a city such as they'd never seen before. The streets were crowded and noisy. People hurried along, heads bent against the wind and the incoming rain. Traffic hooted and roared as cars and buses battled the congestion and the sudden clang and clank of a passing tram made Susan and Sylvia scream and cling on to Sheila and Angela.

'Come on!' Sheila yanked on Sylvia's hand. 'Don't be such a baby! It's only a tram!' But even she kept a wary eye open after that.

Afraid of losing Mrs Manton in the lunchtime crowds, they scurried along behind her, dodging through the pedestrians thronging the pavement. A clock was striking two when they finally reached the railway station. There was no sign of Colin and the handcart.

Rita looked round nervously. 'Where's our cases?' she asked Daisy.

'How do I know?' shrugged Daisy. 'That boy's got 'em.'

Mrs Manton led them into the station, pausing for the girls to gather round her.

'Our train is in an hour,' she told them. 'You'll have to wait here.' She waved them over to some wooden benches that ran along a wall. 'Sit there and keep quiet while I buy the tickets.' As they sat down, she opened her bag and handed Sheila a brown paper bag. 'You can share these out,' she said, 'and make sure no one moves before I come back.'

Sheila opened the bag and found it contained some rather soggy-looking egg sandwiches. There was just one each. It was quite a while before Mrs Manton returned with the tickets and by the time they'd all drunk from a drinking fountain and been to the lavatory, it was time for them to board the train. As they clambered into the second class carriage, Colin appeared and climbed in as well. There was no sign of their suitcases.

'Where's our stuff?' asked Rita, an edge of panic in her voice.

'Yeah, where's my case?' Daisy demanded.

'In the van, of course,' replied Colin, and immediately lay down on one of the bench seats, flipped his grubby cap over his eyes and went to sleep.

They were all tired, and it wasn't very long after the train drew out of the station that most of the girls followed his example. The carriage was unheated, and Rita and Rosie huddled together, trying to keep warm. Rosie was soon asleep, her back curved against Rita's, her hand under her cheek. Rita lay against her, listening to the rhythm of the wheels. 'No way back! No way back! No way back!'

There was no way back for them now. They would live in another home until they were old enough to leave school and earn their own living, and then... what then? There would still be no way back. For the first time for weeks Rita allowed herself to think about home. On the ship she'd managed to keep such thoughts at bay. She'd been surrounded by new and exciting things, new places, new people, but now, on a cold train, rattling through the countryside, Rita was faced with the reality of her future life. She thought of Mum at home in Ship Street with baby Richard. Uncle Jimmy she tried to blot out of her mind. She tried to picture Gran in Hampton Road, but poor Gran had been knocked down by a car. Was she still in the hospital? If you've been run over, Rita thought, you must take ages to get better, specially if you're old, like Gran.

She thought about Laurel House and the Hawk, and shuddered. Surely the spidery woman who had picked them up today couldn't be as bad as the Hawk, could she?

Rosie was muttering in her sleep, and Rita pulled her closer, wrapping her arms round her to help keep them both warm, and at last, with the rhythm of the train unchanged and unchanging, she fell into an uneasy doze.

Carrabunna station was small, little more than a platform and a station house at the edge of the town. The grey light of a chilly dawn was stealing into the sky when the train began to slow and, with a squeal of brakes, stop beside the platform. Mrs Manton, who had been sitting elsewhere, hustled them off the train into the early morning chill, shouting at them to stand still while she counted them. Bleary-eyed with sleep, and shivering with cold, they stood waiting. Colin was busy at the guard's van, pulling out his handcart, still loaded with the suitcases. No one else left the train, and the moment they were all safely on the platform, the guard blew his whistle and the train chugged away into the darkness.

Colin set off up the narrow road pushing the handcart, their suitcases jumping together as the cart bumped its way along the rough road. As they followed in his wake, the grey light grew stronger, but they were able to make out a little of the countryside.

It was very cold, the wind biting, cutting through the thin coats which they had all been given as part of their new wardrobe. Dressed in their best clothes, as Miss Ellen had told them, they were all wearing the short white socks and sandals they'd been given, and the wind beat mercilessly at their bare legs as they trudged along the road into Carrabunna.

The town was silent and it seemed to the girls, trailing along the early morning street, that the whole place was deserted. No one saw the weary little procession as it passed and they saw no one. Somewhere in the distance a dog barked; it was the only welcome they received.

A painted sign, hung beside a wide, wooden farm gate, read: *Laurel Farm EVER-Care Children's Home.* Mrs Manton led the straggling line of tired children through the gate of their new home and across a cobbled yard to a long, low building. She opened a door at one end, and a welcomingly warm light flooded into the yard.

'Follow me,' she instructed, 'and make sure you wipe your feet!'

The exhausted group did as they were told, anxious to get out of the keen wind. Inside they found themselves in a concrete-floored cloakroom. There were pegs on the wall and a line of wooden benches, with wire lockers underneath, ran down the middle. Most of the lockers contained a pair of shoes, and there were coats hanging on some of the pegs. It was hardly warmer than it had been outside.

'D'you think we take our coats off?' whispered Daisy, looking round.

'Dunno,' replied Rita, 'but I ain't going to. It's too cold.' She reached over to Rosie who was starting to unbutton her coat. 'Keep your coat on, Rosie, it's cold.'

For a moment they all stood there, wondering what they were supposed to do, then Mrs Manton reappeared, calling them through into a large room, empty except for a table at one end.

'Sit!' she instructed.

They sat down on the wooden floor and waited. Mrs Manton picked up a clipboard from the table and ran her eye down a list.

'Now then, answer your names.' When this was done, she said, 'Good, we haven't lost anyone. Now, here at Laurel Farm we all live in cottages. You'll each be assigned to a cottage, and that's where you'll eat and sleep. Your cottage is your home. There is a house-mother to look after you, so each cottage is one big happy family.'

Her words were greeted with silence, as no one knew if they were expected to speak. She peered at them over her spectacles. 'Now, I'll tell you which cottage you're in, then you'll be taken there and you can get settled in.' She consulted her list. 'Sheila Nevin, you'll be in Ash Cottage. That's the senior girls' cottage. Angela Gardner, Dora French and Mary Shannon, in Elm. Daisy Smart and Rita Stevens, Oak. Sylvia Brown and Susan Hart, Pine, and Joan Cameron and Rose Stevens, Larch.'

She looked up again and said, 'Everyone know where they're going?'

'Please, Miss...' began Rita. She'd seen the look of fear on Rosie's face when she heard she was not going to be in the same cottage as Rita.

'Mrs Manton,' corrected the superintendent. 'Well?'

'Mrs Manton. Please. Mrs Manton, couldn't I go into Larch with Rosie instead of Joan? Then Rosie and me'd be in the same cottage. We're sisters.'

'Rita, is it? Well, Rita, you're all sisters here, and you, Joan and Rose will live where you're told... just like everyone else.' She paused, and when Rita said nothing she added, 'Is that understood?'

Rita was whispering, 'Yes, Mrs Manton,' when Rosie began to wail. 'I want to be with Rita. Reet, I want to be with you.'

'Be silent, child!' snapped the superintendent. 'What a disgraceful noise. Another sound from you and you'll get six of the best.'

Not knowing what six of the best was, Rosie continued to wail, until Rita grabbed her, pulling her sister against her, so that her cries were muffled. She hissed in her ear, 'Shut up, Rosie, or she's going to spank you!'

Rosie's wails subsided, but her shoulders continued to heave with dry, shaking sobs.

'Now then, where was I?' continued Mrs Manton. 'Oh yes.

Colin has left your luggage in the yard, so you must pick up your own suitcase on the way to your cottage. You'll be fetched in the next few minutes.'

Even as she spoke, there was a knock at the door, and a girl came in. Her dark hair was cut straight and short about her ears, she wore a grey checked dress and no shoes.

'Good, here's the first of our guides. This is Jane, she's in Elm. Dora, Angela and Mary, go with her. She'll take you to your cottage.' As the three girls hesitated Mrs Manton snapped, 'Look lively! We haven't got all day!' And with anxious glances at the others, the three girls stood up and followed their guide from the room.

Moments later there was another knock and a second girl appeared, dressed identically to the first, pudding basin haircut, grey dress and no shoes. Gradually all the girls were taken to their cottages. When Louise arrived to take Joan and Rosie to Larch, Joan stood up, but Rosie continued to cling to Rita.

'Come on, Rosie,' Rita encouraged, softly. 'Go with Joan and I'll come and find you later, when we're all settled in.' She stood up, pulling Rosie up with her, and then disengaged the child's fingers from her arms and gave her a little push. 'Go on, Rosie,' she urged, 'go with Joan. I'll find you later, I promise you.' Rita could see Rosie was about to start crying again, and she gave a beseeching look to Joan, who reached out, took Rosie's hand and saying, 'Come *on*, Rosie,' almost dragged her away. Audrey from Oak arrived as Rosie and Joan disappeared and moments later Rita and Daisy were out in the yard where their suitcases awaited them.

When she had dismissed the English girls to their various cottages Daphne Manton went through to the house she shared with her husband, Joe. He was sitting in front of a smouldering fire, reading a newspaper.

'Everything go all right?' he asked as his wife came in.

Daphne flopped into a chair on the other side of the fireplace and kicked off her shoes, holding her cold toes to the warmth.

'Yes,' she said wearily. 'All present and correct.' She glanced down at the clipboard she still carried, with its list of names and assigned cottages. 'Don't know how they'll fit in, though.'

Daphne had been dismayed when she'd received a letter from her cousin Emily some weeks ago saying that she was sending children out from Laurel House. There had been no migrant children since before the war, and the girls who now inhabited Laurel Farm were nearly all Australian-born, children left orphaned or deserted by their families, cast upon the charity of strangers. One or two of the senior girls had vague recollections of coming over on a ship, but most of the earlier migrant children had moved on now and as always, newcomers would be regarded with mistrust.

Well, Daphne had thought at the time, she'll send them whatever I say, so they'll just have to muck in with the others.

Emily had enclosed a typed list with her letter, naming the children she would be sending, and three of the names had hand-written comments beside them.

Rita and Rose Stevens. Sisters. These girls should be separated. Rita is a difficult child and a bad influence on her sister. Rose is very babyish... time she grew up.

She'd done as Emily had advised when assigning the new arrivals to their various cottages, and separated the sisters, but that was only a short-term solution; she had other plans for Rosie, which, if they came to fruition, would deal with the situation on a permanent basis.

Sheila Nevin. Can be a trouble-maker, but usually comes to heel.

That comment didn't worry Daphne either. She was used to the odd trouble-maker, and was well able to deal with those.

Rita and Sheila. Now she had met them, and already had a run-in with Rita, she would, Daphne decided, keep a sharp eye on those two.

'Emily's sent me a whole pile of paperwork,' she told Joe with a sigh. 'It's so long since we had any kids from England, I'd forgotten how much was involved. And I bet there's a long letter, too. You know Emily.'

'Why not wait till you've eaten?' suggested Joe. 'Irene's come over to cook your breakfast. She's waiting in the kitchen to know what you want.'

'Scrambled egg and bacon,' said Daphne, 'and some toast and tea.'

'I'll go and tell her,' and Joe went in search of the senior girl, Irene, whose job it was to cook for the superintendent and her husband.

Daphne leaned forward and poked the fire, so that the smouldering log blazed with welcome warmth. It was an extravagance, having a fire in the daytime, and one she would never have countenanced in any of the cottages, but she was grateful for its heat today after the long and chilly train journey.

'Be ready in ten minutes,' Joe said, looking round the door. 'Told her to bring it in on a tray so's you can stay by the fire. I'm off out to the chooks.'

Daphne decided Joe was right to suggest that she leave the letter from Emily until she'd eaten. After all it had taken six weeks to get here, another half hour wasn't going to hurt, so she sat back, relaxing into her armchair, her feet to the fire, to wait for Irene.

When she'd eaten her breakfast, she poured herself another cup of tea and finally turned her attention to the foolscap envelope. Inside there was the expected letter from Emily, and all the personal records of the ten girls who had arrived that day. She tackled the letter first.

Dear Daphne,

Well, here they are. Quite a mixed bunch, but all of them children who, for various reasons, needed both a change from Laurel House and a completely fresh start. They're all used to living in a home like yours so they should settle in with you quickly provided you stand no nonsense. I do suggest you keep an eye on Rita Stevens. I think I mentioned her before.

'Yes, you did Emily,' muttered Daphne, 'and I did what you told me.'

Sheila Nevin is a bit of a bully, but like all such she's also a coward, so I suggest you take an extremely firm line with her right from the start.

Things are changing here quite a bit, and the trend is to foster children in families rather than keep them in institutions like ours. The Labour government has rewritten the rule book with lots of socialist twaddle, meaning that society as we've known it is being turned on its head. Of course, we here at Laurel House are working hard to maintain our standards, and would urge you to do the same. It is vital that children such as ours should know their place in the world and keep to it. Too much education can only make them dissatisfied, leading to unhappiness and discontent. I am sure you'll agree with me.

I am arranging for further funds to maintain these children and plan to send another group out to join you in the near future.

Daphne raised her eyes to heaven when she read this. Where did Emily think she was going to put more children? She'd had to squeeze in the ones who'd arrived today.

I know it isn't easy to make ends meet, but I'm sure there are economies you can make. Have you considered you might keep a pig? Could Joe build a sty?

Could Joe build a sty? Daphne almost exploded. Joe was going to have to build another bloody cottage, if Emily was determined to keep sending more children from England. And she was certainly going to have to send more money. Economies indeed! How Emily thought they could all live on the funds provided in such tough financial times, Daphne couldn't imagine. Of course, it was no problem to her and Joe. They had their comfortable house, adjoining the central block, from where she could keep her finger on the pulse of the place. She just took money whenever she needed to. A little work on the books made the deception easy and they lived in comparative comfort, but the rest of the place was run on a shoestring. The five housemothers lacked any qualifications; they were women grateful to find employment of any kind, and would never query the difference in salary. Daphne was, after all, the superintendent, Joe was the outdoor manager, both very responsible jobs. It was only right that they should earn considerably more than a housemother, a gardener or an odd-job boy.

Now she scrutinized the details in front of her. The only two she was worried about were the Stevens girls. Attached to their documents was a handwritten note in Emily's writing.

These girls come from a dysfunctional family. The widowed mother is feckless. She has remarried and has had another child. There is no room for them in the new family, and the stepfather is thought to be violent and abusive. Watch Rita, she's already absconded from Laurel House, taking Rosie with her. Rosie is a submissive child, biddable enough once out of Rita's influence.

I certainly will be watching that Rita, thought Daphne. The last thing we want is girls running away from here.

Attached to each girl's report was her birth certificate, family details, and the legal guardianship document signing her over to EVER-Care. The immigration authorities would have the names of the girls who arrived, but they wouldn't have the more intimate details.

Occasionally Daphne Manton was approached by adoption agencies, representing couples wishing to adopt. Most of them wanted babies, which she couldn't provide, but she had placed one or two of her charges in families. She had no idea if those adoptions had been successful, but she'd never been asked to return the adoption fee, and none of the children had been sent back.

Recently she'd been approached by a couple, older than usual, who wanted a daughter. Gerald and Edna Waters had come to her on a recommendation from the minister at the Methodist church they attended in Fryford, just up the coast from Sydney. He had heard that Laurel Farm was an orphanage run by a Methodist charity, and they had made an appointment to visit. When they arrived, Mrs Manton had sat them down in her sitting room and discussed in detail what they were looking for. With luck, she'd thought, there should be a good-sized fee.

The Waters were both in their forties, but had only been married for a year or so, and wanted to adopt a little girl of four or five.

'Need to have her house-trained,' said Gerald Waters with a bark of laughter. 'Too old to cope with nappies and potty training, aren't we, dear?'

He turned to his wife for corroboration. Edna Waters was a small, whey-faced woman, standing little more than five feet, beside her husband's six feet four.

She glanced up at him with a half-smile and said, 'We'd like a daughter, and Gerald's right, we don't want a baby, but we do want a child young enough to become our own. You know,' she went on earnestly, 'a little girl young enough to forget her early life, whatever it has been, who can truly belong to us.'

'I doubt if any of the children here are the sort you're looking for,' Daphne Manton had said, 'they've been in care too long,' adding as she saw the disappointment on the Waters' faces, 'but there are some children arriving from England in the next few weeks, and one or two of them are the right age. Of course I haven't met any of them yet, but I'd be happy for you to meet them when they get here and see what you think.'

'Oh, yes,' cried Edna, clasping her hands together in delight. 'Yes, we'd love to see them.'

'Are they the sort of girls we'd want?' Gerald sounded doubtful. 'I mean, well, English girls? We don't want a slum kid.'

'They've been living in our Belcaster home for some time,' Daphne told him. 'They are perfectly well behaved... we allow nothing else. But of course if you don't wish to—'

'Oh we do, we do,' interrupted Edna. 'Of course we do, don't we, Gerald? We'll come and see them as soon as they get here, just tell us the day.'

They were coming tomorrow. If they were going to choose one of the new arrivals, Daphne wanted it done and dusted straight away. Daphne considered the girls who had just arrived. Rosie Stevens seemed the obvious choice, but you never knew. She would bring the three youngest girls in for inspection, and Rita. She'd bring Rita in as well. She was pretty sure, from Edna's enthusiasm, that they would take one of the three youngsters, but there was just the possibility that when they saw the Stevens sisters together, they might take both, and that would not only relieve her of one of the problem kids Emily had landed on her, but would also ease the overcrowding their arrival had caused.

If one of the other girls was adopted by the Waters couple, that information would be added to her file, so that records were kept straight, but there would be no mention of the adoption fee that would be paid. That would be a matter purely between Gerald Waters and Daphne Manton.

Chapter 20

Rita lay in bed staring up at the ceiling; grubby white-painted boards sloping from a ridge, meeting the grubby white-painted walls pierced by an uncurtained window. This dreary room was her new dorm. Here she'd crept miserably into bed last night, and here she would go to bed tonight and every night stretching away into the future. She shivered under the thin blanket she'd been given, and the metal springs of the bed creaked beneath her. The grey light of a new dawn seeped through the grimy windows, doing nothing to lighten the austerity of the room, but allowing Rita to see the others, asleep in the other beds. Daisy, lying on her back, was snoring lightly; the two other girls, Audrey and Carol, whom they'd met yesterday, were both buried under their bedclothes, not even their heads showing.

When Rita and Daisy had been dismissed by Mrs Manton, Audrey from Oak had taken charge of them.

'It's over here,' said Audrey, when they'd picked up their luggage, and she led them away through a clump of trees to a small cottage squatting in a patch of garden, behind a wooden fence. The word *Oak* had been scratched onto one of the palings. Audrey led them up to the front door.

'Mrs Garfield's our house-mother,' she warned them. 'Watch out for her. She's mean.'

Inside the cottage they found themselves in a small entrance hall from which a short passage led off to the right. Audrey pointed to a door directly ahead of them. 'That's the living room. We eat in there, and do our homework and stuff. Kitchen's here.' She waved at a door on her right. 'Bathroom and toilets here. Dorm's at the end.'

She led them along the narrow corridor to a small room at the end. 'You two're in here with me and Carol.' She pointed to a metal-framed bed in the corner. 'That's mine. 'Yours is under the window.'

Two more beds, identical to Audrey's, stood, unmade, under the window. Each had a strip of mattress, on top of which was folded a sheet and a grey blanket. There was no pillow and no quilt.

'Them's your lockers.' Audrey indicated two wooden lockers standing against the wall. 'You can put your stuff in there.'

'Where's Carol, then?' demanded Daisy.

'Cooking breakfast. You hungry?'

'Starving,' admitted Rita. 'Will it be soon?'

''Bout ten minutes,' said Audrey. 'Better get your skates on, or you'll be late, and then old Ma Garfield'll be at you.' She looked at the two new girls standing, hesitant, and added, 'I'll come back and get you in ten minutes.'

'This is worse than Laurel House,' said Daisy, plonking her case on one of the spare beds. 'Ma Garfield? What a name for a mother! Ma Gar! Ma Gar, that's what I'll call her.'

Rita laughed, her first laugh since she'd walked down the gangplank at Pyrmont. 'Trust you, Dais, giving her a nickname!'

'Bet it suits her,' maintained Daisy, opening her case. 'And the one what fetched us, I call her Spider. Good name, don't you think?'

'Yeah, just right,' agreed Rita. 'Or Witch. She looks like a witch, don't she?'

Daisy, who liked to do the nicknames, said, 'Yeah,' grudgingly, adding, 'but I like Spider better.'

Rita put her case on the other bed and went to look through the open window. It was full daylight now, and she could see across a kitchen garden to some ramshackle buildings beyond.

Several girls were already out there carrying buckets and she guessed they were feeding chickens.

'That'll cheer Rosie up,' she said.

'What will?'

'Chickens. There's chickens. She loves chickens.'

'You ready?' Audrey had reappeared at the door.

'Nearly,' said Rita, pulling all her things out of her case and pushing them into her locker. She hadn't very much, but even so it was difficult to make the locker door close.

'Don't worry,' said Audrey. 'Most of that stuff gets took.'

'What d'you mean?' demanded Daisy, who had just managed to close her own locker.

'All them clothes you brought, get taken in. Used for everyone.' She glanced down at the socks and sandals the two girls were wearing. 'And you only wear shoes for school and church. They'll get took off you as well.'

Rita remembered the cloakroom, the wire lockers with the shoes inside. She looked down at Audrey's dirty, angular feet. Did everyone really go about barefoot here, and only put shoes on when they went to school?

'But they're new,' she stammered. 'We only just got them.'

Audrey shrugged. 'You'll see. Come on, it's time for breakfast, and if you're late you won't get none.'

Mrs Garfield was waiting for them in the living room. She looked at her watch as they came in and glowered at Audrey. 'You're late. Where've you been?'

'Mrs Manton said to show the new girls,' Audrey replied. 'They're here.'

'So I see,' sniffed Mrs Garfield. She turned her attention to Rita and Daisy, and Audrey slipped thankfully into a place at the table.

'What're your names, then?'

'Please, Mrs Garfield,' answered Rita, 'I'm Rita and this is Daisy.'

'She got no tongue in her head?' demanded the house-mother. Rita reddened and said nothing.

Daisy looked up at Mrs Garfield and said, 'I'm Daisy Smart.'

'Smart, are you? Well, don't you get smart with me!' snapped the house-mother. She turned towards the table where six other girls were already standing, waiting behind their chairs. There were two empty spaces.

'Well...' Mrs Garfield waved a hand, and Daisy and Rita hurriedly took their places.

Mrs Garfield sat at the head of the table with a pile of tin bowls in front of her. Into these she dished porridge from a large tureen. They ate in silence. Rita and Daisy put their spoons into the glutinous mess in front of them, and despite their hunger – they had had nothing since the egg sandwiches at the station the day before – they found it hard to swallow. All round them was the clatter and scraping of spoons as the other girls shovelled the grey mess hungrily into their mouths. Fixed by a baleful stare from the head of the table, Rita and Daisy struggled to finish their portions, but, remembering Audrey's warning, they finally managed clean plates.

This was the only communal room in the cottage, and looking at its dirty white walls and grimy windows, the utilitarian furniture and the cold stone hearth, Rita found it dismal in the extreme. Were they really going to spend the rest of their lives here at Laurel Farm in this dreadful cottage, eating this disgusting food? The prospect was too awful.

Are all the cottages like this, Rita wondered, or just Oak?

When everyone had finished the porridge, Audrey came round the table with a large jug of milk, filling the mugs that stood beside each place. The milk was good, and everyone drank thirstily. Then the meal was over. The whole thing had taken less than twenty minutes.

Mrs Garfield stood up. Though she'd sat at table, she had eaten nothing. 'Get cleared up and ready for school,' she said to the room at large, adding, almost as an afterthought, 'New girls don't go today. You'll start on Monday. You're not to leave the house without permission. I'll see you in here in half an hour when the others have gone.'

'And when she's had her breakfast,' muttered Audrey as the house-mother disappeared through a door beside the fireplace.

'Don't she have meals with us?' asked Daisy.

'What do you think?' scoffed Audrey. 'No, she goes back to her own rooms and has bacon and eggs.' She waved towards the door through which Mrs Garfield had disappeared. 'She lives through there... and you don't want to get called in there, I can tell you!'

Just like the Hawk, Rita thought miserably. There was no escape from people like the Hawk... or Ma Gar, and this time the nickname did not make her smile, it made her shiver.

Another girl approached them and Audrey said, 'Here's Carol. Carol, these are Rita and Daisy. They're in with us. You two better get your beds made,' she added turning back to them. 'Ma Garfield'll be round to check the minute we've gone.'

'Ma Gar!' said Daisy.

'Hey, that's clever,' cried Carol. 'Ma Gar!'

'Yeah, well, don't let her hear you call her that,' advised Audrey. 'Told you, she's real mean.'

It seemed only moments later that the cottage emptied, and Rita and Daisy were left alone. All the other girls disappeared over to the main building, which Audrey told them was known as 'central', to put on their shoes, ready for the walk to school. A strange silence settled over the cottage, and Rita felt they ought to be talking in whispers.

Remembering Audrey's warning about having things taken away from them, Rita pulled everything out of her locker. The picture of Daddy that had travelled safely all the way from England, she slipped into her journal notebook and then slid both of them under the mattress. She'd have to try to find somewhere better later. There was nothing else that was particularly precious except her rose-patterned dress and she wasn't sure if it would still fit. Anyway there was nowhere to hide it. Reluctantly she laid it aside. It would have to take its chances. The rest of her new clothes she folded carefully and put back in the locker.

'Let's have a proper look about,' suggested Daisy when they'd made up their beds with the scant bedclothes provided. So they walked back along the passage, opening doors and looking into rooms. The room next to them was also a dorm. It was identical to their own except that this one had five beds. Each bed was neatly made, night clothes tidily folded and laid where a pillow might have been, each locker-top completely clear. The bathroom held two baths and two basins, but it had no door. Anyone could look in. The two lavatories had doors, but no locks.

'We better go back to the living room,' said Rita. 'Your friend Ma Gar'll be after us.'

'All right,' agreed Daisy, and they went back to where they'd eaten their breakfast. They found the table cleared and the chairs upended.

Daisy wandered over to the window. 'Look, Reet,' she said, 'there's a man in the garden.'

Rita hurried over and peered out through the grubby glass. 'Who is it, d'you think?'

Daisy shrugged. 'Dunno. It's not that Colin, is it? P'raps he's the gardener.'

'Ah, there you are.' Mrs Garfield's voice cut through the air like a knife. The two girls spun round, each of them wondering how long their house-mother had been standing there. Had she heard their speculation about the man in the garden?

'Please, Mrs Garfield,' Daisy asked, 'who's the man in the garden?'

The house-mother gave her an icy stare, as if incredulous at such curiosity, but then she said, 'That's Mr Manton, the superintendent's husband. He's in charge of outdoors. He oversees the work outside, maintaining the garden and looking after the animals.'

Rita was about to ask what sort of animals, but something in Mrs Garfield's expression made her change her mind.

'Now then,' began their house-mother, 'I'm going to tell you what happens round here, so pay attention. I shan't tell you twice. Oak Cottage is your home now, and you'll be expected to look after it properly. You'll help with the cooking and cleaning, all the usual daily chores. You go to school every day, but when you get back there'll be the afternoon jobs to be done.' She looked at them sharply to make sure they were still paying attention. 'You'll have homework, and then after tea each day, you go over to central for prayers and notices. At weekends and in the holidays, you'll be helping outside. All the cottages have vegetable gardens. We have to grow as much of our own produce as we can. That's what Mr Manton is in charge of. There's not much money for extras here, so you all have to pull your weight.

'You can start in the kitchen,' said Ma Gar briskly. 'There's the washing up to finish and then potatoes to peel. Come along,' she snapped. 'I'll have to show you.' She led them across the passage into the kitchen. A scrubbed wooden table filled much of the room, and shelves, stacked with cooking utensils, lined two of the walls. An old range stood against a third, and under the windows was a deep sink, now filled with unwashed breakfast bowls. There were two more doors leading from the room; one, Mrs Garfield told them, went to the vegetable cellar where they would find the potatoes, the other out into the garden.

'Wash those breakfast things,' she said, 'and then fetch potatoes from the cellar and peel enough to fill that pot.' She pointed to a saucepan that stood, empty, by the range. 'You can go outside and look round when you've finished, but there'll be more jobs to do later,' adding as she stalked out of the room, 'We've no time for idleness here.'

'We've no time for idleness here!' mimicked Daisy. 'You all have to pull your weight!'

'Oh Dais, you are a one!' giggled Rita, keeping an anxious eye on the door, afraid Ma Gar might come back unexpectedly. Her laughter died away as she looked round the kitchen and saw the chores awaiting them. 'I got to go and find Rosie,' she said. 'I got to see she's all right.'

'Better do this first,' Daisy said with unusual caution. 'Won't take long, will it? Bowls, spoons and mugs.' She turned on the tap, and a stream of cold water flowed into the sink. 'No hot water,' she said, as she dipped her hands into the sink and began to scrub at the porridge glued to the rims of the bowls. Rita shrugged and picked up a tea towel from the rail in front of the range.

'S'pose you're right,' she said. 'Ain't no point in getting on the wrong side of Ma Gar on the first day. Anyway, the others're probably having to do the same stuff in their houses.'

Daisy was right, the washing up didn't take very long, despite the cold water and the lack of soap. The potatoes Rita had fetched from the cellar took much longer; the pot they had to fill was huge.

The cellar was a dark hole, stretching the width of the house, lit only by a horizontal slit of a window, level with the garden above. There was no artificial light, and Rita had to wait for her eyes to accustom themselves to the gloom before she could see what was there. An accumulation of junk was stacked up at one end, broken furniture, what looked like a rolled-up carpet, a pile of sacks, a heap of logs and some coal. A shelf ran along one wall on which she could see some jars, but it was impossible to tell in the dim light what they contained. She found the sack of potatoes in a corner. The whole place was chilly and had a musty, dank smell. As she hurriedly filled the pot Rita thought she could hear something scuffling about among the rubbish and shuddered.

'It's horrible down there,' she told Daisy. 'Full of junk, and stinks something rotten. And,' she added with another shudder, 'there's rats!'

With small kitchen knives, the two girls laboured over the peeling for nearly half an hour before the pot was full.

'Let's go an' explore,' said Daisy, when they'd finished. 'We'll go out of this door so's Ma Gar don't see us and find us sommat else to do.'

'I got to find Rosie,' Rita said again. 'She's in Larch, wherever that is.'

'We'll find it,' said Daisy, 'come on.'

The two girls slipped out through the back door into the

garden. Beyond the fence they followed a well-trodden path between the trees and found themselves outside another cottage. This one had no fence round it, but the word *Pine* was scrawled on a board beside the door.

There was no sign of life, so they moved on in search of Larch. It was the next they came to. Like Oak, it stood in a patch of garden, where rows of potatoes were earthed up, and spring cabbage grew in straight, green lines.

'Shall we go in?' said Rita apprehensively. 'I got to find Rosie.'

'You go and see,' said Daisy, glancing round. 'I'll keep cave.'

Rita gave her a twisted smile. 'Yeah,' she said, 'you do that.' And leaving Daisy crouched behind a bush, safely out of view, she walked up to the front door. There was no knocker or bell, so she turned the handle and the door swung open. With one backward glance to Daisy, who gave her an encouraging thumbs up from beside the bush, she stepped inside.

The interior was the same as Oak's. Opposite the front door another door stood ajar, and a passage stretched away to Rita's right. The house was quiet, no sound from anywhere. Rita wondered if she should call out, but hesitated to break the silence. She peered into the room in front of her. Like Oak it was a living room, furnished in much the same way. No one there. She crept along the passage, peeping into each room as she passed, and finally came to the dorm that matched her own. Rosie's case was on one of the beds, but there was no sign of Rosie.

She was about to leave the room when a voice said, 'And what do you think you're doing?' Rita spun round and found herself facing a small, fair-haired woman, standing in the doorway. The woman looked her up and down, waiting for a reply.

'Rosie... I was... just looking for Rosie,' Rita faltered, 'my sister.'

'Visiting other cottages uninvited is strictly forbidden,' said the woman, though she spoke mildly enough and didn't sound particularly angry.

'S-s-sorry,' stammered Rita. 'It's just that I promised her.'

'Rose has gone with Joan to feed the chooks,' the woman told her, adding as she saw Rita's look of incomprehension, 'the chickens. If you go round the house, you'll find the path to the hen runs.'

Rita's face lit up with relief. The chickens. Rosie would love feeding them. 'Thank you, miss,' she said.

'I'm Mrs Watson, Larch house-mother,' the woman said. 'And your name is...?'

'Rita, miss.'

'Well, Rita,' said Mrs Watson with a faint smile, 'I think you'd better scoot out to the chooks as well, before I see you.'

Rita looked uncertain for a moment, but then as the woman disappeared from the doorway, she beat a hasty retreat.

'She's feeding the hens,' Rita told Daisy, and set off round the cottage.

She found Rosie and Joan emptying buckets of water into a trough. Rosie glanced up and seeing Rita coming towards her, dumped her bucket and rushed over to her.

'Oh, Reet,' she cried, her face one huge smile. 'Look, they've got chickens, just like at Laurel House.'

'You all right, Rosie?' Rita asked, but she could see she was.

'What's your cottage like?' Daisy asked Joan, as she came up to join them.

Joan shrugged. 'All right, I s'pose.'

'What did you have for breakfast?' demanded Daisy.

'Porridge and bread and butter,' answered Joan.

'Lucky you!' moaned Daisy. 'We only got porridge and it was disgusting.'

At that moment the man they had seen from the window emerged from one of the sheds. 'Hallo,' he said with a smile. 'Who've we got here then? Don't know you two.'

Rita and Daisy told him their names and he said, 'I'm Mr Manton, you'll be helping me in the garden. Everyone has to pull their weight here, you know.'

The new girls were each given another round of egg sandwiches for their midday meal, and as they ate them they exchanged their news. From what Joan told them, it seemed that Mrs Watson was the kindest of the house-mothers. Mrs Yardley in Pine scared the two younger girls.

'She's got big teeth,' Sylvia told them, fear lurking in her eyes.

'And she shouts,' added Susan.

'Mrs Dawes is Ash mother,' Sheila said, 'but I ain't seen her yet. She didn't come in when we had breakfast.'

'Our house-mother's called Mrs Ford,' Dora told them. 'She's the size of a house. Arms on her like a navvy.'

'Voice and language to match,' agreed Mary. 'She roars at everyone. Stood over Ange this morning till she finished her porridge, didn't she, Ange?'

'Said if I didn't eat it she'd hold my nose and force it down my throat,' agreed Angela. 'An' I believed her, an' all!'

'The girls here do talk funny,' remarked Mary. 'The one what showed us round, Jane, she called us Poms. What's Poms?' No one knew exactly, but they all agreed it probably wasn't complimentary.

'Their voices are dead odd,' said Joan.

'That's just their Australian accents,' said Sheila loftily. 'There was an Australian girl in my class at school back home for a bit, and she talked like that. That's how they talk over here. But they don't like us coming, so we stick together, OK? Ain't going to take no stuff from any of them.'

'Yeah,' said Daisy, 'stick together.'

They all agreed, and felt a little more cheerful, knowing they were in it together.

When the other girls got back from school, the newcomers had to return to their cottages, and were soon swallowed up in the routine of each house. When they got home, the girls changed out of their school uniform and put on overalls. Some went to collect eggs, others were set to weed the vegetable plots, others had to collect the discarded clothes and wash them, ready to wear again on Monday morning.

The potatoes Rita and Daisy had peeled earlier were set to boil, and then added to the thin stew, prepared before breakfast.

After the meal, they all trooped over to central for notices and prayers. The full complement of girls gathered in the meeting hall and sat on the floor, where Mrs Manton addressed them all.

'You'll all have noticed that we've ten new girls come to join us,' she said. 'They will quickly learn how we do things here at Laurel Farm. After prayers I wish to speak to Rita and Rose Stevens, Susan Hart and Sylvia Brown.' She did not say why, but simply went on to outline the jobs for the weekend.

Rita was hardly listening. Why did the Spider want to see them after prayers, and why only her and Rosie and the two little girls? Why didn't she want the others? Rita was filled with a dark foreboding.

After a Bible reading and some prayers, everyone was dismissed except the four new girls, who sat on the floor, waiting. As she got up to leave with the other girls from Oak, Daisy whispered to Rita, 'I'll wait for you outside.' And Rita, feeling the Spider's eyes boring into her, could only nod gratefully, while keeping her own eyes lowered.

When the others had gone, Mrs Manton said, 'Tomorrow we've some visitors coming. You'll wear the clothes and shoes you brought from England, and I want to see clean faces and tidy hair. These people are coming especially to see you and I expect perfect behaviour from you all. You'll answer politely, but only speak if you're spoken to.' She looked round at them and said, 'Any questions? No? Good.'

'Please, Mrs Manton,' ventured Rita, 'why do they want to see us?'

Clearly Mrs Manton hadn't expected questions, and she spoke sharply. 'You'll find out tomorrow. Go back to your cottages now. Make sure you're ready after breakfast.'

Outside Daisy was waiting for them in the gathering twilight. The five girls walked back through the dusk, Rosie clinging tightly to Rita's hand, Sylvia and Susan clutching Daisy's.

'What did she want?' Daisy asked. 'Why did you have to stay?'

'She told us some visitors is coming tomorrow and we've got to meet them,' said Rita. 'She said they was coming specially to see us. Didn't say why. She said we had to dress up and look smart.'

Daisy thought for a moment and then said, 'Perhaps they have to check up on children just come from England.'

'Yeah, I thought that,' agreed Rita, 'but why just us four? Why not all of us what come together?'

'Don't know,' shrugged Daisy.

'I don't want to go in there,' Susan whispered to Daisy when they reached Pine Cottage. 'The lady in there is scary!'

'You got to,' Daisy told her firmly, detaching her hand and casting her adrift. 'Look, Sylvia'll be with you, and we'll see you in the morning, all right?' When neither of the little girls moved, she grabbed their hands again, marched up to the front door of the cottage and opened it. 'See you in the morning,' she said again and pushing them inside, she pulled the door closed behind them.

Rosie gripped Rita's hand even tighter as they came to Larch. 'I don't like it here,' she whimpered.

'Nor do I,' admitted Rita, 'but there ain't nothing we can do about it. I'll see you in the morning, after breakfast, OK? You'll be all right. Joan's in there too. You like Joan.'

'But she's not in my dorm,' cried Rosie. 'There's only girls I don't know.'

Rita sighed. 'Come on, Rosie. You got to go in.' She opened the cottage door. 'You got to be a big girl now. I'll see you in the morning, promise you.'

'What's going on here?' demanded a voice from inside. The door was pulled wider and Mrs Watson appeared. She looked at the two girls hesitating on the doorstep and said, 'Ah, you're back, Rosie. Good. Come along in, now. It's time for bed.' She reached down and took Rosie firmly by the hand. 'Goodnight, Rita.'

Rosie was pulled into the house, and Rita was left standing outside.

'I wish she was with me,' Rita said to Daisy as they walked back to Oak. 'She's only little.'

'She's got to learn to stand on her own two feet,' Daisy said. 'You can't look after her forever, you know.'

'Yeah,' Rita sighed, 'but even so, they could have put us together, just at first.'

Why were they to meet these strange people tomorrow? Rita wondered as she lay in the chilly dorm. Who were they and what did they want? A fearful thought had assailed her, but it was so dreadful that she didn't mention it, even to Daisy. She felt that somehow, just saying it aloud might make it come true. But the idea wouldn't leave her. Suppose they were going to be sent somewhere else. Suppose they were going to be split up. Surely she and Rosie would be kept together – they were sisters. Perhaps that was why she, alone of the older girls, had been included. But Rita felt sick with worry. The Spider had already split them up, perhaps she was going to do it again.

With her thoughts in such a turmoil, it had been ages before Rita had finally fallen asleep. It was the cold that had woken her again and for a moment she didn't know where she was, and then it all came flooding back to her. Yesterday had been a miserable day, surely today things could only get better.

Chapter 21

The next morning Audrey, Carol and Daisy dressed in their weekend overalls. When Daisy had returned from the meeting room the previous evening, she'd found that all her clothes had disappeared and all that was left in her locker was one pair of knickers and her nightie.

'Hey!' she cried. 'Where's my things, my clothes?'

'Told you,' Audrey said. 'Told you they'd take them.' She pointed to a pair of overalls lying on the bed. 'That's what you wear now, like the rest of us.'

'They haven't taken mine,' Rita said, peering into her locker. 'They're all still here.'

Audrey had shrugged. 'You got to dress up for the visitors tomorrow,' she said. 'They'll take them after that.'

Rita lifted out her rose-patterned dress, but when she tried it on, it was too tight and too short. The good food on the ship had done its work, and she had grown, not only an inch taller, but she had also filled out.

'You're too fat, Reet,' Daisy remarked as she watched her friend struggling with the dress.

'No, I ain't,' snapped Rita, pulling the dress back over her head. 'I've grown, that's all.' With a sigh she put the frock away and put on the white blouse and tartan pinafore which she'd been given as Sunday best before she left England.

'D'you know why the visitors are coming?' Rita asked Audrey as she put on her socks and sandals.

Audrey, whose feet were bare, and more than a little grubby, shrugged. ''Spect it's for parade.'

'Parade!' echoed Rita. 'What's parade?'

'You stand on parade and people come and look at you,' said Audrey.

'But what for?'

'To see if they want to take you,' chipped in Carol.

'Take you? Take you where?' Rita still didn't understand.

'Take you with them.' Audrey spoke as if explaining to an idiot. 'To live with them. 'Doption, it's called.'

'And they just take you away?' Rita shivered, a sudden chill running through her.

'Yeah, well, they come and look from time to time,' Audrey told her, 'but nobody never gets took. Don't know why they bother, d'you, Carol?'

'I never knew anyone to get took,' agreed Carol, 'and I've been here forever.'

Rita's mind was racing. Could these people who were coming today, could they simply carry one of them off to live somewhere else? Why was it only her and the three little girls who were to be 'on parade', as Audrey had called it? Did it mean what she'd been dreading, that she might be separated from Rosie? She closed her eyes, fighting against the waves of panic welling up inside her.

'Reet?' Daisy had been listening to the exchange with interest, 'Reet? You all right?' She edged towards the door. 'Come on, Reet, we got to go.'

'S'posing they take Rosie,' Rita whispered.

'They won't,' Daisy assured her. 'You heard what Carol said. No one ever gets took.' She reached out and pulled at her friend's arm. 'Come on, Reet, we'll be late.'

At breakfast Rita was the only girl in Oak who was not dressed in her weekend overalls. Wearing her bright tartan pinafore, she stood out like a parrot among a flock of pigeons. Mrs Garfield, standing at the head of the table, sniffed when she saw her come in, but otherwise ignored her. The other girls cast sideways glances in her direction as she struggled to swallow that morning's helping of glutinous porridge. The silence, broken only by the scraping of spoon on bowl, was oppressive, and Rita couldn't wait for the meal to end.

When at last the tin plates had been cleared away, and Mrs Garfield had disappeared to her own quarters to eat bacon and eggs, Irene, from Ash, appeared and said, 'Message from Mrs Manton, Rita. You're to go straight over to central and to wait in the meeting hall, all right?'

Rita gulped and nodded. Irene gave her a reassuring smile. 'Don't worry,' she said. 'You'll be all right. Never know, you might get lucky and get out of this place.' She gave Rita a little push. 'Go on now, don't be late or you really will be in for it... and don't forget to brush your hair!'

Rita went back to the dorm. She brushed her hair as instructed, slipping on the hair band Miss Ellen had made from some tartan ribbon. Just before she left the room, she rescued the photo of Daddy from under the mattress and tucked it inside her blouse, so that she could feel the stiff paper against her skin and know that he was safe.

When she reached the meeting room, she found Rosie already waiting there. Rosie leaped to her feet and with a cry of 'Reet!' ran to hug her sister. Rita returned the hug and said, 'You all right, Rosie?' She looked at her little sister, and the sight of her twisted Rita's heart. It was clear someone who knew she was 'on parade' had taken great care with the little girl's appearance. Rosie was dressed in her rose-patterned dress, which, though a little on the short side, still fitted her. Her fair, curly hair was brushed, parted down the middle and tied with a pink ribbon on either side. She wore clean white socks and her sandals had been polished. She looked bright and clean and... lovable, and Rita felt a sudden burst of affection for her.

'Who did your hair, Rosie?' she asked, gruffly.

'Mrs Watson,' replied Rosie, making a face. 'She pulled.'

'S'pect it was tangly,' said Rita, 'but it looks nice now.' So different from her own hair, dark and straight, held clear of her face by the tartan snood.

The door opened and Susan and Sylvia came in, brought over

by one of the older girls from Pine. They, too, had had their hair brushed, both now wearing neat plaits. They came in nervously, holding hands, and even when they sat down on the floor beside the other two, they kept a tight grip on each other.

'What we got to do, Rita?' asked Susan nervously.

'Don't know. We'll get told.'

'Who's coming to see us?' asked Rosie.

'I don't know, do I?' Rita snapped, her own nerves jangling. 'Just some people.' How she wished this 'parade' was over and they could all go back to their cottages and get on with things.

At that moment the door opened and Mrs Manton came in. 'Stand!'

They stood, a forlorn group of four children, looking anxiously at the superintendent's grim face. Rita and Rosie close together, hands clasped; Sylvia and Susan, each holding tight to the other.

'Stand up straight!' ordered Mrs Manton. 'And for goodness sake, stop holding hands like babies!' She looked them over and seeming satisfied with what she saw, said, 'I'll be bringing our visitors in shortly, so remember what I said: stand still and straight, be quiet, and answer properly if anyone asks you a question. Understand?' When no one replied, she said again, 'Do you understand?'

'Yes, Mrs Manton,' muttered Rita, and the three little girls murmured, 'Yes, miss,' in a whispered chorus.

Mrs Manton gave a brisk nod and left the room. The four children stood as she'd left them, not daring to move. Moments later the door opened again and Mrs Manton brought in a man and a woman.

Rita, her head held high, standing straight as she'd been told, looked at them. They looked quite ordinary, she thought. The lady wore red lipstick and had permed hair; the man had a red face, wore a blue suit and brown shoes, and his smoothed hair was shiny with oil. Just ordinary grown-ups, really, Rita thought.

The couple paused inside the doorway, their eyes resting on the little group of waiting girls. Nobody said anything. No introductions were made. Mrs Manton stood, a silent presence behind them, as they studied the 'parade'. Then the man came forward, and walked up to Rosie.

'Hallo, little girl,' he said. 'And what's your name?'

Rosie edged behind Rita, peering round nervously at this stranger who towered over her, a bear of a man with a red face and wide bristling moustache.

'Tell Mr Waters your name, child,' ordered Mrs Manton.

'Rosie,' she whispered.

The man bent down, thrusting his big face close to hers.

'And how old are you, Rosie?'

Again Rosie hesitated and Mrs Manton prompted her with a brisk, 'Speak up, Rosie!'

'Five.' Rosie had taken hold of Rita's hand again, and Rita gave her a comforting squeeze. She glowered at the man whose face was just inches away from Rosie's. Can't you see she's frightened? she wanted to say. She's only five.

The man glanced up at Rita and asked, 'And is this your friend, Rosie? What's her name?'

Rosie didn't answer, and so Rita said, 'My name's Rita, and I'm Rosie's sister.'

'Your sister, eh?' The man nodded, and stepped back towards the woman who was still standing at the door. He had hardly glanced at the two other little girls, standing stiff and frightened. They didn't have the blonde curls, they didn't have the blue eyes, which was what Gerald Waters liked in little girls, and Rosie, in her rose-patterned dress, was an exotic butterfly beside two moths.

The woman now walked across to the little group of children. She asked each of them her name, and how old she was. Each replied, monosyllabic, always with an anxious eye on the superintendent who hovered, a black crow, in the background.

When she reached Rosie she smiled and said, 'What a pretty dress.'

'My gran made it,' Rosie told her.

'Your gran?' The woman sounded surprised. She'd assumed that these children here had no family.

'She made it from her curtains,' Rosie told her.

'Did she now? From her curtains! How clever!'

Rosie smiled at her, but Rita, listening, didn't think the woman really thought it was clever at all. She said the words, but Rita could tell she didn't mean them.

'Well, Rosie,' smiled the woman, 'you look very pretty in it.' Rosie beamed at her. She loved being told how pretty she looked.

Having finished her inspection, the woman rejoined her husband by the door. They spoke together in hushed tones for a moment and then Mr Waters turned to Mrs Manton.

'We'll take that one,' he said, and pointed to Rosie.

Mrs Manton treated the couple to her best smile and said, 'The perfect choice, I'd say.' She turned to the waiting children and said, 'Rosie, come over here. The rest of you can go back to your cottages and get changed.'

Susan and Sylvia hesitated for a moment and then scurried out of the room. Rosie came forward as asked, but Rita stood her ground.

'Off you go, Rita,' snapped Mrs Manton. 'We don't need you any more.'

'But what about Rosie?' asked Rita.

'What about Rosie?' Mrs Manton's tone was cold.

'Rosie's coming to live with us,' Mrs Waters broke in. 'You'd like that, wouldn't you, Rosie? To come and live at our house?'

'Can Reet come too?' asked Rosie.

'No, I'm afraid not,' replied Mrs Waters. 'We haven't room for both of you. But you can come... I'm going to be your new mother.'

Rosie's sunny smile faded. 'I got a mother,' Rosie told her. 'She's called Mummy.' Then her lip began to tremble. 'But I don't know where she is now.' She looked across at her sister and said, 'Where's Mummy, Reet? I want Mummy.'

It was so long since Rosie had mentioned their mother that Rita didn't know what to say. She wanted Mum, too, but she'd already realized that they were never going to see her again. She stepped forward and put her arms round her sister, holding her close.

'Mummy's not here now, Rosie,' she whispered, 'but I'll look after you.'

'Off you go now, Rita,' snapped Mrs Manton. 'You can say goodbye to Rose before she leaves.'

'But—' began Rita, but the superintendent interrupted before she could protest further.

'Leave the room immediately, Rita. I'll deal with you later. Rose, you'll come with us.' She took hold of Rosie's hand and jerked her away from Rita, saying to the couple as she did so, 'Perhaps you'd like to come through to my sitting room where we can deal with the formalities.'

They left the room, Rosie beginning to wail as she realized Rita wasn't coming with them, wails that were abruptly cut off by the closing of the door.

Rita was left standing alone, icy despair flooding through her as she knew that her worst fear had come true. She was going to lose Rosie. Just like that. Rosie was going to be taken away, to live with people she didn't know. She, Rita, was going to be left here at Laurel Farm, and each of them would lose the last link with Mum and Gran and Ship Street. She was going to lose Rosie and there was nothing, absolutely nothing, she could do about it. She gazed round the empty room in anguish. She didn't even believe Mrs Manton when she said that she'd be able to say goodbye to Rosie before she left.

Rosie'll have to get her things, thought Rita. And Knitty, she'll want Knitty!

Rita ran across the dusty grass to Larch Cottage. When she got there, she banged on the front door. It was opened by a girl Rita didn't know, but she pushed past her and ran along the passage to Rosie's dorm. There, hidden under the blanket, she found Knitty. He was looking the worse for wear after his travels, but she gathered him up, hugging his familiar striped body to her before tucking him under her arm.

'You'll go with her, Knitty,' she said. 'At least she'll have you.'

'And what is going on here?' demanded a voice and Rita spun

round to find herself confronted by Mrs Watson, standing in the doorway.

'Oh, it's you again,' sighed Mrs Watson, when she recognized Rita. 'I told you yesterday about visiting cottages uninvited.'

'They're taking my sister away,' cried Rita, her voice breaking with misery. 'They're taking Rosie away and I can't stop them.'

'No, you can't,' agreed Mrs Watson. 'And you shouldn't want to! She's going to a family where she'll be looked after and loved. You should be happy for her, or are you too selfish?' She arched her eyebrows and looked expectantly at Rita. When Rita didn't reply she went on, 'Come along, Rita, let's go to my room and talk about this, shall we?'

Rita paused uncertainly. Suppose Rosie came back to her dorm and Rita wasn't there? Mrs Manton had promised they'd be allowed to say goodbye properly, but suppose she didn't keep that promise? Supposing they just sneaked Rosie away and Rita never saw her again? The thought made her clutch Knitty to her more tightly.

Mrs Watson held out her hand. 'Come along, Rita, you can't stay here, you know.'

'Mrs Manton said I could say goodbye.'

'And so you shall. Now come along, there's a good girl.' Mrs Watson didn't sound angry, just tired. Still holding tight to Knitty, Rita reluctantly followed her out of the dorm through the living room, and into Mrs Watson's domain beyond.

Though sparsely furnished, an attempt had been made to turn the two small rooms into a home. There were some books on a shelf, and a photo of a smiling baby in a frame on the mantelpiece. An easy chair stood beside the empty fireplace and there was a table covered with a red cloth in the window with a chair on either side.

Mrs Watson waved at one of these. 'Sit down, Rita.'

Rita did as she was told, and Mrs Watson took her place on the chair opposite. She rested her hands on the table and looked across at Rita.

'Now then, Rita,' she said, 'I know you're upset that Rosie's been chosen to be adopted and not you—'

'It ain't that, miss,' interrupted Rita, 'it ain't that I'm left behind, it's 'cos she's going. She's being took away and I don't know where. She's all I got left now. Our dad's dead, miss. Our mum don't want us. Our gran's in the hospital. Don't know if she'll get better. Rosie and me got each other and that's all, see. If I lose her and she loses me, well, we ain't got no one else, have we?'

'No, not just now. But if Rosie's adopted, she'll have a much better life than if she stayed here.'

When Rita remained silent, her face mutinous, Mrs Watson said, 'You do see that, Rita, I know you do. You're not stupid. You're nine years old, and you know how things work. You think it's not fair? Well maybe it isn't, but then life isn't fair and the sooner you learn that lesson the better.' She waited and Rita gave a reluctant nod.

'So you know that Rosie has a chance today that she may never get again. These people want a daughter and they've chosen Rosie. She's still your sister, and it doesn't make her any less so, you know.'

'You should've seen them, miss,' Rita said. 'They walked round us all like we was animals at some market. They looked us up and down and then, bang, pointed to Rosie and said "we'll have that one" like they was buying a dog.'

'I expect she was just the little girl they were looking for. They'll be longing to take her to her new home.'

'But I shan't see her,' blurted out Rita. 'I shan't know she's all right. Gran said to look after her.'

'And you have, haven't you?'

'But if she's took by these people, I won't see her no more. They ain't gonna let me near her.' Rita fought to swallow the lump in her throat. 'She's only five!' she cried, 'She's only little... she needs me.' For a moment she buried her face into the comforting woollen body of Knitty.

Mrs Watson's life had not been easy, she'd battled her way through her early years, and having escaped from an abusive family, borne and lost a child of her own, she had assumed the title of 'Mrs' and applied for the job she now held in the hope of getting her life back together. She did not suffer fools gladly and had no time for tears and regrets, but even she was touched by the depth of pain she heard now in Rita's voice.

'I'm sure she'll be well looked after, Rita,' she said gently. 'And who knows, you may be able to visit her in her new home, if she doesn't live too far away.'

'They ain't going to let me anywhere near her,' Rita said bitterly.

'Well,' Mrs Watson said briskly, 'you're much more likely to be allowed to visit her if you don't make a fuss about her going.'

Rita raised her eyes to the house-mother's face, a look of scorn suffusing her own. 'You don't believe that,' she said, 'an' if you do, you're just plain stupid.'

'Rita, that's quite enough.'

'Yeah, it is,' Rita agreed and getting to her feet she walked to the door.

'And where do you think you're going?' demanded Mrs Watson.

'To say goodbye to Rosie,' replied Rita. 'I been in here too long.'

With Knitty cuddled against her, she walked round to the main gate. A car was still parked outside, but no one was there. Rita sat down, her back against the wall, to wait.

It was nearly half an hour later when she heard voices and people approaching down the path. She got to her feet and turned to confront the group coming towards her.

Mrs Manton was leading the way, talking to the man. The woman followed with Rosie, holding her firmly by the hand. Rosie was hanging back, dragging her feet, and Rita could see that her face was blotched with tears. As Rita emerged from behind the wall, Mrs Manton stopped in her tracks, her face like thunder. Rosie saw her at the same moment and with a jerk broke free of the woman's hold and hurtled towards her, scream-ing, 'Reet! Reet! I want to stay with you.'

She flung herself against her sister, the tears streaming down her cheeks. Rita held her fiercely in her arms, looking over her head at the three adults who now strode towards her. 'Rita!' roared Mrs Manton. 'What do you think you're doing here?' She reached out to pull Rosie away, but Rita's arms tightened round her sister, and she faced the superintendent, defiance in every line of her body.

'You said I could say goodbye to Rosie properly,' she said. 'That's what I'm doing.' She looked down at Rosie, still clinging to her. 'I've brought you Knitty,' she said, giving her the knitted bear. Rosie hugged Knitty to her, but she didn't let go of Rita.

'What a disgusting looking creature!' The woman was beside them now and she wrinkled her nose. 'I can smell him from here! We're not taking *that* with us.'

'But she loves him,' Rita spoke matter-of-factly. She could see that they'd brought nothing with them to the car, and she said, 'It's all she's got to remind her of home, that and her dress.'

'Made from curtains,' sniffed the woman. 'She won't be wearing any more clothes that are made from curtains, I can tell you!'

'That's enough from you, Rita Stevens,' snarled Mrs Manton. 'You've seen your sister, now you can go straight back to your cottage. I'll deal with you later.'

'Don't go, Reet,' begged Rosie. 'Don't go.'

'Now then, Rose, that's enough from you too,' snapped the superintendent. 'You're going to go with this nice lady and gentleman.'

'And have pretty dresses, just like we told you,' added the woman, reaching down to take her hand again.

'I don't want pretty dresses,' cried Rosie, the tears starting to flow again. 'I want to stay with Reet.'

'Come along, now.' It was the man this time. He'd obviously had enough of female tears. Without warning he scooped the little girl up and carried her to the car. Rosie kicked and screamed all the way, dropping Knitty in the process.

Rita ran forward to pick him up, but by the time she had him safe, Rosie was in the back of the car and the woman was sliding in beside her. The man hurried round to the driver's side and started the engine. Rita ran to the car, holding out Knitty, but the windows were closed, and she could only peer in for one last glimpse of her sister who was screaming now, held firmly in the woman's arms as she squirmed to get free. The car began to move, and Rita had to jump clear as the wheels spun in the dust and the car gathered speed. She stood for a long moment, watching the car disappear down the dirt road that led to the town. Rosie had gone and the only thing that connected them now was a tired and grubby-looking knitted teddy, which Rita still clutched in her arms.

A sudden heavy hand fell on her shoulder. 'As for you, young lady,' hissed Mrs Manton, 'you've disgraced us all. Your sister was going along quite happily until she saw you here. I will not tolerate such disobedience, and you will be punished. Go back to your cottage, sit on your bed and wait for me there.' She spun Rita round, her expression icy as she looked into the girl's mutinous face. 'And you can take that look off your face,' she snapped. 'It's time you learned to do as you're told.' She let go, but when Rita didn't move she dealt her a stinging slap, saying, her fury barely controlled, 'Go back to the cottage.'

Rita's hand flew to her cheek, and then without a word she turned and still clutching Knitty, stumbled back to Oak.

Chapter 22

On reaching the cottage, Rita hurried to her dorm, pulled the photo of Daddy out from under her blouse and slid it back into the journal under her mattress. She didn't know what was going to happen to her, but she was determined to keep her photo hidden.

A pair of grey overalls lay on her bed. Rita stared at them for a moment before opening her locker. Just like Daisy, all she found was a pair of knickers and her nightdress. All the clothes she'd been given on leaving Laurel House had disappeared. They had taken everything she had, including her rose-patterned dress, and she suddenly realized that if they saw Knitty, he would vanish as well. There was nowhere to hide him and she knew with a cold certainty that when Mrs Manton came to her, Knitty would be destroyed. 'Oh, Knitty!' she murmured. Nowhere seemed safe. Then she had an idea and hurried to the lavatories. She pulled the chain and as the toilet flushed, she stood on the seat, looking up to the rusty cistern above. It was old and had no top to it, and the water hissed softly as it began to refill. Standing on tip-toe, Rita reached up and tipped Knitty into the cistern.

He'll be very wet, Rita thought, and he'll be difficult to get out again, but at least he's safe for now. She clambered down from the seat and flushed the lavatory again… it still seemed to work… and she went back to the dorm.

Sitting on her bed, awaiting her punishment, made her think of the Hawk and the punishments she'd dished out at Laurel House.

Was she going to get the same again from Mrs Manton? she wondered. She hardly cared as she thought, despairingly, of Rosie being carried off, screaming, in the back of the car to... who knew where? Little Rosie, usually so sunny-tempered, who just wanted people to love her, now frightened and alone in a new place with new people... and no one to comfort her, not even her beloved Knitty. Rita knew now that she would never see Rosie again.

'I did my best, Gran,' she whispered to the empty room. 'I did my best.' And she sat on her bed, awaiting retribution for doing her best.

The retribution was swift and cruel, but it wasn't Mrs Manton who administered it; that she left to Mrs Garfield. While Rita had been waiting in the dormitory, the superintendent paid a visit to the house-mother. Mrs Manton disliked Mrs Garfield, she thought her a slut, and a toper, but she knew that she stood no nonsense, and could be relied upon to bring mutinous girls to heel.

'Rita's a rebellious girl,' she said, as she sat in Mrs Garfield's squalid sitting room. 'I won't have such disobedience. Please deal with her as you think fit. I leave the punishment up to you, but I will not tolerate a repeat of how she behaved today.'

'Don't worry, Mrs Manton, I'll deal with her,' replied Mrs Garfield. 'I'd already marked her down as a trouble-maker, but I can assure you she won't cause any more.'

Rita didn't have to sit in the dormitory for long. Within a few minutes she heard footsteps in the corridor, and she braced herself for whatever was to come. She was surprised it was Mrs Garfield who appeared, not Mrs Manton.

'Ah, there you are, you wicked, selfish girl.' Ma Gar's eyes gleamed malevolently as she stood over the child sitting on the bed. 'Trying to come between your sister and a lovely new home. Jealous, I suppose!'

'No—' began Rita, but Mrs Garfield cut her off.

'Keep silence,' she hissed. 'You were told to come back here. Did you? No! You were *not* told to lie in wait outside the gates and cause trouble! Did you? Yes! Stand up!'

Rita stood, her eyes downcast.

'You're an ungrateful, disobedient girl.' The house-mother spoke softly and her icy voice slithered round Rita, making her shudder. 'Mrs Manton has asked me to deal with you. She has no time to waste on disruptive girls like you. You're going to learn that she will not be disobeyed or defied. And I am going to be the one to teach you.' She paused, looking Rita up and down and waiting for some reaction. There was none. Rita, determined not to cry, stood rigid, her expression blank.

'Get changed!' snapped Mrs Garfield. 'Put your overalls on.' She stood, hands on hips, as Rita took off her white blouse and tartan pinafore, and put on the grey, weekend overalls.

'Take off your shoes. From now on you only wear them for school and church.'

Rita did as she was told, placing both shoes and her socks in her locker. She stood, barefoot, and waited.

'Now, you can come with me.' Ma Gar turned on her heel and led the way out of the dormitory and along the passage. When she stopped at the kitchen door, Rita felt a wave of relief flood through her. She was going to be given extra kitchen chores as a punishment. She could cope with that.

Mrs Garfield opened the door and nodded to Rita to go in. There were two girls, whose names Rita didn't yet know, working at the kitchen table, making sandwiches for the midday meal. They fell silent as Mrs Garfield took hold of Rita's arm and marched her to the cellar door. Still maintaining a tight grip on Rita's wrist, she pulled the door open and giving Rita a push, said, 'Down there.'

Rita had to grab at the door frame to stop herself from falling. 'What do you want me to fetch?' she asked, still thinking she was going to be given extra chores.

'Fetch?' Mrs Garfield gave a snort. 'Nothing. You'll stay down there until *I* say you can come out again.'

Rita looked down the steps to the gloom of the cellar below, remembered the rats and with a rush of panic turned round to face her tormentor. Mrs Garfield took a menacing step towards her, and Rita took an involuntary step backwards onto the top stair. As she did so, the house-mother slammed the door shut in her face, and Rita heard the heavy bolt sliding home. For a moment she was gripped by a silent terror; panic rose inside her at being shut into this dank, dark place, alone with the rats, and then she began to scream, banging her fists on the solid door, but it remained shut.

After a while Rita stopped hammering and sank down on the step, her fist crammed into her mouth. 'I will not cry!' she said through her teeth as she fought down the panic. 'You will not make me cry!'

She sat on the top step, eyes closed, hands balled into fists, rocking back and forth, drawing deep, slow breaths until, gradually, she grew calmer and her heart beat a little more slowly. How long she sat there she didn't know, but after a while she opened her eyes and, as they grew accustomed to the gloom, she looked around her. She thought back to the previous day; there had been no electric light in the cellar, but there had been a window which allowed a little daylight to filter through.

No point in sitting here, Rita told herself, that cow ain't going to open the door for ages yet. Calling Mrs Garfield a cow, out loud, seemed to give her courage and she began to shout, 'Cow! Cow! Cow!'

Holding firmly to the handrail, she made her way down the steps to the cellar below. A blade of sunlight stabbed its way through the dirty window, a pale shaft of yellow, dancing with dust motes, bringing an illusion of warmth into the chilly air. Rita made her way carefully round the cellar. Among the pile of old furniture she found a wooden stool and, dragging it over to the window, she clambered onto it and peered out through the filthy glass. The garden beyond was flooded with sunlight, bathing the rows of vegetables in bright spring light. Because the window was at ground level, Rita could see nothing more of the garden, but she could hear voices, and occasionally she saw the bare feet of the girls working outside. She tapped on the glass, but got no response; either they didn't hear her, or they knew better than to react.

She was hungry, but as far as she could see there was nothing she could eat: all the vegetables stored here needed to be cooked. Despite the shaft of sunlight, the cellar was chilly, and dressed only in her cotton overalls, Rita was soon shivering with cold. She could hardly feel her bare feet, and she sat on the stool rubbing them to try to warm them up. It helped a bit. She stood up again and began to swing her arms as she'd seen tram drivers do in the winter in Belcaster. This did warm her a little, but as soon as she stopped, the chilly air slipped round her again.

Shivering, Rita made a more careful exploration of the cellar and its contents, and found that one of the barrels contained apples, all wrapped in newspaper. She pulled one out and looked at it. It was big and green, tinged with red. She rubbed it on her overalls, took a bite and immediately spat it out again. Cooking apple, she thought, like the ones Gran used to make into apple pie. She threw the apple away in disgust and turned her attention to the jars on the shelf along the wall. They contained preserves of some sort, but when she lifted one down, she found that the lid was so tight that she couldn't open it. She tried each jar in turn, but it was no good.

As the day wore on, Rita got colder and colder. She was hungry and thirsty, and she couldn't feel her feet at all. She tried jumping up and down to get warm, but it was tiring and she couldn't keep it up. She climbed back onto the stool and peered out of the window again. No one was working outside now, no feet passed by, she heard no more voices.

Rita lost track of time, and as darkness began to fall beyond the window, she turned her back on the garden. Among the oddments of furniture was an old table, and underneath it she discovered a piece of carpet, rolled up and secured with string. It was heavy, but she managed to pull it out and stared down at it.

If I can undo that, Rita thought, perhaps I can roll myself up inside to keep warm. With great patience, she managed to ease the string off and the carpet flopped open. It wasn't as big as she'd thought, little more than a hearth rug, but at least she could spread it on the filthy flagstones of the cellar floor.

She needed to go to the lav, but there was nowhere to go. She tried not to think about it, but as the minutes passed, she became more and more uncomfortable. She couldn't remember when she'd last been. Not for ages, and there was nowhere to go. She made another tour of the cellar, but there was nothing she could use as a chamber pot. In the end, in sheer desperation, she crept into a corner, pulled down her knickers and crouched against the wall. Another fear grasped her. What would Mrs Garfield do to her when she discovered that Rita had been excused all over the floor? She could smell the sharp tang of the urine. Surely Ma Gar would smell it too, when she came down, and know what Rita had done.

She returned to the carpet, pulling it as far as possible from the damp patch she'd made. At least she hadn't needed to do number twos, she thought. That would have been even worse. Wee would dry up, number twos would be there in the morning, for all to see.

As night closed on the garden outside, Rita finally drifted off into an uneasy doze. Not really asleep, she could hear a rustling in the rubbish. There was a definite scuffling in the corner where she'd thrown the apple, and something fell over with a crash. Rita sat up with a start. The darkness around her was complete; only the faintest outline of the window showed in the unbroken blackness around her, but she knew now, for certain, that there was something else in the cellar with her. Knew it was a rat.

She grabbed the nearest thing, another apple from the barrel, and hurled it in the direction of the scuffling. There was more scratching and a squeak. Rats!

The rats added another layer to the fear that wrapped her far more closely than the cold air. With her eyes stretched wide, trying to pierce the darkness, she sat on the stool, her feet held clear of the floor, and waited. While there were still scufflings and scratchings, nothing would induce Rita to lie back down on the carpet. S'pose the rats bit her, started to eat her! They were probably big as cats. She'd heard Gran say once that she'd seen some rats on a bombsite that were as big as cats. Rita had been frightened by the idea at the time, but the fear that consumed her now was an entirely different emotion. She sat perched on the stool, her legs drawn up underneath her, her arms wrapped round them, so that no part of her touched the floor.

When the dawn's early light finally began to filter through the window, Rita was faint with hunger and cold, and her throat was parched and dry. She drifted between sleeping and waking, but every time she nodded off, she began to slip and jerked awake again. At last unable to sit there any longer, she gave in and returned to the carpet. The scuffling had stopped, and the cellar was silent. Had the rats gone? She tried to put them out of her mind. She lay down on her side, and despite the cold and feeling faint from hunger and thirst, she finally fell asleep, only to be troubled by the most terrible dreams.

She dreamed she was running, she had no idea where, but she knew she had to run. Rosie. She was looking for Rosie. There were rats all over the path in front of her, so many of them there was nowhere to put her bare feet, but even so she had to keep running. In her dream she was freezing cold, but even so Mrs Garfield was shouting at her, telling her to take her clothes off. She was chasing the car that was taking Rosie away, and the road was covered in broken glass. She was calling to Rosie, but Rosie didn't seem able to hear her, she simply sat in the back of the car clutching a dripping wet Knitty. Rita was screaming at Rosie not to go, and Mrs Manton, looking more like a witch than ever, was waving a stick and threatening to beat her if she didn't stop screaming.

It was Rita's own screams that woke her up, and she lay on the carpet for a moment, bathed in a cold sweat, not knowing where she was, or what she was doing. Then it all came back to her, the fear, the cold, the hunger, the thirst, flooding through her and making her shake uncontrollably. The light filtering through the window had become stronger, lighting her prison with chilly, grey light. It was morning, but still nobody came.

Daisy woke early. She was cold. She pulled the thin blanket closer round her, but it added little warmth. She turned over, curling up into a ball, and as she was pulling the blanket up over her head she caught sight of Rita's bed, empty and unslept-in. It was a moment before she remembered that Rita had disappeared yesterday, Daisy hadn't seen her since breakfast. When she'd asked Audrey, she'd shrugged and said she was probably in trouble with Mrs Garfield.

'She'll be back later,' Audrey said, 'you'll see.'

'But where is she?' insisted Daisy.

'Better not to ask,' chipped in Carol.

The rest of the day Daisy had been set to work outside. Mr Manton had girls from each cottage clearing out the hen houses, fetching water in buckets to water the vegetable gardens, and one team clearing a new patch of ground to be dug over and planted with beans. It had been hard work and Daisy had little time to think about Rita, but when they all sat down to tea in Oak's living room, there was still no sign of her.

'Have you seen my friend, Rita?' she whispered to the girl next to her.

The girl, whose name was Janet, laid a finger on her lips and whispered back, 'Tell you after.'

Two girls brought in a dish of macaroni cheese, but there was no sign of Mrs Garfield. Agnes, the senior girl in the cottage, said grace and they started to eat. As the meal progressed the girls relaxed and began to whisper quietly to each other. Gradually the volume of their talk rose, until there was a general buzz of conversation. Suddenly the door at the end of the room burst open and Mrs Garfield appeared, swaying unsteadily on her feet, clutching the door jamb for support.

'And what is this noise?' she demanded. The chatter ceased abruptly and she went on, her words slightly slurred. 'Just because I have a shlight headache and am unable to take thish meal with you, there is no excush for thish dreadful noise. You will keep shilence from now onwards, and if...' She paused as if she'd lost the thread of what she'd been saying. '... and if... and if... and if you don't, you'll all be in trouble tomorrow.' Still holding the door frame for support, she turned unsteadily and left the room.

The girls remained silent for a long moment, and then Janet muttered, 'Well, she can't lock us *all* up in the cellar.'

'Is that what she's done with Reet?' asked Daisy, wide-eyed. 'Locked her in the cellar?'

Janet nodded. 'She's done it before as a punishment, but she'll let her out later.'

'Shut up, you two,' hissed Agnes. She was sitting on the other side of Janet, and when they'd started to talk again she looked anxiously at the door.

Janet and Daisy shut up, but Janet nodded towards the door and mouthed the word 'after'.

The meal was soon over, and Daisy found herself on washing-up duty. Janet came into the kitchen too, and as they did the dishes Janet told Daisy what had happened.

'I was doing sandwiches with Agnes,' she said, 'ready to bring them out to you lot, when Garsley came into the kitchen.'

'Garsley?'

'Mrs Garfield. Anyhow, she came into the kitchen with Rita, and she locked her in the cellar.'

'Locked her in?' echoed Daisy. 'How did she... I mean, what did she do?'

'She opened the cellar door and just shoved her inside,' replied Janet. 'Told us if we opened the door or even went near it, we'd be put in there too. She meant it, and Agnes was terrified, 'cos she'd done it to her before and left her there for hours.'

'Poor Reet.' Daisy was horrified. 'What did she do?'

'She banged on the door for a bit, and then it went quiet.'

'No, I mean what did she do, that she was put in the cellar?'

Janet shrugged. 'Dunno. Something to do with her sister, I think.'

'Rosie? What about her?'

'Dunno,' said Janet again, 'but Edna over in Larch said that the sister ain't there no more. She was in the parade, weren't she, so perhaps she was took.'

'Rosie was? Poor Reet! Wonder what she did... or said.'

Janet glanced at the cellar door which was still bolted. 'I don't know, but she's still in there, ain't she? I mean the door's still bolted. Old Garsley'll be back to let her out soon. I'm off before she does.'

Daisy hesitated, looking at the bolted door. Rita was locked in. Should I just open the door a fraction? she wondered. Call to her, see if she's all right?

Janet seemed to read her thoughts. She grabbed her by the arm and pulled her towards the door, saying, 'Don't you dare, Daisy. Come on, she'll be let out in a while, you'll see. It'll be the worst for the both of you if Garsley knew you'd opened that door, honest.' She tugged on her arm again. 'Come on.'

Daisy still hesitated, and Janet let go of her. 'Suit yourself,' she said, 'but I'm not stopping here.' With one final, backwards glance at the bolted cellar, Daisy followed her from the kitchen.

'Daisy wanted to let Rita out of the cellar,' Janet announced. This was greeted by exclamations of horror from the assembled group.

'I didn't,' protested Daisy, 'I just wanted to call down to her, see she was OK.'

'She'll be all right,' said Audrey. 'She'll be out and in bed by the time we get back from prayers, you'll see.' But she wasn't.

'She still ain't here,' Daisy said to Audrey when they got back to the dorm.

Audrey shrugged. 'Nothing we can do about it.'

'We could let her out,' Daisy said.

'Not me,' stated Audrey firmly and got into bed.

'Not me,' echoed Carol. 'And you won't, neither, if you know what's good for you.'

Daisy lay awake for what felt like hours, thinking about Rita and wondering what had happened to Rosie. She was fond of the little girl too, had she really gone? At last, exhausted by the hard day, she, too, had fallen asleep. Now, as cold dawn lit the sky and she could see that Rita's bed hadn't been slept in, Daisy knew she must do something.

Surely Reet isn't still in the cellar, she thought. Ma Gar must've let her out. Surely she hasn't been left there all night.

Daisy was horrified at the thought. Had she had anything to eat or drink? No one had dared to open the door, so unless Ma Gar had given her food, she'd had nothing since her breakfast porridge yesterday.

Daisy sat up. There was enough light now to see the other two still fast asleep. Neither girl stirred as Daisy slid out of bed and crept to the door. She eased it open, but the latch clicked, loudly. She froze, but silence still enclosed the house. No one had heard. The cottage was quiet apart from Carol snoring and a snuffling noise coming from the other dorm.

Softly Daisy edged her way out of the room, and along to the kitchen. She paused at the door listening hard before she opened it and crossed swiftly to the cellar door. It was still bolted. Daisy hesitated.

If I open the door, she thought, we'll both be for it. But if I don't... and s'pose something's happened to Reet?

Reet'd come and find me, she thought. Reet's brave. Her hand rested on the bolt. 'I can be as brave as you, Reet,' she said, and summoning all her courage, she slid the bolt across and opened the door.

The cellar was in darkness. Daisy looked down the steps, but could see nothing. 'Reet,' she called softly, 'Reet? Are you there?'

There was no reply. She ain't there after all, thought Daisy, relief flooding through her. Ma Gar must've let her out last night after all. P'raps she weren't ever in there and that Janet was telling lies.

'Reet,' she called again, going down two steps this time, trying to see into the cellar without going right down. 'Reet, are you there?' She was about to turn back to the kitchen when she heard a sound, a faint whimpering, like an animal in pain.

'Reet?' Daisy crept down another two steps, and peered into the gloom.

'Dais?' The voice was little more than a croak, but it was Rita's.

Daisy scurried down the last few stairs, saying, 'Reet? Reet, are you all right?' In the faint light from the window she saw what looked like a heap of... something... on the floor. She was kneeling beside her in an instant, taking her hand. 'Reet,' she said, 'Reet, it's all right. I've come to get you out. Crikey! You ain't half cold.'

'Thirsty,' rasped Rita. 'So thirsty.'

'Come on, Reet,' Daisy said. 'We got to get out of here. You can have a drink of water when we get up to the kitchen.' And when Rita didn't move, Daisy pulled at her urgently. 'Come *on*, Reet. We got to get out of here.'

Somehow she managed to get Rita to her feet, pulling her towards the stairs. Together they negotiated the steps and got back up to the kitchen where Rita collapsed onto a stool; Daisy shut the cellar door and bolted it firmly. Then she filled a tin mug at the sink and handed it to Rita.

Rita gulped down the water, emptying the mug before she paused for breath. She gave Daisy a wan smile. 'Thanks, Dais,' she said.

Daisy looked at her friend anxiously. 'You all right, Reet?'

'Cold,' replied Rita, 'and hungry, but all right.'

'See if I can find you something to eat,' Daisy said and opening the pantry door, she peered inside. There was very little food, but she found the end of a loaf of bread and a heel of cheese wrapped in a piece of cloth, and brought them out. 'Not much,' she said, passing it over.

Rita wolfed down the food, tearing at the bread and cramming the small piece of cheese into her mouth. 'This'll do,' she said. 'Then I'm off.'

'Off?' Daisy was startled. 'Off where?'

'Out of here,' Rita said through a mouthful of bread. 'You should come too. We're in dead trouble now.' She shook her head at Daisy. 'You shouldn't have come down for me, Dais. Now you'll be for the high jump, too.' She swallowed hard and added, 'But I'm so glad you did. You're a real friend.'

'Couldn't leave you there, could I?' Daisy looked down at herself. 'I can't come with you. I ain't even dressed.'

'Go and get your clothes, then,' said Rita. 'I ain't staying here another day, and you shouldn't neither.'

Daisy hesitated. She'd always lived in a place like Laurel Farm, she hadn't the courage to walk away from it, as Rita had from Laurel House, and was planning to do again.

'We ain't got no shoes,' she pointed out.

'No.' Rita looked down at her bare feet, still too cold to feel. 'They took mine as well, I expect. Never mind, that ain't going to stop me. I just got to fetch something from the dorm and then I'm off.' They made their way silently along the passage. It was almost complete daylight now, and soon the rest of the house would be awake.

In the dorm, Rita opened her locker door. Inside were the shoes and socks that Mrs Garfield had made her take off yesterday. She grabbed them, quickly putting them on, then she up-ended the mattress and pulled out her precious journal, checked that her photo was still inside it and tucked it under her arm. To her surprise she realized that Daisy was struggling into her clothes. Just the overalls they all wore, but she had no shoes. 'What you doing, Dais?' she whispered.

'Coming with you, Reet,' came the soft reply.

The two friends hurried down the passage, and out through the back door.

'Just a minute,' hissed Daisy, and turned aside to a little lean-to shed. Moments later she reappeared wearing a pair of rubber boots. They were several sizes too big for her but at least her feet were covered. Rita gave a muffled laugh when she saw her.

'Had to wear them yesterday when we was mucking out the chooks,' explained Daisy. 'Come on.'

'This way,' Rita said, leading the way through the trees. 'Better not go out through the gate. We'll climb out.'

Together they slipped through the trees, past the sleeping cottages, towards the boundary fence.

'And just where do you two think you're going?'

The two girls froze, their hearts pounding. The voice came from the garden in front of Larch Cottage. Mrs Watson had been sitting on an old wooden bench, and now she came across to the two girls.

'Just for a walk, miss.' Rita tried to sound nonchalant.

'Oh, no, I don't think so,' said Mrs Watson. She'd recognized Rita at once. 'Too early for a walk, don't you think?' She reached across and took Rita by the arm, her fingers warm against the girl's chilly flesh.

'Good gracious, child, you're freezing!' she exclaimed. She turned Rita to face her and saw the dirt on her face and her matted hair. 'And you're filthy. What on earth have you been doing, Rita?'

Rita didn't answer, but Daisy piped up, 'She's been locked in the cellar all night. You'd be cold and dirty if you was left in a cellar that long.'

'That's enough,' snapped Mrs Watson. She didn't know the child's name, one of the new kids from England. She turned back to Rita. 'Is that true? That you've been locked in the cellar all night?'

Rita was glowering at Daisy for interfering, but she nodded.

'All night? Mrs Garfield left you in the cellar all night?'

'She did, miss.' Daisy would not be silenced by either of them.

Mrs Watson looked at her. 'What *is* your name?' she asked.

'Daisy Smart, miss.'

'Well, Daisy Smart, will you kindly be quiet? I'm speaking to Rita.' She looked at the two girls for a moment and saw that Rita was shivering.

'You'd better come inside,' she said and still holding onto Rita, led them into Larch. She took them through the living room into her own quarters beyond and made them sit down. Here she stirred the embers in the fireplace, adding some dry twigs as she coaxed the fire back to life.

'You need a hot drink,' she said, 'and then, you'd better tell me exactly what's been going on.'

Chapter 23

'You'll have to sack Garfield,' Joe Manton said. 'The Watson woman is right, that child might have died in that cellar.'

'That's a bit overdramatic,' replied his wife. 'She's all right, a bit cold... hungry and thirsty, that's all.'

'Daphne, if that other child, what's her name...?'

'Daisy Smart.'

'If Daisy Smart hadn't gone down and found her, she might well have been in a far worse state. The woman was dead drunk on the floor when you went to find her. She wouldn't have come round for hours.' He looked across at his wife, his expression serious. 'Let's face it, Daphne, it's not the first time she's been drunk. Oh, I agree,' he said, as his wife tried to interrupt, 'I agree never as bad as she was today... goodness only knows how much she'd had... but we can't keep turning a blind eye.'

'There was an empty gin bottle lying beside her,' conceded Daphne.

Joe shrugged. 'That says it all. You can't leave her in charge of a house full of children. Imagine what would have happened if that girl had been taken really ill, or worse! Doesn't bear thinking about. We'd have had the authorities down on us like a ton of bricks, they'd have crawled all over the place. Probably closed us down.'

'I know,' agreed his wife reluctantly, 'I know, you're right, of course, but I don't like being blackmailed by that woman.'

'Well,' answered Joe, getting to his feet, 'there's nothing you can do about it. You simply sack the Garfield woman. You never liked her anyway!' And he left Daphne sitting in her chair, deciding what to do.

They'd been awoken early that morning by a pounding on their front door. Daphne had got up, still bleary with sleep, and opened the door to find Mrs Watson, fist raised about to hammer again.

'Mrs Watson!' she'd cried. 'What on earth's happened?'

'It's Mrs Garfield,' began Mrs Watson.

'You'd better come in.'

'No,' insisted Mrs Watson, 'you'd better come with me.' She sounded so urgent that Mrs Manton flung an overcoat over her nightdress and followed her to Oak. The girls stared in astonishment as the superintendent, still in her nightclothes, and Mrs Watson entered the cottage, marched through the living room and into Mrs Garfield's quarters.

Daphne Manton stopped short at what she saw. Mrs Garfield lay on the floor, eyes closed, her breath coming in stentorian rasps, an empty gin bottle beside her.

'She's out for the count,' Mrs Watson said in disgust, 'and must have been for hours.'

'Well, at least there's no harm done,' Mrs Manton said calmly.

'No harm done!' exploded Mrs Watson. 'She had a child locked in the cellar all day yesterday and all last night. She was too drunk to remember to let her out. Mrs Manton, that child could have died!'

'Oh, I hardly think so—' began the superintendent.

'You're wrong,' Mrs Watson interrupted. 'That child was left in the dark with no food, no water, no sanitation, in a cellar which, if ours at Larch is anything to go by, has a population of rats, for nearly *twenty-four hours*.' She confronted her employer across the prone figure of Mrs Garfield. 'I will not be party to such treatment, Mrs Manton. Unless you get rid of this...' she prodded the oblivious house-mother with her toe, '... this apology for a woman, not only will I not stay in this place, I will report this to the authorities.'

'Then you'll be out of a job yourself,' pointed out Mrs Manton, surprised at Mrs Watson's temerity. 'I thought you needed this job.'

'I do,' snapped Mrs Watson, 'but not at the expense of a child's life.'

'The child is not dead.'

'No thanks to this woman. Who knows how long Rita'd have been left there if her friend hadn't had the guts to go down and bring her out? None of the other kids dared, and she...' she prodded Mrs Garfield again, '... she probably won't surface again for hours yet, and won't remember the child in the cellar when she does.' She held Mrs Manton's eyes and said softly, 'That is my ultimatum, Mrs Manton. Either she goes or I do, and if I do, my first stop will be the state authorities.'

'Where's the child now?' demanded the superintendent.

'I've given her a hot drink and put her to bed in Larch,' replied Mrs Watson. 'She needs to be kept in bed today to make sure there are no further ill-effects.'

'And the other child, Daisy Smart?'

'She's still at Larch, too. I left her in my room and told her to wait for me there.' She looked at the superintendent and said, a little less brusquely, 'I think it would be a good idea if those two girls moved into Larch. Rosie leaving has left us with a free bed, and I can make space for one more.' Mrs Watson went on, pressing her advantage, 'Those girls have had a bad start with Mrs Garfield. If you are going to get rid of her, all the girls in Oak will have to move into other cottages until you find a suitable replacement, so I'll take Rita and Daisy.'

There had been just the faintest emphasis on the word 'suitable', which was not lost on Mrs Manton, and her lips tightened before she said, 'I will decide where each child will go, if the necessity arises.'

Mrs Watson remained adamant. With her dark blue eyes fixed on her employer, she said firmly, 'The necessity has already arisen, Mrs Manton. My ultimatum stands, and part of my conditions are that Rita and Daisy move into Larch. I shall keep them both for the rest of the day, by which time you will have made your decision. Should you decide to keep Mrs Garfield on, I will leave tomorrow morning, and I will report the happenings here to the authorities.'

'This is blackmail,' snapped Mrs Manton.

'If you like,' agreed Mrs Watson. 'But if she stays, I go. And if I stay, there are to be no more "cellars" in any of the houses. No child should be treated as Rita Stevens was yesterday.'

'Rita Stevens was defiant,' Mrs Manton retorted, 'she deserved to be punished.'

'Very possibly,' concurred Mrs Watson, 'but her punishment was extreme and unacceptable.'

'I am the superintendent here,' said Mrs Manton, 'and I'll be the judge of that.'

'Exactly,' replied Mrs Watson equably, 'that's what I'm asking you to do. If you think Mrs Garfield's drunkenness is acceptable and that she chose a suitable punishment for a little girl, far from home, who'd just lost her sister, then you keep her on as a house-mother. But you know what I'll do if that is your decision.' She gave a half-smile and added, 'I must get back to Larch and make sure the girls are ready to go to church.'

Daphne considered Mrs Watson's ultimatum again now. Damn the woman! Why had she ever employed her? Mrs Manton had made some enquiries and discovered that the so-called 'Mrs' Delia Watson was an unmarried mother whose employers had thrown her out when they'd found out about the child. She had moved from place to place, but then a few months later the child had been found dead in his cot. An investigation proved nothing against the mother, but she had remained under a cloud, and no respectable household would employ her. Mrs Manton took the risk, because Mrs Watson was desperate for a job and she came cheap. In the months that she'd been at Laurel Farm, she'd proved herself a competent house-mother. But now? Now she was holding Mrs Manton to ransom and the superintendent bitterly regretted taking her on. She knew Joe was right. They couldn't risk the authorities being informed and descending on the place. She would have to give in to the woman's blackmail and sack Mrs Garfield. She sighed. Emily had warned her that Rita Stevens was a troublesome child, and she was quite right! Rita had been nothing but trouble from the moment she arrived. She gave another sigh and made her decision. Mrs Garfield would have to go, with all the upheaval that would cause, and Rita and Daisy would stay in Larch Cottage.

After a quick breakfast she went across to Oak to make sure the girls who lived there were ready for church. The buzz of conversation ceased as soon as she walked into the living room, and they looked at her fearfully.

'Mrs Garfield isn't well this morning,' she told them. 'Go over to central and put your shoes on, then line up with the others.'

'Please, Mrs Manton,' stammered Agnes. 'We think Rita is in the cellar and we can't find Daisy Smart.'

'Of course Rita isn't in the cellar,' snapped the superintendent. 'And I know where Daisy Smart is, so you don't have to worry about them. Now, off you go, or you'll be late.'

The girls scurried away to find their shoes, and Mrs Manton closed the door behind them, drawing the bolt. Looking out of the window to check they'd all gone she went through into Mrs Garfield's room. The house-mother still lay on the floor, still snoring.

'You stupid woman!' Mrs Manton told the inert form. 'You had a cushy number here, and now you'll have to go.' As she left the room, she removed the key and locked the door from the outside. She did not want a hungover house-mother wandering round the property when they came home from church.

Everyone was ready for the walk to the church when she returned to central. She crossed to Mrs Watson asking softly, 'Where are Rita and Daisy?'

'Rita's in bed, and Daisy is sitting in my room. I've given her some mending to finish before I get back. It'll keep her busy enough.'

Mrs Manton nodded. She didn't tell Mrs Watson what her decision had been, but simply walked to the head of the line, gave the signal and they all set out for church.

Daisy watched the line of girls disappear down the road, and then, tossing aside the sock she was mending, went in search of Rita. Rita was watching from the window as well.

'You all right, Reet?' Daisy asked as she came into the dorm.

'Yes, course I am,' said Rita. 'She put me in Rosie's bed and told me to stay here till they get back from church.' She suddenly realized that Daisy ought to have gone with the others. 'Why ain't you gone?'

''Cos she left me in her room with a stack of mending to do,' replied Daisy.

'Did you see if Ma Gar was with them? I couldn't see from here.'

'Probably was,' said Daisy, 'not sure. Why?'

''Cos I got to go back to Oak and fetch something... and I need your help.'

Daisy looked apprehensive. 'Don't want to go back there if I don't have to,' she said. 'I don't want to bump into Ma Gar. I'm going to be in enough trouble for letting you out.'

'Don't think you will,' Rita told her. 'Mrs Watson said things were going to be all right and not to worry.'

'All right for her,' groaned Daisy, 'but she ain't the one going to face Ma Gar.'

'Well, I'm going back anyway,' Rita said firmly. 'I got to fetch something.'

'What?' demanded Daisy. 'What you got to fetch?'

'Something I hid,' Rita said, unwilling to say it was Knitty in case Daisy really didn't come with her. 'Something of Rosie's. You going to come and really help me or not?'

'S'pose so,' agreed Daisy reluctantly.

They slipped out of the house and hurried over to Oak, hoping that everyone had gone to church. There didn't seem to be anyone about, and they crept up to the front door.

'It's locked,' Rita hissed in dismay. 'We can't get in.'

'We come out the back door before,' Daisy reminded her. 'P'raps it's still open.'

Rita was relieved when the back door opened. Daisy had

hoped it that would be locked. She was still terrified of being confronted by Ma Gar.

Rita led the way back along the passage towards the bathroom. 'In here,' she said.

'In the *toilet*?' gasped Daisy. 'What for?'

'You'll see,' answered Rita, and pulled the door closed behind them. 'I hid him in the cistern.'

'Hid who?' Daisy was bemused. 'Rita, what are we doing here?'

Rita climbed up onto the lavatory seat and reached up. She could touch the open-topped cistern all right, but there was no way she could reach high enough to put her hand inside.

'That's no good,' she said. 'Wait a minute.' She hurried out to the broom cupboard in the passage and returned a moment later with a stepladder. 'Hold this steady,' she said, and as Daisy put her foot on the bottom rung, she climbed to the top.

'Reet, what are you doing?' demanded Daisy.

'Hid something in here,' panted Rita, balancing precariously on the top step and reaching her hand into the cistern. Her fingers found the sodden Knitty, and grasping him as tightly as she could, she dragged him, dripping, from his hiding place.

'Hey,' cried Daisy, 'you're soaking me.' She let go of the steps and they wobbled violently and Rita jumped to the floor as they crashed against the wall. The sound echoed round the house, and the girls froze in terror, but no one appeared.

'What are we going to do about this mess?' Daisy pointed to the pool of water on the floor.

'Nothing,' said Rita, picking up Knitty and squeezing him so that more water poured from his sodden body. 'Come on, let's go.' Moments later the steps were back in the cupboard and they were creeping into the kitchen.

As they approached the kitchen door they heard a loud banging. Daisy clutched Rita. 'It's Ma Gar,' she whispered. The banging came again, and then they heard someone shouting.

'Scarper!' hissed Daisy.

'No, wait!' Rita grabbed her arm. 'Listen!'

'Let me out,' came the shout. 'I'll thrash the lot of you, you little sluts. Let me out!'

'Come *on*, Reet,' begged Daisy.

'Just a minute, someone's locked her in!' Rita exulted. 'Some brave girl's locked her in.'

'Yes, and I ain't going to be here when she breaks the door down,' Daisy told her, and shot out of the back door. With a gleeful grin Rita turned and clutching the still-dripping Knitty in her arms, scooted after her.

When they reached Larch, they went back into the dorm. Rita leaned out of the window and gave Knitty another squeeze before leaving him on the outside windowsill to dry in the sun, then she went back along the passage to the kitchen.

'Reet!' cried Daisy in dismay. 'What you doing *now*?'

'Back in a min,' called Rita, and returned carrying a pointed kitchen knife.

'Cripes, Reet.' Daisy stared at her friend. 'What you gonna do with that?'

'This,' replied Rita, and Daisy watched in horror as Rita pulled the bedclothes off the bed and up-ended the mattress. With sudden vigour, she stabbed the mattress, slitting the worn and faded ticking with the point of the knife. The shabby material ripped apart easily, exposing a thin layer of crushed kapok. Rita reached inside and, pulling out a handful of the stuffing, she took her precious journal containing the picture of Daddy she'd brought from Oak that morning, and slid it into the hole. Carefully she replaced the stuffing and then put the mattress back onto the bed, the ripped side resting on the wire springs of the bed frame.

Daisy watched the whole process open-mouthed.

'You won't tell,' Rita said to her. It was a statement, not a question, and Daisy nodded.

'Course not.'

'When I got Knitty dry, I'll put him in there, an' all,' Rita said. She gave Daisy a grin. 'You and me's best mates, Dais. We'll look out for each other in this place. Now we better get your mending finished, before that lot get back.'

When Mrs Watson came in from church, she went straight to see how Rita was doing. She found her sitting up in bed, mending a hole in the sleeve of a cardigan. Sitting beside the bed was Daisy, sewing up the hem of some overalls.

'Daisy Smart,' she exclaimed, 'I thought I told you to wait in my sitting room.'

'Sorry, miss,' Rita said before Daisy could answer. 'It's my fault, I felt a bit funny, so I asked her to come up and sit with me.'

'Did you, now?' Mrs Watson said wryly. She was coming to realize that these two girls would stick together, and she found that she respected them for it. She was determined that, if she still had a job at the end of the day, they should be transferred to Larch, so that they would be under her care.

She was outraged at the way Rita had been punished. She had no problem with disciplining girls who were disobedient, indeed she knew that obedience to authority and conformity to rules were necessary if one was to get on in life, but she also liked to see the sparks of independence and courage she'd seen in Rita, and to a lesser extent in Daisy. It would be wrong to extinguish those. The girls in Larch lived under the same strict regime as those in the other cottages, their daily routine was as strenuous and their work as hard, but they were allowed a certain leeway in behaviour. They were allowed to chat during meals and in the dorms before lights out. Mrs Watson had found some old packs of cards, a snakes and ladders board and a draughts set, and she encouraged them to play games in the living room when they'd finished their homework, sometimes even playing with them. She had collected a small selection of books, and occasionally she read to the younger ones. She had taken the job of house-mother, as Mrs Manton knew, because she was desperate, but having taken it, she was the sort of woman who gave it her best shot. House-mother. To Delia Watson it was the second half of her title which was important. Since taking up her position, several things about Laurel Farm had worried her. She knew it was no good confronting Mrs Manton head-on, but she did feel that from the inside she might be able to influence and alter some of the practices; they had certainly softened in her own house. She knew the other house-mothers regarded her as soft, but she didn't care. Her girls usually gave little trouble, and she was always prepared to listen if they came to her, as she had listened to Rita the previous day. This morning, however, she knew that she couldn't ignore what had happened to Rita. Once she had seen to Rita's immediate needs, she went straight to Oak to confront Mrs Garfield and what she'd found had sent her straight to Mrs Manton's front door.

As she sat in the sun that afternoon, thinking over the day, she wondered, not for the first time, what she would do if Mrs Manton called her bluff. No, not bluff, she told herself. If Mrs Garfield wasn't sacked, she, Delia Watson, would indeed leave at once and go to the authorities. She'd manage somehow, but what would happen to the girls in Larch if she had to leave? At that moment, one of the senior girls came running up.

'Please, Mrs Watson,' she puffed, 'Mrs Manton wants to see you over at her house. Straight away, she said.'

'All right, Diane, thank you.' Delia Watson stood up. 'Run back and tell her I'm on my way, will you?'

'Yes, Mrs Watson.' The girl streaked off like a hare, her bare feet thudding on the path as she went.

Mrs Watson did not go straight over to central; first she went indoors to check on Rita. She was still sitting up in bed, Daisy beside her, as they both tackled the mountain of mending Mrs Watson had given them.

Assured now that Rita had in fact suffered no lasting effects from her incarceration, Mrs Watson followed Diane more slowly through the trees. When she knocked on the Mantons' door it was opened by Joe who gave her a smile, and said, 'Ah, Mrs Watson, come in. You'll find my wife in her office.' He stood aside to let her pass and then stepped out of the door himself, adding, 'Off to feed the chooks.'

Mrs Watson went through the house to the office at the back. She knocked on the door, and at the sharp 'Come!' went in.

The superintendent was sitting behind her desk, apparently working on some papers. She glanced up as Mrs Watson came in. 'Ah, there you are,' she said, 'please sit down.'

Mrs Watson took a seat on the upright chair in front of the desk. For a moment neither of them spoke. In the end it was the superintendent who broke the silence.

'I have spoken to Mrs Garfield,' she began, 'and she deeply regrets the events of yesterday.'

I'm sure she does, thought Mrs Watson. But she did not speak, simply sat and waited for her employer to continue.

'However,' Mrs Manton went on, 'I have told her that such behaviour is unacceptable and she must leave Laurel Farm by tomorrow evening. In the meantime the girls who live in Oak Cottage will be assigned new places this evening. I hope that this...' she hesitated, '... arrangement will meet with your approval. Of course, no mention will be made of why Mrs Garfield has left, either to the other staff or the children. It will be announced she's been called away to look after her sick mother.'

Very generous of you, thought Mrs Watson, but all she said was, 'Since they are already in my house, I will keep Rita and Daisy in Larch from now on... as agreed.'

Mrs Manton gave her a long look, as if assessing whether it was worth making an issue of such a small added victory, and decided against it. 'Agreed,' she said. 'If Rita is still in bed, you'd better send Daisy over to Oak to collect their things.'

'I will,' replied Mrs Watson, adding as she got to her feet, 'but I don't expect there's much for them to bring, do you?' And with this she walked out of the room closing the door quietly behind her.

'Insufferable woman!' exploded Mrs Manton to the closed door. 'Just you wait.' She got to her feet and went through to her living room, where she flopped into a chair, feeling suddenly exhausted. It had been one hell of a day, she thought, and Mrs Garfield's reaction to her dismissal had been quite extreme.

'You must see that I can't continue to employ you—' she'd begun, but was interrupted.

'I can't think why not,' snarled Mrs Garfield, 'I was only doing what you'd ordered me to.'

Mrs Manton did not respond but simply told Mrs Garfield that she had to be out of the house by the end of the next day.

The house-mother had been almost apoplectic. 'You told me to deal with that child!' she shrieked. 'You told me you wanted no more trouble from her.'

'Agreed,' Mrs Manton said mildly, 'but I didn't want her dead, either.'

'But she ain't dead, is she?' screamed the woman. 'She's alive and well and making accusations about me.'

'You were drunk,' said Mrs Manton flatly, 'I saw you myself. I told you, neither Mrs Watson nor I could rouse you. Rita Stevens had nothing to do with that.'

'I did what you told me to do,' reiterated Mrs Garfield, 'and now you want to sack me! Turn me off without a reference!'

'I didn't say that,' said her employer. 'But I can't keep you here. If the authorities heard that you'd been dead drunk while in charge of a house full of children, and I hadn't sacked you, they'd close us down without a second thought. Both my husband and I are agreed on this—'

'Your husband!' sneered Mrs Garfield. 'He's just a lapdog. He don't make the decisions round this place.'

'Maybe not,' agreed Mrs Manton smoothly, 'but he concurs with them, and this one in particular.'

'You bitch!' shrieked Mrs Garfield, who, realizing there was no reprieve, gave no heed to her language.

'You will be paid up to date,' went on Mrs Manton as if she had not spoken, 'and be off the premises by the time the children get home from school tomorrow.' She stared across at the enraged Mrs Garfield. 'And should you need a reference, you may write to me for one.'

'Stuff your reference,' snarled Mrs Garfield.

'As you wish,' replied the superintendent, and with her dignity unruffled, she turned and left the room, closing the door gently behind her.

The relief with which Rita and Daisy greeted the news that they were to stay in Larch Cottage was immense. They were back sharing a dorm with Joan, whom they both liked, and though Rita felt a physical ache when she thought of Rosie, alone in a strange place with strange people, there were times when she was so busy that there was no room for Rosie in her thoughts. Knitty had been retrieved from the windowsill and while the other girls were in the bathroom, had been stowed, still slightly damp, in the mattress.

Mrs Watson had taken the two girls aside and told them that from now on they would be living in Larch. 'I've given you a little leeway today,' she said, 'but from now on I expect complete obedience from you, do you understand?' She fixed them with a stern eye as she waited for their 'Yes, Mrs Watson'.

'I hope you do. Tomorrow you'll be starting school with the others, and I expect to hear that you're model pupils. Any reports of bad behaviour and you'll be in more trouble. Understand?'

'Yes, Mrs Watson.'

'Good. Now Rita, you can come and collect clothes for both of you, and then you can get dressed and come down for tea. Daisy, run over to Oak and collect anything of yours and Rita's that's there. You needn't worry,' she smiled as she saw the look of horror on Daisy's face, 'you won't see Mrs Garfield.' When Daisy didn't look convinced she said briskly, 'Come along, Daisy, do as you're told.'

Unwillingly, Daisy went back into Oak, and found a general hubbub as all the other girls were there doing the same thing.

'Which cottage are you going to?' asked Audrey when Daisy came in.

'Larch.'

'Lucky you,' said Carol. 'We've got to go into Pine, with the babies.'

'Better than here,' Daisy said.

'Where's Rita, then?' demanded Audrey as she watched Daisy gather up her toothbrush and flannel from her locker, and then collect Rita's from hers.

'Back in Larch. She ain't well.'

'Bet she was there all the time,' Audrey said belligerently. 'Bet she weren't in the cellar at all.'

'She was, too,' retorted Daisy. 'I let her out, and then Mrs Watson looked after her.'

'Bit of a sissy, if you ask me,' Audrey said. 'She ain't the only one's had the cellar treatment. Agnes had it and—'

'Yeah,' interrupted Daisy, 'and look at her now. She's scared of her own shadow.' She went to the beds that had been theirs and pulled off the single blankets that covered them. Rolling them carefully together, she tucked them under her arm.

'Where're you going with those?' asked Carol, watching open-mouthed. 'You can't take them, they ain't yours.'

'Nobody else needs them,' Daisy pointed out. 'Nobody ain't going to be sleeping in here, are they? Take yours to Pine, I would.'

'That's stealing,' announced Audrey righteously. 'You won't half get it in the neck when they see you walking off with those.'

'Yeah,' echoed Carol, 's'posing we tell!'

'Then,' replied Daisy as she looked round to check that there was nothing else of use she could take, 'you'd be just plain stupid.' As she passed the lavatories she glanced in; one of them had an extremely wet floor. Daisy gave a grin. Reet was a card, and no mistake.

The routine in Larch turned out to be virtually the same as in Oak.

'Our turn first in the bathroom,' cried Sandra, as they hurriedly stripped their beds, folding the bedclothes neatly as they'd been taught back in Laurel House. 'Come on, you lot, get in there before the other dorm do.'

When she'd washed her face and hands, Rita remade her bed, tucking the extra blanket in carefully, hoping it wouldn't be noticed if there was dormitory inspection. Rita and Daisy had each been given one of the grey checked frocks that all the girls wore to school, and they put them on, leaving the grubby weekend overalls in a basket, ready for someone to launder later on.

Chapter 24

'For Christ's sake, Edna, shut that child up,' growled Gerald Waters as he accelerated away from Laurel Farm. The spinning car wheels threw up a cloud of dust as they sped down the dirt track leading to Carrabunna and the main Sydney road beyond.

'Hush now, Rosie,' Edna said as she struggled to hold the child squirming in her arms. 'Be quiet, dear, you don't want to upset Daddy now, do you?'

But Rosie, crimson-faced and her cheeks wet with tears, didn't stop, couldn't stop and went on bawling, 'I don't want you! I don't want you! Go away! I want Reet. Where's Reet?'

'Come along now, Rosie,' Edna tried again. 'Calm down, there's a good girl.'

Rosie didn't calm down and once they had passed through Carrabunna Gerald suddenly slammed on the brakes and the car screeched to a halt. Without a word he got out, opened the back door and reaching in, dragged the little girl from her new mother's arms. He pulled her clear of the car and then, shouting 'Shut up! Shut up! You hear me?' he shook her, hard and long till her head flopped and the screaming stopped.

'That's more like it,' he snarled. 'Now you listen to me, young lady. I'll have no more of that disgraceful noise, understand? Start that row again and you'll get a hiding.' Then he thrust Rosie back into the car and slammed the door behind her. Edna gathered the shaking child into her arms and held her tight, crooning softly to her and stroking her hair.

Rosie's screams had stopped, but heaving sobs still shook her body as she buried her hot, damp face into Edna's neck.

Exhausted by the events of the morning and lulled by the motion of the car, Rosie finally fell asleep, only waking again when the car stopped outside a roadside café. She opened her eyes, for a moment forgetting where she was, and then she saw the frightening man getting out of the car, and she shrank back against Edna's shoulder again.

As he opened the back door of the car, Edna said, 'Look, Gerald, you've terrified the poor child!'

'Well, she needs to learn to do as she's told,' he muttered. Then he held out his hand and twisting his mouth into a smile, said, 'Come along now, Rose. You must be hungry, let's find something to eat.'

'Out you get, Rosie,' encouraged Edna. 'I expect you're hungry, and we're going to have some eggs and bacon and sausages now.'

Once out of the car, Edna took Rosie's hand and they went into the café. The promised food appeared on the table and Edna helped Rosie cut up her food saying, 'If you eat all that like a good girl, you can have some ice cream after. Would you like that?' When Rosie didn't answer Edna went on, 'You like ice cream, don't you?'

Rosie nodded.

'I thought you did,' Edna said. 'Eat up then.' She turned to Gerald who was just finishing, wiping round his plate with a piece of bread. 'Will you order up the ice cream, Daddy?'

'Ice cream for our little girl, coming up,' he cried, jovial now that Rosie was behaving herself, and he waved to the woman at the counter to bring them each a bowl of ice cream.

Somewhere in the back of her mind Rosie could hear Rita's voice saying, 'He's not my dad,' but looking across at the frightening face of the man opposite, she said nothing and went on eating her sausages. They were nice, and she did want ice cream.

'Thank you, Daddy,' Edna enthused when the dessert came.

She beamed at Rosie. 'Aren't you a lucky girl to have such a kind daddy?'

They finally reached Fryford, where the Waters lived, in the late afternoon. Their house was in a quiet street, one of a row of villas. There was a window on either side of the front door and another perched above it under a shingled gable. Mr Waters drew into the kerb and switched off the engine.

'Here we are,' he said, 'home at last.'

Edna took Rosie into the house. 'This is where we live, Rosie,' she said. 'This is your home now. Isn't it nice? Look, we've got a yard out the back where you can play. Now come upstairs and I'll show you your bedroom.' She led the way up a narrow staircase to the floor above where there were two bedrooms. The one at the front looked out through the gabled window onto the street below, while the one at the back, much smaller, had a little window looking out across the single storey scullery roof below and onto the small square of garden beyond.

'Here we are,' Edna said brightly, leading Rosie into the tiny bedroom. 'This is your room.' She went to the window and drawing aside the flimsy curtains, threw it open. 'Isn't it nice?'

Rosie stood by the door and stared into the room. A wooden bed stood along one wall, a chest of drawers topped with a bowl and jug stood against another, and there was a small chair in the corner. Though the room was hot and stuffy, it was stark and unwelcoming.

'I wish Reet was here,' Rosie said, her lip beginning to tremble again as she looked at the cold hard bed where she must sleep alone. 'I want Reet.'

'Well, you can't have her,' said a sharp voice behind her. Gerald had come upstairs carrying her small suitcase. 'You must forget her. You live with us now.'

That night Rosie lay in bed in her new bedroom and with her face under the pillow, cried herself to sleep. She was entirely alone, no Rita, no Daisy, not even Knitty to cuddle as exhaustion overtook her and she finally fell asleep.

Next morning she was given breakfast and then the three of

them walked to the nearby church. The only thing suitable to wear was the rose-patterned dress, and so Rosie was dressed in that.

'Tomorrow,' Edna promised her, 'we'll go shopping you and I. We'll get you some decent clothes, not something made out of curtains.'

Church was boring, but Rosie was used to that. Numerous Sundays spent in church since she'd been taken from Ship Street had taught her to sit still and quiet however bored she was, until it was over and they could emerge into the sunshine again. Outside the church she found herself the centre of attention. People came up to the Waters, smiling and nodding.

'Is this the little girl you're adopting?'

'What a generous thing to do, taking a child like this from an orphanage!'

'What a pretty little girl, such lovely fair hair.'

Edna had spent some time brushing Rosie's hair and had tied it back off her face with a ribbon. Rosie liked the ribbon, and she liked people saying she was pretty, so she smiled at the lady who was reaching out to touch her curls.

'What a lovely smile,' said the lady. 'Aren't you a lucky girl to have been chosen by these kind people.'

The minister was standing by the door, and he came over and shook Gerald by the hand. 'Well done, Mr Waters,' he said. 'A truly charitable act.' He reached down and chucked Rosie under the chin. 'And what's your name, little girl?'

'Rosie,' she whispered shyly.

'Well, Rosie, I hope you're truly grateful for the kindness of your new parents.'

The next few days passed in a whirl. Edna took Rosie on the promised shopping trip, and the little chest of drawers soon held new underclothes, a blouse and skirt, a dress and a cardigan. She was fitted with new shoes, worn over new white socks. Her rose-patterned dress, though still wearable, was pushed to the bottom of a drawer, the last remnant of her previous life.

One evening Gerald came home carrying a small teddy bear

which he pushed into her arms, saying gruffly, 'Thought you might like to have this.' Rosie hugged it to her, and from then on every night she fell asleep with the bear, named Bear, tucked under her arm, just as Knitty had been.

The Waters insisted that she call them Mummy and Daddy; if she didn't, they appeared not to have heard her, and she soon learned that her life was easier if she did what she was told. Rosie had never liked being in trouble, and without Rita to protect her she simply accepted what was happening.

'I always wanted a daughter called Jean,' Edna told her one day, 'so Daddy and I have decided that's what we'll call you from now on.'

Rosie looked confused. 'I'm called Rosie.'

'No, darling, you *were* called Rosie, but now you're called Jean.'

She was enrolled at her new school as Jean Waters, and so everyone there called her Jean. At first, often, she didn't realize she was being spoken to, and was scolded for not answering, but in time she got used to being Jean, and the name Rosie, like the rose-patterned dress, was consigned to her past life and almost forgotten.

'Please will you remember that Jean has been adopted?' Edna said to the principal on her first morning. 'Everything here is a bit new to her. I'll bring her to and from school just until she's used to it all.'

Rosie liked her new school. She liked her teacher, Miss Hughes. She liked Edna, but she was still afraid of Gerald. He had a way of grabbing her from behind and crushing her against him that she found frightening. She'd struggle to pull free and he'd hold on even more tightly saying, 'What, not got a cuddle for your dad?' He laughed as he said it, but she hated the way he held her and nuzzled the back of her neck with his moustache. Mummy laughed too, and said, 'How Daddy loves his little girl!'

Rosie settled in at school quite quickly. Always eager to please, she did as she was told and behaved herself well in the classroom. The first sign of trouble came, however, a few months after she arrived. The children were asked to tell the class about their families. Each child stood up and spoke for a minute or two, telling of mums and dads, brothers and sisters, family pets. Miss Hughes left Rosie till last, because she was aware that Rosie had only recently been adopted and didn't have a family to talk about. When it finally came to be Rosie's turn, she said gently, 'Now then, Jean, can you tell us about your family, you've got a new mummy and daddy, I think, haven't you? But no brothers or sisters.'

Rosie looked at her as if surprised. 'I got a sister,' she said. 'She's called Reet.'

'No, Jean, I don't think you have,' said Miss Hughes. 'You've come to live with Mr and Mrs Waters, haven't you?'

'They took me away,' Rosie said with sudden recollection. 'They pushed me into the car and they left Reet behind.' She began to look wildly round the classroom and with tears flooding down her cheeks called out, 'Where's Reet? I want Reet. I don't like it here. I want Reet.'

The other children stared at her, round-eyed, and Miss Hughes sent one of them to fetch the principal, unable to stop Jean from crying, from calling for someone called 'Reet', from shouting that she didn't like her new home.

She was quickly hustled from the room and made to wait in the principal's office until Edna came to fetch her.

'You're a naughty, ungrateful girl,' Edna scolded. 'Daddy and I have given you a lovely home, and you're telling people you don't like it here. You're a lucky girl that we took you away from that place and gave you a proper home.'

Gerald, when he came home that night, did more than scold her. 'She's got to learn who's boss in this house,' he said to Edna when he heard what had happened. 'And I'm going to teach her.'

'Of course, Gerald,' Edna said. 'You're quite right.' And she waited down in the living room while Gerald went upstairs to find Rosie. Moments later when Rosie's screams echoed through the house, Edna switched on the radio to drown them out.

From then on, Rosie, now Jean, walked in terror of her new father. She withdrew into her own little world, only emerging to do as she was bid, to appear to the world as the spoilt adopted daughter of two kind and generous parents. Beautifully dressed, she appeared at church, sat quietly through the services, spoke only when spoken to. A dutiful, obedient daughter.

Some weeks later, Edna had gone to a meeting at the church to help plan the annual Harvest Festival supper. Rosie was already in bed, tucked in with a kiss by Edna before she left, but as so often, she lay awake, listening to the sounds that came from downstairs. Sometimes she would hear her father come up the stairs and pause outside her room, apparently listening to hear if she had gone to sleep. This particular evening, she heard his feet on the stairs, and lay as still as she could waiting for him to go back down, but he did not. She heard the door open and kept her eyes screwed up tight, so he would think that she was asleep, but he did not simply close the door again and go away as she had hoped. He came into the room and stood by her bed.

'Jean,' he said. 'I know you're not asleep. Open your eyes.'

Not daring to disobey, Rosie opened her eyes and in the faded light still coming in through her little window, found him staring down at her.

'I see,' he said with a smile. 'Pretending again. Never mind, you are awake, so you can give your dad a cuddle, can't you?' He saw Rosie shrink back in fear and his hand snaked out, pulling the covers off her bed and dumping them on the floor. 'Now then,' he said, his voice still jovial, 'let's have a look at you.' He paused for a moment as if listening, then he crossed to the door. 'Don't want Mummy walking in to spoil the fun, do we?' he said, as he turned the key.

Chapter 25

Life in Larch was a great improvement on life in Oak and Rita and Daisy soon settled into the familiar routine. On that first morning, after breakfast, which was shared by Mrs Watson sitting at the head of the table, there were the usual chores to be done. Daisy and Rita were set to making more of the ubiquitous egg sandwiches, which had to be wrapped in paper and taken to school as packed dinner. As well as her sandwich, each girl was given an apple. Rita discovered later that girls from other houses were not as lucky. It was a rush to get everything done, and Mrs Watson was soon clapping her hands and chivvying them over to central to put on their socks and shoes for the walk into town.

Carrabunna School was housed in a long low building set round three sides of a square. There were two blocks of classrooms and a hall used for gym, dancing and any school gatherings, an outside toilet block, and in the middle was a sandy playground. As they came into the yard, the English girls saw there were boys as well as girls playing in the dusty space.

'Didn't know there was boys too,' Daisy said with interest. She watched a game of football being played at one end of the yard, and was soon hopping from foot to foot, longing to join in. 'D'you think I could play?' she wondered.

Rita, who was familiar with boys' playground games, laughed. 'Not a hope. Boys don't let girls play.'

She and Daisy were standing with the other new girls just inside the gate, watching the other children and wondering what to do and where to go. After a few moments Irene came over.

'You lot got to come inside with me,' she said, and she shepherded the new girls into the hall.

Daisy looked round her at the wooden ribs on one wall and the three thick ropes looped up to the ceiling. Through the window she could see the rest of the children out at play before morning school.

'This place don't look too bad,' she muttered to Rita. 'I'd love to have a go at climbing them ropes.'

'D'you know how?' asked Rita in surprise.

'No, but I will.'

The nine girls sat down on the floor and waited. The teacher who came in was a small woman, dumpy, with grey hair cut short, rather like a man's. Her face was round, with a short snub nose and a receding chin. She wore round-rimmed glasses, but through these stared a pair of piercing blue eyes, convincing the seated girls that she was not a person to be trifled with.

'I am Miss Headley,' she announced when she had everyone's attention, 'and I am the principal of this school.'

'What's a principal?' asked someone in a whisper.

'The principal is what you would call a headmistress, back home in England,' she answered, although the question had clearly not been intended for her ears. 'Now then, I'm going to call your names and when you answer I will tell you which classroom you'll be in. Remember the number, and when I dismiss you that is where you're to go. If there is no one in there, you simply wait for the rest of the class to come in from the yard.'

Rita, Daisy and Joan, all being much the same age, were sent to Room 3. The room looked out on the playground, but the four rows of ten desks faced the blackboard and the teacher's table, with their backs to the window. They were greeted by their teacher, Miss Carson, who told them where to sit, and moments later a bell rang, heralding the start of morning school. Another thirty children filed into the room and went to their places, boys on one side of the room, girls on the other. Rita found she had Audrey from Oak on one side of her and Carol on the other, and recognized several others from Laurel Farm, including Elizabeth from Pine and Jane from Elm.

Miss Carson introduced the new arrivals to the rest of the class, who looked at them with interest. They'd come all the way from England... they might as well have come from the moon.

Rita had never had much problem with her school work, though she preferred reading and writing to arithmetic. She knew her tables, and so found the multiplication sums they'd been set quite easy. She could see that Daisy was struggling, but there was complete silence in the room, so she couldn't whisper any help. When the answers were given, Rita found that she'd only got one mistake.

'This is very good work, Rita.' Miss Carson had to glance at the name she'd written on the book to remember which new girl it was. 'Well done. I hope all your work is as good as this.'

Daisy had done the worst and was warned that she'd be tested on all her tables at the beginning of next week. 'That means I got to learn them all in just a week,' she complained to Rita, when they were out in the yard for the mid-morning break.

'Don't worry,' Rita said comfortingly, 'I'll learn them to you.'

After play it was time for composition, a subject Rita really enjoyed. They were told to write about what they'd done at the weekend. Most of the girls were soon hard at work, but both Daisy and Rita hesitated; Daisy because she found any sort of creative writing difficult, Rita because she couldn't write about what had happened to her over the past two days.

'Come along, you two,' chided Miss Carson, 'get writing. You haven't got all day.'

'Don't know what to put, miss,' grumbled Daisy. 'We only just got here.'

'Then write about how you came,' suggested Miss Carson. 'I don't really mind what you write about, as long as you write something for me to read.' That made things easier, and Rita wrote about the ship and the journey out from England. Having recorded most of it in her journal already, the words began to flow and she was still writing when the bell rang for the dinner break, and she had to hand the work in.

The girls were all collected into the hall where tables and benches had been set up, and there they sat, eating their sandwiches. Some of the local children went home for their midday meal, but there were one or two from outlying farms who joined the Laurel Farm girls. One of them was a boy from their class called Patrick, a large freckle-faced boy with flaming red hair that stood up in an untidy tuft on the back of his head. When he'd entered the classroom, Daisy recognized him at once from the earlier football game. Now, she went over and sat down next to him.

'Hallo,' she said. 'I'm Daisy. Can I come and play football with you afterwards?'

Patrick looked at her with undisguised astonishment. 'Football's for boys,' he said at last.

'I can play,' Daisy said, although she'd never kicked a football in her life. 'I'm good at football.'

'Well, you ain't playing with us,' Patrick said decidedly, 'we don't play with girls and we don't play with "homies".'

'I ain't a "homie",' Daisy told him hotly, not at all sure what he meant, but knowing it wasn't complimentary.

'Course you are,' he returned. 'All you lot from Laurel Farm's "homies". Wouldn't be in a home otherwise, would you? Stands to reason!'

'I ain't a "homie",' repeated Daisy. 'I just live there for now.'

''Spect you'll live there forever,' Patrick said. 'My ma says you wasn't wanted in England and you ain't wanted here, neither.' He turned his back on her and as soon as he'd wolfed down his sandwiches, he ran outside, leaving Daisy sitting by herself.

Rita went over and sat down beside her. 'Told you,' she said.

'Can't even pretend we don't come from Laurel Farm, can we,' Daisy said bitterly, 'not when we're all dressed like this.' She held out the skirt of her dress, looking down at its dull grey checks in disgust.

'Never mind, Dais, Miss Carson said it's PT this afternoon,'

Rita reminded her. 'You're good at that. Let's go and play tag in the yard, now. Come on!'

Rita was right, the first lesson that afternoon was PT, the only lesson for which Daisy showed any enthusiasm. Miss Carson led them out into the yard where she had placed bean-bags to mark a makeshift race track. Two children, Daniel and Frances, were appointed team captains and told to pick up teams. At first Daniel simply chose boys, and Frances, girls, but there were more girls than boys in the class, so in the end Daniel had to select a girl. He looked across at the four girls left, the three new girls and Carol. Patrick, already chosen, nudged him and pointed out Daisy. He shrugged; it clearly didn't matter to him which girl, they were all equally useless at running. He pointed a finger at Daisy.

'Her,' he said, and Daisy went across and stood with the boys' team. Rita was chosen by Frances, Joan went to Daniel, and Carol, flushed with mortification at being chosen last, to Frances.

'We'll have a relay first,' Miss Carson told them. 'When I blow my whistle it's twice round the circuit,' she indicated the bean-bags, 'and then touch the next one to go.'

The children lined up ready, and when the whistle went the first pair raced off round the makeshift track, encouraged by shrieks from their teammates. As the race progressed it was clear that it was going to be a close finish, the girls' team in the lead. Then it was Daisy's turn, the last to go for Daniel's team. She was off like a hare, her feet pounding the yard as she chased after Carol, lumbering along half a lap ahead of her.

'Go on, Daisy!' screamed Joan, the only one in her team who knew her name. Immediately the boys joined in, and soon the whole team was bellowing, 'Go on Daisy!' as she overtook the stumbling Carol and hurtled over the finishing line, several yards ahead. Daniel's team cheered, delighted with their victory. Daisy, flushed with success, grinned round at her team-mates, but none of the boys spoke to her.

Joan went over and clapped her on the back. 'Well done, Dais. You won.'

Carol, red-faced and hot, glowered at her as she finally crossed the finishing line.

'Why do we always get Carol?' one of the other girls was heard to ask. Miss Carson looked across to see who had spoken, but couldn't tell.

'Remind me next time that Carol will be a team captain,' was all she said, and Carol gave her grumbling team a look of triumph. Next time she'd be doing the choosing.

There were several more races before they went back inside for the last lesson of the afternoon, and Daisy ran flat out in all of them, never flagging, so that Daniel's team won every one. The boys all cheered for her as she was running, but once the race was over they ignored her.

'You was great!' Rita enthused as they went back inside. 'You was faster than anyone else, even them boys.'

'Yeah,' said Daisy glumly, 'but they still don't want me.'

At the end of the afternoon, all the Laurel Farm girls lined up together for the walk home. Miss Carson had set them some spellings to learn for homework, but Daisy was more worried about the tables she had to master before the next Monday.

'Which ones *do* you know?' asked Rita as they waited for some of the older girls to appear.

Daisy looked uncertain. 'Twice times?' she offered.

'Say it then.'

'What, now?'

'Yes, now,' insisted Rita. 'Come on, I can't help you if you don't try.'

Daisy shrugged and began to chant, 'Twice one is two, twice two is four...' She got to the end without a mistake, and Rita punched her cheerfully on the arm.

'Well, that's one you don't have to learn,' she said. 'Now the three times.' Daisy managed to get through it, and all the way home they chanted the fours, in time with their marching feet.

'If we do that each way, every day, you'll soon learn them,' Rita told her as they came in through the gate.

Tea was the main meal of the day, and Mrs Watson was in

the kitchen to supervise the preparation. She made sure that the vegetables brought in from the garden were properly washed and peeled, and though the mince for the cottage pie was extremely fatty, it was the best she could get, and properly cooked. After tea she set them all to do their homework, and when Rita had learned her spellings, Mrs Watson tested her.

'The Watchdog's OK,' Daisy said, as they lay in bed, warm under two blankets. 'We'll be all right here in Larch.'

'Hmm,' agreed Rita, smiling at the nickname Daisy had given Mrs Watson earlier in the day. It was a good one, she thought. Mrs Watson had certainly watched over them. She just wished Rosie was here for her to watch over too.

Chapter 26

After the first week at school, the days began to run into each other. There was a sameness about each day which made for extremely humdrum living. The routine was unchanging, and despite the severity of the regime, everyone knew what was expected of her, both at Laurel Farm and at school. In Larch, Mrs Watson didn't mind how they passed their short leisure hour at the end of the day. Most of them sat around and chatted, or played the games that Mrs Watson had scrounged from somewhere. Rita used the time to read, and it wasn't long before she had devoured the few books on the living room shelf. Every evening she sat up in bed and wrote her journal. She enjoyed recording the events of each day. She wrote about school and things that had happened at Laurel Farm, but she also wrote about the people around her, the other girls and the staff. And she wrote about Rosie, letting her sadness seep onto the page and ease the ache of her loss. Sometimes she wrote stories. She often thought of Paul Dawson, from the ship, and wondered if he was still writing stories as well. He had finally let her read some of his before they reached Sydney, and she'd thought they were very exciting.

Now that she didn't have to hide what she was doing, she tried her hand at similar stories. Rita thought they weren't as good as Paul's, but she enjoyed writing them, letting her imagination roam across the remembered places of home and the new and unfamiliar landscape that surrounded her now. Her stories were a means of escape from the gritty, grey days that made up her life, and she was never happier than chewing the end of her pencil trying to find the exact word she needed.

Rita had settled into school particularly well. She enjoyed the work, and though she was nothing like as keen as Daisy on the physical exercise, she was happy enough to join in the PT classes with everyone else. Miss Carson had quickly spotted that Rita was an intelligent child, with an enquiring mind; it delighted her, and she set out to foster that intelligence. Rita, Miss Carson saw, enjoyed learning for the sake of it, and it wasn't long before she was encouraging her to borrow books from the school book-shelf. She also noticed that Rita wrote well. From the first day, when she'd written about her journey out from England, Miss Carson had realized that this child had a creative talent which should be nurtured, and she encouraged her to continue record-ing her thoughts and ideas.

Mrs Watson had spotted Rita's potential as well, though she never singled her out for any special attention. Rita might be bright, but she was treated the same as everyone else. She knew Rita missed her sister, but there was nothing Mrs Watson could do about that; Rosie's adoption was something else that Rita must accept and get used to.

One evening a few weeks after Rita and Daisy had moved into Larch, it was Rita's turn to do the ironing and she was warming the iron when Mrs Watson came in and said, 'Ah, Rita. I've some ironing to be done as well. Please come and fetch it now.'

Rita didn't look very pleased. She thought there was enough in the basket already, but she obediently set the iron aside and followed the house-mother. There was, she knew, never any point in arguing with the Watchdog.

When they reached Mrs Watson's quarters, Rita followed her inside, and was surprised when she closed the door behind them.

'I've got something for you, Rita,' she said, 'but I'd rather the others didn't see it.' She fixed Rita with a firm gaze. 'Can I rely on you for that?'

Rita, who had no idea what she was going to be given, nodded. 'Yes, Mrs Watson.'

'Not even Daisy?'

Rita hesitated. She and Daisy had become inseparable. They had been close friends before, but since Daisy had rescued Rita from the cellar, and Rosie had been taken, Rita had shared everything with Daisy, and to Daisy it seemed that at last she had the sister she'd always wanted.

'I'm sorry, Rita,' said Mrs Watson, 'but I must insist. If I give you this, you mustn't show it to Daisy, all right?'

'All right,' Rita said, but she crossed her fingers behind her back.

'Well, I'm going to trust you,' said the house-mother. 'Here you are then,' and she handed Rita an envelope.

The letter had arrived that morning. Mrs Watson had been on her way into Carrabunna to buy some notepaper and stamps, and as she walked to the gate, Mrs Manton had shouted after her, asking her to collect the mail. When she got to the post office, she bought her own stamps and then asked if there was any post for Laurel Farm. Miss Drew, sitting as always behind the counter, swivelled round on her chair and reached into the Laurel Farm pigeon hole.

'Here you are,' she said. 'Not much, but there is one from England addressed to two of the kiddies. They'll like getting that, won't they?'

'I'm sure they will,' agreed Mrs Watson, even as she doubted they'd ever see it. She thanked Miss Drew and took the small bundle of letters. Glancing through them she found that all but one were addressed to Mrs Manton, most looking like bills. Only one was for anyone else, and that was addressed to *Miss Rita and Rosie Stevens*. Mrs Watson stared at the envelope for a moment before tucking it into her bag with the rest of the post.

She finished her errands and then walked slowly back up the lane to Laurel Farm, thinking hard. A letter for Rita... and Rosie. Too late for Rosie, but Rita? Who would have sent it, and how did they have the Carrabunna address? She knew that it was never given out. It was one of Miss Vanstone's strictest prohibitions. Once a child had been taken in by the

EVER-Care Trust, she lost all contact with anyone from her previous life; all ties cut, no further contact with friends or extended family. It was one of the things that Delia Watson most disliked about EVER-Care. To her it indicated a lack of humanity. She knew that many of the children in their care were, perhaps, better off at Laurel Farm, but she felt that cutting them off from everything known and familiar was cruel, leaving them with no roots or sense of identity. But, now, here was this letter for Rita.

It's got the right address on it, she thought, so Miss Vanstone must have allowed it to be sent. She took it out of her bag again and leaning on a field gate, scrutinized it once more. The names, *Miss Rita and Rosie Stevens*, were written in a neat hand, but the address underneath was an untidy scrawl, obviously written by someone different. It had a line of stamps all along the top, the postmark that cancelled them was London, and the date, over six weeks ago.

Mrs Watson had a lot of time for Rita. She knew her to be a courageous little girl, who had braved all that her short life had thrown at her. She thought of what Rita had told her about her family; that her mother had remarried, a baby brother, something about a grandmother? So, who could have written? The address was certainly written in an uneducated hand. Could it be the mother's? If so, surely the child had a right to read what her mother had written.

What am I going to do? she wondered. But in her heart she already knew. 'The address is right,' she spoke aloud, trying to convince herself, 'so it must have been given to the person who wrote the letter, and the only one who could have done that was Emily Vanstone. In which case, I can give it to Rita.'

If she gave the letter to Mrs Manton, she would insist on opening the letter first and might not pass it on. Rita might never know someone in England had written to her.

But, if I give it to Rita directly, Mrs Watson thought, and don't mention it to anyone else, there's no reason why Mrs Manton should ever know. Her decision made, Delia Watson put the letter back into her handbag, but in a different compartment from the rest of the post.

Her chance to give the letter privately to Rita came that very evening. She knew a moment's hesitation, as the girl waited expectantly. Was this a mistake? But looking at Rita's eager face, she stuck to her earlier decision and reaching into her bag, passed the letter across.

Rita took it, staring at it in surprise. 'Who's it from?' she asked.

'How should I know?' asked Mrs Watson briskly. 'I haven't opened it. It's your letter.'

Rita tore the envelope and extracted the letter. She took one look at the signature and gave a little cry.

'Well?' Mrs Watson couldn't contain her curiosity.

'It's from my gran,' whispered Rita, holding it out for the house-mother to see. Mrs Watson did not take it, but she could see that the letter was written in the same neat hand that had written Rita's name on the envelope.

'Well, you'd better read it then.' Mrs Watson spoke more gently this time, and turned away, so that Rita could do so unobserved.

'She thinks we've been adopted, me and Rosie,' Rita said quietly when she'd read the letter. 'She thinks we're together somewhere, but she don't know we've gone here.' She passed the letter over. 'You read it,' she said.

Mrs Watson glanced through the short note. Rita's quite right, she thought as she read it again. This grandmother has no idea they've been sent to Australia.

Mrs Watson felt a wave of relief; at least now she knew that Miss Vanstone had indeed sanctioned the letter. She handed it back and said, 'Did you know your grandmother had been in hospital?'

Rita looked up. 'Yes, she got run over and they took her down the General. We was living with her then, but when she was hurt, Auntie Carrie, next door, looked after us till Mum come home from her honeymoon.'

'I see,' responded Mrs Watson quietly. She waited for Rita to go on.

'And when Mum come home, she was took to hospital to fetch the baby, so we was took to Laurel House.'

'It looks as if your grandmother hasn't been told you're here,' Mrs Watson said carefully.

'No, she ain't,' snapped Rita. 'She's been told a lie. She's been told we're adopted, me and Rosie. She thinks we're together, and,' her voice broke on a sob, 'she's told me to look after Rosie, and I can't!'

The look of total misery on the child's face pierced Mrs Watson's own carefully preserved carapace, and for the first time since she had laid her son in his coffin she pulled a child into her arms and held her close.

For a moment Rita stiffened, about to push her away, and then she relaxed and allowed herself to be held.

After a moment Mrs Watson released her and sitting down on a chair, waved Rita to another. 'Sit down, Rita,' she said. 'We'll have to have a think about what we're going to do next.'

Rita sat, still clutching Gran's letter in her hand, and looked bleakly across at her house-mother. 'She don't know where we are,' she said flatly.

'You could write and tell her,' suggested Mrs Watson. 'How about that, Rita?'

Rita's expression brightened a little, but she said, 'I can't. I ain't got no paper or stamps.'

'I'll give you those, but I'll have to read the letter before you send it. Those are the rules here. All right?'

Rita nodded and looked down to read Gran's letter again. There was no mention of Mum, or baby Richard. Rita wished Gran had said something about them, but at least she knew Gran was all right and getting better from her accident.

'I'll find you some paper and an envelope,' promised Mrs Watson, 'and tomorrow evening you can write your letter.' She got to her feet. 'You'd better get back to the ironing now. Shall I look after the letter for you till tomorrow evening?'

Rita shook her head violently. 'No!' she almost shouted. 'No,' she repeated in a more moderate tone, 'thank you, miss. I'll look after it.'

Back in the kitchen at the ironing table, Rita thought about her letter. She could feel it, tucked into her knickers, and longed to take it out again, but she didn't want anyone to see it. It was too special, too private to be shared with anyone else, even Daisy, just now. She would tell Daisy and show her the letter later, after all, she'd had her fingers crossed when she'd promised not to, so that didn't count, but just for now she wanted to hug the secret to herself. As she ironed the weekend overalls, she thought about what she would say to Gran in her reply. There was so much to tell her, but the most important thing was about Rosie. She'd lost Rosie.

When it was bedtime at last, Rita went into one of the lavatories and shutting the door, pulled out her letter again. It was already looking a bit dog-eared, but she sat on the toilet seat and read it through again. *Remember, wherever you are you are my best girls.* Rita could hear Gran's voice in her head, and despite her determination, she found that, at last, the tears were pouring down her cheeks, and it was some time before she was able to go back into the dorm.

'You been crying?' asked Daisy, looking at her suspiciously. 'What's up?'

'Nothing,' replied Rita as if surprised by the question. She gave a meaningful glance at the others. 'I'm fine, Dais. Do you want to go over your twelves for the test tomorrow?'

They sat together on Rita's bed, chanting the twelve times table, and when it was lights out, Rita slipped the letter from under her clothes and fell asleep with it held tightly in her hand. When she awoke in the morning, she put it in her school bag, so that it would be with her all day.

The letter from Gran filled Rita's thoughts.

Daisy tackled her in the playground. 'What's up with you, Reet?' she demanded. 'You been in a funny mood ever since last night. You ain't thinking of bunking off again, are you?'

'No,' replied Rita. 'Got things on my mind, that's all.'

'Like what?'

'Like mind your own business, Dais,' Rita snapped uncharacteristically. 'I'll tell you when I'm good and ready.'

Daisy's cheeks reddened. 'Suit yourself,' she said, turning away, 'but I thought we was mates.'

Rita, immediately contrite, grabbed her arm. 'Sorry, Dais, sorry. Don't be like that,' she begged. 'Course we're mates, but I just can't tell you yet. I will soon, promise.'

'Promise?'

'I said, promise.'

'OK, only you was crying last night, and I weren't the only one what noticed.'

'I just got to sort something out, Dais, that's all. I'll tell you all about it soon, honest.'

Mrs Watson handed Rita some sheets of notepaper when she got back from school. 'When you've written it, I'll find you an envelope.'

Rita slipped the notepaper into her school bag, and when she had finished her homework that evening, she pulled it out, and began to write.

Once she'd started the words flooded from her pencil, and before she knew it she'd covered three sheets of paper, pouring out to Gran exactly what had happened to them both. As she wrote about Rosie, she felt the tears welling up in her eyes, and she forced them back. One day she would find Rosie again, and that was a promise she made to Gran in the letter.

Delia Watson looked at the letter Rita handed to her and knew at once that she couldn't send it as it was. It would have to be censored. She read it through again and looked up at Rita. 'What a lot you've written,' she said lightly. 'Now, here's the envelope. You address it to your gran, then I'll post it tomorrow. It'll need lots of stamps for England.'

Rita looked anxious. 'But I ain't got no stamp money.'

'Never mind,' Mrs Watson reassured her, 'I'll buy them for you. Write the address, and we'll get your letter on its way.'

Rita wrote the address in Hampton Road carefully on the envelope, adding ENGLAND, when prompted by Mrs Watson. Then she put the letter into it, licked it up and handed it to her house-mother. 'You promise you'll post it?' she said, her eyes fixed on Mrs Watson's face.

'I promise I will.' Rita gave a quick glance at Mrs Watson's hands, but her fingers weren't crossed, and Rita felt reassured.

Later that evening, Mrs Watson took out the letter Rita had written and carefully unsealing it, read it through again. *Dear Gran*, she read...

I got your letter the other day. Thank you for writing to me to tell me you are better. I am glad you ain't in horspidal no more and your leg has got better. Rosie and I ain't with a family like you said, nobody's took us but we ain't at Laurel House neither. We tried to come home to Mum and to see baby Richard, but the horrid lady from the children's office took us back to Laurel House. Soon after that we was told we was going to Australia. We wasn't allowed to tell Mum we was going, but I think she knew anyway. It was cos Uncle Jimmy wanted to get rid of us.

We come here by ship and it took more than six weeks. The ship was lovely and we had a good time on board. The food was lovely. Lots of times the weather was very hot. We learned to swim in the pool on the ship.

We saw lots of places on the way, but we wasn't aloud get off the ship. When we got to Australia some people got off before we did at Perf and Adalayed but we was going to Sidney. When we landed we come to this home. It is in a little town a long way away called Carrabunna.

When we got here we was put into cottages. Rosie was in a diffrent one to me. My cottage mother was called Mrs Garfield. Two days after we got here, we was all called together and had to put on our best clothes. We ain't got many, but Rosie wore the dress you made, but mine was too small. It made us both cry when we thought of you back at home and us so far away. Then a man and a lady come and looked at us all. We had to stand still and strate and then turn round. They walked along the line looking at us all, then they said to Mrs Manton they'd have this one, and the man put his hand on Rosie. Then they took her away. She didn't want to go with them, and she started screaming. I ran over to hold on to her, but they pushed me away. Then we was all told to go back to the cottages. Rosie went on screaming, and they dragged her away. I waited by the gate to say goodbye but Rosie was put in a car and I couldnt. Mrs Garfield shut me in the cellar all night. When I came out I went in a diffrent cottage called Larch.

I ain't seen Rosie no more. She has gone to live with them people, and I dunno where she is. It is very lonely here without her and I hate it, but when I get out of here, I'll go and find her again.

We all go to school here and I am here with some of the girls who came from Laurel House. It was cold when we arrived, because it was winter here, not like England. Spring has come now and it is a bit warmer.

I don't like it here and wish I could come home. I wish Rosie was here too.

Please write to me again soon.

Lots of love from Rita xx

Mrs Watson opened a bottle of Indian ink and working through the letter, blacked out the most damning parts. One page she removed entirely, and when she was satisfied, she slipped it back into its envelope, using some clear glue to reseal it. Next morning she walked to the post office, bought the necessary stamps, and dropped the letter into the box. She had kept her promise. Rita's letter had been sent.

Chapter 27

Lily was having her second cup of tea when the letter plopped through her letter box. It lay on the mat, face down. Stooping stiffly, Lily picked it up and looked at it. It was from abroad, as far as she could tell without her spectacles. The stamps didn't look English, though they had the king's head on them. Puzzled she carried it back into the kitchen and put on her glasses. The king was on the stamps, but underneath was the word AUSTRALIA. Lily stared at it. Who could be writing to her from Australia? Then she looked at the handwriting. For a moment she felt light-headed, and she sat down hard on a chair. In a childish hand, but carefully written, the letter was addressed to Mrs Lily Sharples, here in Hampton Road, and the handwriting was Rita's. Lily recognized it at once. Rita's writing. But Rita wasn't in Australia; she and Rosie had been adopted by a couple here in England, a couple from 'up north'. How could Rita be writing to her from Australia?

With a shaking hand, Lily ripped the envelope open, and confirmed that it was signed, '*Lots of love from Rita*'. She turned back to the beginning and began to read.

Dear Gran,
I got your letter the other day. Thank you for writing to me
to tell me you are better. I am glad you ain't in horspidal
no more and your leg has got better.

Then there were a few lines crossed out so darkly that Lily couldn't make out anything. Then Rita's handwriting again.

We come here by ship and it took more than six weeks. The ship was lovely and we had a good time on board. The food was lovely. Lots of times the weather was very hot. We learned to swim in the pool on the ship.

We saw lots of places on the way, but we wasn't aloud get off the ship.

Another line blacked out.

When we landed we come to this home.

More scratching out. Lily began to be angry. Rita had written to her to tell her where she was, and what was happening to her, but someone must have read the letter after it had been written and censored it.

Just like in the war, thought Lily. Why would they do that? How dare they? What harm was it to write a letter to your grandmother?

She went on with the letter, but it was soon apparent that a whole page was missing. The last page began in the middle of a sentence,

to school here and I am here with some of the girls who came from Laurel House. It was cold when we arrived, because it was winter here, not like England. Spring has come now and it is a bit warmer.

There were several more lines crossed out and then just one line at the end.

Lots of love from Rita xx

Lily read and re-read the letter, her consternation growing by the minute. It was clear that Rita had received her letter, but it had followed her to Australia. Miss Vanstone had said that the two girls had been adopted together. Had their adoptive parents decided to move to Australia? Were they still together? Rita hadn't mentioned Rosie once. Why not? What had happened to her? Had she written about her on the page that was missing? Lily looked at the letter again. There was no return address and no date. How long ago had it been written? She picked up the envelope and studied the postmark, but it was smudged, most of it was unintelligible, the only part she could make out was NSW. What or where was NSW? Lily didn't know. Her grasp of geography was hazy, but she was determined to find out. She'd go to the library and look it up in an atlas. The postmark was a definite clue and one that couldn't be censored by someone the other end before the letter was sent. Switching on the table lamp, Lily held the paper to the light, trying to see if she could make out any of the censored part of the letter, but it was impossible. Whoever had read Rita's letter had been determined to obliterate whatever it was that she'd written and had used Indian ink.

If they were going to black so much of it out, Lily wondered, why did they send it at all?

All the way through Rita had written 'we' but hadn't mentioned Rosie. Surely Rosie must have gone with her. But then, Lily thought, Rita also said that there were other girls from Laurel House, so perhaps she meant them when she said 'we'.

And if she's with a load of girls from Laurel House, and living in this home wherever it is, thought Lily suddenly, then she ain't been adopted. She's just been sent out there to another home. Just been got rid of 'cos she caused trouble.

Lily felt the anger rising up inside her, a fireball of fury, as she realized that she'd been duped and lied to... that they'd all been duped and lied to. Surely even Mavis wouldn't have given her permission for her children to be sent to the other side of the world. Lily got to her feet, gripping the table as she fought for her balance. She felt giddy with rage, her little girls, Rita and Rosie, aged nine and five, had been posted off to Australia without so much as a by-your-leave from the family. Surely Mavis didn't know. Did Jimmy Randall know? Had he arranged it all? What about that fat pig of a woman, that Children's Officer? Did she know where they were going when she took them back to Laurel House?

Calm down, Lily told herself, calm down. This is getting you nowhere. She forced herself to sit down again and think rationally. 'Think it all through,' she said aloud, 'then you can decide what you're going to do about it.'

She squeezed another cup of tea from the pot and considered what to do. Were there any clues in the letter that she'd missed? She picked it up and read it yet again. All the points she'd already noticed came into sharp focus. No mention of Rosie. 'We.' Who's we? 'We come to this home', no mention of a family, or adoptive parents, so adoption was unlikely. NSW. She thought about the postmark. What did NSW mean? Carrie's John worked for the post office, he might know.

Lily found a pencil and paper and began making a list, a plan of campaign to find her missing granddaughters.

1. Talk to John about postmark.
2. Make sure of all the facts.
3. Go to Laurel House and demand explanation.
4. Go and see the Children's Officer woman.
5. Write to the Children's Committee?
6. Find out whether Mavis knows.
7. Tell her if not.

Lily looked at her list. It was a start. She got to her feet again and went slowly back upstairs to get dressed. It was Saturday, so she'd probably find John and Carrie at home. She got washed and dressed, her mind churning with the possibilities, and then, all of a sudden, she began to weep. Slumping down on her bed, she clutched her pillow to her and began to sob, her whole body shaking with grief and despair. Little girls, such little girls. How could anyone send children that age to the other side of the world? How could anyone be so cruel?

Lily looked at the picture John had taken of the girls at the wedding, beaming at the camera, and the ache in her heart was a physical pain. Australia. No one ever came back from Australia. She would never see them again. Lily wept for a long time, great sobs racking her body.

Later, much later, when her tears had run dry, and with stiffened resolve, she finished dressing. Pull yerself together, woman, she told herself firmly. Crying ain't going to help no one. With new determination, she put on her coat, and walked round to Ship Street, not to see Mavis but to visit the Maunders.

Carrie was surprised to see her, but she said, 'You looking for Mavis?'

'No,' replied Lily, 'it's your John I want a word with. Is he in?'

'No, John's at the Lion for his pint,' Carrie replied, putting the kettle on the stove. 'But I 'spect he'll be back soon if you want to wait.'

When John came home, he found Lily and Carrie in the kitchen.

'I've come to pick your brains,' Lily said, 'if you don't mind.'

'Pick away,' said John. 'How can I help?'

'I've had a letter.' Lily showed him the envelope. 'I can't read the postmark, and I wondered if you could tell me where it come from.'

John took the envelope and studied it. 'It's from Australia,' he said at length. 'Some place in New South Wales.'

'New South Wales!' echoed Lily. 'So that's somewhere in Australia?'

'It's a big area,' John said. 'The name of the town's the smudged bit.' He looked up enquiringly. 'Who's it from then, Mrs S? Who's writing to you from Australia?'

'Rita.'

'Rita!' echoed Carrie. 'Rita's in Australia? Does Mavis know?'

'Don't know,' Lily shrugged, 'but I don't think so. She'd never let them be took that far away, would she?'

'No, course she wouldn't,' said John, trying to sound reassuring. 'She'll be real upset when she hears.'

'What's Mav going to say when you tell her?'

'I ain't going to tell her, not yet,' stated Lily. 'I got to find out exactly what's happened to them girls before we say anything to Mavis, right? I know you're her best friend, Carrie, but please don't tell her. Don't even say I've been here. Please.'

'No, all right,' agreed Carrie. 'D'you think it was Jimmy what sent them? You know, wanted them right out of the way?'

'Don't know,' said Lily. 'I went round the home looking for them, didn't I? Said I wanted them back, that they could live with me, just like before. And this woman, the one what runs the place, she said that Rita and Rosie was adopted and had moved away.'

'Did she say where they was taken to?' asked Carrie.

Lily shook her head. 'Just that it was "up north". I asked to see them but she said it'd unsettle them again. She wouldn't even give me an address to write to. Just said if I wrote one last letter, she'd send it on.'

'And did you?' John asked. 'Did you write to them?'

'On the spot,' replied Lily. 'The woman give me some paper and a pen, and I wrote to them there and then.'

'And she addressed it and sent it on.'

'S'pose so. Rita got it, didn't she?'

Lily had been wondering about that. Clearly Miss Vanstone had forwarded the letter as promised, but perhaps she'd broken the other part of her promise and had read it herself first. Perhaps she had crossed out bits she didn't want Rita to read. Lily thought back over the letter she'd written. Was there anything that Miss Vanstone might have thought it necessary to censor? No, all she'd written was that she was out of hospital and getting better. She'd wished them well with their new family and said she loved them and would never forget them. Perhaps, if the woman knew they weren't being adopted into a family, she might have blacked out that bit.

'Anyway,' Lily said, 'I'm going to go to that Laurel House and face that woman for the liar she is.'

'Will it do any good?' wondered Carrie.

'No.' Lily's shoulders sagged. 'Probably not, but I have to try.'

'Still, she might give you the address now that you know they've gone,' suggested John more optimistically. 'So's you can write back.'

Lily thanked them for their help and got to her feet, quite as determined as before to tackle Miss Vanstone at Laurel House.

When she got home again she lit the fire. It was extravagant, she knew, but sitting alone, she felt cold through to her bones.

How strange, she thought as she poked the fire into life, that here I am, freezing cold, on a dark November evening, and where Rita is it's warming up for summer. Thousands of miles away. Thousands of miles from home.

How she got through that Sunday, Lily wasn't sure. Much as she wanted to rush over to Laurel House and confront Miss Vanstone with her duplicity, it was Miss Vanstone she needed to see, not that other woman, and Miss Vanstone didn't live there.

'Want to speak to the organ-grinder, not the bloody monkey,' she announced to her kitchen, as she rehearsed what she intended to say.

Monday morning dawned cold and wet. Lily opened her curtains to a grey drizzle that drifted from the sky, enveloping the houses across the street in shifting mist. It was an outlook that chimed with her mood, grey and dismal. She dressed with care. Today she'd go back to Laurel House and she wanted the Vanstone woman to know that she was respectable and had all her wits about her; that she wasn't a common, ill-educated woman who could be fobbed off again. Today she wasn't going to be misled, lied to or patronized.

Laurel House was silent when Lily arrived, it, too, shrouded in the grey mist of the dull November day. She rang the bell and waited. After several minutes, the door opened and a young girl of about fourteen peered out at her. Not the girl who'd opened the door to her before; this one was smaller, had reddish hair and a pale, freckled face.

'Can I help you?' she whispered.

Lily was about to ask for Miss Vanstone when she hesitated.

Perhaps this girl had known Rita and Rosie, and something could be learned from her, before anyone had the chance to shut her up.

Lily smiled at her. 'Hallo,' she said. 'I'm Rita and Rosie Stevens' gran. Do you think I can see them?'

The girl stared at her in wide-eyed consternation and then said, 'They ain't here.'

'No?' Lily affected surprise. 'Where are they, then?'

'Don't know, miss, they went away.'

'What's your name?' Lily asked gently.

'Pamela, miss,' said the girl, glancing fearfully over her shoulder.

'Well, Pamela, I'm trying to find Rita and Rosie. I'm their granny and I wondered if you, or any of the other girls know where they went.'

'The other girls are at school, miss,' said Pamela.

'And why aren't you at school, Pamela?'

'I left, miss, in the summer. I work here now.'

'How old are you, Pamela?' asked Lily, still speaking softly, as she might to a frightened animal.

'Fourteen, miss.'

'Have you always lived here?'

Pamela shrugged. 'Think so, miss.'

'Pamela! Who's at the door?' The strident voice rang out from inside the house, and Lily saw the girl blench, her faint colour draining from her face.

'That's Mrs Hawkins,' Pamela whispered. 'You'll have to ask her about Rita. I don't know nothing.'

'Don't worry,' Lily reassured her, 'I won't say nothing, neither.'

Pamela looked anything but reassured, as she stood aside to let Lily in.

'Lady to see you, Mrs Hawkins,' she murmured, as the Hawk appeared from her office.

'You should have told me at once, Pamela,' she scolded, 'not left her on the doorstep. Go back to the kitchen now, Mrs Smith'll be needing you.'

The girl needed no second bidding, and with one last imploring glance at Lily, she scurried away.

'I was simply telling the girl that I need to see Miss Vanstone,' Lily said, stepping into the house before Mrs Hawkins could speak. 'You may remember I came before. I'm Lily Sharples, Rita and Rosie Stevens' grandmother.'

'I remember,' replied Mrs Hawkins, 'but I'm afraid that Miss Vanstone isn't here today.'

'And when will she be?' asked Lily sweetly.

'I never know. She comes when she feels it necessary.'

'Well, it's necessary today,' said Lily sharply. 'I've come to see her and see her I must.'

'Perhaps I can help you?' suggested Mrs Hawkins, stretching her mouth in a smile that didn't even come close to her eyes.

'I want to speak to the organ-grinder, not the monkey.' Lily snapped out the prepared line and had the satisfaction of seeing Mrs Hawkins flinch.

'I'm afraid rudeness like that won't get you what you want,' said Mrs Hawkins, her voice cold steel. 'Miss Vanstone isn't here today, and I'm certain that she has nothing further to say to you.'

'Well, I have something further to say to her,' said Lily planting her feet firmly on the floor and leaning on her stick. 'A great deal.'

'I'm afraid I must ask you to leave now,' said Mrs Hawkins, reaching past her and opening the front door. 'You have no further business here.'

'And if I refuse?' challenged Lily.

'If you refuse to leave, I'll have to call the police and have you forcibly ejected. I'm sure you don't want that sort of trouble.'

'If the police is called, I'll tell them how you've sent my granddaughters to Australia, without asking and without telling anyone! I'll show them the letter I've had from Rita, and then we'll see who's in trouble!'

'Miss Vanstone will probably be here sometime tomorrow,' said Mrs Hawkins. 'I suggest you come back then,' and with a sharp push she propelled Lily out through the open door. Lily staggered, jabbing her stick into the ground to maintain her balance, and by the time she was able to turn round, the front door had been slammed. She had to admit defeat for the time being, and turned away, the rage still boiling inside her. She was defeated now at Laurel House but she was still determined to confront Miss Vanstone. Somehow she would find her and throw her lies in her face.

Inside Laurel House, Mrs Hawkins went upstairs and peered out of the landing window watching and waiting for Lily Sharples to give up and leave. Damned woman! How had she had a letter from Rita? Surely they hadn't allowed Rita to write home!

Better warn Miss Vanstone, she thought. I always knew that woman was trouble. Monkey indeed! I'll make her regret that!

Mrs Hawkins returned to her office and picking up the phone, she rang Vanstone Enterprises and asked to be put through to Miss Vanstone.

'Yes? What is it?' Miss Vanstone was, as always, brisk on the telephone.

'That Sharples woman's been round again,' answered Mrs Hawkins. 'She knows those brats are in Australia.'

'How? How could she possibly know?'

'She says she's had a letter from Rita.'

'A letter from Rita? Hmm.'

'I told her you weren't coming here today,' went on Mrs Hawkins. 'Said you might be here tomorrow if she wanted to call back.' She hesitated before she added, 'I think you'll have to see her. She's threatening to go to the police.'

'Leave it with me,' said Miss Vanstone, 'but if she turns up again, tell her I can give her five minutes tomorrow afternoon at four o'clock. We have to sort this thing out once and for all.'

Chapter 28

While Mrs Hawkins had been warning Miss Vanstone of Lily's intentions, Lily herself had been reassessing them. She found a tearoom a couple of streets away and, sitting over a cup of tea and a sticky bun, she considered her next move. If she couldn't get to Miss Vanstone at Laurel House, perhaps she could beard her in her other office. She'd rung her before at some business place. She couldn't remember the name, but maybe she still had the paper with the phone number on it. She scrabbled through her handbag, emptying it out onto the table in front of her, and at last she found it, tucked into the back of her purse.

Now I can ring the Vanstone woman's office, Lily thought and hurried out to find a phone box. She was about to ring when another idea struck her. How much better simply to turn up on the doorstep. She paused outside the phone box and thought it through. She didn't know where this office was, but what if she rang and asked for the address? Once she had that, she could turn up unannounced as she had at Laurel House. Having thought of a plan, Lily went into the phone box, slid the coins into the slot and dialled.

As soon as she heard the words 'Vanstone Enterprises! May I help you?' Lily pressed button A, and spoke in a clear, business-like voice. 'Ah, good morning. Vanstone Enterprises?'

'Yes, good morning. How may I help you?'

'Please could you give me the exact address of your offices? I have a delivery to make, and I seem to have the wrong address.'

Lily tried to keep her voice steady, but she was shaking as she spoke.

'Vanstone House, 21 Broome Street. Just off Main Square,' came the helpful reply. 'It's a big red brick building, with black railings. You can't miss it.'

'Thank you very much,' said Lily, and replaced the receiver. '21 Broome Street,' she repeated aloud, 'just off Main Square,' and she set off to catch the number 37 bus.

Vanstone House stood behind its black-painted iron railings with wide steps leading up to double, glass-panelled front doors. There was a brightly polished brass nameplate. Vanstone House.

Lily stared across at the building with misgiving. How would she get inside a place like that? She'd never get past the front door. She looked up at the three floors of windows overlooking the street. Many were lit from within, and Lily wondered what went on in there. What did Vanstone Enterprises do inside Vanstone House? How would she get to see Miss Vanstone? Better to wait and catch her one day going into Laurel House.

No! Lily told herself firmly. You have to do it today. Every day you leave it will make it more difficult.

As she watched, a man in a dark overcoat walked up to the front door and simply pushing open the double doors, went inside.

So, thought Lily, here goes. She crossed the road and pushed her way through the doors. She found herself in an entrance hall, carpeted in dark green, with several doors opening off it. Two chairs stood against the wall and a gracious staircase rose to the floors above. A smartly dressed woman was sitting behind a desk and as the door swung closed behind Lily, she looked up and smiled. When she spoke her voice was soft and well modulated. 'Good morning, madam. May I help you?'

For a moment Lily faltered in the face of such courtesy. Could she simply demand to see Miss Vanstone and create a scene if she were denied?

'I need to see Miss Vanstone,' she said. 'It is a matter of great urgency.'

'Have you an appointment, madam?' enquired the receptionist.

'No, I haven't,' admitted Lily, 'but it is most important that I see Miss Vanstone today.'

'I see,' the woman replied. 'Perhaps you'd like to take a seat,' she waved her hand towards the chairs, 'and I'll enquire.'

Lily stood irresolute for a moment and the receptionist, smile still fixed in place, repeated, 'Please, take a seat, madam.'

Lily sat down, perching awkwardly on the edge of the chair, as if ready to leap up again. She watched the receptionist lift a phone, and speak in a low voice. Lily couldn't hear what was said, but after a moment she glanced across at Lily and set the receiver down.

'What name shall I say?' she asked.

'Mrs Lily Sharples,' replied Lily.

'Thank you, Mrs Sharples.' She picked up the receiver again and after another brief conversation, rang off.

'Please make yourself comfortable,' she said. 'Miss Drake will be down to see you in just one moment.'

Lily sat back on the chair and waited. One moment turned into ten minutes and she was just about to approach the desk again, when a woman came down the stairs and after a glance at the receptionist, crossed the hall to Lily. She was a small, thin woman, with a sharp, narrow face. Her faded fair hair was cropped short, accentuating her angular features, and her mouth was set in a straight line. There was no sign of welcome in her expression.

'Mrs Sharples? I'm Miss Drake, Miss Vanstone's secretary. Can I help you?'

Lily stood up. 'How d'you do?' she said. 'I'm here to see Miss Vanstone.'

'Yes, so I understand,' replied Miss Drake, 'but Miss Vanstone is unavailable at the moment, so perhaps I can help. What was this in connection with?'

'That's between her and me,' said Lily.

'I see. Well, I'm afraid if you can't give me some idea of your business, I'll simply have to make you an appointment for some time next week.'

'Next week! Next week ain't no good,' retorted Lily. 'It's important. I got to see her today.'

'So you say,' replied Miss Drake, smoothly, 'but unless you give the reason for such urgency, I'm afraid she can't see you.'

'Can't or won't,' snapped Lily.

'Mrs Sharples,' Miss Drake's tone was one of extreme patience, 'Miss Vanstone is a busy lady. She can't simply drop everything when someone walks in off the street and demands to see her. I'm sure you understand that.'

At that moment the front doors swung open and two young men came in. One approached the reception desk, and spoke quietly to the receptionist, while the other, who carried a large black bag, paused just inside the door, looking round.

'What I understand,' said Lily, the anger which had been boiling up inside her finally exploding, 'is that EVER-Care has stolen my granddaughters. Your Miss Vanstone lied to me, lied to me to my face. And I want to see her, now. I want her to tell me where they are, 'cos they certainly ain't where she told me they was.'

Miss Drake gave an anxious glance at the two men standing in the hallway. One was still talking to the receptionist, but the other was unashamedly listening to Lily.

'Excuse me, Miss Drake,' the receptionist called across. 'Sorry to interrupt, but I thought you'd want to know that the two gentlemen from the *Chronicle* are here.'

'Thank you, Miss Pullman,' replied Miss Drake. 'I'll come back down as soon as I've taken Mrs Sharples upstairs.' She turned to the waiting men and said, with a tight smile, 'If you'd like to take a seat, gentlemen, I'll be down again in just one moment. Please come this way, Mrs Sharples.'

Without looking to see if Lily was behind her, she started back up the stairs. Lily followed, taking the stairs slowly. She had no idea what accounted for Miss Drake's change of heart, but she didn't care, she was being taken up to see Miss Vanstone.

Miss Drake led her into an office on the first floor, a strictly utilitarian room, with metal filing cabinets along one wall and two more chairs along another. Across the office a second door led to a room beyond.

Miss Drake waved Lily to one of the chairs and then knocked on the second door and went through. As she waited, Lily looked round, but there was little to tell her what Vanstone Enterprises was all about. This was a secretary's office, functional and sparse.

Several moments passed and then the door opened and Miss Drake emerged. 'Miss Vanstone will see you now,' she said. 'She can give you five minutes.'

Lily got to her feet and passing the secretary at the door without so much as a glance, went through into Miss Vanstone's office.

This was quite a different room. Maroon carpet covered the floor, thick and soft under Lily's feet. The three windows which looked out onto the street below were hung with rich, red, velvet curtains. There was a sofa and two easy chairs set before a fireplace, where smouldering logs gave off a comforting warmth. The room was dominated, however, by a huge mahogany desk, set facing the door. In front of it was an upright wooden chair, and behind it sat Miss Vanstone.

She did not look up as Lily came into the room. Lily paused inside the door for a moment and then strode across the expanse of carpet and placing her hands on its polished surface, leaned across the desk.

'Where's my granddaughters?' she demanded. 'Where's Rita and Rosie?'

Miss Vanstone lifted her head as if surprised to see her. 'Mrs Sharples?' she said, an eyebrow raised. 'I believe we've met before.'

'You know darn well we have,' retorted Lily. 'And you know why I'm here now. You've sent my granddaughters to Australia. Sent two little girls as what have a loving family here to look after them, thousands of miles away without even telling anyone.'

'I have nothing to tell you,' replied Miss Vanstone, evenly. 'As I told you before it's a question of confidentiality, to protect the children left in our care.'

'Protect 'em!' Lily almost shrieked. 'Is sending them to the other side of the world, on their own, little kids like that, protecting them?'

'These children are my responsibility. Where they live and who looks after them is entirely up to me. I do not have to explain myself to you, or anyone else.' She removed her glasses and stared at Lily, her expression hard and uncompromising.

'You don't have to tell me nothing,' snapped Lily. 'I know where they are, 'cos Rita wrote to me, see. They're in New South Wales, and that's in Australia.'

'Then you know all there is to know,' replied Miss Vanstone, calmly.

'No, I don't,' asserted Lily. 'You can give me their proper address for a start.'

'If your granddaughter has indeed written to you, you have the address already.'

'What d'you mean "if"? Course she's written to me, otherwise I would still think she was adopted by some people "up north", wouldn't I?'

Lily reached into her handbag and pulled out Rita's already dog-eared letter, and thrust it at Miss Vanstone, but jerking it away before she could touch it.

'Oh no you don't,' she said. 'You ain't getting your hands on this. This is my evidence that you're a liar. I don't trust you as far as I can throw you.'

'That's your problem, Mrs Sharples, not mine.' Miss Vanstone shrugged and looked away as if the letter was of no interest to her.

'So, I need the proper address,' repeated Lily, 'and you're going to give it me.'

'No, Mrs Sharples, I am not.' Miss Vanstone didn't raise her voice, but it was clear that she was not going to change her mind.

'But you must.' Lily knew that she was pleading now, but

there was nothing else that she could do. 'How can I write back to her if I don't have the proper address?'

'I see your difficulty,' replied Miss Vanstone, 'but I'm afraid I can't help you.'

'But she'll think I don't care.' Lily was desperate now. 'She'll think I didn't bother to answer.'

'As I told you before,' said Miss Vanstone, 'a clean break is the best way. Wherever your granddaughters are, they have embarked on a new and exciting life. It will be far better for them to forget their earlier life and make a fresh start, don't you think?'

'No, I bleedin' don't.' Lily seldom swore and it was a sign of her distress and desperation that she did so now. She saw Miss Vanstone frown at the obscenity and knew she'd done her cause no good. Miss Vanstone would never have used such a word, and Lily having done so marked herself out as being far beneath her, not fit to have the care of children.

'I'm afraid I must ask you to leave now.' Miss Vanstone rang the little silver bell that stood on the desk top and Miss Drake appeared at the door.

'Mrs Sharples is leaving now, Miss Drake,' stated Miss Vanstone and picking up the papers on her desk, she began to read.

Lily got to her feet and stood, irresolute.

'This way, please,' said Miss Drake, and when Lily still didn't move she took hold of her arm.

Lily shook off her hand angrily. 'Don't you touch me!' she growled. 'Don't you lay a hand on me!'

'This way, please, Mrs Sharples,' repeated Miss Drake. 'Miss Vanstone has another appointment.'

Slowly Lily turned and leaning heavily on her cane, walked to the door. As she reached it she turned back to face the woman sitting behind the desk. 'You ain't heard the last of me,' she warned, 'you ain't heard the last of me, not by a long chalk.'

Miss Vanstone ignored her but, addressing her secretary, she said, 'When you've seen Mrs Sharples off the premises, please ask the gentlemen to step upstairs.'

Unable to provoke any further reaction, Lily straightened her back and with her head held high left the room.

'I'll see you to the front door,' said Miss Drake, leading the way to the stairs.

'There's no need,' replied Lily stiffly. 'I can find my own way out.'

'Nevertheless, I will see you to the front door.'

Miss Drake followed her down to the hall where the two men were still there waiting. They watched as Lily was shown out of the front door, and as it closed behind her, Lily heard Miss Drake say, 'Miss Vanstone will see you now, gentlemen, if you'd care to follow me.'

Upstairs, Emily Vanstone set aside her papers. That Sharples woman is a real nuisance, she thought, coming here causing a fuss. Let's hope that's the last of her. After all, what more can she do?

In a way, Emily found herself admiring Lily's determination and tenacity, recognizing traits that ran as strongly in herself. Despite Mrs Hawkins's warning, Emily had been surprised that the woman had turned up, unannounced, at the office. She had assumed that Lily would ring for another appointment, and had already briefed her staff to refuse her. But by turning up and making a scene in front of reporters from the *Belcaster Chronicle*, Miss Drake had had no choice but to bring her upstairs, before the newspaper men latched on to what she was saying.

'She was accusing you of stealing her granddaughters and of lying to her,' Miss Drake had explained. 'I thought it was better to get her out of sight and earshot as quickly as possible.'

'You did quite right, Miss Drake,' Emily had replied. 'Send her in to me, I'll deal with her.'

That Lily had a letter from Rita, posted from Australia, Emily found worrying. She'd been relieved to see, when Lily held out the letter, that a great deal of what the child had written had been blacked out. At least Daphne had had the wit to do that, but why allow her to write at all?

Emily felt no remorse or guilt at having separated the children from their family. She had rescued them from a feckless mother and an abusive stepfather; she had done God's work. Remorse and guilt never came into her mind.

But what will the grandmother do next? wondered Emily. What would I do next, if it were my grandchildren? Then she thought of May Hopkins. I'd go and see the Children's Officer. Emily allowed herself a tight smile. Well, you'll get no luck there, Mrs Sharples. May Hopkins doesn't know where they are.

However, the troublesome woman might make difficulties with the Children's Committee. Emily reached for the phone, but before she could ask the operator for the number, there was a knock on the door.

'Excuse me, Miss Vanstone, the gentlemen from the *Chronicle* are here.'

Emily Vanstone replaced the receiver. Mrs Sharples and Miss Hopkins could wait, the men from the newspaper couldn't. 'Please show them in,' she said, and rising from her seat, came round her desk to greet them.

Terry Knight was one of the senior reporters on the *Belcaster Chronicle*. Tall and slim, he had an intelligent face with deep-set blue eyes. His fair hair was well cut, his face freshly shaved. Snappily dressed in dark suit and white shirt, he was out to make an impression. He was writing a feature article on the rise of women in business since the war. Emily Vanstone was one of the obvious candidates for interview. She had been running her own business empire since the thirties, and he wanted to discuss the changes, particularly in the role of women, that she'd seen over the years.

The interview went well, and as it drew to a close, she posed at her desk for Mike Holden to take his pictures.

'I understand that you are very much involved in charity work as well,' Terry Knight said as he put his notepad away.

'I do what I can,' said Emily modestly. 'If one is in a position to do good, it behoves one to do so. I'm sure you'll agree.'

'Of course,' smiled Terry. 'Wasn't the EVER-Care Orphanage founded by you?'

'Yes,' agreed Emily, 'that is one of my projects.'

'What good work you must do there,' remarked Terry, 'helping children who've been orphaned by the war; your home giving them a new start.'

Statement, not question. Emily liked that and smiling, she nodded. 'Certainly. We give them a home, and when they leave us, we help them find their place in the world.'

'And I expect some children are left with you for just a short while,' suggested Terry. 'That must be very helpful in time of family crisis.'

Emily gave him a wary smile. 'Not often,' she replied. 'We become the legal guardians to the children who come to us, as we have to assume complete responsibility for their welfare.'

'Oh, I see. I assume they stay in touch with their extended families, though. You know, aunts, uncles, grandparents?' He spoke casually, with no notebook in his hand, but hearing this question, Emily knew at once what he was after. He'd heard the Sharples woman sounding off downstairs about her granddaughters and he was fishing, fishing for a story.

She decided to confront him, head-on. 'I expect you overheard the lady downstairs who's looking for her granddaughters. That poor woman, she's a case in point. She's heard that her estranged daughter has placed her daughters in our care, and she's been trying to find out where they are. I wish I could help, she's so distressed, but I could tell her nothing. It would break professional confidentiality. We never reveal details of the children placed in our care.'

'So you do know where her granddaughters are,' said Terry.

Emily gave him a practised smile. 'As I said, Mr Knight, I'm afraid I can tell you no more than I could tell her. We never discuss our children.'

'Not even to say whether they *are* your children?'

'I'm so sorry, Mr Knight,' Emily said sweetly and got to her feet. 'If you've finished, I'm afraid that must be all for today.'

'And the lady downstairs,' persisted Terry. 'What was her name again?'

'I'm sorry, Mr Knight, I'm afraid I can't discuss the subject with you any further.' She rang the bell on her desk. 'Miss Drake will show you out, gentlemen. I'll be so interested to read your article in due course.' She extended her hand and both the reporters shook it before following Miss Drake out of the room.

When the door had closed behind them she sighed. How infuriating that they'd picked up on Lily Sharples so quickly. Still, she thought, at least they don't know who she is, so they won't be able to write anything except in a very general way. Still, she'd better warn Miss Hopkins.

Lily Sharples plodded away from the Vanstone Enterprises building, emotionally exhausted. She had met her match in Miss Vanstone; that lady hadn't got where she was without being ruthless. Lily knew that she'd get nothing more from her. Miss Vanstone hadn't expected her today; from now she'd be surrounded by the protecting ranks of her staff. However, Lily hadn't given up all hope. There were the others on her list that she intended to visit. The next was Miss Hopkins, the Children's Officer.

She probably don't know they've been sent to Australia, Lily reasoned. She's probably been told that they was adopted, same as me. This thought encouraged her. Perhaps the Children's Officer would be as outraged as she was. Perhaps Miss Hopkins and the Children's Committee could make Miss Vanstone say where the girls were.

Feeling another faint flicker of optimism, Lily slowly walked back to the Main Square, and was soon struggling up the stairs to the second floor of the council offices in search of Miss Hopkins. Once again she was forced to sit in the crowded waiting room.

'I'm sorry, but Miss Hopkins has a full diary this afternoon.' It was the same pale, pinch-faced woman behind the glass hatch. 'You can wait if you like,' she sniffed, 'but Miss Hopkins won't finish her list till late, and then she may not agree to see you.'

'I'll wait,' said Lily. Sighing, Miss Parker wrote down her name, and said, 'You'd better take a seat then.'

Lily sat there for two hours before she heard her name being called through the glass.

'Next appointment hasn't turned up,' she was told. 'You can go in now.'

Miss Hopkins didn't get up to greet her new visitor, just gave her a vague smile and waved her to a chair. 'Now, Mrs Sharples,' she said when Lily was seated, 'what can I do for you?'

She didn't need to ask. She already knew why Lily was there. She had been expecting her. An earlier meeting had been interrupted by a phone call from Miss Vanstone.

'Mrs Sharples will be coming to see you,' she'd said. 'She knows that the Stevens girls have gone to Australia, but she doesn't know where. Please ensure that it stays that way.'

'Oh, of course, Miss Vanstone. I quite understand. I wouldn't dream of—'

'The best thing to do would be for you to plead complete ignorance of their whereabouts,' went on Emily, smoothly. 'She may well show you a letter from Rita, the older one, you know? But there's no return address on it, and that's what she's after.'

'You can rely on me, Miss Vanstone,' purred Miss Hopkins. 'Mum's the word.'

'Thank you, Miss Hopkins. Good afternoon.'

'Just one other thing, Miss Vanstone,' the Children's Officer cried as Miss Vanstone was about to put down the phone.

'Yes,' had come the abrupt reply.

'I was going to phone you later today. I've just heard there's to be a full inspection of Laurel House in the next couple of weeks.'

That caught Emily's attention. 'When?' she demanded.

'I don't know, they're unannounced spot checks, but I just thought I'd tip you the wink. Good afternoon, Miss Vanstone.' And this time it was May Hopkins who'd replaced the receiver and cut off the call.

She turned her attention back to the woman in front of her. 'You were saying?'

'I'm Lily Sharples, Rita and Rosie Stevens' grandmother,'

began Lily. 'I came to ask if you know where they are. They ain't at Laurel House no more and they ain't been adopted like I was told.' She paused to allow the Children's Officer to speak, but as she said nothing, Lily went on, 'They've been sent to Australia!'

Still Miss Hopkins said nothing, showing none of the outrage that Lily had hoped for.

'Australia!' repeated Lily. 'The other side of the world! Did you know that, miss? No one told? Not even their mother? Did you know that?'

'No,' replied Miss Hopkins evenly, 'I didn't, but I'm not surprised. I seem to remember that their mother signed the children over to EVER-Care. In which case,' Miss Hopkins held up her hand to silence Lily as she was about to interrupt, 'in which case, that charitable society is entitled to do whatever it feels is in their best interests. If that means sending them to make a fresh start in a new country, well, so be it.'

'But without even telling my daughter? Without even telling their mother?'

'Certainly,' said Miss Hopkins. 'Your daughter gave up her right as their parent when she signed the papers.'

'But that can't be right!' protested Lily.

'I'm sorry, but I'm afraid it is,' Miss Hopkins assured her.

'So you *did* know they was sent to Australia,' stated Lily.

'No. Once they're with EVER-Care, they're no longer my responsibility.'

'But you're the Children's Officer, ain't you? You're supposed to look after children.'

'And so I do.' Miss Hopkins was tired of Mrs Sharples. 'I looked after the Stevens girls. I removed them from a home where they were not wanted; from the influence of an abusive stepfather and a weak and ineffectual mother who couldn't stand up for them. I placed them in the care of a reputable children's home, and my job was done.' She rose to her feet to indicate that she considered the interview at an end. 'And now, Mrs Sharples, it is time for my next appointment.'

'But you must know where this place in Australia is,' said

Lily, sitting firmly in her seat. 'You must know where they've been sent.'

'No,' Miss Hopkins maintained, 'I do not. Australia is a huge country, and there are many homes like the EVER-Care. If your granddaughters have indeed been sent there, they could be anywhere.'

'Oh, they've been sent all right,' said Lily. 'I've had a letter from Rita...' She retrieved the letter from her bag and getting to her feet, held it out towards Miss Hopkins.

'Then you know where they are, and that they're safe and well,' said Miss Hopkins, ignoring the proffered letter. 'I'm afraid there's nothing else I can do for you. Good afternoon!' She brushed past Lily, opened the door, and called out, 'Next.'

Lily walked slowly out of the room, but as the door shut behind her, she looked round the still full waiting room and said, 'Don't let that woman take your children off you.' Heads jerked up as she went on, 'Don't let her get her hands on your kids. They don't look after them for you, they pack them off to Australia, out of the way!'

'Really, Mrs Sharples,' cried Miss Parker, emerging from her cubbyhole behind the glass, 'you've no right to spread such lies.'

'They ain't lies,' snapped Lily bitterly. 'That woman's took my granddaughters, and sent them away, thousands of miles. Don't let her do it to you!'

'Mrs Sharples, you must leave this office at once,' begged Miss Parker. 'You must stop saying these dreadful things and go home... or I'll have to call the police.'

'Yes, why don't you?' demanded Lily, but when she saw that the woman was reaching for the phone, she turned towards the door. 'All right, all right, I'm going,' she muttered, and then with one last look round the waiting room, she added as the tears began to slide down her cheeks, 'but I'm telling you the truth. I was in the hospital and couldn't look after my girls for a week or two, and they sent them to Australia.'

Lily had planned to go round to Ship Street next, to tell Mavis what she'd discovered, but when she reached the square outside the council offices, she was suddenly so tired she wasn't even sure she could make it home. Exhaustion overcame her and she almost collapsed onto one of the stone benches in the square. One or two passers-by, seeing her tear-streaked face, looked at her awkwardly and hurried past. After a moment or two, Lily's pride reasserted itself and ashamed of being seen to weep in the street, she pulled out her handkerchief and wiped her eyes.

The clock on the town hall struck four. Lily stared up at it in amazement. Could it really be four o'clock in the afternoon? She'd left home soon after nine. No wonder she was tired. She thought again about going to see Mavis, but by the time she got there, Jimmy would be coming home for his tea. No, Lily decided, I'll go home, and go round Mavis's first thing in the morning, soon as Jimmy's gone to work.

It was well after nine the next morning when Lily left for Ship Street. The day was still chilly but the drizzle of the day before had disappeared and there was a pale winter sun in the pale winter sky. She walked slowly through the comfortably familiar streets, her mind calmer now, despite the dull ache that she'd carried with her ever since she'd received Rita's letter. She didn't hurry. Lily wanted to be sure that Jimmy had gone before she arrived; she needed uninterrupted time with Mavis.

It was a haggard-looking Mavis who opened the door to her knock. Still in a grubby dressing gown, her feet bare, her hair lank and uncombed, and with a screaming baby on her hip, Mavis was the picture of exhaustion.

One look was enough. Lily dumped her bag and her stick on the hall floor and reached out to take the crying child into her arms, cradling him against her, his hot, sticky face buried in her neck.

'Ssh, now, Ricky,' she soothed. 'Ssh, now. What's the matter with you then, eh?'

Wordlessly, Mavis turned and led the way into the kitchen, where the remains of breakfast lay on the table and last night's supper dishes filled the sink.

'He won't stop crying.' Mavis was almost in tears herself. 'I been up most of the night with him, and he won't stop, and Jimmy's shouting at him and shouting at me. I'm so *tired*, Mum, I don't know what to do.'

It was clear that Mavis was in no state to talk about the girls now, so Lily, still rocking the baby against her shoulder, said, 'You go up to bed for an hour's kip, love. I'll look after him for a while and wake you later.' Mavis needed no second bidding and moments later she was crawling back into her unmade bed.

By the time she resurfaced, Lily had cleaned the kitchen and made a scratch meal from odds and ends she found in the pantry and was feeding a clean and dry Richard.

'Mum, you're a wonder,' Mavis said as she took in the quiet baby and the tidy kitchen.

'Well, we're all right just now,' agreed Lily, 'so you go back up and get yourself dressed. Have a bath and wash your hair. Make you feel much better, that will. Go on,' she encouraged as Mavis hesitated, 'up you go. Then I want to talk to you.'

Half an hour later, a much-refreshed Mavis reappeared in the kitchen. Together they ate the soup and sandwiches Lily had made, while Richard slept in his pram.

'Well,' said Mavis at last, 'you said you wanted to talk to me. What about? You ain't come round here just to clean my house, have you?'

'I come to see how you and Ricky was getting on,' replied Lily, 'but I do need to talk to you about something.' She paused awkwardly, not knowing quite how to go on. She'd rehearsed it at home, but now, faced with Mavis's expectant expression, she wasn't sure where to begin.

'Go on,' urged Mavis, 'spit it out!'

'I had a letter,' began Lily, and then, since there was no going back, she went on, 'I had a letter, from Rita.'

'From Reet?' Mavis sounded incredulous. 'What she write to you for?'

Lily ignored the question and asked one herself. 'Mavis, do you know where your girls are?'

'What d'you mean, "where they are"?' Mavis was immediately defensive.

'I mean where they are now. Where they live.'

'Course I do. You went there, that EVER-Care place, down at Russell Green.'

'No,' replied Lily flatly. 'They ain't.'

'What? So where they gone, then?' Mavis asked, wiping the last of her sandwich round her soup plate and stuffing it into her mouth.

'You don't sound very interested,' remarked Lily, watching her chewing on the bread.

Mavis looked up in surprise. 'Course I'm interested,' she said. 'They're my kids, ain't they?'

Another time Lily might have asked Mavis if she remembered that herself, but now she simply said, 'Then I'll tell you where they are, Mavis. They're in Australia.'

'Australia!' echoed Mavis. 'What d'you mean, Australia? They can't be. We put them in EVER-Care.'

'And EVER-Care put them in Australia.'

'They can't do that,' said Mavis, as if dismissing the idea.

'They can and they have,' snapped Lily. 'Your girls is in Australia.' She reached down for her bag and pulled out Rita's letter. 'Here, see for yourself.'

Mavis took the envelope and pulled out the letter. She stared at the first few lines, and then at the blacked-out words. She turned to the second sheet, fingering the paper as if to feel the words that had been concealed. She read the letter again and then looked up at her mother in disbelief.

'It don't say they're in Australia,' she said. 'It don't mention Australia. Where'd you get that daft idea from?'

'They've gone somewhere in a ship. Reet says it took six weeks.'

'Don't mean Australia,' replied Mavis mulishly. 'It's Reet having a joke, that's what it is. She's made some mistakes, look, and scrubbed them out. She ain't really in Australia.'

'Look at the envelope, Mavis,' said Lily, holding it out. 'Look at the stamps. They've got Australia on them. That's where they are.'

'They can't be,' Mavis whispered. 'They're in EVER-Care.'

'No, they ain't,' Lily repeated. 'I went round the EVER-Care again and they ain't there.'

'It don't mean they're in Australia,' cried Mavis. 'They can't be. How will they get home again?'

'Mavis, they ain't coming home again,' responded Lily, knowing as she said it that it was true. Australia was too far away, their girls weren't coming back.

'What you mean, they ain't coming back?' demanded Mavis. 'Course they're coming back. They're coming home here when Richard's a bit bigger.'

Lily stared at her in disbelief. Surely Mavis didn't still believe that. Didn't she know she'd signed them away when she'd put them into Laurel House? She must know.

'But Mavis, you signed the papers.'

'Yeah, well, just for now, right?'

'No, Mavis,' cried her mother. 'Not just for now. You signed your kids away for good.'

'No,' Mavis burst out. 'It was just till I got sorted with Richard.'

'But they came home, didn't they? They ran away from the EVER-Care place and Reet brought them home. You sent them back.'

'I didn't, it was Jimmy...' stammered Mavis.

'And you let him.'

'I wasn't ready then, was I? Richard was only new. I couldn't look after them and him proper.'

'Mavis,' Lily's voice was icy cold, 'Mavis, you knew you wasn't ever going to have them back. You chose Jimmy ahead of your own kids.'

'I didn't!' Mavis shrieked. 'It was only till I got sorted.'

'But you signed them papers,' Lily repeated in despair, 'to give your kids to EVER-Care.'

'I didn't know what they said, did I?' Mavis protested feebly.

'Then what you sign them for?'

'I don't know! I just signed, OK? I just signed what Jimmy told me to sign.'

'You can bet your life Jimmy knew what they said,' sighed Lily. 'You have to face it, Mavis, he didn't mean them girls to come back.' And nor, if you're honest, did you, she thought.

Mavis was now realizing the truth; she'd lost her daughters for good. She stared at Lily, ashen-faced, and the tears began to slide down her cheeks. 'What am I going to do, Mum?' she whispered. 'How am I going to get them back?'

In the face of Mavis's despair, all Lily's anger at her stupidity melted away. It was all too late. Lily reached out and took her hands. 'I don't know, love. I been to the home and I been to the Children's Officer, and they both say we can't do nothing about it. We don't even know where in Australia they are.'

'But the letter,' Mavis cried. 'The letter from Reet. That must tell us where.'

'There's nothing on the letter to say. And you saw lots of what Reet wrote was censored.'

'What d'you mean, censored?'

'You saw. All crossed out so we can't read it. Like in the war when they blacked out bits of letters so's not to let the Germans know where our troops was. You remember.'

'But why do that to Reet's letter?'

'I don't know, just so we couldn't find her, I s'pose,' answered Lily. 'Still,' she went on, 'they couldn't do nothing about the postmark. It's smudged, but you can read the letters, NSW. New South Wales, which is a big part of Australia, very big, not a town.'

'Well, you can write back—' began Mavis, but Lily cut her off.

'Mavis, I can't write back. Ain't you been listening to me? We ain't got an address to write to, have we?'

'Why'd Reet write to you and not to me?' asked Mavis angrily. 'I'm her mum, not you!'

Lily looked at her in despair, but all she said was, 'I expect she was afraid Jimmy'd find the letter. Look, love, don't worry about that now. We need to be thinking how to find our girls. There's probably ways we can find out more if we put our thinking caps on.'

Mavis had dissolved into tears again, and Richard began to wail as well. Mavis ignored him, and it was Lily who reached over and lifted him from the pram.

'Why don't I take Ricky home with me for the night?' she suggested. 'That way you can get a good night's sleep, eh? And you and Jimmy can have an evening to yourselves.'

An hour later Lily was wheeling the pram down Ship Street on her way home. Tucked in beside Richard was a bundle of clothes and some nappies. The clothes were dirty, but Lily didn't mind. She'd been determined to get the baby out of the house before Jimmy came home. When Mavis told him about the girls, there would be a row, and Lily didn't want Richard in the middle of it. She planned to keep him for more than one night; it would give Mavis time to rest, and Lily wanted to be sure that things had calmed down before he went back home.

When Lily had gone, Mavis dropped her head in her hands in despair. Where were her girls? She'd never see them again. Never. She went to a drawer in the kitchen dresser and pulled out the photograph that Carrie had given her, Rita and Rosie in their new dresses. She'd kept it hidden from Jimmy, tucked into an old magazine at the bottom of the drawer. Now, she looked down at her girls, so happy, so trusting, and it was as if something collapsed inside her. How could she have let them go? For the first time for months she thought of Don. Where was her picture of him? That had disappeared. Jimmy must have taken it and thrown it away. Clutching the snapshot, Mavis began to sob. Later, her tears exhausted, she fell asleep with her head on the table.

Chapter 29

J immy Randall was not in a good mood. He'd had a lousy day,
clearing a bombsite in the teeming rain.

Knocking off at the end of the day, Jimmy and Charlie made
straight for the Red Lion. Charlie bought the first round, and
when they had downed that in double quick time Jimmy went
for the second. He was in no hurry to go home to a miserable
wife and a squalling baby. When Charlie got up to leave, Jimmy
stayed, bought himself another pint and sat, brooding, in a
corner.

'The trouble with Mav,' he'd moaned to Charlie earlier, 'is
that she's let herself go, know what I mean? And she don't want
it no more. Says she's too tired. Too tired for a good fuck? I said
to her, I told her, what she needs is a good seeing to, but, no, she
won't have none of it. Says the baby's making her tired. The
baby, I ask you? How can looking after a baby make you tired?
He sleeps most of the day!'

Charlie, the father of five himself, nodded and taking another
pull at his pint, replied, 'Women get funny about that sometimes, mate. But she'll get over it, you'll see.'

Well, thought Jimmy, as he finished his pint and treated
himself to a whisky chaser, she can bloody well get over it
tonight. She's going to get a bloody good seeing to, and no
mistake. I've had enough. One more drink for me, and then I'm
off to sort her out.

He bought himself another whisky that he couldn't afford,
thinking as he handed over the money that Mavis would have to

go short on the housekeeping this week, but that was tough, he needed a drink.

When he got home, he found the house in darkness. A street lamp gave him enough light to fit his reluctant key into the lock, and when finally Jimmy managed to open the door, he staggered into the dark hall.

'Mavis!' he bellowed. 'Where the bloody hell are you?'

There was no reply, but he heard a sound in the kitchen and slamming his hand on the switch, he flooded the hall with light.

'Mavis!' he shouted again. 'Mavis, what's going on? Where are you?'

A reply came from the kitchen. 'In here.'

'What the fuck are you sitting in the dark for?' he demanded, as he pushed open the door. His words were slurred, his step unsteady and he lurched against the door frame, flicking on the kitchen light, before slumping heavily onto a chair.

Mavis was sitting at the table, her eyes red from weeping and bleary with sleep. He stared at her for a moment, trying to focus his own eyes, then he looked round and seeing no sign of the pram, asked, 'Where's the kid?'

'Mum's got him,' Mavis replied wearily. 'She's keeping him for the night, so's I can get some real sleep.'

'Is she now?' Jimmy gave her a lewd grin. 'Well, that suits us just fine, don't it? Means we can have some fun, you and me. Not have to think about him.'

Mavis still didn't get up from the table, and Jimmy looked round him.

'Where's me tea?' he demanded. 'You ain't got the kid to look after, and you ain't even got me tea on the table when I get home, you slut.'

Mavis got shakily to her feet and reached for the kettle. Jimmy grabbed her wrist as she went past him and jerked her towards him. 'I said, what you been doing all day? Where's my tea?'

Mavis tried to snatch her hand away, but his fingers bit into her wrist.

'Let me go,' she screamed, grabbing at the table to steady herself. Jimmy's eyes swivelled to the table and fell on the photo of Rita and Rosie still lying there. Letting go of Mavis, he snatched it up, waving it at her in fury.

'What the hell's all this?' he roared. 'Where'd you get this? That what you've been blubbing about? Well, you can cut that out. Them kids is nothing to do with us no more!'

'No,' shrieked Mavis, grabbing at the photo. 'Give that to me!'

Jimmy laughed and pushed her away, keeping the picture out of reach. 'Know what I'm going to do with this?' he jeered. 'This is what I'm going to do with this!' He held the photo high above his head, and with great deliberation, ripped it across and across, dropping the four pieces onto the floor and scuffing them with his feet.

Mavis gave a wail of anguish as he trampled them under his boots. 'My babies!' She launched herself at him trying to push him off the pieces of photograph. Jimmy caught her by her shoulders and gripping tightly, shook her so violently that her head jerked back and forth like a broken doll's.

'Them kids have nothing to do with us,' he shouted again. 'Get it? They... don't... live... here... no... more.' And with each word he banged her shoulders against the kitchen dresser.

'Because of you, you bastard!' screeched Mavis, her fury overcoming her fear. 'You sent them to Australia! It's your fault that I ain't got my kids. They're the other side of the world, and it's your fault.'

'Australia! Don't be daft!' snapped Jimmy, giving her a shove so that she staggered sideways and had to grab hold of the gas cooker to stop herself from falling. 'They're in Russell Green, you stupid cow, and you know it.'

'No, they ain't!' screamed Mavis. 'They've been sent away.'

'Good riddance!' snarled Jimmy. 'Australia's welcome to them.' He slumped back onto his chair. 'Now, where's my tea?'

'There ain't none,' Mavis said flatly.

'Ain't none?'

'No, nothing.'

'Then we'll get on with the next thing!' shouted Jimmy. 'And don't you tell me you're too tired, 'cos I don't give a flying fuck.' He gave a drunken laugh as he tried to grab her, 'and that's what we're going to do, you and me, whether you like it or not.'

'Don't you touch me!' shrieked Mavis. 'Get your hands off me.'

'Why? Don't like it no more?' jeered Jimmy. 'Was a time I remember when you couldn't get enough of it. Like a bitch on heat, you was. Couldn't wait to get your knickers off. Well, tonight's your lucky night, bitch.' He lurched to his feet, and made another grab at her, blocking her escape to the door.

'Keep away from me, you bastard!' hissed Mavis. 'You sent my kids away, and I let you. But you'll never touch me again.'

'Says who?' grinned Jimmy. He could feel his manhood stirring in his trousers, growing with excitement as she faced up to him across the table. He'd always enjoyed a bit of resistance, a glint of fear. Oh yes! Once he'd got hold of her, it would be the fuck of all fucks.

'Leave me alone,' she was shouting, backing away from him. 'Get away from me!'

Jimmy laughed aloud now, enjoying her terror. She couldn't escape. He could see the bolt was across the back door, and if she made a dash for it, he'd be on her long before she got the door unlocked. Slowly, deliberately, he walked towards her, looming over her as she cowered into the corner beside the dresser.

'Now, bitch, we're going to have a little fun,' he slurred. He made a grab for her, and catching hold of her by the hair, dragged her, shrieking out of the corner. Her cries excited him even more and holding her against him with one hand, he undid his belt with the other. Twisting away from him, Mavis caught up a kitchen knife from the dresser and slashed it at him, only missing his face by inches. With a roar, Jimmy caught hold of her wrist and wrenching it violently, tried to force the knife from her hand. But Mavis had firm hold, and hampered as he was with his trousers sliding down his legs, he couldn't twist it from her grasp. Together they staggered back against the wall, Jimmy turning the knife away from him as he tried to wrest it from her. Unable to do so, he rammed her hard against the wall, crashing the back of her head against the uneven plaster. Despite the explosion of pain in her skull, Mavis still gripped the knife, and it was only when Jimmy bent her arm back at an impossible angle that she released her hold and he pulled it out of her hand. Still struggling to free herself from his grasp, Mavis kicked out, catching her feet in his loose trousers and together they collapsed into a heap on the floor. Jimmy landed on top, crushing her beneath him, the knife still in his hand. Mavis's scream, cut off, transmuted into a gurgle as a fountain of blood exploded upwards, spraying them both. Jimmy rolled away and heaving himself to his hands and knees, stared down in horror at Mavis and the kitchen knife now protruding from her neck. He knelt, staring unbelievingly as the blood continued to pump from the wound, spreading in a crimson pool on the floor. Mavis stared back up at him, her lips moving, but no sound coming from them, just a few bubbles of blood. Jimmy reached for the knife and with one determined twist ripped it free. With the blade came another gush of blood, and before his eyes Mavis's head lolled sideways as life drained from her.

For a long, stunned moment, Jimmy looked at the knife in his hand and then with sudden rage he threw it across the room.

'Stupid, bloody bitch!' he bellowed. 'What d'you pick up the knife for? Stupid, stupid, bloody bitch!'

He heaved himself up onto his feet and looked down at her again, the familiar anger rising in him once more. Mavis was dead, there was no doubt about that, she lay on the floor like a discarded rag doll, and it was all her fault. If she hadn't said no in the first place, he wouldn't have lost his temper. She was his wife, for God's sake, she had no right to say no. All he'd wanted was his right as a husband, and she'd been screeching at him. Any man would've lost it.

He felt a sudden burst of panic. She was dead, and they'd say he'd done it. That bitch Lily would never believe it was all Mavis's fault.

'Shit! Shit! Shit!' he shouted to the kitchen. 'Shit!'

What was he going to do? For several moments his mind

seemed a blank, but staring down at Mavis, who returned his stare with sightless eyes, he tried to think. A plan. He needed a plan. Christ! He turned his back on her. Couldn't think with her staring at him.

Get rid of her body somewhere? Somewhere she'd never be found. Then he'd say she'd run off and left him. If he could just get rid of her body and clean up the kitchen a bit... Then he looked at the blood all over his clothes, the blood pooled on the floor, the blood spattered on the wall, and knew that it would be impossible to clean up the mess that was Mavis's death.

No, his brain was working now, no, his only chance was to get out, and get out fast. With luck she wouldn't be found until tomorrow or even the next day, if that interfering cow Lily didn't come poking round. Twelve hours, maybe more, for him to disappear into the melting pot of London.

Without looking again at the rag doll that lay at his feet, Jimmy staggered from the room. Had to get out of his blood-stained clothes. Had to clean himself up. He hauled himself upstairs and into the bathroom. There he shed his clothes and standing in the bath, scrubbed himself down. The water turned pink as Mavis's blood was sluiced away, and when at last it ran clear, he towelled himself dry before going into the bedroom and dressing in clean clothes from the skin out. Quickly he packed a grip with another set of clean clothes, neatly ironed by Mavis, his demob suit, and adding his razor and toothbrush, he zipped up the bag and made his way to the front door. Gingerly, he removed his cash from the pocket of his bloody trousers. The trousers he left discarded with the rest of the blood-soaked clothes on the bathroom floor; with Mavis lying in a pool of blood on the kitchen floor there seemed to Jimmy no point in trying to hide them.

He turned off all the lights before opening the front door and taking a quick look along the street. The night was cold, frost sparkling on the pavement, with a new moon and a sky bright with stars. The street was empty, and without a backwards glance, Jimmy stepped out and walked away into the night.

Chapter 30

L ily had had a broken night with Richard. He had woken up several times, apparently crying for no reason. Each time she'd soothed his distress he'd sleep for a maximum of half an hour and then start to cry again.

If he's been doing this ever since he was born, Lily thought, I'm not surprised that poor Mavis is like a limp rag, nor, she had grudgingly to admit, that Jimmy had found it difficult to cope with as well.

At six o'clock she gave up and made up another bottle that Richard guzzled down as if he were starving, after which he fell asleep. With immense relief Lily sunk back into bed and instantly fell into a deep sleep herself. Neither of them woke again until well after nine.

Lily took her time getting them both up and dressed for the day. By ten they were both ready, and she decided to walk back over to Ship Street. Mavis is probably enjoying a well-earned lie-in, Lily thought. Still, by the time we get there, she'll be ready for a cuppa and some breakfast.

When she reached Mavis's front door, there was no sign of life within the house, but the door was on the latch, and leaving the pram outside, Lily picked up Richard and carried him indoors.

'Mavis! Mavis?' she called, but there was no reply. The house seemed eerily still. Lily paused at the bottom of the stairs and looked up to the landing, wondering if Mavis was still in bed. It was getting on for eleven, and even if she was having a lie-in, surely she'd be up by now. She called again. 'Mavis? You awake, love?' Maybe she'd already slipped out to the shops. With luck she'd had a good night's sleep and was feeling better today.

Lily put Richard back in the pram, which she then manoeuvred into the tiny hallway. Mavis would see him there the minute she got in, and meanwhile, she'd pop the kettle on.

Lily pushed open the kitchen door and froze. Mavis was lying in a crumpled heap on the floor, a pool of congealed blood about her head and neck. For a heart-stopping moment Lily stared down at her unable to believe her eyes. She took a step forward, and found herself gazing into Mavis's glazed and staring eyes.

'Mavis?' she croaked. 'Mavis? Oh my God, no!' For a moment the room seemed to spin and closing her eyes, Lily clutched at the table to stop herself falling. She slumped onto a chair and put her head between her knees, feeling the blood pounding in her ears. Once the world stopped whirling, she raised her head again, and with a deliberate act of will made herself look again at Mavis's broken body. Fighting down the nausea that threatened to overcome her, she got unsteadily to her feet and reached down to her daughter's face, stone-cold to the touch. As she withdrew her hand, she felt the stickiness of Mavis's blood on her fingers, and the full horror of what she had found flooded through her, stirring her to action.

The police. She must call the police. Jimmy had done this to Mavis, and must be on the run. They must get after him at once. The surge of hatred for Jimmy Randall that coursed through her brought her new strength, and she groped her way to the front door. As she passed the pram in the hallway she saw that Richard had fallen asleep again. No need to move him, he was safe enough there. Jimmy certainly wouldn't be coming back. She had to get to a telephone and the nearest call box was at the far end of the road. She set off along the pavement, going as fast as she could with no stick to support her. Her legs were shaking, her breathing ragged and the tears were now streaming down her face. At that moment Carrie emerged from her house, almost colliding with Lily as she passed. She grasped Lily's arm to stop her from falling and then saw her face.

'Mrs Sharples?' she cried. 'Mrs Sharples? Are you all right? Oh my God, what's happened?'

'Mavis, it's Mavis.' Lily's breath came in shuddering gasps. 'That bastard's done for her. She's dead. On the kitchen floor. Got to call the police.'

'Dead?' Carrie stared at her, unbelieving. 'Mavis is dead?'

'On the floor. We must get the police. I got to get to the phone box.'

'I'll go,' Carrie said. 'You come into my house and wait, I'll go and ring 999.'

'No.' Lily shook her head. 'You ring 999, I'll go back to Mavis. Ricky's still there, in his pram.'

'But you're in shock.' Carrie looked uncertain. 'You sure, going back there? Being in the house with...' Her voice tailed away.

'With Mavis,' Lily finished for her. 'With my daughter. You get the police, Carrie, and I'll wait for them... with Mavis.' Without waiting for Carrie to agree, Lily turned back towards number 9. Carrie took one look at her stooped but determined figure and raced off down the road to the phone box.

Lily went back into the house and sat on the stairs, one hand on the handle of the pram, rocking it gently although Richard was still blissfully asleep. She couldn't bring herself to go back into the kitchen, but she needed to be near her daughter. Now there was nothing further she could do, Lily's strength drained away and she began to sob.

Constable Chapman found her five minutes later. On his beat, he was met by the distraught Carrie rushing to the phone box. Seeing him, tall and strong, a visible police presence, she'd grabbed him by the arm and blurted out what had happened. He did his best to calm her.

'You go on and dial 999,' he said, 'I'll go and see to the lady. Mrs Sharples, you said?'

'Yes, number 9. It's her daughter, Mavis, what's dead.'

'Go on and ring,' Constable Chapman said. 'I'll go and wait with her until help comes.'

When he reached the house, he knocked on the open door and walking in found Lily sitting on the stairs, sobbing.

'Mrs Sharples?' he said gently. 'Mrs Sharples, I'm Constable Chapman.'

Lily looked up at him and gestured towards the kitchen door, whispering, 'In there.'

The constable pushed open the door, and what he saw made him recoil. Mavis Randall was on the floor, and clearly she'd been stabbed, though from where he stood he could see no sign of the murder weapon. There was no need to check to see if she were dead, the staring eyes and the blood loss confirmed that. Nevertheless he went over to her and touched her cheek, alabaster pale and icy cold. Clearly she'd been dead for several hours. No doubt the police doctor would be able to estimate time of death.

For a long moment he stared down at her. She looked familiar. Where had he seen her before? Then he remembered. It was the house to which he'd brought two lost little girls, and this pale woman had been sitting at the table, nursing a baby. He remembered the misery of both mother and children when they'd been dragged screaming from the house, taken away by some social worker. The memory of that night flooded through him, the anger, the despair, the misery that had filled the little house… and the fear. The mother and the girls had all been terrified of the husband. He remembered standing outside in the street when the girls had been driven away, watching the husband slamming out of the house, headed for the pub. He'd known then that there was no love in that house, but there had been more, a brewing violence which had finally boiled over into murder.

Jumping to conclusions, he reminded himself. We don't know if it's the husband who's killed this woman so brutally, but, he thought as he closed the door again, it seems the most likely explanation.

Lily was still sitting in a huddle on the stairs. Her sobs had subsided, but she was still shaking. The big policeman sat down beside her and took her hand.

'Can you tell me anything about what's happened here?' he asked gently.

'He's killed her, that's what's happened,' Lily replied. 'That bastard Jimmy Randall's been and killed her, my lovely Mavis.'

'How can you be so sure it's him?' asked Chapman.

''Cos he was always knocking her about,' Lily said. 'Often saw her with a black eye, or other bruises. I told her he was a violent bastard, even before they was married, but she wouldn't admit it, not to me, not to no one.'

Chapman looked at the baby in the pram. It must be the one he'd seen Mavis nursing. 'And what about him, or is it a her?'

'Him. Richard. He was with me for the night. I took him home 'cos Mavis weren't getting no sleep. He had her up at all hours, and that Jimmy, all he could do was threaten her and shout at the baby when he cried. Thought I'd give her a break.'

'You don't live here, then, in this house?'

'No, I got my own place. I should have taken the both of them,' she cried. 'If Mavis had come to me last night, he'd still have his mother.'

As she spoke, Richard stirred in the pram, waking up with a whimper. At once Lily scooped him up into her arms, holding him close, burying her face in the soft fluff of his hair, comforted a little by his warm softness.

'Are there any other children?' Chapman asked, wondering about the girls.

Lily raised bleak eyes to his. 'Yes, two little girls, but they've been took to Australia.'

'Australia!' Chapman repeated, startled.

'It's a long story.' Lily was too drained by the events of the morning to say more. In her heart she knew that this was the reason Mavis was dead. She must have confronted Jimmy with the news about Australia and they'd had a fight. 'She loved them,' Lily said softly. 'She wanted them back.'

The insistent clanging of bells announced the arrival of two

345

police cars sweeping into the street. At the same time Carrie reappeared hovering on the pavement outside.

'Wait here,' Chapman said to Lily, and went outside to greet his plain-clothes colleagues. Detective Inspector Marshall listened for a moment and then, with a brief nod, came into the house. Lily was still standing in the narrow hallway with the baby in her arms. She held him closer as the policeman came through the front door, as if afraid he might take him away, but the detective merely nodded towards the kitchen and said, 'In there?'

'Yes,' whispered Lily, averting her eyes. The man paused before opening the door and said, 'Perhaps you'd like to wait outside, madam. We'll need to search the whole house.' Adding in a surprisingly gentle voice, 'And I expect that little chap will be needing a feed soon. Is there a neighbour you could go to?'

Lily nodded. She could go to Carrie, for a while, anyway. Holding Richard tightly in her arms she went outside. A crowd was gathering now, attracted by the police cars, and Constable Chapman was holding them back. More plain-clothes men hurried into number 9, and another car arrived from which a doctor emerged, carrying his black bag. A murmur ran through the crowd as they watched, so far unaware of what had actually happened. The speculation was rife, and several of those at the front of the crowd tried to pump Constable Chapman. He remained solidly silent, his expression blank, giving nothing away. When Lily appeared, one or two recognized her.

'Hey, Lil,' cried someone, 'what's going on, then?'

'Yeah,' called someone else, 'anybody hurt?'

Lily ignored the questions, and turning her back on the crowd joined Carrie and asked, 'Can we wait at your house? Ricky needs a feed and a change.'

'Course you can, Mrs S,' responded Carrie immediately.

'I'll need the pram,' Lily said. 'It's got my bag and Ricky's stuff in it.'

'Don't worry,' Carrie said, 'I'll fetch it.'

Lily paused by Constable Chapman to tell him where she was going.

'Good idea,' he said. 'We'll know where to find you when we need you. I'm sure one of the detectives'll be in to see you shortly.'

It was an hour or so before there was a knock on Carrie's door and a young man with dark hair and a neat moustache came in.

'Mrs Sharples?' he asked.

'In here,' replied Carrie, and led him into the front room. She'd already put a match to the fire, and the room was warm and comforting. Carrie didn't know what John would say about having a daytime fire, but she felt this was an emergency. Lily was in shock and needed to be kept warm. She had refused anything to eat, but Carrie had made sure she drank some tea, adding a generous spoonful of her own sugar ration.

Lily had told Carrie that she'd shown Mavis Rita's letter.

'What did she say?' asked Carrie.

'She was very upset, course she was,' said Lily. 'She was going to have it out with Jimmy...' her voice broke on a sob, '... and I suppose she did. I shouldn't have told her.'

'You had to tell her, Mrs Sharples,' said Carrie. 'It wasn't your fault.'

Lily had dealt with Richard's needs and he was sitting on the floor, propped up with a cushion, happily playing with some toys belonging to Carrie's children. Lily herself sat in a chair by the fire, but despite the warmth from the leaping flames, she felt cold, chilled to the bone.

'Mrs Sharples,' said the detective, 'I'm Detective Sergeant Stanton. I am so sorry for your loss.' He hesitated before going on awkwardly, 'I know it's a difficult time, but I do need to ask you some questions. Do you feel up to answering them now?'

'If it'll help you catch that bastard, Jimmy Randall, you ask me anything you like,' replied Lily vehemently.

'Thank you,' said DS Stanton and drawing up a chair, he sat down opposite her. 'Well, we do suspect that your daughter was probably stabbed by her husband, but of course we aren't sure yet.'

'Aren't you? I am,' snapped Lily. 'He was always knocking her about, weren't he, Carrie?'

Carrie, who was still standing by the door, nodded in agreement.

'Thank you, Mrs...?'

'Maunder.'

'Mrs Maunder. We'll be needing a statement from you in due course.' Stanton turned back to Lily. 'Can you give me some background information about your daughter and son-in-law? It sounds as if their marriage wasn't a happy one.'

'Happy!' snorted Lily. 'It was a disaster from the start and before.' Stanton made a quick note, but he asked nothing more and Lily went on, 'They only got married 'cos he'd got her in the family way.' Her eyes strayed to Richard, sitting between them on the floor. 'And everything went from bad to worse when he got rid of her daughters.'

Stanton looked startled. 'Got rid of her daughters? How d'you mean?'

Lily told him everything, and as she talked he took notes, his pencil flying over the pages, so that he missed nothing.

When at last she lapsed into silence, he asked, 'Can you tell me anything about Jimmy Randall's family, or his friends?'

'Not much,' admitted Lily. 'His father's still alive. Jimmy used to live with him till he moved in with my Mavis.'

'Do you know his address?'

'Not exactly,' replied Lily, 'but somewhere in Leyton Street, I think.'

Stanton nodded and made another note. 'And his name?'

Lily shrugged. 'I only met him once, at the wedding, and I called him Mr Randall. Never heard his Christian name.'

'What about friends?'

'His best man was called Charlie. Don't know his other name, but I do know they worked together.'

'Do you know where he worked?'

'On a building site somewhere.'

'You don't know where?'

'No. I never heard.' She thought for a moment. 'Jimmy drinks at the Red Lion, I expect someone there'll know.'

DS Stanton made another note. 'Thank you, Mrs Sharples. I think that's all for now.'

'No, it ain't,' Lily told him. 'You ain't told me what you found yet, in the house, I mean.'

'Well, I'm not sure—' began Stanton, but Lily interrupted him.

'Well, I am. It's my daughter what's been murdered, I'm entitled to know what you found.'

'I'm afraid all I can tell you, Mrs Sharples, is that the doctor has pronounced her dead—'

'Anyone could see that, for God's sake,' cried Lily in frustration.

'And her body has been removed to the mortuary so that a post-mortem can be performed.'

Lily looked at him, horrified. 'You ain't going to cut her up!' she cried in dismay. 'What you got to do that for?'

'It's just normal procedure,' replied Stanton uncomfortably, 'to establish cause of death and—'

'I can tell you how she died,' exploded Lily. 'He cut her throat!'

'It isn't as simple as that,' Stanton tried to explain, 'there may be clues that will help us identify the killer—'

'But we *know* who killed her.' Lily stared at him in disbelief.

'We know who *may* have killed her,' Stanton said patiently, 'but we have to find the evidence to establish it beyond doubt.'

Lily seemed dumbfounded, and Stanton took advantage of her silence to say, 'Now, if you could just give me your full name and address, Mrs Sharples, someone will be round tomorrow to take a formal statement.'

'What was this then?' demanded Lily. 'Weren't this a statement?'

'Not exactly, Mrs Sharples, we needed some information to work on, and you've given us that. And I can assure you,' Stanton went on hastily, 'that we shall be following up all the leads that you've given us today.' He snapped his notebook closed and getting to his feet, turned to Carrie, who had stood listening to the whole interview.

'Thank you, Mrs Maunder,' he said. 'You knew Mavis Randall well, I assume.'

Carrie nodded. 'Yes, she was my best friend.'

'Then we'll want to talk to you, too,' he said.

'Well, what did you think of that?' asked Lily dully when Carrie returned from showing Stanton out.

'S'pose he had to ask them questions,' Carrie said carefully. She didn't want to upset Lily, but she'd thought the detective had been quite sensitive in his questions. 'They have to find out what's been going on, don't they?'

Richard, tired of sitting on the floor, began to grizzle, and Lily leaned down and picked him up.

'Come on, young man,' she said, 'we'd better get home.'

'Will you be OK,' asked Carrie, 'going home by yourself?'

'Course I will,' retorted Lily. 'Why wouldn't I be? I always go home by myself.'

'Yes, well, I know,' said Carrie, 'but you've had a dreadful shock today, ain't you? Why don't you wait till my John gets in, and he'll come with you? I'd come myself, but the kids'll be home from school directly.'

'I'm sorry, Carrie,' said Lily. 'I've taken up your whole day.'

'Don't be daft,' Carrie took her hand. 'You've had a bloody awful day, and I'm just glad I was here to help you.'

'So am I. Don't know what I'd have done without you, honest. But I need to get home, feel my own things round me; look after Ricky. Let's face it, he ain't got anyone else, now, has he?'

In the end Carrie gave up trying to persuade her to wait for John.

When Lily emerged into the street, she was relieved to see that the crowd of on-lookers had dispersed, but glancing back at number 9, she saw Constable Chapman standing outside it, and on impulse she went over to him.

'Why are you standing outside the house?' she asked. 'Haven't they finished?'

'No one's allowed inside,' he replied, 'still a crime scene.'

'Can I go in?' asked Lily. 'I need to get some things for the baby, clothes and stuff.'

"Fraid not,' answered the constable. 'No one's allowed in.'

'When can I?' asked Lily. 'I need stuff.'

'Few days, I should think. They'll be able to tell you more down at the station. They've taken a whole load of things away to look at. I expect they'll let you back in when they're sure they don't need anything else. What're you going to do now?' Chapman asked.

'Me, I'm going to go home and start bringing up my grandson.'

'Won't the Children's Department offer you some help there?' suggested Chapman. 'I could have a word—'

'Don't you dare!'

Constable Chapman looked taken aback by her vehemence, but before he could say any more, Lily went on, 'We won't be going near them, thank you very much. They've took two of my grandchildren already, and they ain't getting their hands on this one.' And with this she set off down the street, pushing the pram that carried her grandson to the safety of her home.

'That's one brave and determined lady,' Constable Chapman murmured as he watched her go. And thinking back to the courage and determination he'd seen on Rita's face all those months ago, he realized where the little girl had got it from.

Chapter 31

Lily went into her house and closed the door. The warm familiarity of her home enveloped her, and suddenly she felt completely exhausted. She had been running on adrenaline ever since she'd found Mavis, and now, back in her own kitchen, she was so tired she could hardly stand. She lifted Richard out of the pram and holding him close, sank down onto a chair. Although she knew he needed changing, she hadn't the energy to do it. She simply sat on the chair, rocking him in her arms, the tears slipping down her cheeks, soaking into his soft baby hair; and this was how Anne Baillie found her.

She'd heard about Mavis from a customer in the shop and she'd stripped off her apron and gone straight round to Hampton Road.

She reached out and took the baby from Lily's arms. 'I'll see to him,' she said. 'You put the kettle on and make some tea.'

Lily did as she was told, mechanically going through the familiar routine, and when Anne returned to the kitchen with Richard, clean and comfortable, Lily had made tea and set out cups. As soon as she saw Richard, Lily reached out for him.

Anne poured the tea and then said, 'I heard about Mavis, Lily. Is there anything Fred or I can do?'

With Richard cradled in her arms, Lily began to speak. In a low voice she described what she'd found, and as the vision of Mavis lying dead on her kitchen floor filled her mind, she began to sob again. The tea cooled, ignored, on the table as Lily relived the events of the morning and Anne sat and listened in horror.

'She was just laying there,' Lily wept, 'just laying on the kitchen floor. The blood was all round her... so much blood, and her eyes, just staring and staring.'

When she lapsed into silence Anne took the now sleeping Richard and laid him gently in the pram. 'I think I should come and stay with you tonight,' she said. 'You shouldn't be by yourself.'

Lily was about to refuse, but suddenly she knew Anne was right, she didn't want to be alone, not for tonight. She had Richard to look after, and she felt so tired, so very tired. 'You're very kind, Anne. But just for tonight. I'll be all right tomorrow, looking after Ricky and that.'

So Anne stayed the night, and it was she who answered the door to Sergeant Stanton and a Constable Turner.

'We've come to take a formal statement from Mrs Sharples,' Stanton explained.

They sat in the kitchen and Stanton took Lily through the questions he'd asked the day before, while Turner scribbled busily in his notebook, making careful record of her answers.

'I wonder,' Stanton said at last, 'have you a photo of Jimmy Randall?'

'Only this one,' Lily replied, reaching for a framed wedding photo on the dresser. She handed it to the sergeant. 'The bride and groom,' she said bitterly.

Mavis beamed with happiness at her new husband; Jimmy smiling too, his dark head thrown back, his eyes turned away from the camera. A tall man, with strong shoulders and his demob suit looking uncomfortably tight across his chest, he had a tight grip on his bride's arm, as if proclaiming ownership. 'May I take this?' Stanton asked. 'I'll return it to you as soon as we've made copies.'

'I don't want it back,' Lily said. 'I never want to see it again.'

That afternoon Lily persuaded Anne to go home. 'I'll be perfectly all right,' she insisted. 'I've Ricky to look after, he'll give me plenty to keep me occupied.' She grasped Anne's hand. 'You're a true friend, Anne. Thank you for staying last night.'

'We're still here if you need us,' Anne replied, 'if you need help with the baby or anything.'

'I'll remember,' promised Lily, 'but we got to get used to each other, Ricky and me, 'cos I'll be taking care of him from now on.'

'Will the social let you?' wondered Anne.

'Let them try and stop me,' replied Lily fiercely. 'Ricky's mine now, just let them try and take him away.'

Anne was about to go home when there was another knock at the door. She opened it, preparing to send away whoever it was.

'Yes?' Her tone was unwelcoming. On the step was a good-looking man in a smart suit. He greeted her with a disarming smile.

'Good afternoon, madam, I'm Terry Knight from the *Belcaster Chronicle*. Mrs Sharples?'

'No, I'm a neighbour,' Anne replied. 'What do you want?'

'We were so sorry to hear of the dreadful murder of Mavis Randall... Mrs Sharples' daughter, was it?'

Anne nodded.

'Of course the *Chronicle* is leading with the story, but my editor sent me round to talk to poor Mrs Randall's mother, to make sure we had all our facts right.'

'I'm afraid she isn't seeing anyone at present,' Anne told him. 'The police've been here already and that's enough for one day.'

'I suppose you couldn't help me with a little background information about the family?' Terry Knight treated Anne to his most engaging smile.

'No, I couldn't,' Anne said firmly. 'It's not my business, nor yours, neither.' She began to close the door, saying, 'You ought to know better than to come bothering someone at a time like this.'

Unperturbed, Terry smiled again and said, 'Please just pass on my condolences to Mrs Sharples and tell her I called.' He still had others to interview, Mavis's neighbour for instance. She'd been very quickly on the scene.

'Who was that?' asked Lily.

'A reporter,' replied Anne. 'I sent him away with a flea in his ear.'

Terry Knight knocked on the door of number 5 Ship Street and greeted the woman who opened it with a wide smile. 'Mrs Maunder?'

'Yes,' replied Carrie. 'Who are you?'

'Terry Knight, *Belcaster Chronicle*. I wondered if I could have a word.'

'What do you want?' asked Carrie warily.

'I understand that you were poor Mavis Randall's best friend and you were there when she was found.'

'Yes, I was,' said Carrie.

'I'm writing a report for the *Chronicle* and I just wanted to be sure I'd got all the facts straight. Could you help me with that?'

'You'd better come in,' said Carrie.

Half an hour later Terry's notebook was covered in short-hand as he'd written down everything Carrie had told him. 'It's certainly a sad story,' he said when she'd finished. 'And those two little girls are now in Australia, you say?'

'Yes, that EVER-Care place sent them without telling anyone.'

'Thank you so much for your time, Mrs Maunder, you've been a great help. I don't suppose you've got a photograph of Mavis, have you?'

Carrie thought of the snaps John had taken at the wedding. 'I might have,' she said and rifled through the kitchen drawer. She still had a copy of the one of Mavis and Jimmy together. 'You can have this one,' she said. 'It was took on their wedding day.'

Terry Knight thanked her, tucking the photo into his wallet, and extracting two five pound notes. 'For the photographs, Mrs Maunder, and your time.'

Terry Knight was delighted with the interview; it had garnered him far more information than he'd anticipated. The murder was the big story at present, and all the other papers would be on to it soon, but this background story, the story behind the murder, would probably be the bigger story in the end. Terry remembered the encounter with a woman when he'd been to interview Emily Vanstone. She'd been shouting about them stealing her grandchildren, hadn't she? Was that Lily Sharples, Mavis's mother? His interest had been aroused at the time, but he'd never discovered the name of the woman he'd seen at Vanstone House. No one had admitted to knowing it. Now, though, his reporter's instinct told him that it had indeed been Lily Sharples. Now he would make following up this strange story a high priority. A human interest story to tug at the heart strings, he thought, and one that could run for several weeks as he allowed it gradually to unfold.

Emily Vanstone sat at her desk drinking a cup of tea, scanning the papers that Miss Drake had brought in. There was nothing that interested her particularly in *The Times* or the *Telegraph*, and so she turned to the *Belcaster Chronicle*, which she always read cover to cover. She liked to keep up with what was happening round her; keep her finger on the local pulse.

She had been pleased with the piece Terry Knight had recently written about her in his series on rising business women. At the end of it he had also mentioned her charitable work, noting that the EVER-Care Trust, which looked after destitute children, had been founded by her.

A good paper, the *Chronicle*, she'd thought at the time. A good, traditional paper. Trustworthy. Speaking for all right-thinking people, not like the gutter press, stirring up muck at any opportunity.

Turning to this pillar of the community now she saw the two-inch headline blazoned across the front page.

YOUNG MOTHER SLAIN

Below was a grainy wedding photograph of a young couple, under which was printed

Mavis and James Randall on their wedding day.

Shocking! thought Emily Vanstone. Such a horrifying thing...
and here in Belcaster, too. She peered at the picture, but the
names and faces meant nothing to her. She read on.

The Belcaster police are seeking Jimmy Randall (33), labourer,
to help with their enquiries into the vile murder of his wife,
Mavis. Mavis Randall, recently married and mother of baby
Richard, aged five months, was found by her mother earlier
this week, lying in a pool of blood in her own kitchen. She had
been stabbed with a kitchen knife, later found by the police.
Mavis Randall, whose two daughters by a previous marriage
had, without her knowledge or consent, been sent to Australia
by the EVER-Care Trust...

The name leaped out at Emily and she skimmed through the
rest of the article before flinging the paper aside. Colour flooded
her cheeks as rage flooded her mind. How dare they! How dare
they print such things! She'd sue them! She'd ring the editor and
tell him if he made no retraction, she'd see him in court. She'd
demand an apology. She'd... she'd...

Suddenly she felt giddy, a sharp pain behind her eyes, and the
room spun round her. She couldn't catch her breath. She pushed
her chair back, her heart pounding, but she couldn't stand. She
managed to reach the bell on her desk, and Miss Drake came at
once to its summons. She took one look at her employer and
rushed to her side.

'Miss Vanstone! Miss Vanstone, are you all right?'

Clearly she wasn't. She had collapsed back into her chair, her
breathing was ragged and the colour, so high just moments
earlier, had fled her cheeks, leaving her ashen-faced.

Frightened by what she saw, Miss Drake said, 'You must lie
down, Miss Vanstone. Here, let me help you to the couch.' She
took hold of her employer's arm and supporting her as best she
could, managed to get her across to the sofa.

'I'll ring for an ambulance,' she said.

'No!' Miss Vanstone spoke vehemently, though her voice was

scarcely more than a whisper. 'No ambulance!' Then, more gently, she said, 'Just a glass of water. I'll be fine again in a minute. Just felt faint for a moment, that's all. Happened before. Nothing to worry about.'

'Shall I call the doctor?' suggested Miss Drake. 'I really think I should.'

'No,' repeated Miss Vanstone firmly. 'No, thank you. Just the water.'

Reluctantly Miss Drake left her and went to fetch the water. When she came back she was pleased to see her employer looking a little better, colour creeping back into her cheeks. She helped her to drink, holding the glass to Miss Vanstone's lips.

'Thank you.' Miss Vanstone gave her a weak smile. 'I'll be fine now.' She looked at her secretary who was still staring anxiously down at her. 'And I'd be grateful if you didn't mention this little episode to anyone. It's nothing, and I'd hate my family to hear of it and begin to worry.'

'Well, if you're sure...' Miss Drake still sounded less than happy with the situation.

'I'm sure,' said Miss Vanstone, swinging her legs round so that she was sitting up. 'There's no need to trouble the doctor. I'll just sit here for a while and then I'll go home. Be good enough to pass me the *Chronicle*,' she pointed to the paper which was now lying on the floor, 'and then I'd like a cup of tea.'

She was sounding much more her usual self now, and it was with some relief that Miss Drake handed her the paper and left her sitting up on the couch, while she went to make the tea.

Emily was more frightened by her sudden turn than she was prepared to admit, even to herself. This had happened to her once before, at home. Her housekeeper had been on hand that time, and she, too, had been sworn to secrecy. Deep breaths were the thing, slow, deep breaths. By the time Miss Drake returned with the tea tray, Emily was breathing normally and feeling much better. She sipped the tea gratefully, and then turned her attention back to the article in the paper.

Mavis Randall, whose two daughters by a previous marriage had, without her knowledge or consent, been sent to Australia by the EVER-Care Trust, is thought to have confronted her husband over his part in this decision, and it has been suggested that it was this that started a fight that ended so tragically in her death.

Suggested? Suggested by whom, I'd like to know, thought Emily fiercely.

Randall, known to be violent, has not been seen since the evening preceding the murder, when he stopped off at the Red Lion public house on his way home from work. The police are asking for anyone who might know his whereabouts to contact them at Belcaster central police station. He is considered dangerous, and should not be approached by members of the public.

The couple's infant son, Richard, is being cared for by his grandmother, Mrs Lily Sharples.

Lily Sharples! Emily immediately recognized the name. Lily Sharples! So she was at the root of these scurrilous rumours. This Mavis Randall, who'd been murdered by her husband, must be the mother of the Stevens girls; Lily Sharples' granddaughters.

I might have known, she thought. I might have known she'd be behind this. You'd think she'd have more important things to worry about with her daughter dead on the floor, the murderer still at large and her grandson to look after.

She remembered Lily's fury at having the girls sent so far away. Well, thought Emily now, wasn't I right to send them? They were indeed at risk in that dreadful household. Early rescue from that man has probably saved their lives!

She thought about the letter she'd sent to Daphne soon after her last encounter with Lily Sharples, and she felt that what she'd said was now justified by these subsequent events. Yes, indeed, now she'd got over the shock of reading the account of the murder and the suggestion that EVER-Care was responsible in some way, she began to see that once she put her side of the story, she would have the public on her side. Children should not be left in the homes of such violent men, they should be removed and placed where they could be cared for, and brought up in safety. Her belief in herself and the work of EVER-Care was still rock-solid. She knew she had done, and was doing, the right thing.

Feeling revived by the tea, Emily Vanstone went back to her desk and rang the *Belcaster Chronicle*. When the call was put through she demanded to speak to Mr Chater, the editor.

'This is Emily Vanstone of Vanstone Enterprises, and the EVER-Care Trust,' she began when she was finally connected.

'Good morning, Miss Vanstone,' cut in Philip Chater, 'and how may I help you today?'

'It's about the article in today's edition of your paper,' she said. 'I have no idea who's been casting such unsubstantiated slurs on EVER-Care, but I have to tell you, Mr Chater, I expected better of the *Chronicle*. I take great exception,' she repeated the words, 'great exception to such statements being made about the EVER-Care Trust without any reference to me.' She paused but when the editor said nothing she went on, 'The EVER-Care Trust maintains the right to decide what is best for individual girls in its care. We never divulge what those decisions are, to protect the child.'

'I understand your concern, Miss Vanstone, but the *Chronicle* has to keep in mind PUBLIC INTEREST.' Philip Chater spoke the last two words in capital letters. 'Public Interest is what we consider when printing a story. Have these two young girls been sent to Australia without the consent of their family?' It was his turn to pause, but when Emily made no answer, he went on, 'People will want to know, Miss Vanstone. It's in the Public Interest.'

'It has nothing to do with the public,' she snapped, 'and I have no intention of confirming or denying anything about any of my girls. EVER-Care never discusses our children with outsiders.'

'Well, I'm afraid, Miss Vanstone, I don't see that I can be of any help to you,' said Philip Chater. 'Indeed, I'm not at all sure why you wanted to speak to me.'

'I want a retraction, Mr Chater, and an apology for slandering EVER-Care.'

'Out of the question, I'm afraid,' said the editor smoothly. 'If EVER-Care has been sending children to Australia, there is no slander, no libel, as we have simply printed the truth.'

'And what I also want to know, Mr Chater,' Emily went on as if he hadn't spoken, 'is where you obtained this information. Who made these suggestions that there is a connection between this dreadful murder and EVER-Care?'

'I'm sorry, Miss Vanstone,' said the editor, sounding anything but, 'we never reveal our sources. If you would like to make a statement of rebuttal for us to print in our next edition, of course, we'd be happy to have it, but otherwise I fear there is little more I can do to help you.' And he cut the connection, leaving Emily Vanstone gripping the telephone in impotent fury.

'Insolent man,' she muttered as she replaced the receiver in its cradle. 'Insolent and insufferable man! We'll see about you. I'll speak to Martin.'

'Have you seen the paper?' she demanded as soon as Martin answered the phone.

'Which paper?' asked her brother-in-law.

'The *Chronicle*,' replied Emily. 'They're suggesting that there's some link between EVER-Care and this murder.'

'Oh, that,' said Martin. 'Yes, lot of nonsense if you ask me.'

'But it's slander.'

'No, it isn't,' answered Martin. 'It's no more than an idea that's been floated, it's not a statement of fact.'

'People will take it as fact,' said Emily angrily. 'They'll believe what they read in the paper, whether it's true or not. So, what do we do about it, Martin?'

'Nothing.'

'Nothing?' shrilled Emily. 'Why not? We must refute it.'

Martin sighed. 'Emily,' he said, 'the less we say about it the better. Ignore it. Say nothing, do nothing, and it will all be forgotten in a couple of days. Making a song and dance about it will only give credence to the whole thing.'

'But—' began Emily, but Martin cut her short.

'Emily, you asked for my advice and I've given it to you. What you do with it is up to you.' And, for the second time in half an hour, Emily found herself holding a silent telephone.

She thought about what Martin had said. His advice had been sound, she knew that, but it didn't make it any easier to take. Her fury at the *Chronicle* and its arrogant editor was unassuaged. She wanted to vindicate herself and EVER-Care for the decisions she'd made, but she couldn't do that without revealing the way she'd gone about it.

She was about to leave the office, when Miss Drake told her that the *Daily Drum* was on the phone and wanted to speak to her.

'That rag?' said Emily. 'What on earth do they want?'

'They didn't say, Miss Vanstone, they just asked to speak to you.'

Emily thought for a moment and then sighed. 'You'd better put them through,' she said, and picked up her phone.

'Emily Vanstone.'

'Ah, Miss Vanstone, good afternoon. This is Steve Roberts from the *Daily Drum*. I was just ringing to see if you had any comment to make about the murder of Mavis Randall and her connection with the EVER-Care Trust... her children being sent to Australia without her knowledge?'

Emily drew a sharp breath. 'No, Mr Roberts, I have not. No comment whatsoever.' And this time it was Emily who slammed down the receiver.

Chapter 32

'Hey, Betty,' Sean Bennett called as he came into the room. 'What was the name of the place you come from?'

'Belcaster,' replied Betty, not looking up from painting her nails bright red.

'No, I know that. No, the name of the home you was in.'

This did catch her attention and she looked up. 'Laurel House,' she said. 'Why?'

'Here, in the *Drum*.' He held up a newspaper. 'Laurel House, part of the EVER-Care Trust. That the one?'

'Yeah, that's it. Why, what does it say?'

'Says they kidnap kids and send them abroad without asking their families,' answered Sean. He held out the paper. 'Some woman been kicking up a stink about it. Here, have a look.'

'Where'd you get this?' she said, glancing at the date. 'It's a week old.'

'I know, it's my prop,' said Sean.

Sean worked the tube stations, quietly lifting wallets and purses. With a newspaper under his arm as he hurried through the rush hour crowds, he was almost invisible. Sometimes he waited on platforms, and then he read the paper. He had today, and saw the name Laurel House; the place that Betty had told him about.

'But have a read of it, Bet,' he said.

Betty skimmed through the article. It told her nothing she didn't already know and left out much that she did.

Miss Emily Vanstone, founder of EVER-Care, had refused to

363

be interviewed, the *Drum* announced, and declined to comment. Why would she do that, enquired the *Drum*, if there was no substance to the allegations? If there was nothing to hide? 'What,' it asked, 'goes on behind closed doors at EVER-Care?'

Betty tossed the paper aside and blew on her nails to dry them.

'Yeah,' she said, 'that's the place.'

'And do they?' demanded Sean.

'Do they what?'

'Do they kidnap kids and send them to Australia?'

'Not 'xactly, no,' Betty said, 'but they did send kids out there. Telling them it was better. I'd have gone, anything must be better'n that place, but she didn't send me.'

'Who didn't?'

'Old Emily.'

'The one in the paper?'

'Yeah, her. She's the cow what's the boss,' went on Betty, 'she's the one what holds the purse-strings. It's her pays the Hawk and them others to keep the place running, but she don't care what they do, as long as there ain't no trouble.'

'Paper says some woman's saying they took her granddaughters. Said they'd been adopted when they'd really sent them to Australia.'

'Yeah, I know. I knew them kids an' all. They was sisters and their gran come looking for them.' Losing interest in the subject Betty shrugged. 'More important, Sean, d'you get anything today?'

'Nope,' Sean replied, 'nothing.' He flung himself down on the bed. 'How much you got left, then?'

Betty opened her purse. She had precisely three shillings and tuppence three farthings.

'That ain't gonna get us far,' groaned Sean.

Betty had met Sean not long after she first got to London. He was a good-looking charmer who lived off other people. He had got chatting to her in a seedy café in Poplar and soon learned that she was new to London, and even as he smiled at her, his eyes gleamed at the thought of an easy pickings. He'd intended to relieve her of the little money she had and move on, but something about her waif-like figure and the way her brown eyes glared fiercely at him from her pale, pointed face had given him pause.

Tarted up a bit, he thought, she wouldn't be half bad. Not a looker, but she had something, something perhaps that Sean could use to his advantage. Men were always on the lookout for girls, and Sean already had one or two girls he looked after. Betty was, Sean decided, a definite possibility, so he suggested she shack up at his place, 'just till you find yourself somewhere'.

Betty had discovered that in London even menial jobs were hard to come by, and though nervous about his offer, she'd accepted, relieved, at last, to have somewhere to sleep. His 'place' was one grubby room, with a toilet shared by six other lodgers, in a dilapidated house in Shoreditch, but at least it was dry and a huge improvement on the church porches that had been her shelter since she'd arrived. It boasted a narrow single bed, a wobbly table and a scarred bentwood chair.

'It ain't much,' he said as he opened the door and ushered her in, 'but the bed ain't bad. Have a lie down and see.'

They'd both had a lie down and Sean had introduced Betty to another reason to go to bed. Despite being terrified at first, and cowering as far from him as she could, Betty had discovered that she rather liked what he was doing to her, and she shuddered as sensations such as she could never have imagined from her own private fumblings flooded through her.

Not usually a man of great sensitivity where women were concerned, Sean realized that, with a little care, a lot more could be unleashed in Betty. She proved to be a fast learner and to his surprise he found she gave him far more pleasure than the usual quick screw. He decided not to hire her out to his punters but to keep her to himself, at least for now. They'd stayed together and he'd taught her his trade. Already a natural thief, Betty had been a fast learner in this area, too.

'Got to get some cash,' he said now, 'or we'll lose the room. Mickey ain't gonna take no excuses come Friday.'

Betty had been thinking about this, too, and now an idea struck her. She waved her hand at the discarded newspaper.

'There'll be cash in Old Emily's desk,' she ventured.

'What? Her in the paper?'

'Yeah,' Betty nodded. 'Trouble is getting to Belcaster.'

'That ain't a problem. We can hitch. What sort of cash are you talking about?' Betty told him what she'd taken before she'd made her escape.

'That's not much,' scoffed Sean. 'Hardly worth going unless we get at least a fiver or more.'

'It could be worth our while,' insisted Betty, remembering the knick-knacks up in the Hawk's abode. 'There's other stuff worth having in that place.'

'Yeah, but there's always someone there, ain't there? We don't want no trouble.'

'Not on Sundays,' said Betty.

'Sundays?'

'They all have to go to church, and Old Emily's always in church. Shows everyone how holy she is.'

'So,' Sean said thoughtfully, 'no one's home on Sunday.'

'Not in the morning, they ain't,' replied Betty. 'We can watch them all marching along to church, check they've gone. Then we've got a good hour, hour and a half, before they all come back again.'

'Hour's plenty,' said Sean, who was warming to the idea. 'Don't want to push our luck. How're we going to get in?'

'Kitchen window. It don't latch proper. It'll be stiff, but you can pull it open.'

The next morning found them beside the A4, and with Betty standing, thumb out, at the roadside, it wasn't long before a large lorry drew up beside her and they had their ride.

They arrived in Belcaster on Saturday evening. It was cold and dark and there was rain in the air.

'Where are we going to sleep?' asked Betty, reluctant to go anywhere near Laurel House until she had to.

'You tell me, kiddo,' answered Sean. ''S your town.' But Betty had been incarcerated in the orphanage for as long as she could remember, only emerging to go to school and church.

'I dunno, do I?' she snapped. 'We better find somewhere. I ain't sleeping rough here.'

Sean actually had nearly ten shillings he'd removed from the offertory box in a Catholic church in Shoreditch, but he didn't want to use that if they didn't have to.

'I ain't sleeping out,' Betty repeated adamantly. 'Come on, Sean, I know you got money. We got to find a proper room.'

Sean gave in, and they found a room in a pub; two bob each, but no breakfast.

With the key safely in Sean's pocket, they set out to have a look at Laurel House. Following the landlord's directions to Russell Green, they finally reached streets that Betty recognized, and she was able to lead him to the EVER-Care home. They strolled past, arm in arm, a couple walking out on Saturday evening.

'Grim-looking place,' Sean said as he paused to look over the hedge.

'You don't know the half of it!' growled Betty, pulling on his arm. There was a light in the tower room, the Hawk's nest, but otherwise the house stood in darkness.

At last Sean moved on, and with a wave of relief that left Betty feeling weak, they turned the corner into the next street.

'Where do we watch from?' Sean asked.

Betty led him along the familiar route towards Crosshills Methodist Church. 'They have to pass here,' she said. 'You can stand there,' she pointed to the park gates, closed now for the night, 'and count the adults.'

Next morning Sean stood leaning on the gate, smoking a cigarette and watching the world go by. Betty was inside the park, well concealed by the bushy hedge. As she had predicted, the small crocodile of girls came past, led by a hard-faced woman, whom Sean assumed was the Hawk, the last few pairs being chivvied along by two other women. The Dragon and Ole Smithy?

As soon as she saw the Hawk, Betty turned her back. The sight of her arch-enemy make her feel physically sick and the

sight of the girls, many of whom she knew well, walking obediently in twos, made her suddenly angry. She wanted to shout at
them, 'You don't have to stay! Break out! I did!'

When the croc had disappeared round the corner, Sean tossed
his cigarette end on the ground and grinned. 'Well then, kiddo,'
he said, 'let's get to it.'

Betty tested the back gate; it wasn't bolted. A sharp push
from Sean, and they were into the yard, and safe from prying
eyes.

'Where's this window, then?' Sean looked round him, noting
a second escape route through the orchard.

'Round here.' Betty led him to the kitchen window, which, to
her relief, was still open a crack; a fear that it had been repaired
unfounded.

Sean grabbed hold of it and with a screech of un-oiled hinges,
he pulled it wide.

'Here,' he said, 'I'll give you a leg up, then you can open the
back door for me.'

Betty squirmed through and once inside looked round the
all-too familiar kitchen, immediately recognizing the ever-pres-
ent smell of boiled cabbage, and the general air of gloom.

'Open the door!' Sean hissed through the window, and jerked
from her reverie, Betty hurried to let him in. He wrinkled his
nose at the stale smell and said, 'So, where's Emily's office,
then?'

Betty took him through the cold and silent house, memories
flooding back as she led the way to Emily Vanstone's office. Sean
paused, looking round, taking stock of what was there: the polished desk in the middle of the room, the metal filing cabinets
against the wall, the silver clock on the mantelpiece, the paraffin
heater in a corner.

To Betty, Emily's desk looked just as it always had, polished
to a shine, with the pen and blotter lying on the top; only the
paperknife was missing, sold by Betty for half a crown on her
first day in London. She'd warned Sean about the locked drawers
and he'd come prepared with a sturdy pocket knife.

The lock on the centre drawer provided little resistance and when they pulled open the drawer they found the familiar cash box. Sean picked it up and shook it. It clinked loudly and was reassuringly heavy. He pulled a cloth bag from under his jacket and without attempting to open the tin box, stowed it in the bag. 'Let's see what else we've got,' he said and quickly sorted through the drawer's other contents. Apart from a new fountain pen still in its case and a few postage stamps, there was nothing further of value. The pen and the stamps joined the cash box in his bag, as did the silver clock from the mantelpiece, before he looked across at the metal filing cabinets standing against the wall.

'What's in them?' he asked.

Betty shrugged. 'Dunno – papers?'

'I'll have a dekko, you look through them other drawers.'

While Betty worked systematically through the side drawers, Sean set his penknife to work on the lock of the first filing cabinet. 'If she keeps it locked,' he said as he brought pressure to bear with the blade of his knife, 'there might be more valuables. Ah! Got it!'

The cabinet drawer yielded to the knife and sprang open to reveal a range of manila folders, all neatly labelled. Sean ran his fingers through the files.

'Here, Bet,' he called, 'look at that. There's a file here with your name on it.'

'What?' Betty looked up from the last drawer, where she'd found an unused National Provincial Bank cheque book. Sean pulled out one of the manila folders and carried it over to Betty. When he saw the cheque book, he almost snatched it out of her hand.

'We'll have *that*,' he said, as he handed her the folder. He turned his attention to the second filing cabinet but finding it only contained yet more papers, he said, 'Nothing else of interest here. What about the Hawk woman's rooms. You said she had stuff.'

Betty shuddered. 'I ain't going up there,' she said flatly. 'I ain't never going into that woman's place again.'

'OK, OK,' agreed Sean. 'No bother, I'll go and see what's

what. You go on looking downstairs. Never know what you might find, eh?'

Betty knew there'd be nothing else of value downstairs, until she thought of food. They could always do with food, so, with the manila folder tucked underneath her arm, she headed back to the kitchen to investigate the pantry. As she came through the door, she glanced at the old kitchen clock. They'd been in Laurel House only half an hour, but she felt stifled by the place and its memories, and she couldn't wait to get out. She inspected the pantry and took a wedge of cheese from the shelf. There was bread, too, and some sausages.

They'll make us a decent supper, she thought as she gathered them together ready to add to Sean's bag. The huge pot of Sunday stew stood on the range but there was no way they could carry it, so the inmates would have their lunch. Sean was still upstairs somewhere, so Betty perched on the edge of the table and opening the file, she started to read.

Elizabeth Grover
Date of birth: 12/7/32
Father: John Grover (ex-convict) MIA presumed dead
Mother: Alice Grover (deceased)
Paternal aunt: Jane Marks

There were other details which Betty skimmed through and then, held together with a paperclip, there were some letters. The first was dated 4 January 1946, and as she read it, Betty felt suddenly cold. She didn't recognize the address and she didn't know the handwriting, but the letter itself...

Dear Miss Vanstone,
I believe my sister Jane left my little daughter, Elizabeth, with you when my wife was killed in an air raid. As she told you at the time, I was posted as missing presumed dead. She felt that this was best for Betty as she couldn't look after her.

As you see I was not killed, but taken prisoner. Now I am home again and I am longing to fetch my little girl home to live with me. I am about to remarry, and my future wife and I look forward to having Betty home to live with us. Thank you very much for looking after her while I couldn't. Please tell me when I can come and fetch her.

Yours truly,

John Grover

Betty stared at the letter. Her father wasn't dead at all. The Germans hadn't got him, he was alive. He'd come home and he'd asked for her; he wanted to come and fetch her. But he hadn't. Why hadn't he? Why hadn't he come? The letter was dated two years ago; why hadn't he come to find her? Had he changed his mind?

She picked up the next sheet of paper, which she realized with a jolt was a carbon copy of Emily Vanstone's reply.

8 January 1946

Dear Mr Grover,

Thank you for your letter. I was indeed surprised to receive it, and I am pleased to know that you survived the war. However, not knowing this earlier, I arranged for Elizabeth to be adopted. Her adoptive parents are a charming couple from up north, living in the country. They are devoted to Elizabeth and she to them.

I am afraid it is not EVER-Care policy to reveal the names and addresses of the families who have come forward to give our children secure family homes. I regret that Elizabeth is now lost to you, but you may rest assured that she is well and happy herself. I wish you every happiness with your new wife.

Yours sincerely,

The letter was unsigned, but under the space for the signature was typed the name

Emily Vanstone
Founder of the EVER-Care Trust

Betty stared at the letter in disbelief. 'How could she?' she murmured in a grief-stricken whisper. 'How could she do that? How could she tell him all those lies?' With eyes blurred by tears, she turned to the next letter, dated 15 January 1946.

Dear Miss Vanstone,
I can't believe what you told me in your letter. You gave my Betty away without so much as a by-your-leave. Not asking any of her family. You had my sister's address, surely you should have told her what you were going to do. How could you just hand Betty over to strangers without even asking? I'm going to talk to a lawyer and then I shall be coming to see you. Please will you send me Betty's new address so that I can at least let her know I'm still alive. If she has settled so well with these people, maybe she should stay put, but she needs to know I'm not dead and then perhaps we can at least see each other.

The letter was signed by her father.

There was one more letter in the bundle, dated 19 January 1946, the second one from Emily Vanstone.

Dear Mr Grover,
I understand your distress, and regret it, but there is really nothing I can do to lessen it except to repeat that Betty is well and happy with her new family. When Mrs Marks brought her to us at EVER-Care, we became her legal guardians. This gave us an absolute right, as I'm sure any lawyer you may consult will confirm, to settle Betty where we thought best for her, in this case, with adoptive parents.

We never divulge names and addresses of such parents, and
I have no intention of breaking our rule in this case.
  I regret that I am unable to enter into further correspon-
dence with you on this matter.
Yours sincerely,

Again there was no signature, but the carbon copy of the
letter had been initialled 'EV'.

Betty dropped the letters onto the table beside her and sliding
down onto a kitchen chair, buried her head in her hands and
began to sob, deep heaving sobs that convulsed her whole body.
When Sean came into the kitchen, his bag bulging with trinkets
and ornaments from the Hawk's flat, he stopped dead.

'Hey kiddo!' he cried, dumping the bag onto the floor. 'What's
up?'

Wordlessly, still sobbing, Betty handed him the letters. He
skimmed through them swiftly, and then as their import hit him,
read them all again.

'Fucking hell!' he breathed. 'The fucking bitch!'

'He's alive, my dad,' Betty sobbed, 'and she sent him away!'

Sean looked at two other papers in the folder. One was typed,
a brief account of a meeting with 'JG and lawyer', and the other
notes about Betty and her family. A handwritten note had been
added at the bottom.

Entirely unsuitable as a father. Betty stays here. Saved from
a life of depravity.

'We'll take these an' all,' Sean said, stuffing the file into his
bag. 'Come on.' He was about to turn to the back door when he
came up short. 'Shit!' he muttered. 'If she finds your folder
missing, she'll guess who's turned the place over.' He hurried
back to Emily's office. The filing cabinet stood open, revealing
at least a hundred similar files. He pulled out several files at
random and up-ended them onto the floor. Papers flew everywhere, but though it certainly was a mess, if someone did bother

to re-sort them, Betty's file would still be missing. Then the small paraffin heater, standing cold and unlit in the corner of the room, caught his eye and the answer came to him.

'Betty!' he bellowed. 'Come here and help!'

Betty appeared, red-eyed, in the doorway and watched as Sean pulled more and more folders from the cabinets, shaking their contents all across the room and out into the passage.

'Sean!' she cried. 'Sean, what are you doing?'

'Going to have a bonfire!' he announced. 'Going to burn the whole bloody place down. Emily fucking Vanstone kept you from a life of depravity, did she? An' all them girls we saw this morning, too, I s'pose. Well, it ends here. With luck the whole house'll burn down, and them kids'll be took away from her.'

Betty stood transfixed, horrified. 'Sean!' she cried. 'We can't!'

'We bloody can,' retorted Sean. 'Look lively.' He handed her another batch of files. 'Go and empty these all round the hall. We'll go out through the kitchen.'

Betty still hesitated, the enormity of what he proposed enveloping her. ' S'posing it don't catch,' was all she could think of to say.

'Will when I've finished with it,' Sean assured her. 'Now get on with it, girl, or it'll be too late.' He gave her a push, and she took the papers into the hall as instructed and tossed them all over the floor and up the stairs. Once she'd started she felt suddenly reckless. She'd show Emily Vanstone! She'd pay her back for the years of misery she'd lived through in this place. Not allowed up the front stairs? Well, she was going up them now, all right, going up them, strewing papers like confetti, all the way up to the landing.

'Ready?' called Sean, poking his head into the hall.

'Ready!'

'Right, go to the back door and open it,' Sean said. 'Take my bag and wait outside. Be ready to run... I'll be coming out fast.'

Betty did as she was told, picking up Sean's bag and stuffing in the parcel of food she'd packed earlier. She could hear Sean banging about further inside the house, but she followed his instructions and waited outside in the yard. Suddenly Sean erupted out of the door and grabbed her hand. 'Come on, kiddo,' he cried excitedly, 'time to go! We can't hang around, but whatever you do, don't run.'

When they walked past the front gate of Laurel House, neither of them could resist the temptation for a last look at the house. Light flickered in the downstairs windows, and even as they watched, thin coils of smoke began to leak from those on the first floor.

'How did you make it burn so quick?' Betty asked breathlessly, as she scurried along beside him.

'Paraffin,' he replied. 'Tipped the paraffin out of that heater in the office and spread it about a bit. Went up with quite a whoosh!'

'Blimey!' muttered Betty.

'Time to go,' said Sean. 'Someone's going to notice that smoke soon.'

Fifteen minutes later they were safely on the London train.

Chapter 33

When the service at Crosshills Methodist Church ended, chivvied by Mrs Hawkins, the girls formed their usual crocodile and set off, back to Laurel House. As they were passing the park two fire engines swept round the corner, bells clanging wildly. The croc straggled to a halt, staring after them.

'Walk on,' shouted Mrs Hawkins from the back of the croc. 'Mrs Smith, lead these girls on. There's no need to gawp, you've all seen a fire engine before.'

'Mrs Smith, I can see smoke,' cried Janice, one of the pair leading the croc, forgetting the silence rule in her excitement.

'So can I,' cried her partner, Elaine, 'an' I can smell it an' all.'

'Not surprising, is it, dear,' remarked the cook, 'seeing as we've just seen fire engines in a hurry.'

As they continued their walk home the air was rent with more clanging bells, and another fire engine hurtled past them, closely followed by a police car. Above the houses a cloud of black smoke was rising, swirling and billowing in the wind.

Mrs Hawkins hurried to the front of the crocodile and calling a halt, ran forward to the street corner where the police car had pulled up, blocking much of the road.

As she reached the corner and pushed her way through the gathering crowd of by-standers, a large police constable stepped forward and barred her passage.

'Sorry, madam, but you can't go down this way, there's a fire.'

'I can see that,' snapped Mrs Hawkins. 'But I've thirty children with me, and we live in this street. I need to get them home.'

'I'm very sorry, madam, but even so, you can't go down this street. It isn't safe. The fire brigade are dealing with the fire now, but it's still burning out of control.' Then with sudden realization he said, 'Thirty children! Are they the orphanage children?'

'The EVER-Care children. We live at Laurel House... oh my God!' Mrs Hawkins clapped her hand to her mouth in horror as the realization hit her too. 'It's Laurel House, isn't it?' She pushed past him, edging into the road to see for certain.

The constable put a restraining hand on her arm. 'Yes, madam, I'm afraid it is.'

Mrs Hawkins spun round and marched back to the waiting children. Taking the cook and the matron aside she spoke grimly. 'It's Laurel House. That policeman says it's burning out of control.' She glared at Mrs Smith. 'You must have left something on the stove, you stupid woman, and now the whole bloody place is on fire.'

'I certainly did not,' returned the cook with some spirit. 'Nothing was left on the stove, nothing was left in the oven. This fire has nothing to do with me and I won't take the blame for it!'

'For goodness sake,' interrupted the Dragon, 'that doesn't matter now. The important thing now is to decide what we do with this lot.' She jerked her thumb at the waiting children. 'We can't just stand in the street!'

'We'll go back to the church,' said Mrs Hawkins. 'They can wait in there until we find out what we're to do with them. From what I could see there'll be no going back to Laurel House for some time.' She thought for a moment and then said, 'You take them back to the church. If it's locked, one of you go to the Manse and get the keys. I'll go and tell Miss Vanstone what's happened.' She smiled grimly. 'After all, they'll be her problem, not ours.'

When they reached the church, the minister was just closing the doors. The Hawk left the Dragon to do the explaining, and set off in search of Emily Vanstone.

Although she knew the address, Mrs Hawkins had never been to Emily's house. They were not social equals and in all the years she'd been superintendent at Laurel House, she had never received an invitation to Maybury House. As she strode through the town on her way there now, she began to think about what was going to happen to her, now that Laurel House was gone. She had probably lost her home and all her possessions. From what the policeman had said, and from what she'd seen herself, Mrs Hawkins was under no illusions; the EVER-Care home was gone for good.

Wonder how Old Vanstone'll cope with that, thought Mrs Hawkins with a malicious smile, realizing that she was actually going to enjoy telling Emily about the fire. Her resentment at the way Emily had spoken to her and treated her over the years boiled up inside.

It took her nearly half an hour to walk to the more affluent area of Mountjoy where Emily lived. Maybury House was an attractive Georgian house, set back from the road with a broad drive sweeping through a large, well-kept front garden. Mrs Hawkins paused at the gates and looked at it.

Just the sort of house I'd expected, she thought with a sniff. Well, she'd never been invited to cross its sacred threshold before, but she sure as hell was going to cross it now, and she marched up the drive to the front door under its arched portico and rang the bell.

The door was opened by a smartly uniformed maid. 'Good afternoon,' she said.

'I need to see Miss Vanstone,' said Mrs Hawkins without bothering to return the greeting. 'It's a matter of great urgency.'

'If you'd care to step into the hall for a moment, I'll see if Miss Vanstone is at home. Whom shall I say is calling?'

See if she's at home! thought Mrs Hawkins angrily. We both know perfectly well she's at home. But she controlled her anger and said, 'Tell her it's Mrs Hawkins from Laurel House, and tell her I need to see her urgently.'

'Please take a seat.' The maid indicated a straight-backed chair just inside the door, and disappeared into the house.

It was several minutes before she returned, and saying, 'Come this way please,' showed her into a drawing room.

It was a beautiful room, elegantly furnished, with French windows that opened onto a terrace, and from there to a wide expanse of carefully tended lawn. Not wanting to sit down on one of the plush sofas, Mrs Hawkins went over to the windows and looked out. Flowerbeds flanked the lawn, and a smooth gravel path led through a neatly clipped box hedge to an orchard beyond. Everything was beautifully kept, and everything about both house and garden whispered, 'Money.'

She spun round as Emily Vanstone sailed into the room. 'Mrs Hawkins,' she said with some asperity, 'what can be so important that you come to disturb my lunch on a Sunday? You know I'm visiting Laurel House this afternoon. Surely whatever it is could have waited till then.'

'I'm afraid not, Miss Vanstone,' answered Mrs Hawkins. 'You won't be visiting Laurel House this afternoon; there is no Laurel House.' Seeing the expression of bafflement on Emily's face she went on with relish, 'Laurel House has burned to the ground.'

'It can't... When...? How...?' Miss Vanstone tottered forward and dropped down onto one of the sofas. Mrs Hawkins watched her with interest, seeing the colour draining from her cheeks, and sweat breaking out on her brow. Miss Vanstone had clutched at her head and was gasping for breath, but it was several moments before Mrs Hawkins said, 'Are you all right, Miss Vanstone?' Her tone was concerned, but her eyes gleamed with malice.

'I will be in just one moment,' gasped Emily, 'if you could just ring for Freeman...' She waved her hand in the direction of a bell-pull beside the door.

Mrs Hawkins gave the bell a tug, and moments later the maid appeared at the door.

'You rang, madam?'

Emily was looking slightly better now, and though her breath still rasped in her throat, she managed to say. 'Just a glass of water, please, Freeman.'

'Certainly, madam.'

The maid was back almost immediately with a glass of water.

She handed it to Emily who sipped it gratefully. Gradually the muzziness in her head began to clear and her breathing quietened, beginning to return to normal.

Mrs Hawkins watched the colour slowly return to Emily's face, keeping an expression of concern on her own, but with her mind whirling. It was clear to her that Emily Vanstone wasn't well, and not only that but that she must have had such turns before. Freeman knew what to do. She must have dealt with them before. There was no suggestion that they call a doctor, though Mrs Hawkins was tempted to suggest it herself just to see the reaction.

'Sit down, Mrs Hawkins,' Emily said. 'I shall be fine again directly. Just a moment's giddiness.' Then turning to the maid again she said, 'Thank you, Freeman, that'll be all.'

Mrs Hawkins sat down and then wished she hadn't. The advantage of towering over her stricken employer was lost.

'Now,' said Emily, taking one final drink of water and then setting the glass aside, 'tell me exactly what has happened.'

'That I really can't say,' said Mrs Hawkins. 'On the way home from church we were overtaken by fire engines and a police car. When we got to Shepherd Street the police had blocked off the road. The constable there said that it was Laurel House that was on fire, and that it was burning so fiercely that the fire brigade were having trouble bringing it under control.'

'But how did it start?' demanded Emily, sounding more like her usual self.

Mrs Hawkins shrugged. 'I don't know. All I do know is that we have to find somewhere for thirty children to spend the night tonight and for the foreseeable future.'

'Where are they now?' asked Emily, her mind beginning to kick into action.

'In the church with Mrs Smith and Mrs Reynolds,' Mrs Hawkins replied. 'We had to get them off the street, but obviously they can't stay there.'

'Quite right,' agreed Emily, and suddenly she was all action. Her moment of weakness had passed and she was on her feet, and ringing for Freeman.

Mrs Hawkins stood up, too, hardly able to believe the transformation from droopy old woman, turning grey and gasping for breath, to the dynamo that was now Emily Vanstone. Freeman was despatched to the kitchen to make a mound of sandwiches for the children's lunch. Foster, the chauffeur, was called to drive them back to the church and then on to Laurel House.

Within the hour she had contacted Miss Hopkins, the Children's Officer, and demanded placements for all the girls left homeless by the fire. Miss Hopkins, daunted by such a task, protested she couldn't find so many places all of a sudden and on a Sunday, but bullied by Emily, she was persuaded to go into her office and try.

While May Hopkins was beavering away in her office, Emily and Mrs Hawkins returned to the church, handed out sandwiches to the hungry children, and were then driven to Shepherd Street.

The street was still closed to traffic, a fire engine standing outside the remains of Laurel House. The big constable was still on duty and though the car was halted he let the two women pass when they explained who they were.

Together they walked down the street and standing by the fire engine, stared up at the blackened shell, still wreathed in drifting smoke.

Emily was angry. How could the place in which she'd invested so much time and money simply disappear in a matter of minutes?

'Everything I owned was in there,' said Mrs Hawkins bitterly. 'I've only the clothes I stand up in, now.'

Emily turned to her in surprise. She'd been so concerned with EVER-Care, the loss of the house and the immediacy of finding places for the children, she had given no thought at all to the adults who lived in the home and had lost everything.

'I suppose you have,' replied Emily. 'Mrs Hawkins, I'm so sorry.' She thought quickly. 'You and the other staff must move into a hotel at once. EVER-Care will pay, and advance you each some money for clothes.'

'Advance?' Mrs Hawkins pounced on the word. 'What do you mean "advance"?'

'Well, I expect there'll be insurance money, but that won't come through straight away, so in the meantime, I'll advance what you need. I'm sure you can get emergency coupons in the circumstances.'

'I see,' was all Mrs Hawkins said, but inside she was gleeful, planning her claim for all that she'd lost and for much that she hadn't.

Just then two firemen emerged from the front door. 'No doubt about it,' one was saying to the other, 'definitely deliberate. The chief's already in touch with the police.'

'What did you say?' cried Emily, overhearing his words. 'What did you say, my man?'

The fireman stopped short, seeing the two women for the first time.

'What are you doing here, lady?' he asked. 'No one's allowed in here till we've finished damping down.'

'What did you say just then,' repeated Miss Vanstone at her most imperious, 'about it being deliberate?'

'Nothing I can tell you, madam.'

'Indeed you can,' asserted Emily. 'I own this house.'

'I can tell you nothing, madam,' repeated the fireman, looking to his mate for confirmation. 'You'll be told through official channels. Now please go back out of the gate.'

As soon as she got home again, Emily phoned her brother-in-law. 'Martin, Laurel House has burned down,' she began.

'What!' he exclaimed.

She explained what had happened, adding, 'And I overheard one of the firemen say that it was deliberate.'

'He told you that?'

'He wouldn't tell me anything. Said I'd hear about the fire through "official channels". But I heard him say it was definitely deliberate and that the chief was already in touch with the police.'

'Did you speak to the chief?'

'He wasn't there. By the time I got there, they were damping down. Martin, I assume we've got the place well insured.'

'Yes, of course we have,' said Martin, 'but if the fire was started deliberately, it may take a while for them to pay out. They have to be sure we didn't burn the place down for the money.'

'As if we would with thirty children in there,' protested Emily.

'But they weren't in there, were they?' Martin pointed out. 'They were in church. Everyone who lived there was in church, so they were never in danger.'

'Martin, I can't believe you're saying this,' said Emily.

'Emily,' he said patiently, 'I'm only saying what other people will say; and we have to be prepared for it.'

'So, what do we do?' asked Emily testily.

'We put in a claim in the usual way and wait and see what happens.'

Half an hour later Emily received a call from her other brother-in-law, Edward.

'Emily,' he roared down the phone, 'what's this I hear about that home of yours being set fire to?'

'We don't know it was set fire to, yet,' Emily said, irritated as always by Edward's bombast. 'We haven't been told it was arson.'

'Well, Martin seems to think it won't be long before you are, and that's bad. That's very bad.'

'I agree,' said Emily, 'but we'll deal with it when and if it happens.'

'Thing is, Emily, I've been talking it over with Amelia, and I think, well, we both do, that we've had enough bad publicity already, what with that thing about kidnapping children which was all over the papers. Can't go on, you know.'

'But that was rubbish, spread by that rag the *Drum*. It wasn't true.'

'Yes, I know,' drawled Edward, 'but it was mud, and mud sticks. So we've decided, Amelia and I, that we can't lend our names to the association any more. You must see that the good name of the Sherrington family is at stake here. Sorry, Emily, but as from now I am withdrawing my name as the patron of EVER-Care. I shall have to make a brief announcement in all the papers, so that there is no chance that I, or my family, will be associated with anything that transpires.'

'In that case, Edward,' answered Miss Vanstone, 'this will be the last time we speak to each other... ever.'

ARSON AT EVER-CARE! shrieked the headline. *ORPHANAGE BURNS!* was scrawled on the billboard beside the news-stand. Lily stared at the headline and then scrabbled in her purse for coins and bought the paper.

When Terry Knight's article about the background to the murder had been published in the *Chronicle*, Lily had been horrified.

'Who could've told the paper all that?' she'd wondered to Anne as they sat together reading the paper Anne had brought round.

'I sent that reporter away,' Anne said stiffly.

'Oh, Anne,' cried Lily, 'I wasn't suggesting it was you, but I hate the idea of our dirty linen being washed in public.'

'Well,' said Anne, 'I expect it would have all come out in the end. Can't hurt your Mavis now, can it? But never mind that, Lil, how're you keeping?'

Lily didn't know how she'd have managed without the Baillies. She had known them for years, but in the days that followed Mavis's death, their support had been a lifeline and had cemented the friendship.

She smiled at Anne now. 'I'm all right. Bit tired, you know. Ricky don't sleep well at night.' Lily felt tired all the time now, though she wasn't going to admit it, not even to Anne. Looking after Ricky was exhausting; he was a lovely baby, but he certainly wasn't an easy one.

She could see Anne had a point about the newspaper story. It might do some good. Too late for her girls, but it might make another mother think twice before handing her children over to EVER-Care. It wasn't just the *Chronicle*: the *Daily Drum* had also spread the story of Mavis, Jimmy and the two little girls, and it had greatly upset Lily.

'I expect they picked up the story from the *Chronicle*,' Anne said, always the voice of calm. 'That's what them big London papers do sometimes.'

'Well, I wish they hadn't,' retorted Lily. The *Drum* had sensationalized *the foul murder of a defenceless young mother* and what was headlined as *THE EVER-CARE SCANDAL.* It had run for several days before the *Drum* had lost interest.

Now, the 'Arson' headline shrieked at her, another huge EVER-Care story. Lily tucked the paper inside the pram and took it home to read properly.

Under the headline there was a picture of the blackened shell that had been Laurel House, its roof gone, its window frames bent and twisted by the heat. The grey stone walls and the squat little tower topped only by a few charred roof beams, stood stark against the sky, all that was left of the EVER-Care home. A smaller headline proclaimed:

MIRACLE ESCAPE FOR ORPHANS!

The children living at Laurel House, the EVER-Care home in Shepherd Road, Russell Green had a miraculous escape on Sunday when the orphanage was torched by an unknown intruder. Laurel House, recently facing questions about its adoption and migration policies, was empty at the time of the fire. The orphans were at church on Sunday morning when the house was broken into and ransacked. To cover his tracks the burglar used paraffin to set fire to the house. The fire rapidly took hold and by the time the alarm was raised and the fire brigade called, the place was an inferno.

'I can't imagine who would do such a thing,' said Mrs Hawkins, the superintendent of the home. 'What a cruel thing to do to children already orphaned. Laurel House was their security, their sanctuary, and now it has gone. They have lost everything.' Laurel House is now nothing but a shell. The children have all been rehoused by the Children's Committee in foster homes in the area. Asked by the *Chronicle* for an interview, Children's Officer Miss May Hopkins was unavailable. A source has revealed that the records of all children passing through EVER-Care, kept at Laurel House, were lost in the fire. Is this the end of EVER-Care, the charity set up by Miss Emily Vanstone in the thirties to rescue destitute children from the streets? Who can tell? Miss Vanstone, when approached by this paper, was also unavailable for comment.

'We are following several promising leads,' said Inspector Carter, police officer in charge of the case. 'Whoever did this had knowledge of the orphanage's routine. They knew the house was always empty on a Sunday morning.' The police investigation continues.

As Lily read the piece through again she was struck by a dreadful thought. All the records gone. Now there's nothing left to tell me where my girls are, she thought bleakly. I'll never know where they was sent. Who could have done this dreadful thing? And why?

Later that afternoon, Anne looked in, copies of the *Chronicle* and the *Drum* under her arm. 'I wondered if you'd seen this, Lil,' she said, putting the papers on the table.

'Seen the *Chronicle*,' Lily said. 'Has the *Drum* got it too?'

'Yes, here.' Anne pointed to a piece on the front page. The article was not long, and it had a different slant.

INSIDE JOB?

Was it really just luck that no one was inside the EVER-Care home, Laurel House in Belcaster, when it went up in flames last Sunday? The home, recently the subject of another story in our paper, burned furiously for some time before firemen managed to get the blaze under control. Investigators from the fire brigade say that the fire was deliberately set and now the police are hunting the arsonist. Have they got far to look, we'd like to ask them?

In a statement to the press, Inspector Carter of Belcaster, the senior officer investigating the case, said that whoever it was knew the routine of the house, and knew that no one would be at home on a Sunday morning. So, was this really a burglary? Or is it something more sinister?

Could the blaze have been started by a disaffected former resident? A girl with a grudge? A family with a grudge? Or perhaps we should be asking the insurance company who stands to gain from this fire? Miss Emily Vanstone, founder of EVER-Care, when approached by this paper was, again, unavailable for comment. However, the *Drum* notes with interest that Sir Edward Sherrington has publicly withdrawn his patronage from EVER-Care. Does Sir Edward know something that the rest of us don't, we ask? The investigation continues, and we at the *Daily Drum* will be watching the outcome with interest.

'Well,' said Lily when she'd read it, 'someone's keeping the *Drum* up to date.'

'You think it was arson?' asked Anne.

'I don't know, do I?' replied Lily. 'All I know is all the records was destroyed. I'll never find my girls now.'

When Anne had gone, Lily made up a bottle for Ricky. As she fed him she thought about what the papers had said. Someone had set fire to Laurel House. Someone who knew it would be empty on a Sunday morning. A burglar, or was the *Drum* right? Was there a different motive? The children were now all in foster homes. Had that been the motive? To get the children moved from that dreadful place?

Hundreds of kiddies must have been through EVER-Care, she thought. Where are they all now? Had any of them really been adopted, or had they, like Rita and Rosie, simply vanished? Had someone read the story of kidnapped children spread across the *Drum* and realized they'd been lied to? Had someone decided to take matters into their own hands?

No, thought Lily, that really is a bit far-fetched. But a tiny corner of her brain was telling her, 'I might have, if I'd thought of it and I'd had the nerve!'

A tiny part of Lily had hoped that if she persevered long enough, she'd discover where her girls were; that one day she would find them and bring them home. That hope was now extinguished. Laurel House had gone, the children were dispersed and their records were ash.

'Well, Ricky my boy,' she whispered to the baby on her lap, 'it's just you and me now. You're all I have left of Mavis, but I won't forget your sisters.' She glanced up at the photo of the two girls in their rose-patterned frocks, beaming down at her from the mantelpiece. 'We'll remember them together, you and me.'

Lily was not the only one to read both the *Chronicle* and the *Drum* that day. Miss Drake had left both the papers on her employer's desk before going to lunch. Emily came in soon afterwards and finding the newspapers laid out waiting for her, she picked them up, and took them over to the sofa to read in peace. The headline shrieked at her from the front page of the *Chronicle*, but it wasn't the *Chronicle* to which she turned first; it was the *Drum*.

INSIDE JOB!

Inside Job! Inside Job! How dare they! As Emily read the article she felt the rage boiling up inside her. How dare that rag imply that Laurel House had been burned down for insurance purposes? And Edward... Edward had carried out his threat to distance himself from EVER-Care, and had announced as much to the papers, to the *Daily Drum*.

You can bet your life Miss Vanstone wasn't available for comment, Emily thought furiously, as she thrust the paper from her. She has nothing to say to gutter press like the *Drum*, except 'see you in court!' Surely this must constitute libel, she thought, surely they can't suggest such a defamatory thing without a shred of evidence to back it up. I must ring Martin at once.

As she reached for the phone, the familiar dizziness overcame her. A fierce pain lanced through her head and she staggered backwards, the offending papers cascading from her hand as she collapsed in a heap on the floor.

Chapter 34

Daphne Manton opened the letter from England with a sigh. Surface mail and dated six weeks earlier, it was another epistle from Emily. She skimmed through the opening paragraph, and then, unable to believe what she'd read, read it again.

Dear Daphne,

How could you have let this happen? Rita Stevens has written home to her grandmother. Not only that, but it must have been with your permission as there was a fair amount of censorship within the letter. What on earth were you thinking to allow such a thing? The repercussions here have been grave. The grandmother is accusing me of kidnapping her granddaughters. The press were there when she came to my office, but luckily they didn't latch on to what she was saying.

You know my most important rule is that once we have a girl in our care, that girl is to have <u>absolutely</u> [the word absolutely was heavily underscored] *no further contact with her family. I was about to deal with the situation, once and for all, when the matter was taken out of my hands. God moves in mysterious ways, and before I could take any action, the child's grandmother had a stroke, from which she did not recover. She was struck down in her home, but pronounced dead on arrival at the hospital. This is of course very sad (and I know I can rely on you to break it gently to the child), but at least it means there will*

*be no further problems from that quarter. However, I'm
sure I don't have to remind you that the letter occasioning
all this trouble should never have been sent and I wish you
to ensure that there are no further letters.*

Daphne stared at the letter. How had Rita written home? Who had given her the paper, the stamps? And who had censored her letter before it was sent? Only one possible person, Daphne thought in fury, that interfering Watson woman. Well, she'd interfered for the last time. This time she'd have to go.

'So, what're you going to do about it?' Joe said when she showed him the letter.

'I'm going to sack her,' replied Daphne. 'We can't have the house-mothers going behind our backs like that.'

'And who will you get to replace her?' asked Joe mildly. 'You haven't replaced that Garfield woman yet. You can't afford to be without another house-mother.'

Daphne glared at him, knowing he was right. Joe looked up from his paper and added, 'And what about the child? What about Rita? You have to tell the poor kid that her grandmother is dead.'

'Delia Watson can do that,' retorted Daphne, 'that's her job as her house-mother.'

'So you aren't going to sack her?' ventured Joe.

'Haven't decided yet,' replied his wife, sighing, 'But you're probably right, I can't afford to get rid of her just now, it being school holidays and all.'

The long summer holidays were always difficult at Laurel Farm. There was work to be done, but there were times when the girls had little to do and the house-mothers took it in turns to arrange some sort of activity. Mrs Watson often took them for a picnic by the nearby lake. Dusty grass ran down to a small stony strand and there was plenty of room to spread out. Under her supervision, they were allowed to bathe. The little beach shelved gently, and even those who couldn't swim paddled in the cold water. Mrs Watson's 'day' was always looked forward to by everyone.

No, Daphne Manton decided reluctantly, she couldn't afford to let Delia Watson go, but she would certainly reprimand her.

That afternoon, while the girls were playing hide and seek, vaguely supervised by Mrs Yardley, Mrs Manton sent Irene to find Mrs Watson, and waited for her in her office to indicate that this was an official meeting.

The house-mother came in wearing a blue cotton frock, looking cool and comfortable, and strangely younger than usual.

'Good afternoon, Mrs Manton,' she said with a smile. 'You wanted to see me?'

'Ah, Mrs Watson,' Daphne Manton did not return the smile, but looked at her over the rim of her spectacles, 'I have just received this letter from Miss Vanstone.' She passed over the letter. 'I wondered what you had to say about it!'

Delia Watson took the letter and read it with a sinking heart. She and Rita had been found out and it sounded as if there'd be hell to pay, but as she reached the closing paragraph and read of the death of Rita's grandmother, her dismay was replaced by a profound sadness. Poor Rita! As if the child hadn't had enough to put up with.

Still holding the letter she raised her eyes and said, 'The poor child! How very sad. You'd like me to break it to her, would you?'

'I would, yes,' agreed Mrs Manton, 'but that is not why I sent for you. I sent for you because I am extremely angry that you allowed one of our girls to write home to England. How dare you go behind our backs like that?' As her voice rose in righteous indignation, two spots of colour appeared on her cheeks, mottling her skin.

As if she's applied too much rouge, thought Delia, and the irrelevance of the thought made her smile.

'I can assure you, Mrs Watson,' spluttered Mrs Manton when she saw the smile, 'that this is no laughing matter. The letter, which you must have posted, has caused a great deal of inconvenience to Miss Vanstone. The lady who pays your wages!' This last was spoken slowly, as if punctuated between each word. 'So, what have you got to say for yourself, eh?'

'Firstly,' Mrs Watson said, apparently unintimidated by the other woman's anger, 'the letter was sent in reply to one Rita received from her grandmother, in which that lady actually stated that Miss Vanstone had agreed to forward a letter from her to Rita and Rosie. It was addressed to them here at Laurel Farm and so I assumed, apparently erroneously, that it had been sent by Miss Vanstone. I passed the letter on to Rita and she wanted to write back. I saw no harm in it, as her letter had been sanctioned by Miss Vanstone herself. You can see from this,' Mrs Watson waved Miss Vanstone's letter in the air, 'that I took the trouble to censor the letter before I sent it, so that there was little in it to cause alarm.'

'You took a great deal upon yourself, I must say,' snapped Mrs Manton. 'Who, may I ask, is the supervisor of this place?'

'You, of course,' agreed Mrs Watson mildly. There was nothing to be gained, and much to be lost, by antagonizing Mrs Manton further. 'But I am the child's house-mother, responsible for her day to day care. It isn't for me to come running to you with every little query about individual children. You have the responsibility for the whole farm, you have no time for trivialities such as this.'

'I don't consider this a triviality,' retorted Mrs Manton, 'and nor does Miss Vanstone.'

'So I see, and I'm sorry if what I did was wrong, but,' Mrs Watson extended the letter in her hand, 'it would seem that, as Miss Vanstone says, things have been decided for us, and the poor child has lost her grandmother.' She smiled sadly. 'To me that is the most important thing about this letter, the sad news it brings Rita.'

'Well,' said Mrs Manton, 'it seems you had reason to think that Miss Vanstone had sanctioned the letter from England, so, anyway, all's well that ends well.'

All's well that ends well! Delia Watson wanted to shriek. All's well for who, you unfeeling bitch. Not for poor little Rita Stevens, and not her grandmother either, dead on arrival at the hospital. God moves in mysterious ways, indeed! If that's how

God works, she thought furiously, then I'm glad I no longer believe in Him!

'And you'll break the news to Rita, will you?'

Forcing her voice to remain calm, Mrs Watson said that she would and that she would choose a suitable time at which to do so.

'Fine,' said Mrs Manton briskly, 'I'll leave it to you then.'

Back at Larch Cottage, Delia Watson went to her own quarters, pacing the room until her rage had subsided a little. Then she went to the window and looked out into the garden, where the desultory game of hide and seek was coming to an end. The girls would be coming back to the cottage for their tea before very long. The two on duty today to prepare the evening meal were Rita and Daisy.

'Hurry up, or we'll be late,' Daisy was saying as they came in, 'and the Watchdog'll be after us.'

Mrs Watson smiled. She was quite proud of her nickname, the Watchdog. She did watch over them, she watched over them all, and just wished there was more she could do to make their lives happier, but she was confined by the strict EVER-Care rules as much as they. And now she had to find a way to tell Rita that her grandmother was dead.

'Whose day is it tomorrow?' asked Daisy as they spread marge on slices of bread.

'Can't remember,' said Rita. 'Hope it's not Old Dawes.'

'So do I,' agreed Daisy fervently, 'her days are *soooo* boring.'

'Never mind,' Rita said, 'at least it's the Watchdog the day after that. Her days are always fun. I love going to the lake, don't you?'

That's the answer, Mrs Watson thought as she listened to the conversation from the hallway. That's what I'll do. I'll take Rita to the lake tomorrow and tell her then.

'Rita, I need you,' Mrs Watson said the following day. 'I've told Mrs Dawes you won't be joining in the scavenger hunt.'

'Lucky you!' cried Daisy when she heard. 'What does she want you for?'

'How do I know?' asked Rita, sounding a little anxious. Was there another letter? she wondered.

'Well, whatever it is, it's got to be better than whatever Old Dawes has got lined up.'

After lunch Rita waited in Larch, wondering what Mrs Watson wanted her to do. When the house-mother appeared she was carrying a basket.

'Right, Rita, off we go.'

Surprised, Rita followed her out into the garden, through the orchard, and onto the path that led across the dusty paddock towards the lake.

'Please, Mrs Watson, where're we going?'

'You'll see,' replied the house-mother, and strode on so quickly that Rita almost had to run to keep up with her.

When they reached the lake, Mrs Watson took a rug from her basket and spreading it on the ground, sat down. Rita, surprised but delighted, ran to the water and paddled her hot feet in the cool water. Then turning back she said, 'Why've we come here, miss? What do you want me for?'

'Come and sit down here, Rita,' said Mrs Watson, patting the ground beside her. 'I want to talk to you.' Reluctantly, Rita came out of the water and flopped down on the dusty grass.

'Rita, Mrs Manton asked me speak to you,' began Mrs Watson, and then she paused. It was so difficult, breaking yet more bad news just as Rita seemed to have settled down to her new life. 'She's had a letter...'

Rita, staring at her wide-eyed, murmured, 'Is it Rosie? What's happened to her?'

'No, no,' Mrs Watson said, 'it's not Rosie. As far as I know she's fine. No, I'm afraid it's your grandmother—'

'Gran? What's the matter with her?' A note of hysteria crept into Rita's voice. 'Gran got better, she wrote to me. Gran got better.'

'I know she did,' Mrs Watson said gently, 'but then she had what's called a stroke, sudden bleeding in her head, and though they took her straight to hospital, I'm afraid she didn't get better this time.' She reached out and took hold of Rita's hands. 'I'm so sorry, Rita.'

'Is she dead?'

'Yes, my dear, I'm afraid she is.'

Rita pulled her hands away and got to her feet. 'Then I ain't got no one now, have I?'

Mrs Watson let her go, watching a little anxiously as she took the path that ran along the lake shore.

Rita followed the stony track beside the lake, staring unseeingly out across the smooth expanse of water. She had no tears, but there was an unbearable pain in her throat, and despite the heat of the afternoon, she felt cold. She passed some trees that threw silver shadows to dance on the water, and found another tiny beach in their shade. Sitting on the strip of shingle, she heard the words again in her head... *I'm afraid she didn't get better this time.*

Rita looked out miserably across the lake. She thought of home, of Mum and Gran, remembering them as she'd not allowed herself to do for weeks. She thought of Gran waiting for them at the school gate on a Thursday, and playing snap and snakes and ladders in her kitchen after tea. She could still conjure up her mother's face, tired and strained, Gran's smile that crinkled her eyes, even Uncle Jimmy's face, fierce and threatening, but not their voices, their voices had all slipped away.

A wave of desolation swept through her. Daddy was a vague memory, only kept alive by the precious photo still hidden under her mattress. Mum didn't want her, and Rosie had been taken from her, vanishing into the vastness of Australia, and now Gran, beloved Gran, had had this stroke thing and had died. There'd be no more letters from Gran, no possible chance that one day in the far distant future, when Rita was grown up and had left Laurel Farm, that she might manage to go back and find her. There was no going back.

The painful lump in Rita's throat finally erupted and she began to sob. Sitting in the shade of a tree, alone in Australia, she wept for all she'd lost, the tears pouring down her cheeks, her body wracked with sobs, until there were no more tears to come and a strange calm overtook her. She had no handkerchief to wipe away her tears, so she went to the water's edge and scooped up handfuls of water to cool her burning cheeks. She remembered the promise she'd made herself that they wouldn't make her cry, ever again. Well, she'd broken that promise now, but it was for the last time.

'You're on your own now, Rita,' she said, and standing by the lake she made a new promise. 'You don't need no one else.'

Slowly she threaded her way back through the trees, to where Mrs Watson still sat, waiting for her, on the grassy slope.

'We can go back now, miss,' Rita said. 'Thank you for telling me about Gran.' And without waiting for her house-mother to reply, she ran, barefoot through the hot, dusty grass, back the way they'd come.

Daphne Manton heaved a sigh of relief when the long summer holidays ended, and the girls reverted to their tighter term-time routine.

Mrs Watson had broken the news of her grandmother's death to Rita Stevens, but though the child seemed withdrawn and looked a little wan, Daphne could see very little difference in her; she was simply relieved that Rita was causing no more trouble. No more letters came from Emily, so no more news from England. That was, until the phone call that completely changed her life.

Daphne and Joe had been going to bed one night when they heard the phone ringing downstairs. Daphne put on a robe and went down to the office. When she picked up the receiver she was greeted with a hiss and a whistle, and then an operator's reedy voice. 'Putting you through, caller. Go ahead, please.'

'Hallo?' Daphne almost shouted into the receiver. 'Who's there?'

'I need... Manton.' The line was bad, crackling with static, and she could hardly hear the man on the other end.

'Daphne Manton speaking. Who's there?'

This time the voice was a little clearer, and she heard him say, 'This is Martin Fielding, trustee of EVER-Care. I'm ringing from England. Is that Mrs Daphne Manton?'

'Yes,' Daphne replied loudly. 'Yes, Daphne Manton speaking.'

'I'm a trustee of EVER-Care. I'm ringing from England. I'm afraid I have some bad news. Emily had a massive stroke a fortnight ago, leaving her in a coma, and she died yesterday.'

'Died,' echoed Daphne, stunned.

'A stroke,' repeated Martin. 'Look, I haven't much time before we'll be cut off. She has died, and so we're winding up EVER-Care, here in England. There've been problems recently, so, as the sole trustee, I've decided that enough is enough.'

'You can't... I mean, what about—' began Daphne, but Martin Fielding ignored the interruption.

'With regard to Carrabunna, obviously we have a duty of care to those children already living at Laurel Farm, and funds will be available for their upkeep until they turn sixteen and are able to leave school to make their way in the world.'

'But...' stammered Daphne Manton.

'Please hear me out,' said Martin Fielding firmly. 'As the girls leave your care, they will not be replaced. As the numbers fall, there will naturally be fewer staff required to look after them. The cottages will be amalgamated and house-mothers given notice. You and your husband will be able to stay on at the farm and EVER-Care will make it over to you in recognition of your hard work. I'm sure you'll agree that this is an equable solution for everyone concerned.'

Martin gave Daphne no chance to comment. 'I will be putting all this in writing,' he went on, 'you'll get it in the next few weeks, but I wanted to tell you of Emily's death, and about the changes. So, I think that covers everything for now, Mrs Manton,' Martin continued briskly, 'except to offer you my condolences at the death of your cousin. I'll be in touch. Goodbye.' And the line went dead.

Daphne replaced the receiver. So, Emily was dead. Daphne felt no sadness at the news, she'd never particularly liked her. No, what she felt was more akin to anger, anger that Emily should have died so unexpectedly and left EVER-Care to the mercy of her dry stick of a lawyer brother-in-law. Was Martin

Fielding really going to wind up the trust? Could he? Just like that?

Slowly she went back upstairs. Seeing the shocked expression on her pale face, Joe said, 'Who was it?'

'Martin Fielding, Emily's brother-in-law. She's dead, Joe.'

'Who is? Emily? Thought she was indestructible.'

'She had a stroke. She died yesterday.'

'That's sad,' said Joe, cheerfully.

'It's more than sad,' retorted his wife. 'It's disastrous. He's going to close us down.'

'Close us down?' echoed Joe. That piece of news really did grab his attention. 'He can't do that, can he?'

'He says he can,' insisted Daphne. 'He says that he's winding up the trust and not replacing girls as they leave.'

'That'll take some time. Nothing to worry about yet.'

'I'm not so sure. But at least he said they were going to make Laurel Farm over to us, to you and me,' Daphne told him. 'We shall still have somewhere to live.'

'That's all right then,' said Joe. 'We can sell it and move somewhere decent.'

'For God's sake, Joe, grow up,' snapped Daphne. 'The next few years are going to be incredibly difficult as the farm winds down.'

'You could always resign,' suggested Joe. 'Let them find someone else to take it on. Their headache then, not ours.'

'Don't be obtuse, Joe. If I do that, they certainly won't give us the property. Anyway,' she said as she got back into bed, 'this Martin Fielding is going to send me all the details.'

'Then I should wait for his letter,' Joe advised. 'Don't do or say anything to anyone until you've got it all in writing.'

Daphne's brain was whirling. How could Emily not have made provision for the continuation of the trust after her death? Emily was practical, organized. Surely she'd made a will, and surely, in it, she'd stipulated what was to happen to EVER-Care. She would never have left anything that was so important to chance. Was Martin Fielding the only trustee? she wondered. If he was, was it really, entirely, his decision? Laurel Farm had been a comfortable billet for them, with a salary from EVER-Care and all the other perks and extras that she skimmed off the budget. Mrs Garfield had not been replaced. Her departure hadn't been mentioned to EVER-Care in England and her salary had been syphoned off into the Mantons' bank account.

The Mantons had quite a nest egg in their account, but even so, it wouldn't be enough to live on. At last she fell asleep, but in the morning the force of the problem came back to hit her again. Laurel Farm was a fair-sized property, but she and Joe would be hard-pressed to make it pay as an actual farm. Could they sell it? Might Martin have second thoughts?

Now his letter had come, and as she read it, Daphne's heart sank. Martin had no second thoughts, and his new proposals were even more stringent.

We shall, of course, require copies of the accounts for the past five years, as there are none in our files. Also details of all the children now accommodated with you, as their records here were destroyed in the fire at Laurel House...

Fire at Laurel House! Daphne knew nothing about a fire at Laurel House.

... their names, ages and the expected date that they will leave Laurel Farm. We encourage you to find foster place-ments for the younger children if no adoptive parents can be found. It is our intention to close Laurel Farm within the next six months.

'Six months!' cried Daphne. 'For God's sake, how do they think I'm going to get rid of more than twenty children in that time?'

Should this not be possible, funding will continue for the girls still living at Laurel Farm, but we shall expect progress in establishing those children elsewhere. No doubt the New South Wales authorities will assist you in finding suitable homes, either with foster parents or in other institutions.

The property of Laurel Farm will revert to you and your husband on the day that the last child leaves. This will be subject to a signed statement that you will make no further demands whatsoever on the EVER-Care Trust or the Vanstone family in the future.

All documentation with regard to the children who have passed through the farm is then to be destroyed, and no information contained in that documentation is to be disclosed to any third party, now or in the future. Please consider this letter as notice given to you and all your staff. As the numbers of girls decrease, and the house-mothers become redundant, a small amount of severance money will be paid to each. EVER-Care thanks you for your hard work in the past, and I know that I, and Sir Edward Sherrington, who is now a co-trustee, may rest assured of your ready cooperation in the proposal outlined here. I look forward to receiving all the documents I have requested at your earliest convenience.

'Six months!' Daphne said again, and went to find Joe.

'Better get cracking, then,' he said when he'd read the letter. 'You sort out the children, I'll sort out some accounts. Did you send any to Emily recently?'

'No, not for some time,' answered his wife.

'Good,' Joe said with a grin, 'that'll make it a lot easier.'

Chapter 35

From that day things began to change at Laurel Farm. Gradually the children were found places elsewhere, many of them leaving the only home they'd ever known. In ones or twos they disappeared to other children's homes, or occasionally a foster home was found. As the numbers dwindled, two of the cottages were closed, the disgruntled house-mothers forced out into the world, and the remaining children spread among the remaining houses.

Rita was still there, but Daisy had gone. She was sent to a children's home south of Sydney. Delia Watson begged Mrs Manton to send someone else, any one of the other children, as she knew that, since Rosie had gone, both girls were desperate to stay together.

'Do I have to go?' Daisy cried, distraught. 'Can't Reet come with me?'

'Couldn't we both stay here?' begged Rita. 'We absolutely promise not to get into any more trouble, don't we, Dais?'

'Yes, we promise!' Daisy agreed fervently. 'Honest!'

But Mrs Manton was adamant. Daisy should go and Rita should stay.

'I'm surprised you aren't sending Rita,' Delia said. 'You've always disliked her.'

'Don't be ridiculous!' snapped Mrs Manton. 'There's only one place there, and Daisy Smart is going. I'll find a place for Rita eventually.'

Was it pure spite? Delia wondered. Because the woman

regarded Rita as a trouble-maker? Did she want to make Rita's life as miserable as possible? Could anyone be that malicious? Yes. Daphne Manton. Delia had never seen her commit a single generous act, or show a moment's kindness to any of the girls in all the time she'd been at Laurel Farm.

Well, Delia decided, that was enough. She, too, would leave Laurel Farm and return to Sydney. She didn't particularly want to live in the city, but the chances of finding work there were much greater, and when she thought about it she realized she'd had enough of living out in the sticks and needed normal people, living normal lives, around her. She began writing for jobs, letter after letter, but though she had worked with children most of her adult life, she had no qualifications on paper and no one wanted to employ her. Eventually she received the offer of a job as a general assistant in a children's day-care centre. The salary was minimal, but the proprietor offered a little house in Randwick at reduced rent as part of the deal. Life would not be easy, money would be short, but the chance of shaking the dust of Laurel Farm from her shoes seemed heaven-sent, and Delia leaped at it.

The very next morning, when the children had left for school, she crossed over to the Mantons' house and knocked on the door.

Daphne, having a late breakfast, was less than pleased to see Mrs Watson on her doorstep.

'Can't it wait, whatever it is?' she demanded petulantly.

'No, I'm afraid not,' Delia Watson replied.

'Oh, very well,' sighed the superintendent, 'you'd better come in.'

She led the way into her office and seating herself behind her desk, looked across at Mrs Watson, her least favourite house-mother. Her least favourite, but, as Joe was always reminding her, her most efficient. 'Well?' she said. 'What is it?'

'I've come to give you my notice,' Delia replied.

'Your notice?' Mrs Manton was startled. 'What do you mean, "your notice"?'

'Just what I say.' Delia spoke calmly. 'I've been offered another job, and I intend to accept.'

'And what is this job?' demanded Daphne. 'Who would employ you? You have no qualifications.'

'I only have to give you a week's notice,' Delia said, ignoring the superintendent's rudeness, 'and it starts today.'

Daphne Manton was extremely put out by this turn of events. She had already decided Mrs Watson should be the last house-mother to leave Laurel Farm, and now it was clear that Delia Watson had other plans. She glowered at her across the desk.

'You must suit yourself,' she said coldly. 'I only hope you don't live to regret it.'

'I understand,' Delia interposed, 'there's a small severance payment.'

'There would be if we made you redundant,' agreed Mrs Manton sourly. 'But,' her eyes gleamed with malice, 'as you're giving notice, that won't apply.'

Delia was furious. She couldn't afford to wait to be made redundant, she'd lose the job in Randwick. She had to seize this opportunity; it might be the only one. She had a little money saved out of her pittance as Larch's house-mother; she'd have to live on that until she received her first pay cheque.

'In that case,' she returned, 'I shall work out my notice and leave at the end of next week,' and she stalked out of the office without another word.

That evening, as she supervised their tea, Delia looked at the eight girls still living in Larch as they sat round the table and knew a feeling of guilt. She was leaving, escaping from the miserable institution that was Laurel Farm, while these poor children were forced to stay here at the mercy of Daphne Manton. Since Daisy had gone, Rita had lost her spark. She clearly missed Daisy dreadfully. The two girls had been inseparable, each keeping the other afloat in the muddy waters of Laurel Farm. Delia hadn't seen Rita as quiet as this for months. When Rosie had been taken, when her grandmother had died, each time Rita'd withdrawn into herself, but with Daisy staunchly beside her, her natural courage and determination had reasserted itself and she had gradually re-emerged and settled back into the familiar, if strict routine of Laurel Farm.

Delia had done her job as the 'Watchdog', and watched over all her charges, but particularly over Rita. She admired the girl's courage. She encouraged her to work hard at school. A decent education would be a stepping stone out of the mire of an EVER-Care home to a much happier life.

'If you go on working as you are now,' Delia had told Rita, 'you'll pass your exams with flying colours and you'll have lots of opportunities when you leave school.'

How will they all manage without me? Delia wondered as she watched them eating their tea. But in truth Rita was her particular concern.

I could always take her with me.

Where had that thought sprung from? As an idea it seemed to burst, fully formed, into her mind. Could I? Could I really take responsibility for her for the next seven years? Why not? You've got a job to go to and a house to live in. The Manton woman doesn't want her here. The idea of leaving this dreadful place, taking Rita with her, filled Delia with a peculiar sort of exhilaration. What a commitment to take on, the fostering of a child; but not impossible given that she already loved that child. She'd never thought she could love another child since the death of her own son, but now she discovered Rita had crept, almost unnoticed, into her heart. Surely Rita'd want to go anywhere that took her away from Laurel Farm. But, Delia knew that she couldn't ask her. If she so much as hinted at the possibility and then was unable to carry it through, poor Rita would have to cope with yet more disillusionment, another desertion, another apparent rejection. No, Delia decided, if she was going to do this, she must do it, officially, through Mrs Manton.

That night she lay in bed thinking of the obstacles Mrs Manton would surely put in her way. Children were only to be fostered by couples or families. It would be better for Rita...

when had she ever cared about Rita?... to be brought up in an environment she was used to, with other children around her. Delia wouldn't be able to support her on the wages she was to receive.

Delia found an answer for each difficulty. No couple or family had come forward to give Rita a home. She, Delia Watson, was doing so now. The child needed somewhere to go when Laurel Farm finally closed, and Delia was offering that somewhere. She was offering Rita a proper home and somehow they would manage on her money.

'And,' Delia spoke the words out loud, 'there is no possibility that I shall fail. I will not allow that child to be brought low again.'

Next morning when the girls had gone to school, she marched back into the superintendent's office.

'I'd like another word with you, Mrs Manton,' she said without preamble.

Mrs Manton looked up from the letter she was writing, startled at the intrusion. 'Second thoughts, I suppose,' she said tersely. She'd wondered if Mrs Watson might have them when she heard there would be no severance money. She had already decided not to accept a change of heart; she and Joe would keep the severance pay.

'No,' snapped Delia, 'certainly not. I shall be gone by the end of next week, and I shall be taking Rita Stevens with me.'

'Taking Rita Stevens?' echoed Daphne Manton, incredulously. 'Taking Rita Stevens where?'

'I shall take her to live with me in Sydney.' Delia had finally decided in the early hours of the morning that the way to handle this was to state her intention rather than ask permission. So, she spoke calmly but firmly. 'I have a job to go to and a place to live. Rita needs a home and I intend to provide her with one.'

'You can't just—' began the superintendent.

'I can and I will,' declared Delia. 'We shall both leave Laurel Farm at the end of next week, and you need never think of either of us again. EVER-Care will have discharged its responsibility towards the child by ensuring her a loving home to go to, and I will provide that loving home.'

'The state authorities may have something to say about this,' said Mrs Manton sourly.

'If you handle this properly, the state authorities will be delighted to have one less child on their books,' replied Delia. 'All I require is for you to sign the requisite forms, entrusting Rita to me as her foster mother. Of course she'll be a ward of state, but I'll be her day to day guardian. You've already done this for at least four other children. There is absolutely no reason why you shouldn't do the same for Rita.'

'And if it all goes wrong?'

'It won't,' said Delia. 'I won't let it.'

The two women regarded each other for a long moment, then Daphne Manton shrugged. 'If you really want her, take her,' she said dismissively. 'Let's hope you're not making a big mistake. I will not take her back.'

'I have no intention of sending her back.'

'Have you talked to Rita about this?'

'No, not yet,' admitted Delia.

'Supposing she doesn't want to go with you. Have you thought of that?'

'Of course I have,' returned Delia. 'It'll be her decision, but let's face it, Mrs Manton, what child in her right mind wouldn't want to get out of this hell-hole?'

For a moment Delia thought she'd said too much. Daphne Manton's pinched face took on a vicious look, the twin spots of colour reappearing on her cheeks. This time, however, Delia did not smile; her own eyes met and held the superintendent's, challenging and defiant... and the battle had been won.

When Rita came home from school that afternoon, she was on her way out to work in the farm garden with the other girls, but Delia called her aside.

'Rita,' she'd said when they were safe from inquisitive ears, 'can you keep a secret?'

'Yes, miss,' Rita answered, round-eyed. 'What secret?'

'I'm leaving Laurel Farm next week,' began Delia and as the colour drained from Rita's face, she hurried on, 'and I'm taking you with me.'

Rita stared at her. 'Me, miss? But where are we going?'

'Sydney,' replied Delia. 'We're going to live in Sydney.'

'Live in Sydney?' repeated the child. 'For a holiday, miss? When are we coming back?'

'Never!' answered Delia firmly. 'Never, never, never.'

Rita gazed at her in silence, and Delia went on, 'I've got a new job and a little house to live in, and I thought you might like to come and live in it with me.'

'Just me, miss? What about the others?'

'I'm afraid there isn't room for the others,' explained Delia, 'so it'll be just us, you and me. Would you like that, Rita?'

The colour had flooded back into the little girl's cheeks and her eyes sparkled. 'You mean it, miss?' she breathed, not daring to believe. 'You really mean it?'

'I really mean it,' Delia assured her. 'I'll be working at a nursery, and you'll go to a new school.'

'And never come back here?'

'Never, I promise you.'

Rita's reaction had brought tears to Delia's eyes and she swore then that she would never, never let her new daughter down.

They had left Laurel Farm, as arranged, at the end of the following week, carrying all their worldly possessions in two suitcases. Delia had retrieved the rose-patterned dress from the common clothes cupboard and tucked it into her own suitcase. Apart from Rita's picture of her father, the letter from her grandmother and an extremely battered-looking Knitty, Delia knew it was the only link Rita had with her life in England.

On the day they were leaving, Delia went to the office to collect the necessary paperwork, checking the forms carefully to ensure that they were correct.

'Thank you for sorting this out,' she said, managing to smile at her ex-boss. 'But there is just one more thing I wanted to ask you before we go.'

Daphne Manton raised an eyebrow. 'Well?'

'Please will you give me the name and address of the couple who adopted Rosie, Rita's little sister?'

'No,' answered Mrs Manton. 'I will not.'

'But surely it can do no harm now?' pleaded Delia. 'Just to know the name, so that maybe, one day, Rita can find her.'

'She is nothing to do with Rita,' snapped the superintendent. 'All Rita has now is you, and I wish her joy of you.'

'I don't know how you can live with yourself, Daphne Manton,' exploded Delia. 'I don't know how you can face yourself in the mirror. You're a callous, cruel, mean-minded old woman, and I hope you rot in hell!' And leaving Daphne Manton spluttering with rage, Delia stalked out of the door.

Daisy Smart jumped off the bus and walked the last two blocks to the hostel where she had a room. She had just spent the day with Rita, who now lived with Mrs Watson in Randwick. Daisy thought Rita extremely lucky to be living in a proper home, but she didn't begrudge her luck. Somehow, Daisy felt, it was due to her. Rita had always had more courage than Daisy, to stand up for herself and Rosie. Since Rosie had been adopted, Daisy and Rita had become inseparable, until Laurel Farm closed and Daisy was sent to a children's home outside Sydney. Even then Rita had not abandoned her friend. As soon as she and Mrs Watson moved into the little house in Randwick, she'd insisted that they visit Daisy and take her out for the day.

'I wish she could come and live with us,' she said, pleading in her voice.

'I know you do, darling,' Delia Watson replied, 'but not only do we not have enough room for her,' she raised a hand to cut off Rita's protest that she and Daisy could share the tiny bedroom that was hers, 'but I really can't afford to keep her. You know how careful we have to be with our money.'

Rita did know and sadly, she let her protest lapse. She knew how incredibly lucky she was to have a legal foster mother to live with instead of being moved to yet another children's home like poor Daisy.

'I know, Deeley,' she sighed, 'but I feel so sorry for poor Dais stuck in that awful place.'

The day they walked out of Laurel Farm, Delia had taken Rita's hand and said, 'Since you are now officially my foster daughter, I don't think you can call me Mrs Watson any more, do you?'

Rita looked at her in surprise. 'What shall I call you then? We used to call you the Watchdog, Dais and me.'

Delia laughed. 'I know you did, but I don't think you can call me that either. My name is Delia. I know you won't want to call me Mum or Mother, but what about Aunt Delia?'

'Aunt Deeley,' repeated Rita, tripping over the unfamiliar name.

'Deeley,' cried Delia. 'I like that. Call me Deeley.'

Rita had been enrolled in the local school as Rita Stevens, but she was proud to be known as Deeley's daughter.

Once a month on a Saturday, they took the train together and rescued Daisy from the grim institution where she lived. They took a picnic and went to the beach, played in the woods or went to the cinema. When Rita turned thirteen, Deeley let her go by herself and despite their different circumstances the two girls remained firm friends. At fifteen Daisy left school. She had to stay in the home until she was sixteen, but with more freedom and a little cash of her own in her pocket.

Rita stayed on at school until she graduated and was able to go to teacher training college, but they continued to meet on Saturdays.

As soon as she was allowed to, Daisy left the home and moved into Sydney.

'Where will you live?' Rita asked when Daisy told her of her plans.

Daisy shrugged. 'Dunno, I'll find somewhere. An 'ostel or somefink.'

She found a room in a girls' hostel in Kings Cross.

'Not a very salubrious area,' Deeley remarked doubtfully when she heard.

'It's all she can afford,' Rita pointed out. 'And at least she can come and go as she likes. She's got a new job at Woolworths, so she's got her own money.' Which is more than I have, she added silently. Rita didn't envy Daisy her new freedom, it had been long enough coming, but she did envy her the small wages she took home each week. Deeley's tiny income was stretched to the limit to allow Rita to stay on at school rather than get a job and bring in a regular wage, as Rita suggested she should.

'No,' Delia insisted, 'it is most important you stay on. Education is everything.'

So Rita stayed on, passed her exams and went to college, and occasionally as she sat on the bus and looked out at the bustling streets of the city, at the crowds who thronged the pavements and crushed themselves into buses on their way to and from work, she would think about Rosie and wonder what had become of her. She must be out there somewhere, Rita thought despondently. I could pass her in the street and never know it.

Delia told her that she'd tried to get the name of Rosie's adoptive parents from Daphne Manton. 'I'm sorry,' Delia said, 'but she refused point blank to tell me their name, let alone their address.'

'Oh, I know their name,' Rita replied, 'it's Waters.'

Delia stared at her in amazement. 'How on earth do you know that?'

'Mrs Manton called him Mr Waters.'

'And you've remembered all this time?'

'I wrote it in my journal,' Rita said, and she went and found the old exercise book that had been her first diary, and showed Delia what she'd written.

Today Rosie was took away to be adopted by some people called Mr and Mrs Waters. I wasn't let say goodbye proply and Rosie was screaming becos she didn't want to go, but they pushed her into a car and drove away. When I'm grown up I'm going to find Rosie and rescue her from them.

After that, without telling Rita, Delia had searched for Mr and Mrs Waters, but could find no trace of them. Eventually, when she had finally given up, she told Rita what she'd been doing. 'I'm afraid they could be anywhere,' Delia said. 'Australia is so big, I don't think we'll ever find her now.'

Rita hugged her tightly. 'I know I've lost her,' she said. 'And I think we have to accept that, but thank you, dearest Deeley, for trying to find her for me.' She sighed. 'She'd be quite different from the Rosie I remember, anyway, wouldn't she? But thank you, thank you for looking.'

'We'll never find Rosie now,' Rita had confided to Daisy one day as they sat in Centennial Park, sharing the sandwiches and bottle of ginger beer Daisy had brought with her from Woolworths. 'Deeley's done all she can, but we can't find Rosie anywhere.'

'You need a private dick,' Daisy said.

'Oh yeah?' laughed Rita. 'An' where we going to find the money to pay one?'

Daisy shrugged. 'I dunno, do I? Maybe when you've finished all this college stuff and get yourself a job.'

'Well, I sold another story the other day, so maybe when I'm a rich and famous author I'll hire one then.'

Daisy laughed at that. 'You and your writing,' she teased. 'I meant a proper job.'

Chapter 36

Jean lay, rigid, on her bed and listened as the key turned in the lock. As always, Dad was locking her in after his evening visit. She heard him go downstairs, but she didn't move. She heard her mother come in from her church meeting, but still Jean didn't move. It wasn't until she heard them come up the stairs together, go into the front bedroom and shut the door, that she slowly sat up and swung her feet to the floor. She could feel the stickiness between her legs, she knew the smell of him, on her body and lingering in the room.

She crossed to the chest of drawers and pouring water from the jug into the bowl that stood beside it, she took her flannel and scrubbed herself violently between her legs, across her stomach, round her breasts. As always she cleaned her teeth, brushing the taste of him from her mouth. It was what she always did, but tonight it was different. Tonight would be the very last time. Tonight she would leave this horrible house once and for all. She had made her plans over the last couple of months and now it was time to carry them out.

Her adoptive father had been a regular visitor to her bedroom for nearly ten years. At first he had only wanted to cuddle her, to kiss her, to have her fondle him, and if she did not he simply put her over his knee and spanked her. She was terrified of him, but her fear seemed to excite him. As she began to comply with his desires, he found he needed to become more violent, simply to see the fear in her eyes, her fear increasing his arousal.

On one occasion he made a mistake and she was left with a black eye. It was clearly visible in the morning, and Edna said, 'Poor Jean, you've bumped you eye. I thought I heard you fall down the stairs. You must be more careful, darling.'

Gerald had threatened Jean that if she said anything to Edna about his visits to her room, she would be sorry. 'It's our little secret, Jeannie,' he soothed after one of his more brutal visits. 'Very private. If you say a word to anyone, even your mother, I'll have to punish you. You do realize that, don't you, little girl?' He was gripping her face between his hands, forcing her to look at him.

Terrified, Jean nodded, and he had smiled his crocodile smile and said, 'That's a good girl.'

But when Edna commented on her black eye, Jean burst out, 'I didn't fall down stairs, Mum, Dad hit me.'

Edna looked amazed. 'Dad did? He'd never hit you.'

'He does,' Jean insisted, 'when he comes into my bedroom and makes me do things.'

'He doesn't come into your bedroom,' exploded Edna. 'He doesn't make you do anything. You're a wicked, wicked girl to say such things about your father.'

At that moment the door opened and Gerald walked in. 'What's this?' he began, jovial as he always was when they were all three together. 'What's my little girl been saying about me?'

'She's got a bruise on her face,' Edna said. 'She says you came to her room and hit her.'

'She what?' Gerald's joviality fell away. 'Says I hit her?'

'She says you came to her room, made her do something, and hit her,' repeated Edna.

'And you believed her?' Gerald was incredulous.

'No, of course not,' said his wife. 'She's a very naughty girl to tell such lies.'

'She certainly is.' Gerald took hold of Jean's wrist and pulling her out of the room, dragged her back upstairs. Once inside he locked the door and took off his belt.

After that, however, though the bedroom visits continued, he was more careful and there were seldom marks which couldn't be explained away at school. His final warning, as he returned his belt to his trousers, had been, 'If you tell lies like this at school, I'll beat you till you beg for mercy. Understand?' And Jean, sobbing with pain and fear, had nodded, so that he turned away satisfied. 'You're not going to school today,' he said. 'It's better, as you've had a fall down the stairs, that you spend the day quietly here, just so we're sure you haven't hurt yourself too badly. I'll phone the school and explain that you'll be back on Monday.'

Now, aged nearly fifteen, Jean was going to escape. Over the previous months she had been collecting money. She wasn't given pocket money as such, just the occasional sixpence or shilling, perhaps to be sure she had no cash, but she set about acquiring more and wasn't too fussy where it came from. Often she raided Edna's purse, taking a few coins here and there, hoping it wouldn't be noticed. At school she went through the pockets of coats hanging up in the cloakroom, classroom desks, collecting odd pennies and shillings. Never taking all she found, though thieving was suspected, she'd never been caught and the coins joined her stash in an old flowerpot in the garden shed. She was certain Edna would've found it if she'd hidden it in her bedroom. One Sunday she was given a whole pound by a visitor to the church after she'd told him the history of the building. He had folded her hand round the note and said softly, 'Put that in your money box.' He gave her a wink and said, 'Our secret.' The familiar words chilled her, but she managed to smile and the pound joined the coins in the flowerpot.

Recently, on a day when Edna was out when Jean got home from school, she took her chance to pack some things into her old suitcase. With her ears cocked to hear the sound of the front door, she pulled it out from under the bed where it had been ever since she arrived. Opening it she found a childish frock lying in the bottom. She remembered that Edna had particularly disliked the dress, and Jean had for some reason loved it and had hidden it. She'd forgotten all about it over the years, but now here it was again. She knew it was special, but couldn't quite remember why.

Had she brought it with her when she was adopted? Yes, probably that was it, indeed that was probably why Edna didn't like it. She shook it out, about to chuck it into a corner when she suddenly changed her mind and refolding it, placed it in the bottom of the case. Carefully she chose a few of her clothes that she thought would not be missed. She had no idea when she would be able to leave, but knew it must be soon. To the case she added some biscuits and a bottle of Edna's sleeping tablets. She had stolen these some months ago to take after Gerald's visits, helping her drift into deep sleep and fend off the nightmares which haunted her. Once the case was packed she took it out into the yard and hid it under the shed. Now she was ready to go the moment the opportunity presented itself.

Two nights later that opportunity came. Edna was out and Gerald appeared in her room as he always did on such occasions. He still maintained the pretence that Edna didn't know what he was doing, what he was subjecting their adopted daughter to. As always Jean bore with his attentions, but thought with a jolt of angry triumph as he locked the door behind him, That's the very last time he'll do that to me.

Now all was quiet, she dressed quickly, pulling on slacks, a blouse, two jerseys for warmth and a light rain jacket.

She listened again at her door, but the house was silent, and sure that both parents must now be asleep, Jean opened the tiny window and peered out into the night. There was fitful moonlight as clouds drifted across the face of a quarter moon; enough to see without, she hoped, being seen. She hoisted herself up onto the sill and squeezed through. Gripping the opening, she lowered herself first onto the flat scullery roof below and then dropped down into the garden. The noise of her descent sounded very loud to her ears, and the moment she was on the ground she scurried to the shelter of the shed. She glanced back up at her window, but there was no sudden light in her bedroom, no light anywhere in the house, so taking her courage in both hands, she stuffed the money from the flowerpot into her pocket, picked up her case and slipped out onto the road. A quick glance up at her parents' bedroom window assured her that it remained dark, and she set off down the street. Most of the houses were in darkness, and by staying in the shadows Jean hoped to escape any inquisitive eyes. Moments later she was out of her own street and cutting through another towards the centre of the town. She'd looked up train times to Sydney, for she'd decided she must disappear into the anonymity of the city, and knew the first train was at 4.30 a.m. She could only hope that Gerald didn't discover her flight before that and follow her to the station.

She hid in the domain across the road until the station clock showed 4.20, then she picked up her case and walked across the road. When she presented herself at the ticket office, the clerk looked at her in surprise.

'You're an early bird,' he said.

Prepared for such a remark, Jean said, 'Yes, got a job interview in Sydney. Exciting, isn't it?'

'Job, is it?' said the man as he took her money and gave her the ticket. 'Good luck to you, then.'

There were several others on the platform awaiting the early train, but they paid no attention to her, and when the train came into the station Jean hurried to board. Once inside the carriage she kept her head down; she was still terrified that Gerald might appear at the last minute and haul her off the train. But he did not. The whistle blew and the train drew out of the station, heading for Sydney.

When Jean alighted at Sydney Central Station, she was immediately engulfed in the crowds that thronged its concourse. People hurrying in every direction on their way to work pushed past those who stood looking at timetables, or ambled along at a more leisurely pace.

Determined to put as much distance between her and any pursuit as possible, Jean emerged from the station, case in hand, and started to walk. She trudged along the streets, turning down side roads and keeping away from the main thoroughfares. Now she had made the break and she was actually in Sydney, she had no idea where to go or what to do. Her planning had stopped at the actual escape, perhaps because she'd not really thought she would succeed. At length she stopped at a coffee bar and bought herself a sandwich and a cup of tea. As she sat at a metal-topped table in the corner, she looked out at the busy streets beyond. The first thing to do, she decided, was to find somewhere to sleep. She took her money from her pocket and looked at it. Five pounds and a few pence left. She took her time eating her ham sandwich and drinking her tea, but the place was filling up and eventually she had to leave. Further along the road she saw an information office and went inside. The woman behind the counter provided her with a map and when Jean asked her where she might find a cheap hostel, she tutted a little saying, 'You shouldn't be on your own, duck.'

'Just for a night or two,' Jean said quickly, 'then my parents will be here.'

The woman looked at her askance, but she wrote down the names of two women-only hostels and marked them on the map. As she left the office, Jean looked back and saw the woman reaching for the telephone, and certain that she was reporting her to someone, she hurried away. She spent the rest of the afternoon wandering through the town. The woman had told her that hostels weren't generally open during the day, and it was near to six o'clock when she finally risked going to one of those marked on her map. The door was opened by a woman dressed in a housecoat, a cigarette hanging from her lip who, in answer to her query, said, 'No, nothing here. You might try Lawsons, in Flint Street, Kings Cross.'

Jean thanked her. Lawsons was the other one marked on her map. She trudged the extra mile to Flint Street, only to be met with the same answer. 'No rooms free here. Sorry.'

'Can you suggest anywhere else?' she asked wearily.

The woman considered for a moment and then said, 'Marks House, two streets over. They might have something.' Jean thanked her and crossed the road.

Marks House was a decrepit-looking building and she paused

outside, unwilling to go in. She knew she had to find somewhere, but the grubby windows and the peeling paint made her hesitate. Just then a young woman came up behind her and started up the steps to the front door.

'Excuse me,' Jean called, 'do you live here?'

The woman turned round and looked down at her. 'Sorry,' she said, 'you talking to me?'

Jean nodded. 'I just wondered if you lived here.'

'Yup,' replied the woman, ''fraid so.'

'Do you think they might have a room free?' asked Jean.

The woman thought for a moment and then said, 'Actually you might be in luck. I think someone moved out a couple of days ago. Want me to go and ask?'

Jean stepped forward, still clutching her suitcase. 'Would you?'

'Sure,' came the reply. 'Wait a mo.' She pushed her way through the door and minutes later came back, beaming. 'You're in luck. Come on in.'

Jean hurried up the steps and went inside. In the hallway beside the young woman was another, older, woman.

'This is Mrs Glazer, our warden,' the young woman said. 'She does have one room free.'

'Name?' said Mrs Glazer, giving Jean a penetrating look.

'Jean.' She hesitated a fraction of a second before adding, 'Smith.' She'd so nearly said Waters.

'Well, Miss... Smith,' she, too, lingered on the name, 'thirty bob a week... in advance.'

Jean took out her money and counted out the thirty shillings.

'She'll have Miss Crawford's old room, Miss Smart. Will you take her up?'

Taking her acquiescence for granted, Mrs Glazer handed her a key and disappeared through the door to her own quarters.

'Typical!' grinned Miss Smart. 'Lazy Glazy don't do anyfink she can pass on to someone else.' She looked at the thin girl waiting beside her, her fair hair lank, her face pale with a wary expression in her dull blue eyes. 'Come on then,' she said. 'My name's Daisy,' she added, as she led them up the stairs. 'My room's just across the landing from yours.'

When they reached the second floor Daisy unlocked a door and Jean followed her into the pokey room.

'It ain't too bad,' Daisy said. 'None of these rooms is much cop, but at least you can shut the door and call it your own.'

Jean looked round the room. It certainly wasn't much of a place, but it had a bed and a chest of drawers and to her it was a refuge. Most importantly, it had a lock.

'Thanks,' she said and dumped her case on the floor.

'I'm just across the landing,' Daisy said, 'if you want anyfink. Kitchenette's just down the passage and the bathroom is one floor down.'

Jean simply nodded and said, 'Thanks.'

'You got any food with you?'

'Not hungry,' Jean said, not meeting her eye.

'OK,' shrugged Daisy and crossing the landing to her own room, she left her to it.

As soon as Daisy disappeared, Jean shut and locked her door. For the first time since she had climbed out of her bedroom window, she felt safe from pursuit. Even if Gerald Waters chased her to Sydney he'd surely never find her in the myriad of streets and houses. Daisy'd asked if she had food, and she realized that she had had nothing to eat since her sandwich hours ago, and had nothing except the few biscuits in her case until she could go out and find something in the morning. Still she didn't care; hungry or not she wasn't going to venture out into the darkening streets again. She put her case onto the bed and unpacked the few things she'd brought with her.

As she was eating her biscuits, there came a knock at her door, followed by Daisy's voice, 'Jean?'

Jean didn't answer and Daisy knocked again. 'Jean? You hungry?'

'No.' Jean's reply came loud and clear offering no further opening for conversation. She had no intention of getting to know anyone else who lived in this house. She wanted to keep herself entirely to herself, leaving no trail for Gerald to follow.

'OK, suit yourself,' Daisy called, and Jean heard her go along the landing to the tiny communal kitchen.

Maybe she's just being kind, Jean thought. But kind or not, Jean would trust nobody, certainly nobody she'd only met a few minutes earlier.

In the kitchen, as she heated up baked beans and made toast for her own supper, Daisy thought about the new girl. There's something odd about her, she decided. Her name was probably Jean, but whether it was Jean Smith, that was another matter. Looks pretty down, thought Daisy. Wonder where she's come from.

Over the next few days Jean saw nothing of Daisy. She heard her leave for work in the mornings, and though Mrs Glazer didn't allow anyone to remain in the hostel during the day and Jean had to be out by 8.30, she was usually back before Daisy in the evening.

The following week Jean had to find another thirty shillings. Her money had dwindled to almost nothing and she was desperate to earn some somehow. All week she'd been trying to get a job, but she could find nothing. No one wanted to employ a young girl with no experience and no qualifications. She was getting desperate, for she knew that if she didn't find the rent for her room Mrs Glazer wouldn't hesitate to turf her out onto the street.

She was walking home later than usual, through the backstreets of Kings Cross, when a man suddenly materialized out of a doorway and grabbing her by the wrist hissed, 'How much?'

Jean froze. The man smelled of Gerald. 'What... what d'you mean?' she faltered.

'What d'you think I mean?' growled the man, still gripping her wrist. He jerked his head at the dark doorway. 'Quick plunge, eh? I'll give you a pound.'

A pound. It would save her from being chucked out by Mrs Glazer. Jean realized bitterly that she wouldn't be doing anything she hadn't done, or been doing for years, only this time she'd get paid for it.

'Show me the pound,' she said, and the man laughed.

'You're a one,' he said as he pulled her into the doorway.

It was all over very quickly, and as the man zipped his fly he put his hand in his pocket and pulled out the promised pound. 'You're all right,' he said. 'Same time next week.'

'What!' Jean grabbed the pound note, hitching up her knickers as she did.

'I'll be round here same time next week,' said the man. 'Another pound, doll, if you're here too.'

'You make it sound like a dentist's appointment,' Jean said, edging away.

The man gave a shout of laughter. 'Better than the dentist!' And with these words he disappeared into the darkness.

It was two weeks later that disaster struck. Her punter had come back the next week, and though she knew she was stupid but in desperate need of money, Jean went back and earned another pound.

'When I come next week,' he said as if it were a regular arrangement between them, 'I know a place we can go; do it properly, not just a quick knee-trembler.' He cocked an eye at her as she snatched the pound from his hand. 'Pay you more, too,' he said, and as before he melted into the dark even as she was still adjusting her clothes.

So she went again, and when they met he took her hand and led her along the road, just as if they were friends out for a stroll. Jean, tense as a bowstring when they met, began to relax. It's easy money, she thought. Isn't as if I don't know what to do.

They turned into a narrow street and walked to the far end where a light shone above a door. The man took a key from his pocket and opening the door, pushed Jean inside.

'Upstairs,' he said, and Jean, beginning to realize just how stupid she had been to leave the safety of the open street, stumbled up the steep staircase ahead of him. At the top was another door, and when he opened it and shoved her into the room, she was confronted by three men, all of them eyeing her eagerly.

'You was right, Clive,' one said as he reached forward and ran a hand down Jean's leg. 'She is a young'un. Just as I like 'em.'

Jean flinched away and turned for the door, but Clive was barring the way.

'Now then, doll,' he said, 'don't be like that. You done it with me. Now my friends want a turn.'

They all laughed, and Clive said, 'You first, Jerry.'

He propelled Jean into the arms of a man with ginger hair that stuck up round his head like a bottlebrush. She could smell the alcohol, the stale sweat and his putrid breath as he began to pull at her clothes. Jean screamed and he gave her a backhander across her face, before pulling her down onto a bed in the corner.

When they had all finished, Clive, the last to take his turn, gave her a shove towards the door. 'Beat it,' he said, 'I can see Jerry's up for it again.'

Clutching her clothes, Jean staggered to the door and almost fell down the stairs. She had coped with the rape as she had always coped with Gerald, closing her mind, leaving her body to the abuse it was suffering, but now it was over she was shaking with terror. When she reached the street she stumbled through the darkness towards the lights of the broader thoroughfare beyond. Twice she tripped and fell on the muddy cobbles, grazing her hands and bruising her knees, and by the time she reached the hostel she had tears streaming down her face, and knew she couldn't face Mrs Glazer in such a dreadful state. She didn't climb the steps to the front door, but slipped into the alley that ran down one side of the building and sat curled up against the wall sobbing, and that was how Daisy found her half an hour later. Daisy had been to the flicks and was coming home when she heard the sobs. Pausing on the corner, she peered into the darkness and called softly, 'Anyone there?' No one answered but there was a scuffling in the deep shadows, where the light from the street couldn't penetrate.

Daisy flicked on the torch she always carried in her bag and directed its beam into the alley. There she saw a crumpled figure, a hand shielding her eyes from the light. For a moment Daisy didn't recognize her, but there was something familiar about the cowering shape and she said, 'Jean? Is that you?'

There was another sob and Daisy hurried to kneel beside her. The beam of the torch picked out the cuts and bruises on Jean's grimy face, a swelling black eye, a gash across the back of her hand.

'Jean!' Daisy exclaimed in horror. 'Whatever happened? Who did this to you?'

Jean didn't answer, but tears streamed down her face as she heard the kindness and concern in Daisy's voice.

'Right,' said Daisy, taking charge. 'Let's get you indoors.' She helped Jean to her feet and supported her as they walked up the steps to the front door. Letting herself in, Daisy called out, 'Only me, Mrs Glazer, Daisy. Goodnight.'

As she'd hoped, Lazy's door stayed closed and they were able to get up to Jean's room unseen. Once inside Daisy closed and locked the door.

Leading Jean to the bed, she said, 'Lie down and I'll get some water to clean you up.'

It took a while. Daisy carefully wiped away the blood, mud and grit, bathing the grazes on Jean's cheeks and hands, pressing a cold towel gently against the swelling eye. Then she made a cup of tea, ladled sugar into it and, placing it into Jean's hands, said, 'So what happened, Jean? Who done this to you?'

Jean, now propped up on her bed, looked at her warily for a minute or two and didn't reply.

'Come on, Jean,' Daisy urged. 'You can tell me. I ain't going to dob you in, am I?'

'Dunno,' murmured Jean.

'Well, I ain't,' said Daisy stoutly, 'so come on, tell.'

'There was a man,' began Jean, 'and I...' She hesitated and then shrugged as if to say what did it matter anyway.

'And you went with him for money,' supplied Daisy.

Jean nodded. 'Yes,' she whispered. 'I hadn't got the money for my room. Mrs Glazer'll turn me out.'

'So you sold yourself for this poxy little room,' Daisy said flatly.

'Why not?' demanded Jean with a spark of defiance in the eyes. 'Why not? I done it before. I know what to do. Christ, I been doing it for years!'

'Doing it for years?' echoed Daisy faintly. 'How old are you, Jean?'

'Nineteen,' replied Jean.

'Pull the other one,' scoffed Daisy. 'Fourteen, more like!'

'Fifteen,' admitted Jean sullenly.

'OK, fifteen,' agreed Daisy, knowing this was, at least, closer to the truth. 'So how come you been doing it for years, for Christ's sake?'

Jean took a gulp of the hot, sweet tea and a touch of colour came back into her cheeks.

'My dad,' she replied.

'Your dad? You been fucking your dad?'

'No,' said Jean fiercely, 'he's been fucking me. Ever since I was a little girl.'

'But what about your mum?' demanded Daisy. 'I mean, didn't you tell her?'

'Course I told her,' snapped Jean, 'but she called me a liar and slapped my face. '

Daisy took Jean's hand. 'Tell me.' So Jean told her, of her life with the Waters and her final escape.

'So you're on the run,' said Daisy. 'I thought you might be.'

'Yeah, well, my money's gone,' Jean said, 'so I thought I'd make some more. Done it a couple of times and it was OK. Enough money for my room and some food.' She spoke defiantly, but Daisy ignored what she'd said.

'Won't they be looking for you?' she asked. 'Your mum and dad?'

'Maybe,' said Jean, 'but if I keep my head down I'll be OK. If they do find me,' she added defiantly, 'I won't go back. Not ever. I'd rather kill myself than go back there. If they find me I shall tell the police what the bastard's been doing to me... fucking his own daughter for the last ten years! But I won't go back, I swear it.'

'No,' said Daisy gently, accepting as true what Jean had told her, 'course you won't.'

Silence lapsed round them as Jean finished her tea, and Daisy tried to get her head round what she'd just heard.

In the end Daisy said, 'So what happened tonight?'

'Took me to a room,' replied Jean bleakly. 'There was four of them.'

'You're lucky they didn't kill you, Jean.'

'Am I?' sighed Jean. 'Not so sure of that myself.'

'Well, you ain't going back on the streets no more,' Daisy said firmly.

'All right for you to say that,' snapped Jean. 'You got a job to go to. I seen you go off every morning. And the other girls.'

'Well, we'll have to try and get you a job, an' all,' said Daisy. 'You go back out on them streets, you'll end up dead in a gutter.'

When Daisy went into work next day she approached her supervisor to ask if there were any jobs going.

'Might be some part-time,' her supervisor said. 'Why?'

'Know a girl what's looking for a job, that's all,' replied Daisy casually.

'Bring her in to see me,' said her boss, 'and I'll see what I can do.'

'I'll take you to see her when your face is better,' Daisy promised Jean. 'And in the meantime stay in. I'll bring in food for the both of us. You just make sure old Lazy don't see you with your face messed up. Steer clear of her, Jean. We ain't meant to be here in the daytime, remember? So, stay in your room and stay quiet. OK?'

Jean promised, and all that week she stayed in her room. Daisy brought in food for both of them, and as they ate their meals Daisy told Jean a little about her own life.

'Brought up in a kids' home, me,' she said. 'Never had a proper home. Me mum dumped me on a doorstep and I ain't a clue who me dad was. At least you know who your dad is.'

'Yeah, well, Dad isn't my real dad. I was adopted as a kid. Don't remember much before that. Think I was on a ship.'

'On a ship?' Daisy looked at her sharply. 'What sort of ship?'

'Dunno, just a ship. Think there was lots of us kids.'

'When? When was you on a ship?'

'When I was a kid. Then I was adopted by these people, the Waters, and I went to live with them.'

Daisy's mind was racing. She thought about Deeley's and Rita's fruitless search for Rosie and her adoptive parents. What had their name been? Daisy couldn't remember.

'You told Lazy that your name was Jean Smith,' she said.

'Well, I'm not stupid, am I?' scoffed Jean. 'I'm not going to tell her my real name, am I?'

'But you've always been called Jean,' Daisy said casually.

Jean shrugged. 'Suppose so. I remember Mum telling me she'd always wanted a daughter called Jean.'

'So, did she change your name to Jean, then? When you was adopted?'

Jean shrugged again. 'Maybe. Christ, Daisy, I dunno. It's all so long ago, what does it matter? I only have the haziest memory of any of it. Can *you* remember what happened when you were five?'

'Some of it,' answered Daisy. 'My life was pretty much the same, always in a kids' home. Except when we come to Australia. I come on a ship, too.'

'Did you?' Jean seemed uninterested. 'Wonder if it was the same one?'

'Doubt it,' Daisy said. 'There was lots of them.'

At the end of the week Daisy took Jean to Woolworths and she was offered a job as a cleaner, working in the evenings when the store had closed. To Jean it was marvellous. The anonymity of the work, hidden away until all the paying customers had gone, with a wage packet at the end of the week, was the security she'd dreamed of.

Chapter 37

Jean settled into her work at the store and as she received each pay packet she handed her rent over to Mrs Glazer. She began to relax, feeling safe behind the locked door of her room. Surely Gerald Waters could never find her there. But she reckoned without Gerald's determination to trace her.

Several weeks later she was walking home from work, and as she passed the police station at the end of the road, she saw a poster on a board outside which brought her up short.

HAVE YOU SEEN THIS GIRL?
JEAN WATERS, MISSING FROM HOME.
REWARD FOR INFORMATION

Underneath was a photograph of her in her school uniform, and though it made her look much younger, it was undeniably her. In panic she hurried back to her room and locked herself in. She wanted to tell Daisy what she'd seen, but when she banged on Daisy's door, she wasn't there.

The knock on her own door came next morning when she was still in bed. Sleepily she went to the door and opened it a crack. Mrs Glazer stood on the landing and when the door opened she put her foot into the gap so Jean couldn't close it again.

'Mrs Glazer...' began Jean.

'Miss Smith,' sneered Mrs Glazer, 'or is it Miss Waters?'

'What?' Jean managed to look puzzled. 'Who?'

'You're a runaway, Miss Jean Smith Waters,' said Mrs Glazer. 'You're a runaway, and the police are looking for you.'

'No,' said Jean, though the truth showed in her face. 'You're wrong. My name's Jean Smith.'

'Not what it says on the poster,' said Mrs Glazer, triumphantly. 'Says you're Jean Waters and you're missing. There's a reward, too!'

'Don't be so silly,' Jean said, rallying. 'Who'd offer a reward for me?'

'That's what we'll find out, isn't it,' crowed Mrs Glazer. 'Your poor parents maybe.' And in one smooth movement she had shoved Jean backwards into the room and snatched the key from the inside of the door. 'You're going to stay there till the police come and have a look at you,' she said and slamming the door, she locked it behind her.

Jean sank down on her bed, her head in her hands, tears of despair coursing down her cheeks. Mrs Glazer had seen the poster and recognized her. The police would recognize her, too, and Gerald and Edna would come and claim her, drag her back to the nightmare of her former life.

'No,' she shouted at the empty room. 'I won't go. I'd rather die.'

She tried banging on her door in the hope that Daisy or one of the other residents might come to see what the matter was, but Daisy and the other girls had all gone to work and wouldn't be back until the evening, and by then, Jean knew, it would be too late.

She went to the window, wondering if she might get out that way. It was almost as small as the window through which she'd escaped from the Waters' house, but even if she could squeeze through, she was on the third floor of the hostel and the drop to the pavement was thirty feet or more. She tried leaning out of the window and shouting, but her voice was lost in the sounds of the street below, and though one or two people did look up, no one paid any attention to her cries. She went to the door and rattled the handle, but there was no way it would open. She could see through the keyhole that Mrs Glazer had taken the key with her.

She flung herself back down on her bed as visions of Gerald's face, smiling with anticipation, filled her mind. She buried her head in her pillow to blot him out, but his face was imprinted on her memory. She could hear his voice, chilly with contempt, saying, 'You've been a very wicked girl. I'm going to have to punish you. Take your clothes off.'

Jean blocked her ears, but she could still hear his voice, hissing his intent. All her safety, so carefully achieved, was gone. The police would come, Gerald would come, and the nightmare would begin again.

I must do something, she thought, but what? Her mind spun as she tried to think of something, some means of escape. Perhaps when Daisy comes home... But that'll be too late. There's nothing I can do.

Despair flooded through her and she lay back on her bed and wept. 'I won't go back,' she moaned, 'I'll never go back.'

She went yet again to the door, hammering on it with her fists, but there was no response. If Mrs Glazer could hear her she certainly didn't change her mind and come back. With her hands bruised and aching Jean finally gave up and turned back into her room. It was then that the bottle of sleeping tablets she had stolen from Edna caught her eye. It stood beside the bowl and ewer on the chest of drawers. Occasionally Jean still took one of the tablets, as she had on the night she'd been beaten up, a night she needed to sleep dreamlessly and forget, for a few hours, what had happened to her. Now she picked up the bottle and looked at it. It was still more than half full. She had the means to do as she'd threatened, but did she have the courage? She shook it gently, a bottle of tablets that would be the ultimate escape from Gerald Waters, the ultimate escape from a life of abuse and misery that had brought her to this despair. Had she ever been happy? Jean couldn't remember. All recollection of her early life had been blotted out by the misery of later years. The only connection she had with it was a rose-patterned dress, something she was sure came from happier days.

Gerald's malevolent face floated before her again and with sudden determination Jean poured herself a glass of water and opening the pill bottle, began to cram the tablets into her mouth, gulping and swallowing, until she had consumed every one. Then she opened her little case stored under the bed, and pulled out the dress. 'My gran made it.' Somewhere from the depths of her mind, Jean knew she'd said this. When, she didn't know, but the very thought of it comforted her and she clutched the dress to her as she drifted off to sleep. She'd had a gran and that gran had made her a beautiful dress with roses on it.

Chapter 38

After hearing that Jean thought she'd come to Australia by ship, an incredible idea was beginning to grow in Daisy's mind. Could Jean, by any miraculous chance, be Rosie? She didn't want so much as to hint at it to Jean; not until she'd been to see Deeley, until she'd been told the name of Rosie's adoptive parents. No word to Rita, either. Raising her hopes only to have them dashed again would be the ultimate cruelty. Studying her carefully, Daisy wondered if she could see the childlike face of Rosie in the gaunt and scared face of Jean. She had fair hair, though scraped off her face and lacklustre it had none of the youthful curls Rosie had had. Her eyes were blue, but shadowed with permanent fear, nothing like the bright, round eyes of the five-year-old Rosie.

I'm just trying to make what she's told me turn her into Rosie, thought Daisy despondently. There must be hundreds of little girls who arrived on a ship and were adopted by Australian families.

So, she kept her thoughts to herself, deciding that the best thing to do would be to speak to Deeley in private.

On her next half day Daisy managed to get off work early and went to catch Deeley as she left the nursery.

'Daisy!' Delia greeted her in surprise. 'Hallo! What brings you here?'

'Need to talk to you, Mrs Watson. Private. Without Reet.'

'Rita's got a late lecture at college,' said Delia. 'We can go home.'

'No,' Daisy insisted. 'She might come back early.' She glanced along the street and seeing a tearoom further along, said, 'Can we go there?'

Delia shrugged. 'If you really want to, Daisy. What's all this about?'

They ordered a pot of tea, and once it was poured, Delia looked expectantly at Daisy. 'Well, Daisy. Come on, tell me.'

'What was the names of them people what adopted Rosie?'

Delia looked at her sharply. 'Waters. Why do you want to know?'

'I think I may have found Rosie,' Daisy said. She spoke calmly, trying to suppress her rising excitement when she heard the name.

'You what?'

'I think I may have found Rosie.' And she told Delia all about Jean.

Delia listened in horrified silence until Daisy had finished. 'And you think this could be Rosie?'

'Dunno, Mrs Watson, but she said her new name was Jean Waters. I couldn't remember the name of the people you'd been looking for, but...'

'It's the same,' murmured Delia.

'We can't tell Reet, not till we're sure,' Daisy said, 'so will you come and see her? Come and talk to her?'

'Of course,' Delia agreed at once, and picked up her bag. 'I'll come now. Is she at your hostel?'

'I hope so,' Daisy said. 'She should be. She'll go out to work, but not till later.'

They arrived at the hostel door to be greeted by Mrs Glazer.

'Ah, Miss Smart,' she said, her eyes gleaming. 'I think we've got a runaway upstairs.'

'What?' Daisy stared at her. 'What d'you mean?'

'I think you know what I mean, Miss Smart,' Mrs Glazer smirked. 'I'm not green, Miss Smart. I'm not stupid. You've been hiding her, pretending not to know her when she first came here.'

'I didn't know her,' protested Daisy.

'So you say, but I know better. This is a respectable house, Miss Smart, and I won't have runaway girls here.'

'Why do you think she's running away?' asked Daisy, wondering if it was just a guess and Lazy was expecting her to confirm it.

'There's a poster with her picture on it outside the cop shop up the road. Looking for Jean Waters.'

'But her name is Jean Smith,' Daisy said.

'She *says* her name is Jean Smith, but it's her all right. When I went up and faced her with it, I could tell. So I told her I was calling the police,' Mrs Glazer said righteously. 'Her poor parents must be out of their minds with worry. I locked her in and I called the police.'

'And what did they say?' asked Daisy.

'Said they'd come as soon as they could.'

'And did they?'

'Not yet, but I expect them anytime.' Suddenly aware of Delia standing behind Daisy, she said, 'And who's this, may I ask?'

'A friend...' began Daisy.

'Friends of any sort must be out by nine o'clock,' sniffed Mrs Glazer. 'And if I find you've been hiding a runaway child, Miss Smart, you'll have to go, too.' With this parting shot, Mrs Glazer retired to her own quarters to await the police, leaving Daisy and Delia to hurry upstairs to Jean's room.

Daisy banged on the door. 'Jean! It's me, Daisy. Can you hear me? Jean? It's Daisy.' She tried the door, but as Mrs Glazer had said, it was locked. Daisy called again, banging on the door with her fists, but there was no response.

'What do we do now?' Daisy turned to Delia in despair.

'We go and demand the key,' Delia said.

'We can try, but she won't give it us,' Daisy said, 'she's a real mean bitch.'

'Can but try,' Delia said.

'Perhaps mine'll fit,' Daisy suggested, taking out her key. It fitted the keyhole, but wouldn't turn the lock. 'No, no good.'

'You go on trying to get Jean to answer you,' Delia said, 'I'll go back down to Mrs Glazer.'

At that moment there was the sound of boots on the stairs and a puffing Mrs Glazer appeared followed by two uniformed police officers. The first, a sergeant, paused at the top of the stairs and glanced enquiringly at Delia and Daisy.

'Well,' he asked, 'what's going on here?'

Before Mrs Glazer could catch her breath to speak, Delia stepped forward. 'Mrs Glazer has locked a young girl into this room,' she said, indicating Jean's door. 'We've tried knocking, but she doesn't answer.'

'And who are you, madam?'

'My name is Delia Watson and this is Daisy Smart. We are friends of this girl and are extremely concerned that she has been locked in her room all day.'

'They're just busybodies,' Mrs Glazer began to bluster. 'That girl ain't answering 'cos she's hiding. That's what. She's that runaway you lot're looking for.'

The policeman looked at her. 'Perhaps you'd be good enough to unlock this door, madam.' He spoke politely enough, but it was clear he did not approve of what she had done. Disgruntled, Mrs Glazer stepped forward and did as he asked.

Daisy pushed past her into the room and then stopped short with a cry of dismay. Delia and the policemen crowded in behind her and both stopped in horror at what they saw. Jean lay, curled up on her bed, eyes closed, her breathing stentorian, and on the floor beside her bed lay a small glass bottle.

The sergeant caught it up and looked at the label. 'Sleeping pills,' he said, and turning to his companion he barked, 'Ambulance, Andrews! Sharpish!'

Andrews disappeared downstairs, as Delia and Daisy ran to the bedside, kneeling beside the unconscious girl. Delia tried to turn her over, and then they saw it, clutched in Jean's arms, a child's rose-patterned dress.

Daisy burst into tears and Delia held her close as the policeman tried to resuscitate the girl on the bed.

'Anyone know her name?' he asked.

'Rosie Stevens,' Delia said firmly before Mrs Glazer could say anything. 'Her name is Rosie Stevens.'

The ambulance arrived and two sturdy ambulance men carried the unconscious Rosie down the stairs. Delia and Daisy went with her in the ambulance and as the ambulance streaked through the streets, siren blaring, they watched as the medic continued to work on Rosie, trying to bring her round. Daisy was clutching the glass bottle, its label telling them what drug Rosie had taken. When they reached the hospital, Rosie was rushed inside, and Delia turned aside to deal with the admission formalities. She stuffed some money into Daisy's hand and said, 'Fetch Rita. Take a taxi.'

Daisy raced outside to the taxi rank and gave the address in Randwick. 'And please be quick,' she cried, as the driver pulled away from the kerb. 'I think she's dying.'

Daisy had never been in a taxi before, but she had no time to think about the new experience. The sight of Rosie lying, unmoving, on the bed, filled her mind. She had to find Rita and get her to the hospital before it was too late.

'Wait here,' she called to the driver as they drew up outside the house. She leaped out of the cab, and running to the front door she kept one hand on the bell and banged on it with the other.

'Hey,' called Rita in surprise as she opened the door. 'Dais? What's all that about?' Then she saw the expression on Daisy's face. 'Deeley,' she cried. 'Has something happened to Deeley?'

'No,' Daisy said, grabbing at her hand to pull her out to the waiting taxi, 'but you got to come now, Reet. Deleey's at the hospital, she's with Rosie.'

Rita stopped short, and the colour drained from her face. 'Rosie?' she whispered.

'Yeah!' Daisy pulled at her again. 'With Rosie. She's took an overdose. Come on, Reet, come on!'

Rita allowed herself to be dragged into the taxi and within moments they were headed back the way they'd come.

When they reached the hospital Daisy paid off the taxi while Rita dashed inside to where Delia was waiting for her.

'Where is she?' Rita cried. 'Where's Rosie?'

'They've pumped her stomach out,' said Delia, putting her arms round Rita and holding her close. 'They've done everything they can, but darling, I think you must prepare yourself for the worst.'

'Can we see her?' Rita begged. 'I must see her.'

'They said they'd call us, but I'll ask again.'

Delia went in search of someone to ask as Daisy joined Rita in the waiting area.

'Where did you find her?' Rita asked. 'How...?'

Before Daisy could start to explain Delia reappeared with a doctor in a white coat.

'I believe you're her sister,' he said, taking Rita's hand. 'You can come in and see her now, just for a moment or two,' adding as Delia and Daisy moved forward, 'only one of you.'

He showed Rita into a side ward and said, as he closed the door behind her, 'Just a few minutes.'

Rita looked down at the girl in the bed. She was thin and angular, her face the colour of putty, her fair hair, now tied back off her face, greasy and lank. The sheet covering her scarcely rose and fell as she breathed with faint, shallow breaths. Rita crossed to the bedside and gently took one of her hands and pressed it to her cheek. It was cold as ice.

'Rosie,' she whispered, 'it's me, Reet. Can you hear me, Rosie? I've come to get you. To take you home. Rosie? It's Reet.'

Rosie's eyelids flickered and for a moment Rita thought she was going to open her eyes, to see her there beside her, but then the hand in hers seemed to relax and with a last sigh her breathing ceased. With a wave of desolation Rita knew that though they had finally found Rosie, they'd found her too late.

Later, much later, when Rosie was properly laid out on a bed, her hair washed and brushed, her eyes closed in eternal sleep, Delia, Daisy and Rita were able to come back and sit with her for a while.

'Poor Rosie, poor darling Rosie,' Rita wept, holding her sister's cold hand between her own. 'What a dreadful life she had. What a cruel, cruel life.'

Daisy, ever practical, said, 'Do we have to tell them, them Waters, what's happened to her?'

'No,' Delia replied firmly, 'we do not. They have no claim on her. She's Rita's sister, she's formally identified her and we will take care of her now.'

'Won't the police tell them?'

'No, I don't think so,' Delia replied. 'We told them her name is Rose Stevens, not Jean Waters, and they seem to have accepted our identification.'

It was strange, Daisy thought as she looked down at the pale, peaceful face, framed by the soft golden hair, but now I can see it's Rosie, just Rosie grown up. Why couldn't I see it before?

They sat in silence for a while and then Rita reached into a bag at her feet and pulled out Rosie's beloved Knitty. Carefully she tucked him under Rosie's arm, then replacing her hand under the sheet that covered her, she reached down and kissed Rosie's smooth, cold cheek. 'Bye, Rosie,' she said softly. 'I'm sorry I didn't look after you better, but you're safe now. Nobody can't hurt you any more.' Then she turned round and said, 'I'd like to go home now.'

Delia nodded and taking her hand, said, 'Come on then, darling,' before reaching out her other hand to Daisy and saying, 'you too, Daisy.'

D elia came in from the day-care centre and dropped into her chair. She was getting older and the days spent with a roomful of toddlers seemed longer and more tiring. Still, this afternoon, Rita was popping in after school for a cup of tea on her way home to David, and Delia was looking forward to seeing her. She'd missed Rita dreadfully since she'd got married and moved into her own home, but Delia knew she was happy, and that was all-important, all she needed to know.

In a minute, she thought, I'll get things ready, but for a moment I must sit down.

Rita was now the centre of Delia's life. She had watched her change from an abandoned child alone in the world, into a hard-working teenager, a student, and now a committed teacher. Rita had been courageous as a child, coping with all the unhappiness that the world threw at her, rejection by her mother, Rosie's adoption, the death of her grandmother. Later she had had to come to terms with the nightmare that was Rosie's life and her suicide; the dreadful night they'd found her, an empty bottle of sleeping tablets by her bed. Each time Rita had retreated into herself, but in the end, with Delia's love and support and Daisy's friendship, Rita had overcome her anguish and moved on with her life. Delia knew Rita would never forget Rosie, but she hoped that Rita had now let her sister linger in the caverns of her mind, remembering her with love, but allowing her to slip into the past.

Life certainly hasn't been easy since we moved here, Delia

thought now as she waited for Rita to arrive. But thank God we did.

Cash had always been very tight, but the two of them had grown ever closer over the years, truly mother and daughter. Rita had left school with excellent exam results, trained as a teacher and now worked in a local primary school. Encouraged by her high school teachers and Delia herself, Rita had continued to write, and in her last year at school she had won a New South Wales short story competition for under eighteens. Since then, in addition to her teaching, she regularly had stories accepted by various magazines, which had helped boost their meagre income. Delia knew it wouldn't be long before she had to retire from the day-care centre, and she wondered what she'd do with her life then. The boss had promised she could stay in the house, but how would she fill her days?

'Deeley,' Rita's voice broke into her thoughts as she burst in through the front door, and sunshine filled the house. She gave Delia a huge hug and flopped down onto the sofa.

'Lovely to see you, darling,' Delia said. 'Tea?'

'In a minute,' replied Rita. 'I've got something to ask you first.'

'Ask away.'

'How do you feel about being a grandmother?'

'What!' shrieked Delia. 'Oh, darling, are you sure?'

'Yup,' beamed Rita. 'Just been to the doc. Says I'm about three months.'

Delia found there were tears in her eyes. 'Oh Rita, that's wonderful! What does David say?'

'He doesn't know yet,' admitted Rita. 'I'll tell him when he gets home tonight.'

'You should have told him first,' scolded Delia, though secretly delighted she hadn't.

'I know,' Rita agreed airily, 'but I'm so excited – I had to tell you.'

'Well, I'm glad you did,' Delia admitted, 'I'm thrilled to bits for you.'

She made a pot of tea and produced a cake she'd made the previous day, and as they sat together in the familiar kitchen, they shared the wonderful news of the baby.

David Harris was over the moon when Rita told him the news. It still seemed a miracle to him that Rita was really his, and now there was going to be a baby as well. Life was so wonderful he wanted to sing, or dance, or both.

He had met Rita in the offices of *The Sophisticate*, a magazine that had been publishing Rita's stories for some time. He worked in the advertising department, and in what Rita described as 'true corny style' one day they had met at the coffee machine.

David had heard of *coup de foudre* and never believed in it, but then it happened to him, a stroke of lightning, blazing through him. He saw a girl with straight dark hair and wide brown eyes standing by the machine, trying to fathom how it worked. He'd asked if he could help, and when she'd turned and smiled at him and said, 'Oh please, could you? I've never used one of these stupid things before,' he was lost. He didn't know her name, he didn't know why she was there, but he did know that she was the woman he wanted and would wait for, however long it took. Rita had seen a good-looking young man, with smiling green eyes and a head of fair curls that sprung in an unruly halo about his face.

It had taken David nearly two years to persuade Rita to marry him. Determined not to scare her away, he was patience itself, wooing her gently, gaining her confidence slowly. As she gradually allowed him closer, occasionally permitting him glimpses of the life she had lived, he realized that she was afraid. Afraid, that if she let herself love him, he would disappear or die, as others had disappeared or died, and she'd be bereft once more. He didn't rush her, he was simply there, David, strong, firm and comforting, until Rita realized, in quiet surprise, that he was part of the very fabric of her life.

Delia had watched as the friendship that was established blossomed into love. She had seen the depth of David's love, had seen how gently he'd pursued Rita, for, despite his softly-softly approach, it was pursuit, and she'd waited to see if Rita could respond.

On the day that Rita slipped into his arms, holding up her face to kiss and be kissed, David thought his happiness could know no bounds, and Delia knew she had to let go. She had been Rita's rock for the past thirteen years, but from now on, it would be David to whom she clung.

When they came to tell her that they were getting married, Delia hugged them both, tears bright in her eyes. 'I know you'll make her very happy, David,' she said, a statement of fact, though both of them knew that it was also a warning. Don't you dare let my Rita down!

'I'll do everything in my power,' David promised, and as they smiled at each other, they both knew that the pact had been made. Nothing should be allowed to hurt Rita again.

They'd been married, now, for two years. Rita continued to teach at the primary school and to write in her spare time. David had been promoted and now ran the advertising department at *The Sophisticate*. Their house was a comfortable home, and their lives were busy and fulfilling, but they both wanted a family.

Rita was in the kitchen cooking when David got home. She'd meant to wait until they were having tea before breaking the news, but when he walked in the door, looking hot and tousled, she was overcome with such a surge of love for him that she simply dropped the spoon back in the mixing bowl and ran to him.

'Are you sure?' David asked, not daring to believe the amazing news she'd just whispered into his ear. 'Sit down, put your feet up. I'll cook tea.' He took her arm, leading her to a chair in the living room. She laughed and hugged him.

'Darling, I'm not ill. I'm perfectly capable of cooking your tea.'

'I know, I know,' he said. 'But you mustn't get tired.'

She submitted to his demand that he should finish the cooking, but sat in the kitchen to watch him.

As they ate their meal, they talked about the baby, and the wonderful fact that they would soon be a family.

'Do you want a boy or a girl?' Rita asked him.

'Both,' replied David promptly.

Rita laughed. 'Well, I hope it's not twins. I think one baby'll be quite enough to start with, don't you? So, son or daughter?'

'I can't quite believe those words will apply to us,' David said. 'I'm going to have a son... or a daughter, and I promise you, darling, I don't mind which... do you?'

Rita gave a gurgle of laughter. 'Not in the least, but the idea takes some getting used to, doesn't it?'

'You must give your notice in tomorrow,' David said. 'You don't have to work any more.'

'But I like my job,' protested Rita. 'And it's ages yet.'

'I know you do, but you have to think of the baby now. You mustn't get overtired.'

'I won't, I promise you. I'll give notice for the end of the term. Gracious, David, what would I do with myself if I didn't go to school every day?'

'You could stay at home and write,' David replied, not so easily put off. 'You've always said you want to try your hand at a novel, rather than short stories.'

Rita laughed. 'You just want me to write a bestseller, so that you can live on the proceeds.'

'Quite right,' David agreed with a grin. 'And when you sell the film rights to Hollywood, we'll neither of us ever have to work again!'

'What does Deeley think?' David asked as they sat over their coffee. 'Is she pleased?'

'How do you know that I've told her?' asked Rita, defensively, aware that she was blushing.

David laughed. 'Of course you've told her,' he said. 'How could you not?'

David had got used to the fact that Delia and Rita never had secrets from each other. At first he'd been jealous of their continued closeness. After all, he was going to be Rita's husband, he'd take care of her now. Of course Rita still loved Delia, but she shouldn't be using her as a crutch. But, as he got to know them better, David realized that neither used the other in that way. Neither of them had anyone else in the world, so it was only natural that they were so close. He came to recognize that they were simply part of each other; not to the exclusion of him, or of Rita's peculiar friend, Daisy, who turned up from time to time, but that the bond between them was strong, woven with the fibres of shared sadness and hardship, and would never loosen.

'She was delighted for us,' said Rita. 'She can't wait to be a granny.'

'We must tell my parents, too,' David reminded her.

'Of course,' Rita agreed. 'I thought we could go and see them this weekend, or if they're busy, next. More fun to tell them face to face, don't you think, rather than over the phone?'

David's parents had been more than a little dubious about his choice of wife. Andrew Harris was a barrister, and much in demand as a defence lawyer in the city, and his wife, Norah, was very conscious of their social position. When she heard about Rita, she'd been horrified. A girl like Rita did not fit in with the plans she had for her only son.

'Where does she come from?' she asked David. 'What do we know about her? Her family? Her background?'

'I don't care where she comes from, mother,' David replied. 'All I know is that I'm going to marry her, and she'll have my children.'

When his mother had simply stared at him, pouting her lips in the way that so irritated him, David said sharply, 'I don't care about her family, mother, any more than I care about yours.'

Norah, descended from two convicts who had stayed in Australia when their sentences were over, had been silenced, but she still eyed her prospective daughter-in-law with misgiving.

As he'd got to know Rita, Andrew Harris had gradually thawed, and began to see who it was his son was marrying. He recognized her qualities of steadfastness, courage and determination, and began to think his son had made an excellent choice.

Norah remained distant and chilly, though always, as her breeding dictated, scrupulously polite.

'She really doesn't like me,' Rita confided to Delia.

'I expect she'd find it difficult to give her son to anyone,' Delia soothed. 'It isn't just you.' But Rita hadn't been so sure.

'They'll be thrilled to bits about the baby,' David assured her. 'The problem with being an only child is that you have to carry all the hopes and dreams of your parents. There's no one to share the load. Mum's always wanted grandchildren.'

They went for lunch that Sunday, and as they took the ferry to Parramatta and passed under the harbour bridge, Rita had a sudden vision of herself, Daisy and Rosie, staring up in amazement as they arrived on the *Pride of Empire*; Daisy wondering if they'd fit underneath it, and Rosie asking in a tiny voice if it would fall down. Tears sprang to her eyes as she thought of poor Rosie, brutalized by her adoptive father, running away and trying to survive on the streets of Sydney. It was seven years since Rosie had died, but the sight of her sister, lying pale and still in a side ward of the hospital, was as vivid in Rita's memory as the night she'd seen her, the night she had held her hand and said goodbye.

'You all right?' David asked as he saw Rita's eyes were bright with tears.

'Yes, of course,' answered Rita quickly and looked away, staring at the houses climbing the hill above Lavender Bay. 'Wind in my eyes.'

David made no further comment. He knew that Rita had the occasional emotional moment, for no apparent reason, and he'd learned she recovered more quickly if he appeared not to notice.

When they reached his parents' house, they were greeted at the door by his father. 'Lovely to see you both,' cried Andrew. 'Come in, come in. Your mother's in the kitchen.'

They trooped inside and Norah joined them a moment later, stripping off her apron and giving each of them a powdery cheek to kiss.

'Now, how about a drink before lunch?' Andrew suggested. 'What would you like, Rita?'

'Got any champagne, Dad?' asked David casually.

'Champagne?' Andrew was startled. 'I expect so. What are we celebrating?'

David glanced at Rita, but she just smiled and nodded. He should be the one to tell his parents.

'How do you fancy being grandparents?' David beamed.

'What?' exclaimed Norah, her eyes swivelling to Rita's stomach, as if searching for signs it was true. 'Really?'

'Really,' replied David with a grin.

'Well, congratulations, both of you,' cried Andrew, and having pumped David's hand, he hugged Rita, kissing her on both cheeks. 'What lovely, lovely news, isn't it, Norah?'

'Lovely. When's it due?'

'June,' replied Rita.

'And how are you keeping?' Norah asked. 'Not being sick, I hope.'

'No, thank goodness,' answered Rita, 'just a little queasy in the mornings, but that's wearing off now.'

'That's good,' Norah said. 'Now if you want any advice from me, don't hesitate to ask. Not having a mother of your own to go to, there may be—'

'I've got Deeley,' said Rita sharply.

'Yes, of course you have,' agreed Norah, 'but she's not the same as your real mother—'

'She is to me,' asserted Rita. 'She's far better than my real mother. *She* loves me.'

'I'm sure she does, dear,' said Norah, and rather startled at Rita's vehement response, she glanced at David.

'A kind thought, Mother,' he said briskly, 'I'm sure Rita's grateful for the offer.'

Rita had seldom seen her mother-in-law disconcerted. She was often dictatorial, but that never seemed to worry Andrew. Just occasionally Rita had seen him put his foot down and then there had been no further argument. David, on the other hand, often appeared to agree, but then did exactly what he'd always intended.

The awkward moment passed as Andrew reappeared with champagne. 'Here we are,' he said cheerfully. 'I thought I had a bottle somewhere waiting for a special occasion, and what could be more special than this, eh?' He turned to Norah. 'How about some glasses, chicken?'

Andrew poured them each a glass and then raised his. 'Here's to your son or daughter, our first grandchild!'

The rest of the day passed easily enough, and when they finally boarded the ferry for Circular Quay, David took Rita's hand and gave it a squeeze.

'That wasn't too bad, was it?'

Rita shook her head wearily. 'No,' she said, 'it was fine.'

'Better than you thought?'

Rita sat back against him, her face turned to the evening sun. 'You know me too well,' she said with a contented sigh.

David slipped his arm round her, holding her close. 'I'm learning you better every day.'

That night as she lay in bed, with David snoring gently beside her, Rita thought of what Norah had said about not having her own mother. Deeley was her mother now, she told herself, but for the first time for several years, she thought properly about her real mother and what Mavis had allowed to happen to her.

Rita laid a hand on her own stomach where she could almost feel the baby growing in her womb. There was nothing much visible yet, but Rita felt different in herself. With the baby growing inside her, she was already a mother, and as the responsibility of motherhood had enveloped her, she found herself looking at the world from a different perspective. David felt protective of her, constantly telling her to sit down, to put her feet up, to have an early night, but Rita knew it wasn't she who needed protecting, it was the tiny creature living inside her.

A baby is so helpless, she thought now. A mother's job is to care for him, keep him safe. She thought of her little brother, Richard. He would be sixteen now, and she'd only seen him once. He was Jimmy's baby; perhaps her mother had been protecting him from Jimmy.

She didn't protect us, Rita thought. Maybe she thought we were OK, or that I could look after Rosie. Perhaps it was either us or Richard, and he needed her more.

Rita knew, now, what it was to love a man, to want him with her always, to have his children. Could Mum really have felt about Jimmy what Rita now felt about David? Jimmy, a brute, who knocked her about, shouted at her, frightened her with his sudden rages? Rita couldn't imagine being in love with a man like that. She wondered if her mother was still with him. Perhaps she'd left him. Rita hoped so; or more likely he'd pushed off and left her. He was the sort of man who'd do that, Rita thought. How had Mum managed with Richard when Gran had died? Had she had any more babies? Have I got brothers and sisters I know nothing about? she wondered. When she finally drifted into sleep, the questions which had begun to torment her had found no resolution.

For the next few weeks Rita was continually buffeted by thoughts of her mother.

'Put her out of your mind,' David said when she mentioned her to him. 'You have to face the fact that, for whatever reason, however good it seemed, she gave you up.'

'Perhaps she had no alternative,' said Rita.

'Harsh as it sounds, darling,' David replied gently, 'I don't think that can be true. You and Rosie were her children, and should have been her first priority.' He placed his hand on her stomach. 'You'd never give away this little chap.'

'Or chap-ess.'

'Or chap-ess.'

'No, never.'

'No, never,' David agreed.

'What's brought this on?' Delia asked when she talked to her. 'Why this sudden interest in your mother and her motives?'

Rita shrugged. 'I don't know, really,' she admitted. 'Perhaps because I'm going to be a mother myself. It's made me more conscious of the difficulties she faced when she found she was expecting my brother, Richard.'

'Other people have three children and manage without giving

two of them away to look after the third,' observed Delia. 'Other people lose their children through no fault of their own and would give everything they have in the world to have them back.'

Rita put her hand on Delia's arm, knowing she was thinking of her own son, Harry, who'd died so tragically young.

'I know,' she said. 'I do know, Deeley, really I do. It's just that I'm trying to understand what went on in her mind. She must have been under immense pressure.'

'You're being very generous to her, darling,' said Delia. 'Far more generous than I'd be, or than I am, for that matter. *I* can't forgive her for doing what she did to you.'

'But I've got you,' pointed out Rita.

Delia took her hand and gave it a squeeze. 'Always,' she said.

'Perhaps she thought we'd have a better life somewhere else. It would have been hell with Uncle Jimmy.' She fell silent for a moment and then added softly, 'It turned out hell for Rosie anyway.'

She talked things over with Daisy, too. Daisy had come over to Randwick one Saturday afternoon and they'd gone for their usual picnic lunch together in Centennial Park. As they sat under the trees, munching cheese sandwiches, Rita told Daisy about the baby and how, since she'd known she was expecting, her mother had somehow invaded her thoughts.

When Daisy heard this, she was characteristically forthright in her opinion. 'Put her out of your mind, Reet,' she said, 'you ain't been in hers for years.'

'You don't know that,' Rita objected. 'She might have been thinking about us all the time, wondering how we are, regretting what she did.'

'Yeah, well, regrets ain't no good, are they? Waste of time, 'cos you can't put the clock back.'

'No, I know that,' sighed Rita. 'And let's face it, I've been very lucky, really, luckier than you.'

'You was lucky the Watchdog took you,' Daisy agreed, not for the first time. 'God knows where the Manton bitch'd've sent you if you was left there with her.'

'I wish Deeley'd had room for you, too,' replied Rita.

Daisy laughed. 'So do I, sunshine, but it weren't to be, were it? You both did what you could, coming to see me an' that, taking me out, an' I'm grateful, so there's an end to it.' She gave Rita a playful punch on the arm. 'So, what're you thinking about then, Reet? What you going to do?'

Rita shrugged. 'Don't know. Did wonder if I might write to her.'

'Whatever for?' demanded Daisy.

'Well, tell her about the baby and that... you know.'

'No, I don't,' said Daisy roundly. 'I wouldn't let her near no baby of mine, not after what she done to you and Rosie.'

'Well, she wouldn't get near, would she? I mean, she's in England and the baby'll be in Australia.'

'There's planes,' Daisy said, darkly.

'Yeah, well, I can hardly see her getting on one of them,' laughed Rita. 'She ain't got no money.'

Delia had often noticed that when Rita and Daisy got together, Rita slipped back into her childhood vernacular. It made Delia smile to hear them talking, but she was glad that Rita had learned to speak better English as she'd gone through school, and had picked up on Delia's own, precise, use of language. Most of the time Rita spoke good, colloquial, English, her childhood accent replaced by an Australian one, but when she wrote, her language was fluent, flowing from her pen in a style both descriptive and well expressed. When Rita wrote there was little trace of her earliest years.

'She might borrow some, or steal some,' suggested Daisy cheerfully.

'Not likely. Who'd lend it her? She won't come, Dais!'

'Then why write to her? Forget the silly cow, and get on with your life here. Ain't it good enough for you?'

'Course it is,' cried Rita.

'There you are, then. Hey, Reet, did I tell you?' Daisy went on, determined to change the subject.

'Did you tell me what?'

'That I met this bloke...'

'Oh Dais, you haven't...'

'No,' laughed Daisy, 'nothing like that. Honestly, Reet, you got a one-track mind!'

'No, I ain't,' retorted Rita. 'What is it like, then, if it ain't "like that"?'

'He's called Pete and he come in the store,' explained Daisy, 'and we got talking...'

Daisy's diversion had worked. For the rest of the afternoon they talked about Daisy and how Pete had got her into the athletics club 'for peanuts, 'cos I'm so good, see?', and chatted in the easy way they always had. Rita's mother wasn't mentioned again, and when they parted, Daisy to return to her bedsit in Kings Cross, Rita to walk home to David, it seemed that Mavis was forgotten.

Chapter 40

Carrie Maunder came out of her house and looked down the road. Maggie had promised to look in today after she finished work, but she was so much later than usual, Carrie was beginning to wonder where she was. As she looked along Ship Street once again, she saw her neighbour. Madge Holt had moved into number 9 about six months ago, and been avid to learn more of its gruesome history.

When Mavis had been murdered there was talk of the council pulling the house down, but there was such a housing shortage after the war, with so many streets having been flattened, that the house had been reprieved and contract cleaners sent in. Following the big clean-up there had been several tenants, but none of them had stayed more than a couple of years.

Gradually most people forgot that number 9 was the scene of a murder, the horror of that dreadful day becoming a distant memory, slipping back into the recesses of even Carrie's mind. Until, that was, Madge Holt moved in.

'I'm not afraid of ghosts,' Madge asserted roundly. 'The dead's dead, and that's an end to it.' But gradually, over the following weeks, she returned to the subject of Mavis's death, asking Carrie, as Mavis's closest friend, exactly what had happened.

Eventually Carrie started avoiding Madge, ducking back into the house if she saw her. Now as she spotted her bearing down on her, overall flapping like a ship in full sail, she turned back to her own front door.

'Mrs Maunder! Mrs Maunder!' Madge cried. 'Wait!'

Carrie sighed and waited. 'Mrs Holt,' she said with thinly veiled impatience, 'whatever is the matter?'

'I need a word, just a quick word.'

'Have to be quick,' Carrie told her, 'Maggie'll be here in a mo.'

'Just need a word,' repeated Madge. 'Don't know what to do, you see.'

'Do?' echoed Carrie. 'Do about what?'

'I'm trying to tell you,' puffed Madge. 'I got a letter.'

'Yeah, so? Who from?'

'Don't know, but it's addressed to Mrs Mavis Randall, you know the woman—'

'I know who Mavis Randall was,' interrupted Carrie, so sharply that Madge flinched.

'Yeah, well, all right,' she said. 'Anyhow, the letter's addressed to her, but at my address. Which was her address, of course, all them years ago.'

'A letter? For Mavis?' Carrie was incredulous.

Having finally managed to capture Carrie's attention, Madge beamed at her. 'It's got Australian stamps on it, and an Australian postmark.'

'Then I suspect,' observed Carrie, 'that it's come from Australia.' The irony in Carrie's voice passed over Madge's head entirely.

'Yes,' Madge said, nodding vigorously, 'yes, I think you're right. But who would be writing to her now, d'you think?' She drew a blue airmail envelope out from the pocket of her overall.

Carrie took it and turning it over, saw the sender's name on the back. *Mrs R Harris*, and an address in Sydney. 'R'? Could it possibly be Rita, or Rosie? Surely not. Surely someone would have told them of their mother's tragic death.

'It's got a name and address on the back,' said Madge, 'so I'd better send it back, don't you think? Put, "not known at this address"… or,' she suggested with a gleam of intense curiosity in her eyes, 'perhaps we should open it, and write back explaining.'

She held out her hand for the letter, but Carrie stuffed it quickly into her trouser pocket.

'No,' she said firmly. 'No, it's not for us to open. I'll take it round to Mrs Sharples.'

Madge flushed with annoyance, angry that she'd lost the initiative. 'And who's she, when she's at home?'

'Mavis's mother.'

'Her mother!' Madge was incredulous. 'Is she still alive?'

'Very much so.'

'Gawd, she must be ancient.'

'Not at all,' said Carrie. 'She's about sixty-five and alive and well. I'll take it round hers. Up to her to open it.'

'But—' began Madge.

'Thank you for bringing it over, Mrs Holt,' Carrie said, ignoring the interruption, 'that was very kind.' And Madge Holt was left standing in the street, wishing she'd opened the letter herself before showing it to anyone else.

'Mrs Maunder's here, Gran,' Rick called, as he stood aside to let Carrie in. 'Go on through. Gran's in the kitchen.'

'Carrie!' cried Lily, getting to her feet, 'What a lovely surprise. What brings you here?'

'Don't get up, Mrs Sharples,' Carrie said, and Lily subsided gratefully onto her chair. She had some arthritis in her hips now, and getting up from a chair was becoming more difficult.

'Lovely to see you, Carrie,' she said. 'It's been too long. How are you, dear? How're John and the children? Well, not children of course now. Did I hear that Maggie got married last year?'

Carrie let Lily run on about the children, her own answers automatic as the aerogramme seemed to be burning a hole in her pocket. She'd wanted to rush round and give Lily the letter, but now she was here, Carrie wasn't quite sure how to go about it. Perhaps she should have opened it first, after all. What if it *was* from Rita or Rosie? What if Lily had such a shock she had a heart attack? You never knew with older people, did you? She was suddenly aware of a silence and looked across at Lily and found her regarding her quizzically.

'Well, Carrie,' she said, 'you didn't just come round to talk about our children, did you? What's up?'

'It's difficult,' began Carrie.

'Then spit it out,' said Lily. 'Difficult things should always be said straight out. Makes them less difficult, I always find.'

Carrie drew a deep breath and said, 'OK. A letter came today. My neighbour brought it round. It's addressed to Mavis....'

Lily stared at her, unable to speak.

'It's from someone in Sydney, in Australia...' said Carrie, and when Lily still said nothing, she went on, 'someone called R Harris. So I've brought it round to you.'

She pulled the letter from her pocket and passed it across to Lily. For a long moment, Lily held it, looking at the name and address on the front, then she turned it over and read the name and address on the back. Then she handed it back to Carrie.

'You open it,' she said. 'You open it and see who it's from.'

Carrie slit the aerogramme along its sides, and flipped it open. She glanced at the opening and then at the bottom. She saw the words *Dear Mum* and then that it was signed, *your daughter, Rita Harris.*

'It's from Rita,' she said softly. 'And she don't know Mavis is dead.'

Lily stared at her for a moment, tears flooding her eyes. 'Read it me,' she whispered.

Carrie began to read.

Dear Mum,

I expect you'll be surprised to hear from me after all these years. You didn't want me and Rosie, well, not enough anyway, and maybe you don't want to hear from me now. I expect you've got lots of other kids now, but I only know about Richard. Gran did write to me once, before she died, but though I wrote back to her I never heard from her again. I'm not really sure why I'm writing to you now, except that I'm going to have a baby in June, and I thought about you and thought you might like to know you are going to be a grandmother. Perhaps you are one already, but anyway, I thought you'd like to know.

My husband, David, wasn't very keen on me writing to you, but I felt I had to do it, just this once. If you don't answer you'll never hear from me again, but if you do, then I will write to you occasionally and tell you how your grandchild is doing.

I also have to tell you poor Rosie is dead. She was adopted by some awful people when we first got here and they made her life hell. She ran away and when they were coming to find her she took sleeping pills rather than go back. She died because she came to Australia, because you didn't want her.

I'll say this to you only once. I don't know how you could possibly have given us away like you did. Thrown us away, more like. I haven't even had this baby yet, but I know I could never, ever, part with him or her. Still, I suppose it's all water under the bridge now and it's no good going on hating you. David says hatred twists your soul. I think he's right. So, I don't hate you any more.

From your daughter,

Rita Harris

Carrie looked up from reading and saw the tears streaming down Lily's cheeks. She was at her side immediately, her arms round her, holding her tightly until her sobs began to subside.

'Carrie,' she whispered, 'oh Carrie, we got our Rita back.' And her tears began to flow again. 'But Rosie, poor darling little Rosie...'

At that moment the door opened and Rick came back in carrying a book. 'Gran,' he began and then stopped short when he saw her in tears. He looked at Carrie. 'Mrs Maunder? What's going on?'

'Your gran has had some good news.'

'*Good* news?' queried Rick. 'Don't look like good news to me!'

'I've brought her a letter that came today. It's from Rita.'

'Rita!' gasped Rick, his eyes flying to the photo of the two little girls in rose-patterned frocks on the mantelpiece. 'My sister, Rita?'

'Yes,' confirmed Carrie. 'And you can see your gran's a bit overcome.'

Rick dropped into a chair and Carrie handed him the letter. He read it through and then read it again.

'She don't know our ma's dead,' he said, 'and she thinks Gran *is*.'

'Nobody told her about her mother,' Lily said through her tears. 'Nobody bothered to tell her. It's that bloody Vanstone woman again.' Lily's voice shook with rage. 'But she must have told her *I* was. How could she? How could she have done such a wicked thing? Rita's thought I was dead, all these years. What an evil, evil woman!'

'Well, she's dead an' all,' said Rick.

'And I hope she burns in hell!' Lily said viciously.

'Forget her, Gran,' Rick said. 'She's long gone.'

'She killed our Rosie,' said Lily bitterly. 'She killed our Rosie as surely as if she'd stuck a knife into her. Our Rosie killed herself 'cos she was sent to Australia, 'cos some family what took her and was supposed to look after made her life hell. That's what Rita said. An' that woman sent her there instead of letting me look after her.'

'Yeah, I know, Gran.' Richard sat down beside her and took her hand. 'But at least you've found Rita. Cry for poor Rosie, Gran, of course, but smile for Rita. Now you know where Rita is we can write to her and tell her you ain't dead. We could go and see her. We could go to Australia.'

Lily did manage a smile, then, through her tears. 'Steady on, lad,' she said with a shaky laugh. 'We ain't made of money.'

'No, all right,' Rick agreed, 'not go, not straight away, but we can write and send photos and stuff, and she can do the same for us. And I've got my paper round, I'll start saving!'

'You do that, love,' Lily said. She looked across at Carrie who had been watching the two of them, while trying to come to terms, herself, with what she'd read in the letter; the dreadful news about Rosie, the wonderful news about Rita.

'I can't believe this,' Lily murmured. 'I can't believe that there's a letter from Rita after all these years.'

'It's wonderful to hear from her,' Carrie said. '*And* you're going to be a great-gran!'

Lily smiled. 'Yes, I s'pose I am.' Then her smile faded. 'But Rosie? Our lovely Rosie. And how am I going to tell Rita about her mother? About what happened to her?'

'Don't know,' said Carrie. 'That's a hard thing. Just write and tell her, I s'pose. No way of breaking it gently, is there?' She reached over and took the old lady's hand. 'But just think how thrilled she's going to be to find that you're still here! That'll make it easier for her.'

'Will it?' wondered Lily. 'Whatever she did, Mavis was still her mother, and hearing that she was murdered, well, it ain't going to be easy for her, is it?' Silence lapsed round them as they all reflected on Mavis's horrifying end.

When Carrie left, Lily and Rick went over and over the letter from Rita.

'I just can't believe it,' Lily said, 'Rita, married and having a baby. Just fancy that.'

'When're you going to write back?' asked Rick. 'Can I put a letter in too?'

'Course you can, love,' said Lily. 'I'll get one of them airmail letter things tomorrow and we'll write it together in the evening. Now, finish your homework. You've got exams coming up.'

Rick retired to his bedroom to try to finish his history essay, and Lily slowly cleared away the tea things. Rita's married, she thought as she stacked the dishes in the sink. And to a nice man by the sound of it, a man with sensible ideas, anyway. And going to have a baby; little Rita who'd only been nine years old when Lily had last seen her. But Rosie, her bright, sunny, trusting little granddaughter, was dead; literally frightened to death. Alone in the kitchen Lily buried her head in her hands and wept.

Over the years she had tried to imagine her granddaughters growing up, girls in their teens, young women grown, but she'd never really managed it. In her mind Rita and Rosie were frozen in time, remaining as they were in the photograph on her mantelpiece, two little girls in rose-patterned dresses. Now one was about to become a mother and the other was in her grave.

Rick is right, she thought when, finally, her tears ran dry, I've cried for Rosie, but I have to rejoice at finding Rita.

Stiffly she got to her feet and went to the drawer where she kept the letter she'd had from Rita all those years ago, and pulled it from its envelope. Dog-eared and torn down its folds, she spread it out carefully on the table, to read once more. It had been her only link with Rita for sixteen years, and now, now at last, she had another, and this time there was an address on the back; this time she could answer, she could write back and tell Rita she'd been lied to, that she, Lily, was still alive.

She lay in bed that night, trying to compose the letter in her head. There was so much to say, about Rosie, about Mavis, all of it difficult, and when Lily finally drifted off to sleep, she was no nearer to framing the words that would tell Rita that Jimmy Randall had murdered her mother, nearly sixteen years ago.

Chapter 41

It was a sunny afternoon as Rita struggled home carrying a bag of school books to mark and two bags of shopping. When she got to her front door, she collected the post from their mail box, stuffing the handful of envelopes in with the books.

Deeley was coming round for supper, and Rita had stopped off to buy the ingredients she needed for the meal. She was not an adventurous cook, but she liked to try the occasional new recipe, and tonight it was beef stroganoff.

With the recipe book propped up in front of her, she was chopping the onions and mushrooms, when David came in, early for once.

'Hallo, darling,' he said, dropping a kiss on the top of her head. 'What's all that?'

'Beef stroganoff,' said Rita. 'Deeley's coming for tea. I did tell you.'

'So you did,' he agreed, 'I'd forgotten.'

'You're nice and early,' Rita said with a smile. 'Good day?'

'Yes, my last meeting was cancelled. Any post?'

'In my school bag.'

David took out the post, flipping through the envelopes. Buried among them was an air letter. It was addressed to Rita and came from England, postmarked Belcaster. He stared at it for a moment and then turned it over to look at the sender's name and address on the back. He glanced across at Rita, who was paying no attention to him.

She had told him that she'd finally decided to write to her

mother, just the once, and though he'd thought it was a mistake, and had told her so, he also understood why she felt she must.

'Rita,' he said, and then paused.

Rita looked up. 'Yes?'

'What was your gran's name?'

'Gran? Lily Sharples. Why?'

'Leave that for a minute, can you?'

Rita wiped her hands on her apron. 'What's up? I've got to get on, Deeley'll be here soon.'

'Come and sit down, darling,' answered David, and held out his hand to her. She took it and he drew her to the table, pulling out a chair for her and then sitting down next to her.

'David?' Her eyes were anxious. 'Is something the matter?'

'No,' David replied, carefully. 'Something here for you.' He held out the letter. 'This was in the post.'

Rita took the aerogramme with shaking hands. 'From my mother,' she breathed.

'I don't think so,' David said gently. 'Look at the sender's name.'

Rita turned the letter over, and as she saw the name *Lily Sharples*, and the address in Hampton Road, the colour drained from her face. White as a sheet, she looked up at David.

'It's from Gran,' she whispered. 'It's from my gran.'

'Looks like it.'

'But she's dead,' cried Rita. 'Deeley told me she was dead! Why did she lie to me? Why did Deeley lie to me?'

'I don't suppose she did,' David said gently. 'Deeley would never lie to you. I'm sure she believed it to be true.'

'But why? Why would they tell me she was dead when she wasn't?'

David shook his head. 'I don't know, darling. Perhaps she explains in the letter. Aren't you going to open it?'

Rita continued to stare at the letter and David asked, 'Shall I open it for you?'

'No,' replied Rita. 'No, I'll open it.' With hands still shaking, she slit open the aerogramme and began to read. Within moments, tears were flooding down her cheeks, and she couldn't read any more. Wordlessly she handed it to David.

'You read it, David.'

David took the letter and glanced through it to see what had upset her so much, then he began to read.

My dearest dearest Rita,

Your letter arrived yesterday, and was such a wonderful surprise. We're so dreadfully sorry to hear that poor darling little Rosie has died. I'll never forgive that dreadful Vanstone woman for sending you both away when I'd told her I'd give you both a home. My heart broke when I read in your letter that Rosie had killed herself, poor dear child. But to have found you again, Rita, is a miracle. We knew you was in Australia, but we didn't know where and the EVER-Care people wouldn't tell us, so we thought we'd lost you. How wonderful to find you again. It seems from your letter that you thought I had died. No, my darling girl, I'm still alive and well and just so thrilled to have found you again. The sad news that I have to tell you is that your poor mother is no longer with us. She died many years ago at the hands of Jimmy Randall. It seems they had a fight and Jimmy killed her in a fit of rage. I am so sorry to be the one to tell you, but clearly as you wrote to her, you did not know. Since she died I have been looking after your brother Richard. We call him Ricky, and he has been looking after me. He is getting some snaps together to send you, but I couldn't wait for them to be sorted, I wanted to write to you straight away. He's going to add a bit to this letter.

I send you all my love, my dearest, and can't wait to hear from you again, to hear about your David and perhaps see some pictures of you both.

And of course I'm thrilled to bits about the baby.

Gran

'He killed her,' Rita murmured, the tears continuing to stream down her cheeks. 'That bastard, Jimmy, killed my mum.'

David dropped the letter on the table and took her into his arms. 'Oh, my darling girl,' he murmured, 'I'm so sorry.' He held her close, her head on his shoulder, as she wept for the mother who had been murdered all those years ago.

'I never knew,' she sobbed. 'I always thought she'd forgotten us and... and... and she wasn't even alive. Why didn't they tell me? Why?'

'Perhaps they thought it would upset you too much,' soothed David, stroking her hair.

'They needn't have said he'd killed her, just that she'd died. After all they told me Gran had,' she added bitterly, 'and that wasn't even true! They didn't care about upsetting me then, did they?'

'My darling, I don't know,' answered David, feeling completely helpless in the face of her distress.

Gradually, Rita's sobs subsided. 'She was always frightened of him, Uncle Jimmy, we all were,' she said. 'I can't bear the thought that he beat her up so badly that she died. Poor Mum. Poor Mum.'

'It was all a long time ago,' ventured David, offering her his handkerchief.

Rita blew her nose. 'I know, but it doesn't really make it any easier, does it? She was my mother, whatever she did, and I did love her.'

Silence fell between them and they sat, their hands clasped in mutual support as they thought about what they'd just learned.

'Perhaps,' said Rita after a while, 'perhaps that was why Mum let him send us away. Why she signed the papers to put us into Laurel House, to get us away from him. Perhaps she was scared for us... d'you think?'

'Maybe,' David agreed, though privately he thought it unlikely. But if the thought comforted Rita, then he was happy to go along with it.

Now she was calmer, he picked up the letter again. 'There's a bit written by Rick at the end. Shall I read that to you?'

Rita nodded. 'Yes,' she said, 'he's my brother.'
David started to read.

Dear Rita,
I'm your brother Rick, and I live with Gran. She never forgot you and there is a picture of you and Rosie on the kitchen shelf. It's always been there. I'm sorry Rosie died, I'll never meet her now, but I'm longing to meet you. I am so glad you have written and I hope you will keep on writing to us. I am going to send some snaps of Gran and me. We are both well. Please send some pictures of you as I don't know what you look like now you're grown up. Lots of love from your brother, Rick.

P.S. I've got a paper round and I've started saving so that we can come and see you.

Hearing this last, Rita gave a wan smile. 'Bless him,' she said. 'What is he, sixteen? It'll take him forever, but it's a lovely thought.'

At that moment there was a knock on the door, and without waiting for an answer, Delia walked into the house. 'Only me,' she called. 'Can I come in?'

'Course you can,' David called back. 'We're in the kitchen.' He gave Rita a quick hug and then turned to welcome his mother-in-law.

Delia breezed into the kitchen, coming up short as she took in Rita's tear-streaked face. She glanced from one to the other, and demanded, 'What's happened? What's the matter?'

David said nothing, waiting for Rita to speak. He was very aware that Delia thought he'd done something to upset Rita, and he wanted Rita to be the one to set her straight.

'Rita?' Delia spoke gently. 'What's the matter, darling? It's not the baby, is it?'

'No,' Rita assured her, 'not the baby.'

'Well then?' Her gaze turned back to David.

Rita saw it and said quickly, 'And it's not David either, so don't look at him like that.'

'I'm not looking at him like anything,' retorted Delia, though she knew she had been. 'So, why the tears?'

'Give her the letter, David,' Rita said. 'You can read it for yourself, Deeley.'

Delia took the letter and began to read, glancing up at Rita as she reached the bit about her mother, and then returning to it again.

'Oh my darling,' she breathed, 'what a dreadful thing! And this is from the grandmother we told you was dead?'

Rita nodded.

'But I don't understand,' said Delia dropping down onto a chair. 'I don't understand. There was a letter from Emily Vanstone in England, saying that your grandmother had had a stroke and died. I saw it myself.' There was a break in her voice. 'My poor girl. I believed it was true, why wouldn't I? It was there in black and white. Oh, Rita, I'm so sorry.'

'It wasn't your fault, Deeley, I know that,' Rita said softly.

'Even so,' Delia's shoulders sagged under the weight of this new knowledge, 'and your mother...' Her voice trailed off as she couldn't find the words.

'My mother has been dead for years,' Rita said bravely, 'but I'd already lost her before she died, hadn't I?' Still clutching David's handkerchief she blew her nose again. 'But I've got my gran back, Deeley, and a grown-up brother. I've got a family again now.'

Rita didn't see David's expression at this remark, but Delia did and sympathized; they had both done all they could to make Rita feel part of a family. But she knew what Rita was really saying, that she had her childhood family back, that she hadn't been forgotten over the years, and she understood how important that was. She just hoped David did, too.

'I think we could all do with a drink,' David said, and without reference to either of them he poured three large gin and tonics.

'Here's to your gran and your brother,' he said, raising his glass to Rita. 'To our English family.' And Delia knew it would be all right.

Over the following weeks there was a flurry of correspondence between Rita and her family in Belcaster. Rick had sent her recent photos of her grandmother and himself. Gran certainly did look older, but Rita wasn't surprised, after all she was in her sixties now, but she still had the same smile that crinkled the corners of her eyes, and though her hair was grey, it was still done in the same style, making her endearingly familiar, bringing the ready tears to Rita's eyes. Rick, she decided, was a good-looking boy, intelligence lurking in his eyes and a shy smile on his lips. She studied his face to see if she could see echoes of his father, but Jimmy Randall's face had dissolved into a merciful blur, and she could see no likeness.

She showed all the pictures to David, and he dutifully admired his new in-laws. Delia took far more interest. And Daisy? Families meant nothing to Daisy and she evinced no interest at all, simply saying, 'Good snaps, Reet,' and then telling her about the next athletics meeting she was going to.

When David's parents heard about the surprising response to Rita's letter, they were somewhat taken aback. Now the reality of Rita's family back home had been exposed to all. Norah said as little as possible about them, simply saying that Rita must have been pleased to hear from them after all this time. She did not want to know that Rita's mother had been murdered by her husband, nor, as they'd subsequently learned, that the murderer had never been caught. Her daughter-in-law the daughter, or at least the stepdaughter, of a murderer, was too much for her to accept with equanimity. It was bad enough that Rita's sister had committed suicide years ago, and Norah was determined that if she had anything to do with it, the news should go no further than the immediate family.

Andrew had been shocked, too, at first, but when he'd seen the difference it made to Rita, the happiness that had infused her on learning that her beloved grandmother was still alive and well, he had hugged her and told her how pleased he was. He had become increasingly fond of his daughter-in-law, and her happiness delighted him.

'I may never see them again,' Rita confided in him, 'but I'll know they're there.'

'Oh, you never know,' he said cheerfully, and then changing the subject said, 'Not long to go now, have you? Thought of any names yet?'

'Yes,' replied Rita.

'And we're not saying,' David put in firmly. 'You'll have to wait and see.'

Rita gave up work at the end of term, and after Easter spent her time at home, preparing for the new arrival. Delia came round and helped her turn their tiny second bedroom into a nursery. Together, they made new curtains and painted the walls a restful apple green.

'Can't have pink or blue,' David said, 'in case it's the wrong one.'

Once a week Rita went to antenatal classes, doing exercises, learning to feed and bath the baby, practising changing nappies on a life-sized doll.

'Won't be as easy on a real baby,' laughed Delia. 'They're all arms and legs and won't lie still!'

'I thought you were going to start work on your novel,' David teased her one evening when he came home from the office and inspected the ongoing work on the nursery.

'No time for that,' Rita said cheerfully, 'though I did send in another story to your editor the other day.'

'Certainly won't be time for writing novels when the baby's here,' said Delia. 'You won't have time for anything then!'

As her time drew nearer, Rita became increasingly anxious about becoming a mother. Supposing she was no good at it. She'd had no experience with babies, she didn't know what to do with them. Many of the other girls in the antenatal class already had children, or had helped with nephews and nieces.

They all know what to do, she thought, in panic. Supposing I can't cope.

She was afraid Norah would think her inadequate, and sweep in to take over and David would realize that she, Rita, was a useless mother. She confided her dread to Delia, who hugged her and said, 'Don't worry about it, darling, everyone's nervous at first, but you'll be amazed how quickly you get the hang of it.' And when she saw that Rita wasn't convinced she added, 'And don't worry about Norah, David won't let her bully you. He won't want her in the house any more than you do!'

It was one night, three weeks later, that Rita was jolted awake from a restless sleep as a contraction seized her. She sat up in bed, gasping as the pain lanced through her, trying to relax and breathe her way through it, as she'd been taught. As the contraction passed and she felt herself relax, she announced to the darkness of their bedroom, 'Well, all that deep breathing stuff's a waste of time, ain't it!' And having checked the time on the bedside clock, she lay back waiting for the next contraction. She'd been having twinges on and off all day and not knowing quite what to do, had rung the maternity hospital.

'First baby, dear?' asked the midwife on duty.

'Yes.'

'Fine,' replied the woman. 'No need to come in until the contractions are about fifteen minutes apart. First babies always take their time.'

Now they were definite contractions and they seemed to be coming pretty often. The next made its attack exactly eighteen minutes after the last.

This is it, Rita thought, surprised at how calm she was feeling. I'm going to be a mother, and it's time we went.

She reached over and shook the still-snoring David awake. 'Think we'd better go, David,' she said and then groaned, clutching herself as another contraction gripped her.

David shot out of bed, panic in his eyes. 'OK,' he said. 'All right, now, all right, yes...' and started dragging on his clothes.

As the contraction released its grip Rita said, 'It *is* all right, David, they aren't that close yet. We've plenty of time. First babies always take their time.'

But David wasn't having any of it. As soon as he was dressed he picked up the suitcase that Rita had packed, ready. 'I'll just put this in the car and then I'll come back and get you. All right?'

Rita assured him that she was, but stopped in the middle of dressing to get through another contraction. David reappeared at the door.

'Come *on*, darling,' he said, panic in his voice. 'Oh Rita, you aren't even dressed yet!' He helped her struggled into her coat. It was cold outside, and she shivered as she walked to the car, David clutching her arm to steady her.

'It's all right,' he kept saying, 'it's all right. Won't be long till we're there. It's all right.'

It wasn't far and one contraction later, they arrived. At the front door Rita was gathered up by a smiling nurse.

'All right, dear? First baby? Don't worry, first babies always take their time, and we'll soon have you nice and comfy.' She looked at David standing awkwardly by the door, holding the suitcase. 'Hubby can wait here,' she said, and pointed to a small room off the hall. She gave David a little push and taking Rita's case from him, said, 'I'll be back in a while to tell you how things are going.'

David pulled Rita to him and hugged her tightly. 'Love you, darling heart, love you always.'

Rita reached up and kissed him. 'Don't worry, David, I'll be fine,' she assured him a little tremulously. 'You'll be a dad very soon.'

It wasn't as soon as she'd hoped.

An hour later the nurse went back to David and said, 'It's going to be some time yet, Mr Harris, I suggest you go home and get some sleep, and come back in the morning.'

But David knew he could never sleep with Rita going through whatever it was she was going through upstairs, and said he'd rather stay.

'Up to you, of course,' returned the nurse, 'but it may be a long wait. First babies always take their time.'

If anyone else says that... David thought, gritting his teeth, but he knew the nurse meant to be kind and he managed a smile. 'Thank you, nurse. I'll wait.'

She smiled back. 'Difficult for the dads, I know. I'll get someone to bring you a cup of tea, shall I?'

It was more than seven hours later when the nurse finally reappeared in the tiny waiting room and beaming at David, told him that he had a beautiful son.

'Is Rita all right?' demanded David. 'Can I see her?'

'She's fine,' the nurse assured him. 'We're just getting her tidied up and then you can come in and see them both. You can't stay long, though. She's very tired and needs her sleep.'

David crept into the delivery room and found Rita, pale but radiant, sitting up in bed, a tiny bundle cradled in her arms. She held the baby up a little and murmured, 'Say hallo to Daddy, little one.'

David bent over and kissed her cheek, his face pressing against hers. 'Oh darling,' he whispered, 'you're safe. You're safe, and you're beautiful.'

He looked down at the red, crumpled face of his son, topped with a head of thick, black hair, and added, 'and he's beautiful, too.'

'Isn't he?' Rita agreed, her face alight with joy. 'Just beautiful. Oh, David we're so lucky.' For a long moment they both stared down at the tiny form in the blanket, marvelling at the wonder of him.

'Are you still happy with the names we chose?' Rita looked up and asked, and David nodded.

'Yes.'

'Donald Andrew,' she said, smiling down at her son, 'for your two grandfathers.' She held him out to David. 'Here, you hold him,' she said and looked on with love and pride, as David took the little bundle awkwardly in his arms.

'He's too small to be called Donald just yet,' she said softly, 'so I've been calling him Donny.'

'Donny he is then,' agreed David. He looked down again into

his son's face, saw the wee snubbed nose and the eyes screwed up in slumber and whispered, 'Hallo, Donny, mate. I hope you have the most wonderful life.'

The nurse bustled back into the room. 'Time for Mother to get some sleep. You'll have to go now, Mr Harris. You can come back and see them again later, after lunch. Fathers only the first day, other visitors from tomorrow.'

David could see that Rita was exhausted and made no demur. He placed Donny back in her arms and then leaned down and kissed them both.

'I'm so proud of you both,' he said softly, 'you're the two most special people in the world and I swear I'll do everything in my power to look after you.'

Rita caught his hand to her cheek, and for a moment their eyes locked. Then David pulled his hand away gently and said, 'I must go.'

'You will ring Deeley, won't you?' Rita reminded him. 'Straight away?'

'Course I will,' he promised, 'and my parents. I can't wait to tell them all. You get some sleep now and I'll be back to see you both after lunch. Promise.'

When he left the hospital he headed straight for a phone box and dialled Delia's number. There was no reply, and he realized that it was now mid-morning and she would be at work so he headed for the nursery.

'Delia's in the Yellow Room, with the fours,' he was told. 'Don't be too long.'

David went in and found Delia beside a sink, wiping red paint off a little girl's face. She froze for a moment and then, seeing the broad smile on his face, crossed the room and was enveloped in a massive bear-hug.

'It's a boy,' he told her ecstatically, 'a beautiful boy, with a mass of dark hair. Mum and Baby both fine.'

'Oh David,' cried Delia, 'that's fantastic news! Oh, I'm thrilled to bits! It's so exciting, I can't believe it. And, Rita, is she really all right?'

'She's fine,' David assured her. 'A bit tired, that's all. She's asleep now, but I can go back again after lunch.'

'When can I go?' demanded Delia. 'When can I see them? I can't wait to hold my grandson.'

'Tomorrow,' promised David. 'Grandparents are allowed to visit tomorrow.'

'Have you got a name for him yet?'

'Yes,' replied David proudly, 'he's called Donald Andrew for his two grandfathers. Rita's calling him Donny.'

'Donald Andrew Harris,' Delia said slowly, as if trying it for size. 'Little Donny Harris. Oh, David, I'm so happy for you both. Give Rita all my love when you go back, and tell her how thrilled I am.' She beamed up into his face. 'And if you want to, come round this evening, after visiting, and I'll cook you tea.'

'Thanks, Deeley,' he said, 'that would be great. I must go now, I've got to tell my parents the news.' He drew her to him, kissed her on the cheek and then left her standing in the middle of the Yellow Room, exulting in the news he'd brought, and the fact that he'd brought it to her first... because she was, truly, Rita's mother.

David had rung his office and told them he wouldn't be in, and now he had the rest of the morning to fill before he could go back to the hospital. He didn't know if his father would be at home, but he was pretty sure his mother would be, and decided to go and tell them in person too, rather than give them the news over the phone.

By the time he reached his parents' house he'd begun to wish he had phoned. It would be an awful anti-climax if they weren't there; but a car was parked in the drive. Dad must be working at home today, he thought. Brilliant!

His mother opened the door and one look at his beaming face told her that she had a grandchild, and she was shouting for Andrew almost before David had got into the house.

They were as thrilled as Delia, both of them hugging him in delight.

'Tell me all about him,' Norah begged. 'Is he beautiful?'

'Absolutely.'

'And what does he weigh?' she demanded.

'Seven pounds thirteen.'

'A good-sized baby, then. You were only six pounds eight ounces.'

'And how's Rita,' asked his father. 'No problems for her?'

'Rita's fine, Dad,' said David. 'Tired, but absolutely... well, you can imagine.'

'Donald Andrew, you said?' queried Norah.

'Yes, Mum,' David answered. 'Donald was Rita's father's name, and Andrew for Dad of course.'

'I'm honoured,' his father said simply. 'Tell her so, when you go back in to see her. And give her my love.'

'You can go and see them both yourselves, tomorrow.'

'Not too early in the day for a glass to wet young Donald Andrew's head, is it?' asked his father, and minutes later they were raising glasses to the new arrival.

Just before David left to return to the hospital, his father said, 'There's something I want to show you in my study, David, if you've got a minute before you go.'

David was itching to be back at the hospital, but with only a glance at his watch, he dutifully followed Andrew into his study.

'Sit down for a moment, son.' Andrew closed the door behind them. 'I've had an idea I want to run past you, just to see what you think. Haven't mentioned it to your mother yet, as I wanted to know what you thought about it first.'

David was intrigued. 'What is it, Dad?'

'You know I'm very fond of your Rita, don't you?'

David nodded. 'Yes, and I'm delighted. It's made things easier for her than they might have been.'

Andrew laughed. 'Oh, you mustn't mind your mother, she's coming round now she knows her better. And young Donny will be a big help. No, what I had in mind was something I hope will please Rita, but I wanted to see what you think before I did any more about it.'

When David left the house his mind was reeling.

'Talk to Mrs Watson about it, if you like,' Andrew had said. 'Don't want to put my foot in it.'

'No,' agreed David. 'I'll have a word with her. I'm seeing her later.'

Back at the hospital David found Rita sitting up in the ward with Donny in a crib beside her. She had more colour in her cheeks now, and looked a little less tired. When she saw David her face lit up with such happiness that his heart contracted with love for her.

'I've just fed him,' she told David as he peered into the crib. 'He's a hungry monkey. I'm quite sore.'

'You don't have to feed him yourself,' David said. 'You could give him bottles.'

'No,' returned Rita firmly, 'I'm going to feed our baby myself. Part of the job. Were they all pleased?' she asked when he'd drawn up a chair to the bedside.

'They're all thrilled to bits,' he told her. 'They all send you their love and I think all three will be in to see you, and admire Donny, at visiting tomorrow afternoon.'

'Will you bring me in an air letter when you come next time?' Rita asked him. 'I must write to Gran and Rick to tell them about Donny. They'll be so excited.'

'Of course,' David promised. 'You must write and tell them all about him, but I've already sent a telegram with the news.'

Rita looked at him, her eyes sparkling with love and happiness. 'Oh David, have you? Oh darling, thank you.'

The next afternoon both his parents and Delia came trooping into the ward. Norah was carrying a teddy bear wearing a blue bow, Andrew a huge bunch of flowers, and Delia with a blue, crocheted matinee jacket, wrapped in white tissue paper.

'Oh, Deeley, it's beautiful!' cried Rita when she unwrapped it. 'Were you that sure it was going to be a boy,' she teased, 'or did you make another one in pink, just in case?'

'No, darling,' Delia said, 'this was Harry's. It was the only thing I kept.'

Tears sprang to Rita's eyes as she reached up to hug her

mother. 'Oh Deeley,' she whispered, 'thank you. Thank you for everything.'

As Norah was at the bedside, gazing down at her new grandson, trying to see a likeness to David in his tiny features, Andrew drew Delia to one side.

'Has David had a word?' he asked.

'Yes,' replied Delia, 'we discussed it last night.'

'Do you think she'd like it?'

'I think it's a wonderful idea,' Delia told him.

'I'll go ahead, then,' he said. 'Mum's the word.'

Chapter 42

The letter arrived in Hampton Road one Saturday morning. 'Hey, Gran,' Rick cried, passing it over, 'there's one from Australia.'

'Not Rita's writing, though,' Lily said, putting on her glasses and looking at the name of the sender. It just said *Harris* with an address in a place she'd never heard of.

'Perhaps it's from David,' she said. 'I hope Rita's all right, and the baby.' Sudden fears flew through Lily's mind. Suppose something had happened to Rita, to the baby. Complications after the birth. Unexpected infection. Were Australian doctors any good?

'Shall I open it, Gran?' asked Rick.

'No,' she said, 'I will,' and slitting open the envelope she pulled out the letter. Glancing at the bottom she saw the signature. 'Andrew Harris,' she read. 'It's not David. Perhaps it's his father? Wasn't he called Andrew?'

'Can't remember. Come on, Gran, read it out,' begged Rick. 'What does he say?'

'He says… "*Dear Mrs Sharples, I am your granddaughter Rita's father-in-law.*"'

'You were right,' said Rick. 'It's him. Go on, Gran.'

Lily continued to read aloud.

You'll know by now, that Rita and David have a beautiful son, born a couple of weeks ago. I'm sure Rita will be sending you some photos of him very soon. I have become very fond of Rita, she is a girl of great character, and I know she had to travel a difficult road in her childhood. I would like to reward her for her courage and steadfastness, and I wondered if you and her brother Richard would like to fly out and see her and the baby...

'Wouldn't we just,' groaned Rick. 'Chance'd be a fine thing.'

'Just a minute,' said Gran, her eyes widening as they took in the rest of the sentence.

'What?' demanded Rick seeing her expression. 'What?'

'"... and if so,"' Gran read, '"*whether you would consider accepting your airline tickets as a gift from me.*"'

'What!' shrieked Rick. 'Gran, we're going to Australia!'

Lily looked up at him, equally incredulous, but said, 'Wait a minute there, Ricky, let's finish reading the letter, eh?'

Nothing would give me greater pleasure than to see Rita reunited with you both after all these years. I have discussed it with David and Rita's foster mother, Mrs Watson, and they both think it would be the most wonderful surprise for Rita if you agreed to come.

I hope you won't be offended by this offer. I've heard from Rita that Richard is working hard to save up to come over sometime in the future, but I am fortunate enough to be in the position to send you tickets immediately. I know it is a long journey, taking nearly two days, but if you were able to come, you would be able to stay for several weeks and so make that journey worthwhile.

Obviously we've said nothing to Rita about this. We didn't want to get her hopes up, in case you didn't feel able to make such a long journey. One way or the other, we'd be glad if you would keep the secret too. Perhaps you'd reply to the address at the top of this letter, and if you have a phone number, let me have it, so I can ring you and we can discuss arrangements more easily. I would be happy to phone you at a convenient time in the future.

I hope that you will feel able to accept this gift, and that we shall all see you in Sydney before very long.

Yours sincerely,

Andrew Harris

Lily put the letter down on the table and looked at Rick.

'That's fantastic,' he breathed. 'Just amazing. Us going to Australia!'

'It would be wonderful,' agreed Lily, 'but I'm not sure it's on.'

Rick stared at her stupefied. 'What d'you mean, not on, Gran? Why not? This bloke, Rita's pa-in-law, is offering to pay for us to go. Don't you want to go, Gran?'

'Course I want to go,' replied Lily, 'but it ain't that easy, Rick. It's a lot of money to take from someone you don't know.'

'Oh, come on, Gran,' cried Rick. 'We *do* know him. He's Rita's dad now.'

'Not quite, and even so, it's too much money,' maintained Lily.

'But he ain't doing it for us, Gran,' Rick pointed out. 'He's doing it for Rita. What did he say...' Rick picked up the letter and squinted at it. 'Yeah, here we are... "*I have become very fond of Rita, she is a girl of great character, and I know she had to travel a difficult road in her childhood.*" This is the bit, "*I would like to reward her for her courage and steadfastness.*" There you are, see,' Rick said triumphantly. 'He's doing it for her, not for us.'

'It's for us as well.'

'I know, but it's for her mostly. Look, Gran, he can afford it. He says so, don't he? He says he knows I'm saving up to come, well OK, but he also knows it'll take me years to save enough for the both of us. And let's face it, Gran, you ain't getting any younger. Don't want to wait until the journey is too much for you, do you? He sees that, this Andrew bloke. He knows that if we don't go soon, if *you* don't go soon, it could be too late.' He looked across at his grandmother and flushed red, as he realized what he'd said. 'Sorry, Gran,' he muttered, but when she said nothing, he added a little defiantly, 'It would be dreadful if we didn't go now and then couldn't go later, wouldn't it?'

'All right, Richard,' said Lily tartly, 'you've made your point.'

He got to his feet and went to the door, adding as his parting shot, 'Just think how Rita would feel if she found out we could've gone to see her and we didn't.'

When he'd gone out, Lily sat looking out of the window and thinking about the letter and its offer. She thought back to the day when she'd got the telegram about the baby, and how anxious she'd been when it arrived. Telegrams were bad news, everyone knew that, except those special greetings ones that came at weddings, so when Lily had opened the door to the telegraph boy, it was with a shaking hand that she took the proffered buff envelope. Rick was at school, and she was on her own in the house. She'd looked at the envelope, wondering if perhaps she should wait till Rick came home to open it. But on the other hand, she thought, if it's urgent enough for a telegram, then perhaps I shouldn't wait.

She retreated to the kitchen and sitting down at the table, tore the envelope open. When she read the message, she found she was crying, crying with joy at the news it brought.

DONALD ANDREW HARRIS BORN 3 JUNE. MOTHER & SON DOING WELL. LETTER FOLLOWS. DAVID.

Within moments Lily was on her feet, pulling on her coat and closing the front door behind her. Bursting with the news, she hurried to Baillies' to tell Anne.

'It's a boy!' she cried as she flung open the shop door. 'Rita's had a boy!'

Anne came round the counter and gave her a hug. She and Lily had become very close over recent years. 'That's wonderful, Lil,' she cried, 'I'm so pleased for you.'

'Donald, after Rita's dad. Don't you think that's lovely? I do. Donald Andrew. David's father's called Andrew, I think. Oh, Anne! That I should live to see the day!'

Lily decided she wouldn't mention Andrew Harris's generous

offer to anyone yet, not even to Anne or Carrie. She would think about it and make her decision, then, if they were going, she'd tell them.

'Have you thought yet?' Rick demanded when he got home from school.

'Sort of,' replied Lily.

'Does that mean we can go?'

'I ain't decided yet,' Lily answered, 'I'm still thinking on it. But, if we do decide to go I'll have to speak to Mr Harris.'

'We could get a phone put in,' suggested Rick.

'That'd take too long, wouldn't it?' Lily hadn't bothered with a phone, but now she quite liked the idea.

'No, honestly, Gran, it'll be done in no time.'

'I'll see, but I'll tell you one thing, young Ricky-me-lad,' she said firmly, 'we ain't going nowhere, not till you've finished them exams.'

Rick grabbed her hands and, holding them tight, said, 'But we are going, Gran, yes?'

'Yes,' replied Lily. 'We're going, Rick. 'Course we are.'

'Fan-*tas*-tic!' cried Rick, enveloping her in a hug.

'But we keep it to ourselves for now,' she reminded him, 'and certainly no hint to Rita if you write to her again. Right?'

'Right,' agreed Rick.

There was no question of them going for at least a month. Neither of them had passports, and Lily had stuck to her guns about Rick having to sit his O-levels.

The phone was put in, and when Andrew Harris rang to discuss the arrangements Lily was still having difficulty accepting such a generous offer.

'I'd like to try and pay you back,' she said, 'for the tickets. It ain't right for you to pay all that money out for us.'

'It's my pleasure, Mrs Sharples,' he replied gently. 'I know your grandson is saving up to come, but he can always use that money for a second visit.'

'It's too generous,' Lily said, 'but I do want to see Rita and the baby.'

'Of course you do,' Andrew said, 'and I know they'd love to see you, so, that's settled.'

The plans were made and at last Lily was ready to tell her friends.

Characteristically, Anne and Fred were delighted for them. 'Ain't that great news?' Anne said. 'Fancy! Flying all the way to Australia to see Reet!'

'Flying,' confirmed Lily. 'Rita's father-in-law has sent us the tickets.'

'When you off, then?' asked Fred.

'Soon as Rick's finished his exams,' answered Lily. 'We got our passports and that, so we're all set to go.'

Carrie was delighted for them too. 'How long are you going for?' she asked.

'Not decided yet,' replied Lily. 'We'll be back here for Ricky to start in the sixth form.'

The day they were leaving arrived at last. John Maunder had offered to drive them to London Airport. Rick could hardly contain his excitement, but Lily was extremely apprehensive. 'D'you think I'm stupid to go on such a long journey at my age?' she asked Carrie. 'S'pose I got took ill?'

'No,' cried Carrie. 'You're as fit as a flea, and there'll be air hostesses to look after you on the flight, and when you get to Australia, well, Rita and her family'll be there, won't they?

Lily had listened to Carrie and tried to dismiss her fears, but as they drew near to London Airport, she began to have serious misgivings. She was glad that Carrie had come with them, especially when they went to the airline desk to show their tickets and hand over their luggage.

'It will get on the right aeroplane, won't it?' she asked anxiously.

'Certainly, madam,' replied the girl at the desk. 'I've labelled it for Sydney.'

'And it'll go there all by itself?'

''Course it will, Gran,' said Rick. 'Don't worry about it, it's all took care of.' He took the tickets back and stowed them in the leather money belt he'd bought for the purpose. 'Safe in there, Gran,' he assured her, giving the pouch a pat, 'all strapped round my waist, see?'

At last it was time to go through to the lounge. Rick pranced on ahead, turning back now and then to be sure they were all coming.

Lily paused and turned to Carrie and John. 'Goodbye,' she said, giving Carrie a hug. 'Thanks to you both for bringing us up.'

'Pleasure, Mrs S,' Carrie assured her, returning the hug.

'You look after your Gran, young man,' John said to Rick.

'Will do,' promised Rick.

'He will,' said Lily and turning away, she walked through the gateway into the lounge.

'Give our love to Rita,' called Carrie.

Lily turned and waved once more before she and Rick disappeared from sight.

Chapter 43

As Lily and Rick finally struggled out through the customs area at the airport in Sydney, Lily was afraid she wouldn't make it. She had lost track of the times the aeroplane had taken off and landed on the way. Sometimes they had to leave the aircraft, other times they stayed in their seats. Passengers left the plane, others boarded; there seemed to Lily to be continual bustle. When the captain had finally welcomed them to Sydney, she hardly believed they'd actually reached their destination.

It was early morning as they emerged into a wintery sunlight. They stood for a moment, looking round, and then Rick pointed.

'Look, Gran,' he said. 'Over there.'

Two men stood together, one holding a handwritten sign: *Mrs Sharples*. Rick picked up the two cases and led the way across.

'Hallo,' he said to the younger of the two, 'How d'you do? I'm Rick.'

'And I'm David,' replied the other. 'Here, let me take those cases.'

Lily, following behind, saw the two men glance over Rick's shoulder, looking for her. This time it was the older man who stepped forward, hand extended.

'Mrs Sharples?' he said. 'Welcome to Sydney. We're so glad you could come. I'm Andrew Harris, and this is David, Rita's husband.'

David shook hands as well, and said, 'You've had a very long journey, Mrs Sharples, are you all right?'

THE THROWAWAY CHILDREN

'Tired,' admitted Lily. 'Tired to the bone.'

'We guessed you would be, so we're taking you straight to my parents' house. You can rest there and have a good sleep. I'm sure you need it.'

'Where's Rita?' asked Rick, looking about him. 'I thought she'd be here.'

'She still doesn't know you're coming,' replied Andrew. 'Look, let's get you into the car, and then we'll explain the plans on the way home.' He hailed a porter to take the luggage and led the way to the car. There was a chilly wind, and Lily shivered.

'It is a bit cold today,' Andrew said, 'but we'll soon warm the car up. It's winter here of course.'

Once they reached the car, Andrew installed Lily comfortably in the front seat, while David dealt with the porter, the luggage and Rick.

'Comfortable now?' Andrew asked Lily.

Lily nodded wearily, 'Yes, thank you, sir,' she said.

As they drove into the city Andrew explained what they hoped to do. 'What we thought was that, as you'd be so tired when you first arrived, it would be better to take you to my home where you can catch up on a bit of shut-eye, have a shower or a bath, and generally recover from the journey. We'll look after you, and then as it's Saturday tomorrow, David will bring Rita and young Donny over for lunch. She won't know you two are there, so it'll be a real surprise when she walks into the room and finds you.'

'So we ain't seeing her till tomorrow,' muttered Rick.

'No, I'm afraid not,' answered Andrew. 'I'm sorry if you're disappointed, Rick, but we thought your grandmother would need a while to get over the journey. It would be a pity to spoil her reunion with Rita just because she was too tired, don't you think?'

''S'pose so,' he grumbled, 'I just thought she'd be here, you know.'

Lily directed a quelling look at her grandson.

'Please don't listen to him, Mr Harris. I'll be very pleased to

483

have a good rest before I see Rita, I can tell you,' she said firmly. 'It's very good of you both to have thought about it all, isn't it, Rick?'

'Yes, Gran,' came the rather mutinous reply, but Rick's disappointment faded as he turned his attention to the city, wide-eyed at the buildings, the traffic and the bridge. He heard no more of the arrangements as he pressed his nose to the car window, drinking in the sights and sounds of Sydney.

'Rita's foster mother will be coming too,' David was telling Lily. 'Delia. You'll like her. She was the one who got Rita off that dreadful farm.'

'Yes,' said Lily. 'Rita's told me all about her. I shan't be able to thank her enough for looking after her when there weren't no one else.'

When they reached the house in Parramatta, Norah was waiting to greet them at the front door. She wasn't sure what she'd been expecting Rita's grandmother to be like, but when she saw her, tired and pale from the long journey, she hurried out to welcome her.

Lily spent most of the day asleep, as did Rick, despite his best efforts to stay awake. She woke as evening approached, and as she and David's parents sat down to supper, Norah began to ply her with questions about Rita and her childhood.

'What happened to her parents?' Norah asked. 'All we know is that she was an orphan and was sent out here to start a new life.'

'Yes, well, that sort of happened,' agreed Lily. 'Her dad was killed in the war. Her mum looked after her and her little sister...'

'Yes, her sister...'

'Norah,' interposed Andrew mildly, 'I don't think you should be interrogating Mrs Sharples like this. These are questions you should be asking Rita, not her grandmother.'

'But Rita won't talk about it,' objected Norah. 'She never tells me anything.'

'Then they're probably things she doesn't want to discuss,'

said her husband. 'So I expect Mrs Sharples doesn't want to either.'

'No, I don't,' agreed Lily with a firmness in which Andrew heard an echo of Rita. Then fearing she'd been rude to her hostess, Lily went on, 'You can imagine these things are painful to Rita, so if she's managed to put them out of her mind, then I'm delighted.'

Lily turned to Andrew, sitting at the head of the table. 'I'm sure you both realize how difficult it's been for her. I'm just so happy that she's found herself a lovely man like your David. After all, it's the rest of her life what matters now, ain't it?'

Nobody mentioned Rosie again. Rosie was at peace. Rita was the important one now.

Rita woke on Saturday morning, still feeling tired. She'd been up with Donny twice in the night, once at midnight, and again at four in the morning.

'Do we really have to go to your parents' for lunch today?' she asked David. 'Couldn't we cry off, just this once?'

David was alarmed. 'Don't you feel well?' he asked anxiously.

'I'm all right,' Rita said, 'just tired. I thought we'd have a nice quiet weekend just doing nothing. Not that I haven't got loads to do,' she added. 'I need to wash nappies and the ironing's reaching the roof.'

'I'll do the ironing,' David offered.

Rita gave a shout of laughter. 'You? Ironing?'

David looked offended. 'Can't be that difficult,' he said, 'just running an iron over a few shirts.'

Rita put her arms round him and gave him a hug. 'Sorry, darling, I didn't mean to laugh at you. It's sweet of you to offer, but I can do it. I just thought I'd give your mother a call, and suggest we came next week instead.'

'I really don't think we can do that at such short notice,' argued David. 'She'll have got food in, and prepared things.'

'She didn't think of that two weeks ago when they were coming here for dinner and then didn't because she had a headache,' retorted Rita.

'Oh, come on, Rita,' David said. 'She really was ill. You know she went to bed for two days with one of her migraines.'

'Yeah, well, they seem pretty convenient to me.'

'Look, Rita, I'm afraid we've got to go—'

'Why?' snapped Rita. 'Why have we got to go?'

'It's been in the diary for more than two weeks.'

'So what? We can still not go. Suppose I had a raging fever, we couldn't go then, could we?'

'Come on, darling,' implored David. 'Be reasonable.'

Rita knew she wasn't being reasonable, but somehow she couldn't help herself. She was tired and cross, and the thought of listening to her mother-in-law telling her how to look after Donny was more than she could cope with. 'I don't *feel* reasonable,' she said petulantly.

'Look, I'm going to let you into a secret,' David said, 'and then you'll see why we've got to go.'

'Well?'

'Dad's got a special present for Donny. 'He's got it specially, as a surprise, and he's going to give it to him today.'

'What sort of present?' demanded Rita.

'It's just a present, a surprise. Something that Dad thought Donny would like. He's gone to a lot of trouble to get it for him. He'll be most disappointed if we don't go.'

'Couldn't he bring it here?' asked Rita.

David sighed. What a day for Rita to be so awkward all of a sudden.

'No,' he said, 'not easily. Look, I'm going to go, and I'll take Donny with me. You don't have to come if you don't want to. I'll tell Mum you weren't up to it, she'll understand.' He waited anxiously, afraid she might call his bluff.

'Don't be silly,' Rita said sharply. 'You can't take him on your own. How will you feed him?'

'Oh, Mum's got a bottle and some powdered milk,' answered David, playing his ace. 'It won't hurt him just this once not to be breast-fed. I'm not going to let Dad down, Rita. We'll manage.'

Rita stared at him obstinately, then she shrugged. 'Oh, all

right, I'll come, if it's that important to you. But we're not going to stay all afternoon, are we?'

'Not if you don't want to,' said David evenly, relief flooding through him at her capitulation.

'I shan't want to,' Rita told him. 'OK, I'll be ready to go at twelve.'

On the dot of twelve, David put the carrycot into the car, picked up the bag that contained everything they could possibly need for Donny and waited in the driver's seat with the engine running. Moments later the front door slammed and Rita, smartly dressed in navy slacks and a red jumper, climbed into the passenger seat.

David turned to look at her. 'You know,' he remarked conversationally to her stiff profile, 'I think I love you even more when you're cross, that stern expression makes you even more beautiful.'

For a moment Rita didn't move, then she looked at him, a rueful expression on her face. 'Sorry,' she said in a small voice and she leaned over and kissed him on the ear. 'Come on, David,' she chided, 'let's get going, or we'll be late.'

When they drew up at the house, David lifted Donny, still fast asleep in his carrycot, out of the car. Rita grabbed the change bag and together they walked to the door. Norah opened it before they could ring the bell. She must have been standing at the window waiting for us, Rita thought, a little of her earlier anger creeping back. We aren't late, well, not much, and here she is on the doorstep.

'Come on in,' Norah said, smiling. 'We're in the lounge.'

David stood back to let Rita precede him into the room, and the first person she saw was Delia.

'Deeley,' she cried in delight, 'I didn't know you were going to be here! Why didn't you say, we could have given you a lift.' As she went to hug her mother, Rita was suddenly aware of other people in the room and paused to look round. There was an elderly lady sitting in a chair by the fire, and a young lad perched on the window seat.

'Oh,' said Rita, 'sorry, I didn't realize there were other guests.'

'Rita.' It was the old lady in the chair who, very softly, spoke her name.

Rita froze and a waiting silence enveloped the room. She stared at the old woman, who was now struggling out of her chair.

'Gran,' she whispered. 'Gran? Is it really you?'

'It's Gran all right,' said a voice from the window seat, 'and I'm Rick.'

Rita spun round. 'Rick? My brother, Rick?' She looked wildly round the room and found they were all smiling at her. David, his mother and father, Deeley, and miraculously her gran and Rick, her brother.

'Gran,' she croaked, 'oh Gran, I don't believe it,' and finally she moved towards the grandmother she hadn't seen for more than sixteen years, gathering her into her arms, clinging to her, weeping on her shoulder as if she were a little girl once more.

Lily sat down again, and Rita sat at her feet on the floor, still clutching her hand. Having greeted her with an awkward kiss on the cheek and then a bear-like hug, Rick sat beside her. There was so much to say that they didn't say anything. There were so many years missing, they didn't know where to begin.

Rita remembered David's words from earlier in the day, *Dad's got a special present for Donny. He's gone to a lot of trouble to get it for him. He'll be most disappointed if we don't go.* She looked up at Andrew, who was standing by the door smiling broadly, and getting to her feet, she went over and put her arms round his neck.

'You did this for me, Mr Harris,' she whispered. 'I don't know how to begin to thank you.'

Andrew hugged her. 'I think you could start by calling me Andrew, or if you can't manage that, how about Grandad, like young Donny?'

Rita reached up, and kissed him on the cheek. 'Thank you, Andrew,' she whispered, tears shining in her eyes, 'thank you so very much.'

There was an excited buzz of conversation in the room as everyone began to talk at once. Andrew produced another bottle of champagne, and when everyone had a glass, he said, 'I'd like to propose a toast. To young Donald Andrew and all his family, from both sides of the world.'

'Donald Andrew,' they chorused, and raised their glasses.